A DETECTIVE CHIEF INSPE

CW01636536

CHEATING MY DESTINY

NEW YORK TIMES #1 BESTSELLER **TONY LEE** WRITING AS

JACK GATLAND

Hooded Man MEDIA

INSPIRATION • PRODUCTION • PUBLICATION

Published by Hooded Man Media.

First Edition: December 2024

PRAISE FOR JACK GATLAND

'Fast-paced and action packed, Jack Gatland's thrillers always deliver a punch.'

'This is one of those books that will keep you up past your bedtime, as each chapter lures you into reading just one more.'

'This book was excellent! A great plot which kept you guessing until the end.'

'Couldn't put it down, fast paced with twists and turns.'

'The story was captivating, good plot, twists you never saw and really likeable characters. Can't wait for the next one!'

'Totally addictive. Thoroughly recommend.'

'Moves at a fast pace and carries you along with it.'

'Just couldn't put this book down, from the first page to the last one it kept you wondering what would happen next.'

Before LETTER FROM THE DEAD...
There was

LIQUIDATE THE PROFITS

Learn the story of what *really* happened to DI Declan Walsh, while at Mile End!

An EXCLUSIVE PREQUEL, completely free to anyone who joins the Declan Walsh Reader's Club!

Join at bit.ly/jackgatlandVIP

Also by Jack Gatland

DI DECLAN WALSH BOOKS

LETTER FROM THE DEAD

MURDER OF ANGELS

HUNTER HUNTED

WHISPER FOR THE REAPER

TO HUNT A MAGPIE

A RITUAL FOR THE DYING

KILLING THE MUSIC

A DINNER TO DIE FOR

BEHIND THE WIRE

HEAVY IS THE CROWN

STALKING THE RIPPER

A QUIVER OF SORROWS

MURDER BY MISTLETOE

BENEATH THE BODIES

KILL YOUR DARLINGS

KISSING A KILLER

PRETEND TO BE DEAD

HARVEST FOR THE REAPER

CROOKED WAS HIS CANE

A POCKET FULL OF POSIES

CHEATING MY DESTINY

STAND AND DELIVER

TOM MARLOWE BOOKS

SLEEPING SOLDIERS

TARGET LOCKED

COVERT ACTION

COUNTER ATTACK

STEALTH STRIKE

BROAD SWORD

ROGUE SIGNAL

SNIPER ALLEY

ELLIE RECKLESS BOOKS

PAINT THE DEAD

STEAL THE GOLD

HUNT THE PREY

FIND THE LADY

BURN THE DEBT

LIAM HARPER BOOKS

FINAL CLAIM

DAMIAN LUCAS BOOKS

THE LIONHEART CURSE

STANDALONE BOOKS

THE BOARDROOM

As Tony Lee

STANDALONE

TWELVE TASKS

THE PLAYING CARD WAR

KNAVE OF SPADES

For Mum, who inspired me to write.

For Tracy, who inspires me to write.

CONTENTS

PROLOGUE

THE DOUGHNUT THAT JOSEPH LAWRENCE HAD EATEN THE NIGHT before still weighed heavily on his mind the following morning, and it pissed him off.

He was annoyed at himself, if he was being honest. A moment of temptation, a cheat meal he didn't need, and one that had probably thrown him backwards in his quest. He had avoided sugar for months, doing his best to stick to a strict diet, but last night's fall off the wagon meant he woke up sluggish, tired, and, more importantly, bloated.

The first thing Joseph did on waking was check his sleep score. It was ninety-six per cent out of one hundred. He had dropped four points, most likely because his digestive system was trying to get that goddamn doughnut out of his system. He was angry and wanted to throw something, shout at somebody, but he knew the only person guilty of this was himself. Even his wife, the temptress who had provided it – the Eve to his Adam – hadn't forced the doughnut down his throat. He had done that quite happily himself.

Joseph Lawrence's days were quite uniform in their style. He would wake up at five in the morning and begin his day with meditation. But before he even did that, waking up was a very important part of his routine. He'd lay back on his expensive water-pumped mattress, feeling the temperature cool as it did so.

The room was pitch black, exactly how he needed it. In fact, even his wife didn't sleep in his bedroom. Her snoring over many years had caused him, a light sleeper, to repeatedly wake up during the night, often breaking his sleep to the point where, even though he was in bed for over eight hours, he was only sleeping for six, maybe seven of them at best. Eventually, he had made the decision that they should have separate beds in separate rooms.

Unsurprisingly, his wife had agreed with this, probably because she too was sick of having to sleep next to such a perfectionist.

His sleep score back then had been in the late seventies and maybe early eighties, nowhere near what it needed to be. And so, when he had the opportunity to create his own bedroom, his "sleep pod" as such, he'd gone all out. He'd placed noise-dampening wooden slats against the walls to make sure that the outside world didn't affect him as much as it should. Blackout curtains didn't completely remove the outside light – there was a streetlamp near his apartment, and the neon lights of Canary Wharf would still shine into his window. He'd fixed this by securing a piece of plasterboard to the wall itself, effectively blocking off the entire window. He'd screwed it deep into the wall and, bar a couple of tiny, minuscule gaps, gaps he'd filled with Polyfilla, the room was now completely dark when the door was shut.

The door too had been fixed so that, when closed, no

light pollution streamed in. Once closed, it was as dark as an isolation pod.

All that was in the room was Joseph's double bed and a side table with a lamp on it. There was an Alexa device to the side, but it didn't light up when contacted, staying dark like the rest, thanks to black electrical tape around the outside, covering the blue LED line. When he turned the lamp off, the room went black, and even if he woke up at seven, eight, or even nine the following morning, it would look exactly the same. He would never know what time it was, and that was good.

Beds were for sleeping in.

The only way he knew it was time to wake up was that the bed had a temperature-related timer. It was one of the newer ranges of water-pumping thermal bedding; a topper that lay across a mattress and had water pumped through it from a machine to the side. He'd picked the most expensive because it was also the quietest, and the water that pumped through the tubes attached to the topper would either heat up or cool down, depending on what he'd requested. It would sense the changes in his body temperature during the night and effectively adjust accordingly, using AI to keep him at the optimal temperature for sleep. Only when it was time to wake up, at a set time arranged in advance, would the mattress change the temperature, altering it to bring him out of sleep and wake him naturally.

Once awake, the lamp would slowly build in light, allowing his eyes to adjust. When he woke and saw the light was on in the room, he knew it was time to get up. He didn't need to check his watch, currently monitoring his sleep patterns. He would rise, open his door, and enter the real world.

He had gained one hundred percent scores for the last week through this.

A streak ruined by last night's doughnut.

Joseph Lawrence didn't have breakfast, preferring to intermittently fast from six the previous evening until one in the afternoon. Then he would have a five-hour window in which to eat his lunch and dinner. It wasn't a strict rule – often he would eat up to eight or even nine at night, and as long as he had several hours to digest, he was fine with that. It also meant he could exercise without food in his stomach – fasted cardio and fasted weights would help him burn any fat that had crept onto his body, keeping it lean and at peak fitness.

First, however, following his meditation, he walked over to his apartment's patio, opening the doors and stepping out into the morning air. By now, it was almost five-thirty in the morning, and Joseph sat on a chair, letting the light of the sun gradually wake him up, helping remove the cortisol from his system and building his circadian rhythm as he wrote in his gratitude journal. He made sure he was fully awake before doing anything else; he wouldn't drink coffee until at least ninety minutes after waking, so he sipped on a glass of mineral water, flavoured with lemon, while taking the first batch of his many supplements and vitamins; entire handfuls of small pills rammed down his throat. He knew that, by doing this, he was technically breaking his fast – the glucose in some tablets surely contained enough calories to count as such. But it wasn't food, and Joseph didn't classify it as such.

The doughnut he ate the previous night, however, was definitely food.

It hadn't been his wife's fault, he wrote in his gratitude diary; a friend of hers at work was leaving, and they'd had a party. Cake was provided, and when she left, she'd brought back three doughnuts in one of those twelve-doughnut boxes that often arrived at these kinds of events. Nobody else had wanted them.

Joseph's wife wasn't as bothered about the whole anti-ageing market as Joseph was. She'd eaten one but didn't have the stomach for the other two. Joseph had had a bad day, a couple of finance deals falling through, and he needed a dopamine hit.

This had been it.

Stupid.

His mind wasn't focused. He didn't want to meditate today; he just wanted to go straight to the gym. He'd had his greens – powdered vitamins and minerals stirred into his drink – and he'd downed that with a methylene blue chaser. Methylene blue was an electron donor that helped him focus; it worked well with his nootropic stacks that he'd also taken that morning, giving him a small kick later in the morning, especially in the gym.

The gym itself wasn't far from his apartment, right in the middle of Canary Wharf. Joseph worked nearby; he was a finance executive for a top five company, and although it was tough work and long hours, the money he made provided him with the life he had. Every other day, he stayed in his apartment to exercise, usually calisthenics or a P90X session. But today, after the doughnut debacle, he needed to do more. He needed to burn those stolen calories before they could attach themselves to his stomach.

The next-level gym he was a member of was cutting-edge, perfect for a man like Joseph. There was a swimming pool, weights, cardio machines, even an infrared steam room and a plunge pool, giving him the heat and cold therapy he often liked. The gym also provided a variety of AI-related devices – new technology aimed at the anti-ageing market. If he wanted, he could go up to the second floor and bathe on a bed of red lights, reduce lymphatic swelling with PEMF mats, or cycle on an AI-controlled exercise bike that could give him forty-five minutes worth of exercise in the space of five. Such technology was enough to make an ordinary man feel like a god, if he so desired.

Today, however, he wasn't feeling it, even after his workout.

He knew he should have shaken it off by now, but that sodding doughnut was still on his mind. Interestingly, as if reading his mind, a notification came up on his phone – a last-minute space had opened up a couple of doors down, in *Ionosphere*, the cryogenic centre along the mall. So, he checked the app for Ionosphere and saw that there was indeed a session first thing because of a cancellation. The plunge pool would've been fine, but he needed something *more*. Cryotherapy was the option. He used the cryotherapy sessions once a week, having a rolling subscription for them, but today he needed a top-up.

So, he booked the spot there and then before someone else could take it, and, after showering, he bypassed the cold plunge and went straight next door, to Ionosphere.

Even though it boasted a variety of options for the active bio-hacker, Ionosphere was small and focused. There were two rooms, each with a built-in cryochamber at the back. Before you reached them, there was an office on one side of the corridor that led to them, and a larger room on the other that held the hyperbaric chamber, the red-light session lamps and a couple of massage beds—although Joseph didn't go in for that sort of new-age crap.

But as for the cryochambers ... well, essentially, each chamber was like a walk-in freezer with a glass window. In front of the window was a large countdown clock on the wall, so you could see how long you were in there for, and a small speaker at the top blasted out music of your choice.

Joseph didn't like listening to music. Music meant you could time how long you'd been in there by the verses and choruses. He preferred listening to audiobooks or podcasts – something random and unknown – where he could let his mind drift for the four minutes he'd be inside. He'd been doing cryotherapy for a while now, and even had the fan on during the session, so the wind instantly cooled the skin. He didn't know if it did anything more than the usual, but sometimes minus ninety or so degrees *wasn't enough* for him, it seemed. The shorts, socks, ski shoes, ski gloves, and even a little fluffy band for his ears were all provided, as well as a mask.

He'd never really understood why the mask was necessary, but he guessed it was probably to stop the air from freezing as it left his mouth. It was cold, after all. The whole point of a cryo-session was to shock your body, effectively. Your temperature would start at around thirty degrees, and by the end, it would have dropped to about fourteen degrees. Your body, not understanding what was going on, and not really having much of a memory for these things, would instantly believe that you were dying, trapped somewhere cold, and would start trying to find ways to heat you back up. It would burn calories, creating heat. It would eject senescent cells – those that weren't doing their jobs effectively – to free up more energy to use, effectively clearing the toxins out of your system. Joseph had heard it said that a good cryo-session could burn up to seven, maybe even eight hundred calories.

That was about the same as the bloody doughnut he'd eaten.

Even though he was first in line for the day's treatments, that didn't mean he wanted to be late; you only got a twenty-minute slot there, and all it took was someone showing up late to throw everything off – although, by being the first of the day, that shouldn't have been much of an issue. He also hoped that by arriving a little early, he'd be able to sneak in early, maximise his morning rather than waiting around. Stephen Kline, the owner usually opened up first thing, and during the day would likely let him start as soon as the previous customer left, even if there was time on the clock. It was a perk, and Joseph knew this was primarily because he'd sorted out some financial deals for Stephen.

But then he'd also screwed Kline over, too. However, that was business. And some clients took preference over others.

Anyway, from there, he could head straight to the office. He'd already had a shower at the gym, and the cryo session was a cold, dry experience rather than a wet one.

He was still thinking about the doughnut, though, as he approached the building, pushing on the double glass doors and frowning as they stayed locked. Looking through them, he could see that the main reception was lit up, the TV at the back showing icy fjords and freezing lakes – basically Wim Hof's wet dream on a loop.

But, for some reason, no one was answering his knocks. It was eight in the morning – his session had started. Someone should have been there.

I'm not paying for a half session, he thought to himself irritably, even though the "session" was technically just the four minutes he stood in the chamber. It was the principle of the matter, after all.

There was a doorbell to the side, so he pressed it. He even called the office number and watched as the phone on the other side of the door rang endlessly with no one answering. Now past the "getting in early" stage, and ten minutes into what would have been his twenty-minute session, Joseph was getting annoyed; this was wasting serious time here.

However, just as he was about to give up, Alexis, one of the assistants, arrived. She was twenty-one, and working here when she wasn't at university in Greenwich; blonde, slim, pretty, and sickeningly healthy. Joseph was over twice her age and wished he'd known in his twenties what she knew now.

He also wanted to sleep with her *so badly*.

Just not in his bedroom, that was for sleep only.

'Running late, aren't you?' he muttered irritably, expecting an apology.

Alexis frowned, trying the door herself.

'I don't understand,' she said. 'Stephen's supposed to be opening up this morning.'

She rattled the door again, shouting Stephen's name through the gap in the doors, as if her voice would summon the elusive owner. When no one arrived, Alexis reached into her pocket and pulled out a set of keys on chains. As one of the assistants, it was likely Alexis either opened or closed up at set times, so *of course she had a key*, Joseph realised, before irritably wondering why she hadn't pulled the key in the first place.

Eventually finding the correct one, she then dropped them to the floor, apologising as she scrabbled around to pick them up, unlocked the glass doors and pushed them open, glancing around.

'The alarm's not on,' she said. 'Stephen has to be here. He was closing up last night; he wouldn't have left it like this.'

'Maybe he was in a hurry,' Joseph said. 'Just like *I* am.'

His comment didn't go unnoticed, and Alexis sighed and nodded, walking over to the system and opening up the laptop on the reception desk, opening the calendar.

'I see you have the first session today,' she said. 'Sorry, we had someone else booked at this time, so I assumed you were the eight-twenty.'

'The app said eight was free.'

'Yes, looks like there was a cancellation last night,' Alexis read the screen. 'Eli Green isn't back from Thailand until today, so it was moved. No worries. Because we're running late, we'll comp you another session later this week as well.'

'Damn right you will,' Joseph replied irritably, noting the name mentioned; he knew Green. 'This wasn't *my* fault.'

'Let me gather the things together, and we'll have you ready in a jiffy,' Alexis smiled and walked to the end of the hallway. There were two wooden doors, placed almost side-by-side, each leading to a separate cryotherapy chamber. Inside each cryotherapy chamber was a bench where the customer's private and personal items were placed, allowing them to get changed in private. The rooms were mirrors of each other, with a wall between them.

But, no sooner had Alexis entered the first room than a piercing scream echoed down the corridor.

Joseph ran without thinking. He didn't know what had happened, but the scream wasn't the kind you'd hear if something small had occurred. This was pure terror. As he opened the door, his breath caught in his lungs. Even though he was the first client that day, Joseph Lawrence wasn't the first to enter the cryotherapy chamber.

Through the misted, frosted glass, a figure lay on the floor.

Joseph moved forward, pushing Alexis to the side.

'Wait,' he said. 'Let me.'

He reached for the door, pulling at it. The glass doors of the chambers were always left unlocked, so that if something went wrong or you didn't enjoy the session, you could simply push it open and walk out, meaning there was no need to wait for someone to let you out. But this time, the door wasn't moving.

Frozen shut? No, it didn't work that way.

Frowning, Joseph examined the door and noticed a bolt at the top; a flat metal slat had been slid into the frame, locking it from the outside. The only way out would have been to smash the glass door, but Joseph had been told the glass was effectively bulletproof.

There was a similar lock at the base of the door. These locks hadn't been there during his last session, and from the look on Alexis's face, they were unfamiliar to her as well. She trembled as Joseph worked at the bolts, unscrewing them, and opening the frosted door.

Inside, lying dead on the floor, was Stephen Kline.

The body lay stiff and lifeless in the centre of the cryotherapy chamber, frozen to the core after what looked to be hours in the sub-zero environment. His skin had turned an unnatural shade of pale blue, almost translucent in the harsh light of the room. His features were locked in a rigid, deathly expression, lips slightly parted, with ice crystals clinging to the edges. Frost had formed on his eyelashes and eyebrows, giving them a frosty, brittle appearance. His hands, curled slightly as though grasping for warmth, were stark white, with the telltale signs of frostbite showing on the tips of his fingers, where the skin had blackened. The rigidness of his posture and the sheen of ice covering his body suggested he had frozen in place, no hope of warmth or movement.

His clothing, now stiff as cardboard, was dusted with a fine layer of frost. It clung awkwardly to his form, the moisture from his body having turned to ice in the severe cold. Any hint of life had long since been stripped from him, and the room, once used for therapeutic rejuvenation, had now become his icy tomb. Even the air seemed to hang with a biting chill, the scent of something sterile and cold, mingling with the unnatural stillness of death frozen solid.

Joseph pulled away from the door, closing it quietly, before turning back to face the horrified Alexis.

'When did you last see him?' he asked.

'Yesterday,' she replied, her voice only a whisper. 'I finished at seven-thirty. He was closing up. There was one more booking.'

She stared at the frosted glass.

'He's been there all night, hasn't he? It should have turned off.'

Joseph couldn't help himself. He nodded, a morbid curiosity overtaking him. He looked back at the glass, then gently grabbed Alexis by the arms, pulling her gaze away once more as he guided her out of the room.

'Phone the police,' he said.

'Should we phone an ambulance?'

'I think we're well past ambulances here,' Joseph replied.

'Should we turn off the machine?'

Joseph shook his head.

'They're going to want to see the body, and in a way, he's perfectly preserved. We'll let them make that decision.'

As Alexis walked over to the phone and started dialling 999, Joseph Lawrence looked again at the door to the cryotherapy room and the body of his onetime client.

The doughnut he'd eaten last night was now completely forgotten, as was everything else he intended to do that day.

1

DAY TRIP

Detective Chief Inspector Declan Walsh travelled down to Canary Wharf with a perpetual scowl on his face. Usually, the Last Chance Saloon would take on jobs more suited to the City of London's remit, preferring not to venture outside their usual area. However, lately, they'd investigated cases all over London; cab drivers down mysterious London Knowledge routes, dead Roman soldiers re-enacting events on the London Wall – although that one had technically still been within the City of London boundary – but there had also been the more *personal* cases; Robin Hood actors killed by arrows at conventions, ex-military police partners found dead, and the serial killer who'd murdered Declan's parents. The list went on, and often with these ones, there was a personal connection.

Today's case seemed more in line with *that* than anything else.

The Last Chance Saloon had been attending their usual daily briefing; Detective Superintendent Alex Monroe, as always, taking the lead. Detective Inspector Anjli Kapoor sat beside Declan, Detective Sergeant Billy Fitzwarren in his usual spot at the laptop, and Doctor Marcos, the divisional surgeon, sat on the back row, with her sort-of assistant, Sergeant Morten De'Geer, and PC Esme Cooper alongside her. They'd been discussing the previous few weeks, primarily discussing a longtime case that had hung over Anjli's head, when Detective Chief Superintendent Sophie Bullman arrived.

Bullman had been a Detective Chief Inspector when Declan first met her, working alongside Monroe on the second case Declan had taken with the Last Chance Saloon. She had then served as Declan's *Police Federation Representative* when he was accused of terrorism, and had travelled with Monroe to Germany when they were hunting Karl Schnitter. After that, she'd taken on the role of Detective Superintendent, effectively becoming the boss of the Last Chance Saloon.

This was until the City of London Police Commander Edward Sinclair, the third-highest ranking police officer in City of London police retired – well, retired before he was *fired* – and his second-in-command, Chief Superintendent David Bradbury, moved up in Guildhall. Bradbury had worked closely with Bullman for a while by then, and when his old position became vacant, Bullman moved up as well. There had been rumours of nepotism, whispers of a personal relationship between the two, but Declan believed it was a well-deserved promotion. Bullman was an outstanding officer – she had solved some solid cases and had saved his life on multiple occasions. So what if she was being fast tracked?

But it was also Bullman who interrupted their briefing, bringing them their next case: a frozen body found in Canary

Wharf. Apparently, it was a location she frequented once a week, before attending her weekly numbers' meetings. There was a personal attachment to the body, the victim, and the location. An attachment so strong that as Declan drove to Canary Wharf, it wasn't Anjli Kapoor sitting beside him, but Bullman herself.

'HOW ARE YOU HOLDING UP?' SHE ASKED AS THEY HEADED towards the A13. 'It's been a bit of a hectic time for you.'

'It would have been nice to have a break, Ma'am,' Declan commented flippantly, teasing her gently about the sudden rush into a fresh case.

'You'd be bored,' Bullman replied. 'And bored detectives find mischief. Do you want to find mischief, Deckers? Or would you rather be a solid superstar detective like me?'

Her tone was mocking, using the nickname "Deckers", one she'd adopted since taking charge of the Last Chance Saloon. Declan accepted the ribbing.

'What can you tell me about this place?' he asked.

Bullman shrugged.

'It's a cryotherapy chamber and spa. They've got red light therapy, PEMF mats—'

'You're just making up words now, aren't you?' Declan raised an eyebrow as he interrupted.

'No, no, absolutely not,' Bullman replied. 'There's a hyperbaric chamber too, if you want to sit in one.'

'Do you get many people with the bends in Canary Wharf?' Declan asked. At Bullman's blank expression, he sighed. 'Hyperbaric chambers are for when scuba divers come up too fast. They get oxygen in their blood – it's called the bends.'

'Oh,' Bullman replied with a tone that suggested she didn't really care. 'Yeah, this isn't for that. This is more for oxygenating the blood and healing injuries. You know, most Premier League football clubs have one or two of them now. An hour at one-point-three pressure actually heals you up quicker. It calms you down, too.'

'And do you use it a lot?'

'Christ, no,' Bullman laughed. 'I don't go there to relax. I go there to get fired up. Four minutes at minus ninety-two degrees, standing in the cryotherapy chamber.'

'Are you allowed to wear a big coat?' Declan smiled. 'A pair of gloves, maybe some earmuffs?'

'You're not too far off, actually,' Bullman replied. 'They give you a headband to cover your ears, and you get to wear ski gloves and boots.'

'And the large winter coat?'

'No,' Bullman smiled. 'But they give you a nice pair of shorts. The whole point is to shock your body. It's a great way to wake up.'

'But not so great that you'd do it every morning.'

Bullman shook her head.

'It's also an incredibly *expensive* way to wake up, especially on a police salary. But I've known Stephen Kline, the owner, for years. When he first started up, he was up in Manchester when I transferred there as a DCI. When I moved down here, he was already set up, and offered me a police discount.'

Declan wanted to make a comment about how it seemed to be a *particular person* kind of police discount, but decided against it. He didn't want to take up the offer anyway.

Almost as if reading his thoughts, Bullman looked over.

'I thought you'd have been all for it,' she said. 'I remember you did your intermittent fasting and your bulletproof coffee.'

'I don't do it that much anymore,' Declan replied.

'How come?'

'No time,' Declan said. 'I'm often on the run, straight out the door. Coffee in hand is fine, but mixing the butter in is just a hassle.'

He shrugged.

'I still use MCT oil, though. Really concentrated coconut oil.'

'Sounds horrid,' Bullman smiled. 'Let me guess, you do this because you're a masochist?'

'Says the woman who stands in freezers for fun,' Declan muttered.

'Go on, why do you do it?'

'The olive oil's great for heart health – it helps lower bad cholesterol and has antioxidants that fight inflammation. It's a simple way to keep everything running smoothly.'

As he spoke, Bullman narrowed her eyes.

'Do you follow this stuff a lot?' she asked.

'What do you mean?'

'Well, you must pick this up from somewhere. Podcasts? Books? There's always some guru telling you to take weird stuff, or show your bumhole to the sun, right?'

'Something like that, I suppose, although I'm not sure where the "bumhole" idea comes from,' Declan said. 'I listen to podcasts. There's a guy who talks about getting sunlight in your eyes first thing and waiting an hour and a half before having coffee.'

'Sounds like the most boring killjoy ever,' Bullman muttered, typing on her phone.

There was a long moment of silence in the car after the

comment, and Declan took the opportunity to glance over at the Detective Chief Superintendent beside him. They weren't driving fast; there was no need to – the body had already been discovered, and the local police were holding down the fort. In fact, the only person likely speeding with sirens flashing right now was Doctor Marcos, who, the moment she heard there was a case to be looked at, grabbed De'Geer and made her way as quickly as she could towards Canary Wharf, complaining that the City Police forensics were far superior to the "local plod".

Declan knew that even if they *were* the best forensics in the world, she'd find a way to be unhappy. Doctor Marcos was a consummate professional in all matters, and by now, they would have already arrived, and she'd probably removed most of the people standing around, complained about the levels of lockdown in the area, and forced everybody to wear PPE suits or at least booties and gloves, which was strangely lacking in a lot of police investigations these days. He even went to comment on this to Bullman—

But Bullman was staring out of the window, in a thousand-yard stare.

'I know you said you knew him in Manchester before you came down,' Declan asked. 'Was there more to it?'

At this, Bullman raised an eyebrow in surprise.

'That's a rather personal question, Mister Walsh,' she said, almost amused by the way he spoke. 'Not that it's any business of yours, either.'

'Sorry, ma'am,' Declan replied sheepishly. 'I wasn't looking for gossip or anything like that, it's just, I know—'

Bullman nodded.

'You want to know how close I was to him, and how close I am to this case?'

Declan nodded, looking at her briefly as he spoke.

'You're a Detective Chief Superintendent, ma'am,' he said. 'You shouldn't be out here with me. Realistically, *I* shouldn't be out here. It should be DI Kapoor. As it is, Monroe's annoyed that he's not the one—'

'It's my case, Declan,' Bullman replied. 'And while we're in the field, you can call me Guv.'

'With all due respect, *ma'am*,' Declan continued. 'I call Monroe Guv because he's my Guv. You're *his* Guv.'

He glanced back at her.

'Also, can I ask a question? In Guildhall, when Ch Supt Bradbury had the role, he was pipped and uniformed—'

'Detective Chief Superintendents don't have to wear the uniform,' Bullman replied calmly. 'And before you continue about how I shouldn't be involved in something personal, you should reconsider exactly what's been happening with the Last Chance Saloon in the years that you've been with them. Victoria Davies, your first ever case with them? That was personal for you – it was a case your father failed to solve properly. Kendis Taylor's murder. Karl Schnitter, a serial killer who killed your parents. Eddie Moses, your onetime partner in the Royal Military Police.'

'In fairness,' Declan repeated, 'I was on the run and suspended from the force when Kendis was murdered. I was still suspended when I took on hunting the Red Reaper, and I'd quit the unit when I helped solve my partner's death.'

'Johnny Lucas,' Bullman replied.

'What of him?' Confused, Declan frowned.

'How many times have you helped him? A man that has connections personally to you, Kapoor, Monroe? You weren't suspended when you recently took down Karl Schnitter's daughter, and in the process you almost caught Karl

Schnitter himself, before he jumped to his death. You weren't suspended when you assisted your partner to take down a killer from her past ...'

Bullman's voice had grown softer and colder now.

'I knew Stephen Kline. And yes, we'd had a small fling years ago, but that doesn't necessarily mean that I'm going to go all teary-eyed the moment I see the body. Some bastard killed him, and I want them to pay. And with the best will in the world, DCI Walsh, if I'm going to find who killed him, I want the best detectives beside me as I do so. I don't know who would take the case on the Metropolitan Police side, but I do know that *you* would take the case if I brought you on personally.'

For the first time in a while, she actually gave a small smile.

'And unfortunately for you, Declan, you're too good a detective to be put aside.'

Declan took the faint praise as they arrived at one of the security cordons into Canary Wharf. Security cordons had become commonplace following terrorist attacks two decades earlier; the area's concentration of high-profile financial institutions making it a potential target. These measures included checkpoints and vehicle searches; the cordons allowed for screening of people and vehicles entering the area, aiming to protect the thousands who worked and visited the district daily.

Pulling out and showing his warrant card, the security officer waved them through, and they carried on into the Wharf itself, heading towards the car park for the shopping centre ... and for the cryotherapy centre within.

As they did so, Bullman checked her phone and smiled.

'Perineum sunning,' she said triumphantly.

'Sorry?'

'It's where you aim your bumhole at the sun,' Bullman read from the phone. 'In ancient Taoist beliefs the perineum, or as they call it the "Hui Yin" is said to be an important portal in the body where energy can enter. It's great for Vitamin D.'

'I bet the sunburn must be excruciating,' Declan muttered. 'I think I'll give that one a miss, if you don't mind.'

THE MAIN WALKWAY THROUGH THE REAR OF THE CENTRE HAD been blocked off with blue and white crime-scene tape, and PC Esme Cooper, having travelled with Doctor Marcos and now on scene of crime duty, was blocking people from passing through, patiently enduring the complaints from suited "finance" and "legal bros" in Ralph Lauren shirts and loafers with no socks, who were annoyed that their shortcut up the nearby steps to their offices was now out of use, and they had to go the long way around.

She nodded as Bullman and Declan approached.

'Ma'am, Guv,' she said, nodding through the glass doors. 'It's not that big in there, there's quite a few people already. If you want, I can get people to come out.'

'No, we can go inside,' Bullman replied.

But Cooper, even though she was diminutive and dwarfed by the taller Detective Chief Superintendent, stood in her way, standing her ground.

'Ma'am, the body hasn't been removed yet,' she said. 'I think it might be better—'

'I've seen bodies before,' Bullman snapped.

Declan placed a hand on Bullman's shoulder.

'I think what PC Cooper's trying to say,' he started, 'is that she knows you knew the victim and she's giving you an opportunity to *not* have to see the body.'

Bullman, realising, nodded at this, giving a tight smile to Cooper, a "thank you", before looking back at Declan.

'I have to be there for this,' she said.

'The Detective Superintendent running the case is in the back of the building and she's not exactly happy when she heard your name, or when she realised that Doctor Marcos was here,' Cooper, giving what was either a sigh of relief or a sigh of resignation, continued.

Declan frowned. He hadn't pissed any Detective Superintendents off recently – well, unless you counted Monroe. But he chalked it up to yet another thing he was going to have to deal with later on that day. He'd intended to find Doctor Marcos and ask what had happened, but she was already in the midst of a huddle of PPE-clad forensics, and Declan didn't want to interrupt her. So, he walked into the back office of the spa, Bullman beside him.

There, talking to one of the uniformed officers, was a young woman, her eyes red-rimmed with tears.

Declan showed his warrant card to the officer, who nodded, stepping back.

'Guv,' the officer said, 'this is Alexis. She works at the spa. She was the first to find the body.'

'Sorry for that,' Declan said to her, almost as an automatic response. Alexis, however, had seen and recognised Bullman, likely from her sessions as a customer, and almost as if discovering a lifeline, had run over and embraced the woman, crying into Bullman's sleeves.

'He's dead,' she cried. 'He's dead. They killed him.'

'Who killed him?'

'We don't know, but they locked the door. He couldn't get out. He died,' Alexis wailed.

Bullman, obviously embarrassed by this, tried to pull Alexis away from her.

'We'll do what we can to find out who killed Stephen,' she said. 'But in the meantime, I need you to keep giving your report to this officer, yes?'

Alexis, wiping her eyes, nodded, and Bullman turned to the uniformed officer.

'PC Quinn, ma'am,' the officer said. He was slim, young, with black hair cut into a trendy haircut., but his eyes looked haunted. Declan wondered if he'd also seen the body.

'I understand there's a Detective Superintendent around?'

'She popped out for a coffee,' PC Quinn said. 'I can check if she's back?'

'Please.'

'You don't need to,' a woman's voice spoke behind them. And Declan couldn't help it, but gave an involuntary groan as he turned to face the woman in the doorway.

She was in her forties, stocky, the kind of woman who could easily play rugby – and play it well. Her once-greying hair was dyed a dark-raspberry, curly and pulled back into an incredibly frizzy ponytail.

She was a battle-axe in every sense of the word.

And, as she stared at Declan, he forced himself into a smile.

'Congratulations on your promotion, Detective Superintendent Warren,' he said.

2

OLD ACQUAINTANCES

BULLMAN HELD HER HAND OUT.

'Detective Chief Superintendent Bullman,' she said. 'I guess you and DCI Walsh know each other?'

'Only in passing,' Warren replied. 'He once trampled all over a crime scene of mine in Newbury.'

'In fairness, Guv,' Declan said, 'that was mainly Monroe. And it was also to get Doctor Marcos past you, to have a look at the crime scene—'

'Before you took that case from me,' Warren muttered, interrupting.

Declan's smile became weaker, more sickly, as he realised that this *wasn't* going to be a fun conversation.

'Ma'am, when we met then-DCI Warren,' he said to Bullman, 'it was during the Victoria Davies case, in Savernake Forest. They'd found a body and, well, Doctor Marcos wanted to see it—'

'And she was banned from crime scenes back then, wasn't she?' Bullman nodded. 'Yeah, I heard about this. Sorry you had to deal with it.'

The last part was spoken to Warren, who shrugged.

'You deal with Monroe, you get shit, ma'am,' she said.

'Warren also helped us with the Adam Harris re-enactor case,' Declan continued on. 'Nicholas Stephens was passing along information on the death of Bridget Farnsworth at Pennington Hall three years ago.'

'Well, your help with our cases is appreciated,' Bullman said. 'I have to ask, though, why is a Newbury officer here?'

'I'm no longer with Newbury,' Warren replied matter-of-factly. 'I was offered a transfer and a promotion. Nothing much was happening up there, and you can only stay a DCI of a provincial area for so long.'

She looked over at Declan and her eyes narrowed.

'And I heard that in London anybody can get a promotion,' she said. 'I didn't get a chance to mention it when I last came to your Unit, but congratulations on *yours*, DCI Walsh. I suppose I should go and congratulate Alex Monroe as well, as I didn't bother last time. Is he around?'

'No,' Bullman replied, now noting the bitterness in Warren's tone, and apparently not caring for it. 'But you can congratulate me. Until recently I was the same rank as you.'

Declan had realised already that Warren and Bullman *really* weren't going to get on together.

'Look, I'm sorry for us taking over your case,' Bullman continued. 'But—'

'But nothing,' Warren put her hands on her hips. 'You're Detective Chief Superintendent. You can do what you want. If you want to take a case on, off you go. If you want to bring the City of London police out of their jurisdiction and into mine and take it over, go ahead. It's not the first time I've seen them do this.'

She glanced at Declan.

'All it takes is a friendly higher-up, maybe a Prime Minister who owes you a favour or two, and it seems you can go wherever you want.'

'We're not taking the case from you, Detective Superintendent Warren. We intend to work alongside you,' Declan gave a smile. It was as fake as his expression, and he knew that Warren would know this.

'Oh, really?' Warren replied sarcastically and then paused, frowning. '*Really?* I assumed Monroe would just want me out of the way. We've never really got on.'

'I'll be honest, Guv, I don't think he even realises that you're here.'

'So this wasn't a deliberate "screw you"?' Warren now looked from Bullman to Declan, and then back. 'When I heard you were coming, and the witch doctor arrived, I assumed—'

'When you *assume*, you make an ass out of you and me,' Bullman replied coldly. 'Alexander Monroe did not choose this case, I did. I knew the victim.'

'Surely that gives you a conflict of interest then?' Warren didn't move, standing in the doorway.

Bullman shrugged.

'Most likely,' she replied. 'But, let's be honest, it's not the first time someone's done this.'

'I should push this up the ladder.' Warren didn't move. 'With you being the Detective Chief Superintendent of the City of London Police, I think the Met should know what's going on as well.'

'The Met *are* aware of what's going on,' Bullman said, cutting off Warren mid-flow. 'But I'm more than happy to have someone contact you, show you the paperwork, and make sure that everything's sorted. Until then, how about you tell me what's going on?'

Warren nodded, looking at Quinn.

'I'll finish here with the witness,' she said. 'Give the nice people here a tour.'

Declan understood why Warren would pass it on to subordinates, but he did feel a little slighted as PC Quinn led Bullman and Declan out of the back office and into the main reception area.

'Does Warren do a lot of these?' Bullman asked him.

He shrugged.

'She's only been here a month,' he replied. 'She likes to keep on top of things, hands-on approach.'

Declan was typing on his phone, and Bullman spied this, tapping him on the shoulder.

'Are we keeping you from something?' she inquired. 'A little midnight tête-à-tête, or something that you need to organise?'

Declan smiled as he looked back up, finishing the message.

'Just telling Monroe that an old friend is involved here,' he murmured. 'I would have preferred to have said it to his face, see the expression, but the chances are Doctor Marcos will be there to tell him first, and I wanted to make sure—'

'That you were the one to provide the joy,' Bullman shook her head as she looked back at Quinn. 'Come on then, PC Quinn, tell us all about the popsicle in the freezer.'

There was a moment of stunned silence. Bullman looked from Declan to Quinn.

'Hey,' she interjected, 'he was my friend. If anyone's going to say it, it's me.'

Swallowing and opening his notebook, PC Quinn began.

'Stephen Kline, age fifty-five, owner of Ionosphere. He was the last in the office last night, closed up after the last session at seven-thirty pm, although the assistant reckoned there was one more booking after she left for the day. She'd agreed to open up this morning, but the first booking was cancelled. Well, sort of.'

'Explain sort of.'

'The eight am that'd been booked was delayed until later in the day, so there was an open spot,' Quinn continued reading. 'Usually these don't get taken, but this morning another customer, Joseph Lawrence, took the spare spot for a last-minute session.'

'We have that confirmed?'

'Yes, Guv. Took the spot, and arrived this morning to find no answer. When Kline's assistant turned up, upon entering, they found Mister Kline in the cryotherapy room.'

'How did they get in?' Declan queried.

'The assistant, Alexis Kovalenko, has keys to get in,' Quinn responded, reading from his notes. 'She also has the code for the alarm, but she said it hadn't been placed on last night.'

'Do we know how long he was in the freezer – room – chamber – whatever you call these things?' Declan asked.

'Your surgeon, Doctor Marcos is informing our forensics on how to do that right now,' Quinn explained.

Declan could detect the slightest hint of irritation in the

police constable's voice, which was understandable. People who met Rosanna Marcos for the first time often felt the same way.

'The estimation, however, is that he's been there for about twelve hours,' Quinn continued.

'So, realistically, from the moment he was closing shop to the moment somebody turned up to open shop,' Declan pulled out his notebook, noting this down as well. 'What was he wearing?'

At Quinn's surprised expression, Declan continued, glancing slightly at Bullman to push the point home for the constable.

'We've not looked at the body yet,' he explained. 'I'd rather we did that at the end, if I'm being honest.'

'Why hasn't he been removed?' Bullman interrupted.

Quinn looked uncomfortable.

'Problem is, ma'am, he was in minus ninety-two degrees for twelve hours,' he admitted. 'He was collapsed in the corner of the cryotherapy booth and, well, he's not ... flexible.'

Declan grimaced as he heard this, understanding exactly what Quinn was explaining. There was no way that Stephen Kline was going to be wheeled out on a gurney. Chances were they'd probably have to wait for him to thaw out a little, before they could bend him into position – or find a different way to get him to the morgue.

'Okay, so let's go back a moment. What was he wearing?' Bullman repeated, looking at Declan. 'As I said on the way here, when you do cryotherapy, you have shorts and boots and gloves and a mask and a little thing to go around your head to keep your ears warm. I'm curious if this was a session that had gone bad.'

Quinn shook his head.

'Body was fully clothed,' he replied. 'No shoes, but he was wearing socks. They've stuck to the base of the booth – it's another reason we haven't moved the body yet. He was wearing jeans, a polo shirt, socks and, well, maybe underwear?'

'Rings, watches, things like that?' Declan asked. 'Could he have been robbed?'

'He was wearing a watch which had stopped, had a ring on, and a wallet with credit cards and cash was still in his back jeans pocket,' Quinn continued reading from the notes now. 'To be honest, it just looked like he'd just taken his shoes off and stepped in.'

'Which is probably what happened,' Declan muttered, 'until someone placed locks on the doors, apparently.'

'Yes, sir,' Quinn nodded. 'Two bar bolts slid in at the top and the bottom. They effectively blocked the door from being able to be opened from the inside. Apparently, you could usually push the glass door open and it would let you out, but with this you couldn't get out without anybody coming in and unscrewing the bolts on the other side. There was no way he was going to get out and, after a couple of minutes, he would start losing the ability to do it anyway.'

Declan didn't want to consider how long Stephen Kline would have been hammering on the door.

'Do we know who he was here with?' Bullman continued.

'We have the last booking, Aria Milton. We were going to bring her in for questioning, but now it's your case, you might want to do that,' Quinn replied. There was no sense of anger in his voice; he was simply stating a fact. 'We have footage that shows her arriving for her session and then leaving about eight minutes later.'

'So the sessions don't take long then?' Declan asked.

'Oh, not at all,' Bullman interjected, now speaking from experience. 'You arrive, you change into the clothing, you stand in a freezer for four minutes, get changed back and leave. It's a quick turnaround; they can do three, sometimes four in an hour.'

'Good money if you've got it,' Declan observed. 'Maybe that's where this is coming from. Do we have anything on the CCTV footage?'

'Security footage was wiped, sir,' Quinn responded, and Declan could see that he was also irritated by this.

'Define "wiped"?' Declan asked.

'I mean that we have security footage of Miss Milton leaving,' Quinn shrugged. 'There's about another few minutes of footage of the main reception, which is the only place where the camera is. They don't film the cryo-sessions, mainly because people get changed in there, and it's a privacy issue.'

'Likewise, probably the hyperbaric chamber or the sauna area,' Bullman continued.

'About five minutes after Miss Milton leaves, we see the assistant, Miss Kovalenko leave, and then a few minutes later the footage simply cuts out,' Quinn replied. 'If somebody had killed Mister Kline, they could have gone to the security footage, reversed it to a set point before they arrived, deleted it, and then turned the cameras off.'

'You say "if" someone killed him,' Declan said, narrowing his eyes. 'Surely this is a straightforward murder case?'

Quinn shook his head.

'We thought that, but your Doctor Marcos ... she thinks there might be something different going on. She thinks the lock could have been made in such a way that the moment the door shut, it instantly stopped it from being opened again. This could have been a suicide attempt.'

'How the hell is this suicide?' Bullman's face darkened, and Quinn, realising he was probably overstepping, shrunk back against the wall a little.

'Ma'am, when people want to kill themselves,' he explained cautiously, 'and I'm not saying that Stephen Kline *wanted* to kill himself, I'm just saying what I was told – when people want to kill themselves, they often make sure they can't back out at the last moment. It's why people jump from buildings or ... well ... you know. If Mister Kline had wanted to commit suicide and he wanted to do it this way, there's every opportunity for him to place those locks on the door to prevent escape, if he so wanted to.'

'So, you're saying that Stephen Kline, a man who had no real reason to kill himself, simply attached two locks to his door, clambered in, shut it behind him, and then waited out his death?' Bullman's tone was icy.

'I'm saying, ma'am, that we don't know what it is yet,' Quinn answered hesitantly.

Bullman looked like she was about to speak again, but Declan, noticing her rising anger, decided to step in.

'Surely there has to be a cutoff?' he asked. 'The machine must realise there's a problem and stop?'

'Checking into that,' Quinn read the notes, flipping the page. 'Apparently, as he hadn't set a session going, the machine probably didn't realise it was being used, and stayed at temperature.'

Declan shuddered, as if the room had dropped its own temperature.

'Any enemies?' he asked.

'Did Kline have any? Oh, everybody,' Bullman started, but then stopped as Declan raised a hand to pause her.

'Ma'am, I know you knew him,' Declan said gently, 'but

what you're doing right now is exactly what I commented on earlier. If you're going to run this case, you have to do it impartially. The data we have on Stephen Kline cannot come from you. If it does, then you become a witness, not an investigator.'

Bullman sighed, nodding and waving to Quinn to continue.

'We're still checking into that, sir,' Quinn continued. 'At the moment, it doesn't look like Kline had any enemies – unless Ma'am here has other intelligence.'

'It's okay,' Declan said, his tone calm. 'Our own people will look into that.'

There was a buzz, and Declan looked down at his phone. A message from Monroe had arrived.

> Jesus Christ, you're kidding, right? Kill me now.

Declan decided it was best not to show this to Bullman, and instead stretched, looking around the lobby as he did so. He saw Alexis Kovalenko emerge from the office, walking over to them.

'Miss Kovalenko, sorry to ask this, but can you think of anybody who was unhappy with Stephen?' he asked.

Alexis didn't reply at first, glancing nervously at Bullman. Bullman gave her a nod.

'It's okay,' she said gently. 'We need you to be honest.'

'There was a lot of stress,' Alexis said finally. 'Not hatred or anger, but irritation.'

'And why would that be?' Declan pressed.

'The contest,' Alexis spoke as if it was the most obvious thing in the world. 'People were angry with him that he wasn't helping them with it. There was talk that he himself was trying to get involved, even though he'd claimed at the start he was impartial. He even removed himself a couple of months back.'

Declan looked around, wondering if he was the only person missing a vital point here.

'I'm sorry,' he said, pausing his note-taking. 'What contest are you talking about?'

Alexis looked at Bullman, who shrugged, also as confused as Declan was.

'I assumed you'd know.'

'Let's, for one second, pretend that we don't know,' Bullman suggested.

Alexis nodded.

'The ... well, rejuvenation thing,' she explained. 'You know, the "who can live the longest" anti-ageing contest. Stephen was one of the people helping with it.'

'The what?' Declan wrote the name down.

'The Rejuvenation Royale Tournament, or RRT,' Alexis repeated. 'Basically, Stephen said it was a bunch of super-rich folks competing to see who can make themselves the youngest using all these wild, cutting-edge biohacks. Everything from extreme diets to experimental tech, just to shave years off their biological age. It's like a super intense, futuristic version of a beauty contest, but way more hardcore.'

Declan nodded. 'And hypothetically, if you were the winner of this contest,' he asked, 'what would you get, apart from immortality?'

'The same as it's always been,' Alexis said. 'The top ten global contestants get two million dollars, a trip to Vegas and a chance to win in the finals.'

Declan looked back at Bullman. A man dying in a cryotherapy chamber was different, that was for sure. But a man dying while part of a competition where you could win two million dollars, just to start with – that was way more familiar.

'I think we need to know a little more about this contest,' he decided.

3

CONTESTANTS, READY

Ladies and gentlemen, let's get ready to rumble in the Rejuvenation Royale Tournament!'

Billy Fitzwarren stood at the front of the briefing room – an unnatural position for the young man to be in. Usually, he sat beside his laptop, pressing keys on the keyboard to change the image behind him as someone else, usually Monroe, gave the briefing. This time, however, the laptop was at an empty seat, with Monroe sitting beside it, Bullman next to him, and Declan and Anjli in their usual places. Cooper and De'Geer were at the back, with a rather irritated Detective Superintendent Warren between them.

The only person missing was Doctor Marcos, who was still examining the body, but had promised to be back with an update within the hour. It was now approaching lunchtime; Canary Wharf had been reopened, the body had eventually been removed, and life was returning to normal.

For the Last Chance Saloon team, however, everything was different, and not just because of their new arrival, who glared at everyone as if she expected them to attack her at the first opportunity.

'Go on then, lad, amaze us with your knowledge,' Monroe said, crossing his arms, his expression set in a scowl.

Billy, standing a bit nervously, pressed a remote held in his fingers – a tiny stick no larger than a pen as he cleared his throat.

'Okay then, the Rejuvenation Royale Tournament, or RRT for short. This isn't just some vanity project for the rich and famous – it's a serious competition that's been running for about seven years now,' he began to explain hesitantly, unused to the spotlight. 'It was started by a guy named Rupert Cray, a tech billionaire who got obsessed with the idea of beating the ageing process after a near-death experience. His idea was to gather some of the wealthiest and most ambitious people from around the world, to see who could reduce their biological age the most using the latest in biohacking and anti-ageing technology.'

'If this is so big, why hasn't it had more news out there?' Anjli asked.

'The whole thing is pretty hush-hush, happening behind closed doors in exclusive circles,' Billy replied, clicking his remote and showing a website page on the plasma screen behind him. 'Anyone who puts their head above the parapet gets laughed at or called a scam artist. But the stakes are real; two million dollars to whoever manages to knock the most years off their biological clock by the end of the year – with local rounds across the globe leading to a motherlode event in Vegas next year, and a further ten million in prize money.'

'How's that work then?' Declan frowned. 'How can you tell how many years are knocked off?'

'I'm glad you asked,' Billy smiled, waggling the remote as

he pressed it, pulling up a list of names on a leaderboard. 'In the RRT, participants' progress towards reducing their biological age is tracked using a combination of advanced scientific techniques and cutting-edge health assessments.'

'Which you understand, of course?' Monroe raised an eyebrow.

'Hell no, Guv. I'm just reading this from their media kit,' Billy grinned. 'And the media kit says these methods aim to provide a comprehensive picture of each individual's biological age, which may differ significantly from their chronological age.'

'Such as?'

'First, they look at your biomarkers – stuff like telomere length and DNA methylation from your blood or saliva. These tell scientists how old your cells really are. Then, they use something called an epigenetic clock, which measures changes in your DNA to figure out your biological age compared to your actual age,' Billy explained. 'They also do imaging, like MRI and DEXA scans to check your muscle mass, bone density, and fat distribution – basically, how your body's holding up physically. Then, they test your metabolism and heart health by looking at things like VO_2 max and insulin sensitivity. And since ageing isn't just physical, they also evaluate your cognitive function – memory, reaction times, stuff like that. In the end, they combine all these results into a single score that represents your biological age. The goal is to lower this score as much as possible. The person who can reduce their biological age the most wins the whole thing.'

'How does the score work?' Warren asked from the back.

Surprised at the direction the question came from, Billy paused, looking back at the leaderboard.

'So, in the RRT, participants are scored based on how much they can lower their biological age, which reflects how old their body is on a cellular level, not just their chronological age. The goal is to achieve the greatest reduction possible,' he explained, nodding up at the board. 'When you see a score like 0.65, it means the participant has reduced their biological age by thirty-five percent, compared to where they started. Suppose you start with a biological age of forty years, yeah? After various treatments and lifestyle changes, your new biological age is calculated. If your score is 0.65, it means your biological age is now sixty-five percent of what it was. In this example, your biological age would now be twenty-six years.'

'That'd be nice,' Declan smiled.

'It also means that for every year you age, you're technically only ageing two thirds of that year,' Billy continued. 'Every three years, you only age two. The score is a simple way to express how much younger your body has become as a result of the treatments, with "one" representing no change, and lower percentages indicating greater success in reversing the ageing process. Zero means you're not ageing at all. You've succeeded in immortality.'

'Or you've been bitten by a vampire,' Anjli muttered.

'So, who are the people on the board, then?' Monroe asked. 'And why isn't Kline on there?'

'Stephen Kline wasn't competing, but he was heavily involved in promoting the London round of the RRT,' Cooper now spoke up. 'Alexis, the assistant said people were suspicious of his motives, claiming he was looking to make an entrance to the contest as soon as he was low enough on his score, but he seemed to change his mind.'

Billy nodded at this, before nodding up at the list, all showing variances between 0.65 and 0.72 beside their names.

'As for the top five UK contestants, here's who we've got,' Billy said, and as he named each one, an image appeared beside them, taken from social media accounts. 'Top is David Lester. This guy's a Silicon Valley heavyweight. He's throwing every piece of tech and data at this competition, from gene therapy to advanced health tracking. For Lester, this is about proving that technology can outsmart ageing.'

'If he's Silicon Valley, why's he in a London contest?' Monroe frowned.

'Because he's banned from the West Coast one for "problematic behaviour",' Billy replied. 'I'm still looking to see what that is. He has offices in the City, so he's moved over while the contest is on ...'

'And while he has a London postcode, he's eligible,' Declan nodded. 'Next?'

'Selene Carter. She's a former Olympic triathlete who's transitioned into wellness coaching. Carter's all about natural methods – fasting, epigenetics, and fitness routines designed to keep you young. She's here to show that you don't need high-tech gadgets to stay healthy, and is probably the only one spending less than fifty grand a year on this.'

'Fifty grand a year is low?' Declan's eyes widened.

'Lester's paying out two million a year for his.'

'Two million to win two million,' Monroe tutted. 'That's bad finance.'

'It's also the potential ten million extra in prize money,' Billy added. 'But he doesn't want that. Chances are he wants the kudos of being the "Immortality King" or whatever they call the winner, to start selling his own machines and products. This is an industry worth *billions* right now.'

'I'm in the wrong job,' Monroe said, shaking his head in disbelief. 'Go on, laddie. Continue.'

'Third is Aria Milton—'

'This is the one who was last in the chamber yesterday?' Declan looked back at Warren, who nodded.

'Milton's a big name in biotech, running her own company focused on anti-ageing products,' Billy continued. 'She's known for pushing the envelope with experimental treatments, as well as luxury smoothies and serums, and she's in this tournament to prove her products are the real deal.'

'She could have been angry to hear Stephen was looking to enter, and decided while they were alone to fix this,' Anjli muttered. 'We should chat more with her, and not just as a witness. She is, after all, the last person we know to see Kline alive.'

'In fourth, we have Leon Brecht, a data scientist from Switzerland, who lives in the UK now,' Billy forced onwards. 'Brecht uses AI and machine learning to monitor his health. He believes that by crunching the right numbers, you can extend life significantly, and sees the RRT as the perfect stage to validate his theories.'

'Isn't that the same as Lester?' Declan asked. 'Tech and all that?'

'More AI specific, I think,' Billy shrugged. 'I've not yet seen if they know each other outside the contest. Finally, in fifth place, we have Mira Nakahura, an investment banker who's been pretty secretive about her motivations as, unlike the others, she doesn't seem to have any kind of company to benefit if she wins.'

'Maybe she makes the money in endorsements,' Anjli

suggested. 'Why make the machines when you can be paid a ton to advertise them?'

'How many go through?' Declan asked. 'To Vegas?'

'The top twenty lowest percentages, globally,' Billy replied. 'So, if nobody else beats their scores, then all five would. Maybe even the top six or seven. Currently, Mira is fifth in the UK, but sixteenth globally. All it takes is a bad score to lower her ...'

'And, if Kline came in lower, with a couple of other sudden changes, it could push Mira out of the top twenty global,' Declan considered. 'So, these are the top players?'

'In what's shaping up to be a pretty intense competition,' Billy nodded. 'And, with Kline out of the picture, the dynamics could shift—'

'And we need to keep a close eye on who might stand to gain the most from his death, laddie,' Monroe nodded.

'These were all part of this competition, but we also know that Aria Milton was the last person to effectively see Stephen,' Warren now spoke up from the back. 'Are there any other connections they have?'

'Actually, yes,' Billy replied. 'Aria Milton isn't just a contestant who uses his cryotherapy. Some of the technology that the spa holds was actually manufactured by her company; the hyperbaric chamber was, for a start. It's created by *Luxor Aesthetics*, which is the wellness company she founded.'

'She's a business partner?' Warren suggested.

'I don't know if she's a business partner, more of a supplier, really,' Billy mused. 'And obviously, during that time, she's developed a relationship with Stephen Kline that has led her to use his equipment.'

'She creates these kinds of things. Surely she has her own cryotherapy devices?' Declan suggested.

'Maybe she prefers to use someone else's, or it's stupidly expensive on the electricity bills,' Monroe replied, looking back at Billy now. 'Anyone else?'

'Mira is a client of the spa,' Billy said, reading through some notes on the laptop, turning it to face him, as he stood on the opposite side of where he usually would be. 'She's been going there on and off for the last year and a half. But although the others probably connect to him somehow, it might not be specifically through the spa.'

He paused, scrolling through a page on his screen.

'There's a biohacker event that happens in London every six months,' he said. 'The Energy Optimisation Summit usually gets held in the Business Design Centre in Islington. Stephen Kline is a sponsor of it. So is Aria Milton, and from the looks of things, so is Leon Brecht, but not as much. At the last one of these events, two months ago, Brecht was a speaker, and I can check if the others attended.'

He read his notes, pausing.

'There was one thing that might be relevant, and it goes to your question about whether there were people who didn't like Stephen or not – Eli, full name Elias, Green.'

He tapped on his keyboard, and on the plasma screen behind him, the image of another man appeared. This man was in his forties, salt-and-pepper hair cut short, in an almost army cut. He was tanned and fit, built like a gymnast, or some kind of callisthenics expert.

'Green is another high-profile UK competitor in the RRT, although only just out of the top ten in the UK, so way down the line globally,' he continued. 'From the looks of things, he was also a close business associate of Stephen Kline. Green is deeply invested in biohacking and anti-ageing technologies, made his fortune in the health and wellness industry, focusing on groundbreaking supplements and alternative therapies. The blurb says they were "essential components of a holistic anti-ageing regimen, complementing the cryotherapy treatments with internal support for cellular regeneration and longevity."

'I remember those,' Bullman nodded. 'They stopped selling them, though. And I remember Green being around back in Manchester, too.'

'That makes sense,' Billy replied, looking up at her. 'Apparently, Eli Green pulled his products two months ago, after a spat with Stephen during the Summit. According to witnesses, quite a few people were involved.'

'We know about Eli,' Warren said from the back. 'When we looked into the spa itself, Eli Green was one of the original directors of the company.'

'Hold on,' Monroe rose, turning to face Warren. 'Are you telling me this Eli chap, who had a fight with Stephen Kline two months ago at some event in Islington, who then pulled out all of his product from the spa – the one he bloody created with Stephen – you didn't think that this guy could be a suspect?'

'Of course we thought he could be a suspect,' Warren snapped back. 'However, on checking, he's been in Thailand, and he's landing today. '

'Oh,' Monroe slightly deflated as he sat back down. 'Well, that's okay then.'

'But feel free to tell me I'm not doing my job in other ways, Alex,' Warren snapped. 'I don't get tired of it.'

'I just thought our cyber expert would have picked up on this as well,' Monroe muttered.

'The cyber expert did, Guv,' Billy spoke up now, his voice tinged with irritation as he looked across at his boss. 'He had motive and opportunity, even if he wasn't in the country. He also worked side by side with Stephen Kline in the first years of his Ionosphere existence, up in Manchester. He stepped away, selling his shares in the business last year, right after bringing it to London, but before that he had access to the building, security, everything. If anybody was able to get in, screw around with the CCTV, and stick Stephen Kline in the cryotherapy chamber, it would have been him.'

He shrugged, however, looking back at Warren.

'But, as the Detective Superintendent says, he wasn't in the country. In fact, he only landed an hour back.'

'He could still have sent somebody to do it,' De'Geer suggested, the first time he'd spoken in that meeting.

'That's possible,' Monroe mused. 'We should meet with him now he's back from Thailand. Find out exactly who he's been talking to recently.'

As they had been talking, Billy had clicked to a second photo of Green, this time with a younger man beside him. They both wore futuristic training vests, and were holding up plasma bags in some kind of press shot.

'Who's the kid?' Declan asked.

'Sorry, it jumped a photo,' Billy reddened, checking his notes. 'Green recently made it into the industry press by injecting his son's plasma into himself, in an attempt to reverse the ageing process.'

'And the tournament was okay with that?'

'Doesn't look like it, as he stopped the procedure soon after.'

Declan leant forward, staring at the screen.

'You wouldn't know they were father and son,' he said, a hint of sulkiness creeping into his tone. The sight of the two well-toned men on the screen, one several years older than he was, seemed to make him feel a bit insecure. 'Green does look younger ... but not by much. What's the son's name?'

Billy smiled.

'Elias.'

'Didn't you say that was Eli Green's name as well?'

'I'm guessing it's Elias Green Junior. Either way,' Billy continued, 'Eli Green *senior's* the one we're really interested in. His son doesn't seem to want to be involved in any of this. In fact, he's just started an internship at an investment bank. Same one as Mira Nakahura, but that's probably just by chance, as they'd be in different areas.'

'A bit of a change of pace for someone whose father is one of the next generation of anti-ageing hackers, isn't it?' Declan raised an eyebrow.

'Just because you followed your father into the family business doesn't mean everyone else does,' Monroe gave Declan a wink. 'Anyway ...'

He shifted in his seat as he started to plan ahead.

'Anjli, speak to Aria Milton. Find out if she saw anything or noticed anything that could have piqued her interest last night. If you can, chat to Selene Carter, too. And let's look into these other people.'

He frowned.

'And somebody have a chat with these Energy Optimisation Summit people, whoever they are. Find out everything you can about any fights that happened at the last talk. If there was a bit of a confrontation with a few people, including Eli ... that means there were other people involved. I'd like to know exactly what was going on.'

4

OLD GHOSTS

As they drove in Anjli's car down to Streatham, Anjli couldn't help but feel that she was being observed critically. Eventually she turned to face Detective Superintendent Warren, who, seeing this, spun to face forward as if she hadn't been looking at the woman beside her.

'Do we have a problem?' Anjli asked, painfully aware of the relationship the woman had with her superior.

Warren turned, looking back at Anjli.

'How do you do it?' she asked. 'Working with them.'

'I don't quite know what you mean,' Anjli replied honestly. 'You're a strong woman, Guv, you're a Detective Superintendent. If you're worried about working in a man's world, I think you're doing slightly better than me.'

'Call me Lennie,' Warren replied. 'And yeah, I might have the rank over you, but I also have the years.'

She looked out of the window, watching the A13 go past.

'You're lucky, working in London. There's more scope for promotion. Bigger jobs, quicker movement. People transfer to the countryside for a quieter life.'

'Do they get that?' Anjli asked, surprised at the statement.

'Christ no,' Warren laughed to herself. 'Half the DCs and DIs I know who move to various provincial villages find that there are more murders going on there than there were in London. Shows like *Midsomer Murders* are like a how-to documentary to those guys.'

Anjli nodded.

'We've had our share of countryside issues,' she said. 'So, I know exactly where you're coming from.'

At this, Warren's face darkened.

'Yeah, I heard about Walsh's parents and the serial killer,' she said. 'I also saw the news a couple of weeks ago about how he'd gained the house in a will and all that.'

Before Anjli could angrily answer, she held her hand up to pause her.

'I didn't say I *believed* it, I said I'd seen it. Big difference,' she settled back in the passenger seat. 'Your husband might be a bit of a nightmare, but he doesn't look like he's corrupt. Seems a nice man.'

'Oh no,' Anjli quickly said, 'we're not married.'

'Really? You carry yourself like a married couple. Although I wouldn't know,' Warren waggled her fingers. 'Never had the ring on mine.'

'Is that why you moved to London?' Anjli asked. 'No ties to keep you in Newbury?'

'That and the fact that I was watching others get promoted time and time again while I got to do nothing, went nowhere – while doing a bloody good job, I'll have you know.'

'By others, do you mean Monroe?'

Warren didn't answer for a moment, staring out the window.

'And if I did?'

'I'd like to know what your problem is with him,' Anjli replied. 'He's been my mentor for many years, he's helped both myself and Declan. Does he have his problems? Sure, but not enough to make someone hate him the way you seem to. Especially as you've never worked with him.'

At the comment, Warren turned to face Anjli, raising an eyebrow at this.

'You don't think we've worked together?'

Anjli shrugged.

'He was at Mile End for fifteen, twenty years before moving to Vauxhall. Then after that, he came here to the Last Chance Saloon. I mean, I'm sure he's been here and there, I know he started off in Glasgow. But he's never been a provincial detective.'

'Provincial detective ...' Warren shook her head sadly. 'You guys even say it like we're your country bumpkin partners.'

'I didn't mean it that way,' Anjli quickly added.

'I know what you were saying,' Warren said, and the smile that she'd had moments earlier was now gone. 'I did work with Monroe. I was a detective sergeant. Actually, I was pretty much you. Just promoted from detective constable. Shiny and excited. I worked under DCI Parsons, but she went off on maternity leave. And for about five, six months, Alexander Monroe was brought in, in her place.'

'Monroe did maternity cover?' Anjli shook her head. 'Now that I *can't* believe.'

'No, I'm sure you can't,' Warren smiled, but this time it was a humourless, dark one. 'I think it was more of a case that he was told he *had* to do this, rather than anything. I mean, we're talking almost fifteen years ago. He was still at Mile End and his wife had disappeared a couple of years earlier. The man had a drinking problem. And I don't mean that he drank a lot, I meant his problem was he just couldn't find places to put all the bottles he held. Vodka, gin, whisky, you name it, he had them. Walking into his office was like walking into a speakeasy.'

Anjli said nothing. Monroe in the past had mentioned that he'd had a drinking problem, claiming he was a functional heavy drinker rather than an alcoholic. His line had always been that alcoholics hid their drinking, where he was quite happy to let anybody in the area know that he drank. He was Scottish, and he claimed it was part of his heritage.

Anjli knew it was an excuse. Warren, however, hadn't finished.

'He lasted with us for five months,' she continued. 'In that time, I think he was sober for three days. I get he was having a bad time, but I don't care. I'd just been promoted, and I was nervous, worried I was going to make mistakes. Detective Constable to Detective Sergeant is a bit of a jump, and I wasn't ready for it.'

She held her hand up to pause Anjli from adding to this.

'I'm not stupid, Kapoor. I know I wasn't ready for it. I'd bullied my way to the role. Politically angled myself as the candidate from a very small batch of opportunities. Monroe saw that when he arrived. He didn't think I was good enough.'

She shrugged.

'He was right, of course. But he didn't have to treat me the way he did. He took the piss out of me. Any time I was wrong, he made sure everybody knew. It was like I became his whipping girl.'

She was staring off as she spoke, her mind lost in arguments from years earlier.

'The worst bit is, I don't think he even realised he was doing it,' she said. 'I had a friend who passed away a year or two ago. Brain cancer. Horrid thing. But, in the last few months, nobody recognised her. The personality was completely different, she would argue things she would never usually be concerned about. It was a complete Doctor Jekyll and Mister Hyde – you never knew who you'd get. In Monroe's case, he thought he was Doctor Jekyll while he was *being* Mister Hyde. You ask Monroe, he'll say those five, six months he spent at Newbury were a holiday, a change of scene, a chance to make new friends. He'll remember me as a grumpy, overbearing Detective Sergeant. He won't remember what *he* was.'

'I get that,' Anjli said.

'Do you?' Warner asked. 'When Monroe, Walsh and Marcos turned up at my crime scene in Savanake Forest, I almost got fired. I allowed Monroe and an uncleared divisional surgeon to enter my crime scene to take clues and leave. When Nicholas Stephens was found dead and that whole re-enactor thing came to life, I was blamed for not following it up at the time. But Monroe screws up left and right and what happens with him? He gets promoted. He gets fired but then the Prime Minister says he should stay. Even the one *before* Charles Baker said that Monroe could hang around a bit longer.'

She shook her head.

'It must be great having people like that looking out for you.'

'The Monroe you knew, the drunk, still grieving a wife who disappeared – and I mean she literally disappeared; she didn't walk out the house one day, she completely evaporated, joining MI5, scrubbing her identity – he's honestly gone now,' Anjli said as they pulled into the sports centre car park, where Selene Carter was, according to her PA, teaching inner-city girls how to run, or something. 'I'm not making excuses for him, he can be a prick and it sounds like he was one of the greatest levels of prick going when he worked with you, but don't sit there being pissed at him about it. Confront him, tell him what happened. Let the Monroe of today deal with the Monroe of fifteen years ago, because while you've got that chip on your shoulder, you're always going to believe that you're not worthy of what you get.'

She smiled as they both got out of the car.

'And trust me, Detective Superintendent Warren, you wouldn't be in the role you're in, if people didn't believe you could do it.'

'You're a good kid,' Warren smiled, even though there was only about ten years between them. 'Thanks for letting me hang along.'

'That's fine,' Anjli said, with a slight hint of crispness. 'It's your case, after all.'

'Yeah, but you're not happy about it,' Warren said as they walked out onto the wharf itself, marching along in rhythm together. 'I can tell that.'

'It's not you,' Anjli eventually replied. 'It's the situation. The last case we were on we ended up having to work alongside other detectives. It's very difficult to get into a groove when you know there's somebody else that you don't know watching over you, judging your every move.'

She chuckled.

'In a way, it's probably how you were when Monroe turned up.'

'Well, if I start drinking from the bottle while grabbing the next in my free hand, you know you've got a problem,' Warren smiled as they arrived at the entrance to the sports centre. 'Is this the place?'

'I believe so,' Anjli replied, opening the door and waving her superior through. 'Shall we?'

SELENE CARTER WAS DRESSED IN A TRACKSUIT WHEN ANJLI AND Warren finally found her, standing in the one hundred-metre section of a four-hundred-metre track at the back of the sports centre. Her blonde hair pulled back, she had a group of teenage girls in front of her, clearly in the middle of a training session. The moment Anjli appeared, however, Selene immediately curtailed whatever she was doing, walked over, and before Anjli could even show her warrant card, indicated for them to walk away – a clear signal she wasn't keen on being seen with a police officer.

Obviously, Anjli thought, *she'd recognised Warren's gruff demeanour for the police.*

Selene shook her head as Anjli went to speak and indicated that they could talk at the finish line.

'Not here,' she said. 'The kids – some of them come from broken families. They have brothers or sisters in prison.'

'I see,' Anjli said, glancing back at the youths. 'Outreach programme?'

'Kind of,' Selene replied. 'I do a lot of these. You know, I was the same before I found swimming and, you know, triathlons.'

'You were?' Warren asked, unable to hide her surprise. 'I read your Wikipedia page. It says you grew up in High Wycombe, the daughter of a successful film producer. That doesn't sound the same as someone from inner-city London.'

'We all have our pasts,' Selene said. 'Sure, my dad was well-off. That didn't mean I was looked after.'

'But he did pay for all your training, didn't he?' Anjli cut in, siding with her colleague. 'I mean, you were what, thirteen when you started doing triathlons? His company even sponsored you.'

Selene glanced back at the girls to make sure none of them were listening.

'Look,' she muttered, 'if you've got something important to go through here, just get to it.'

'We're here because of Stephen Kline,' Anjli decided to just get on with it; small talk was out of the window now. 'You've heard?'

'I have,' Selene responded, a little too defensively. 'It's a shame, but he hadn't exactly showered himself in grace recently. You kind of expected it, you know?'

'You expected him to be locked in a cryogenic chamber and left to freeze to death?'

'Well, no, but I expected a bad end. I thought it'd be more stabbed in an alley, or hit in a drive-by shooting. He didn't exactly hang out with the Chipping Norton crowd.'

Anjli pulled out her notebook, writing this down.

'And how long have you known him?'

'Since the Olympics where I won silver, so what, eight years ago,' Selene shrugged. 'Met him through a friend. David Lester.'

'The biohacker?'

'Among many other things,' Selene nodded. 'He helped me train. David, not Kline. I couldn't see Kline helping anyone if it didn't benefit him in some way.'

Anjli noted this down.

'Do you know anybody who could have wanted him dead?' she asked.

'Have you met him?' Selene shrugged. It was a snarky, throwaway comment.

'I never had the chance, no,' Anjli replied emotionlessly. 'However, my superior knew him quite well.'

'Oh,' Selene said, realising her comments weren't landing as expected. 'Well, let's just say he was an acquired taste. Always on the lookout for a way to make money. Anti-ageing was perfect for him.'

She shrugged again.

'There's a sucker born every minute, after all.'

'And would you class yourself as a sucker?' Anjli asked, her tone sharp.

'I'm only in the tournament because I was asked to be,' Selene snapped, her temper flaring. 'I want to prove you don't have to spend millions to live healthily.'

She gestured to the track.

'I spent my life in places like this, honing my skills, becoming the Olympian I eventually became. I won a silver medal on my own – by blood, sweat, and tears. The rejuvenation tournament is a chance to show that what I know, what I've learned over decades, can help others, just like I'm helping these girls here.'

'Can you tell us where you were last night around eight pm?' Warren now asked, probably tiring of the lecture.

'Sure,' Selene pulled out her phone from her tracksuit bottoms, scrolling through until she found what she was looking for, holding it up so they could see. It was a Facebook advert, with a photo of her on it.

Selene Carter appearing tonight at Waterstones Piccadilly

'I was there from six until nine. After that, I did a podcast. Left Piccadilly around ten.'

'We'll need to confirm that,' Anjli said, making a note.

'Of course you do,' Selene replied. 'I wouldn't expect anything less. So, are you speaking to the others?'

'Others?'

'Sure, the London biohacker crowd. They're an incestuous bunch. As I said, I've known Stephen for nearly a decade, and many of the others have known him just as long. If you're looking at suspects ...'

She trailed off, her eyes drifting to the girls who were beginning to lose focus.

'Look, as much as I want to help, those girls are about to check out. Once they do, it's hard to get them back. So, if we're done ...?'

Anjli understood the hint.

'We might need to call you in for more questions,' she said, handing Selene her card. 'If you think of anything else, please let me know.'

'Of course,' Selene said. 'You've spoken to Aria Milton and Mira Nakahura, right?'

'Why would we want to speak to them?' Anjli asked, not revealing that she already knew who they were.

'They both used his Ionosphere spa,' Selene replied. 'Might also want to talk to Eli Green. He was around when I first met Stephen. Still is.'

'We understand Eli Green is currently abroad,' Anjli said.

'I don't keep track of him. Just offering suggestions,' Selene shrugged. 'Now, if you'll excuse me?'

With that, Selene turned back towards the girls, clapping her hands and calling for them to get into position.

Warren watched her go.

'What a lovely lady,' she muttered. 'If she *really* wanted to impress the girls, we could always arrest her, stick her in cuffs in front of them.'

Anjli chuckled before looking back at her notes.

'Seems like Stephen Kline wasn't exactly well liked,' she said thoughtfully. 'Which makes me wonder – why did Bullman like him so much?'

'From what I've seen of your boss,' Warren said as they walked back towards the main building, 'she likes to go against the grain. She's got a soft spot for Alex Monroe, and I've already told you how much of a prick he is.'

Anjli ignored the obvious bait here.

'Come on,' she said. 'Let's go talk to Aria Milton.'

5

THE AI GUY

WHILE ANJLI AND WARREN TRAVELLED TO FIND SELENE Carter and then Aria Milton, both around South East London, Declan and Monroe headed out towards Kingston-upon-Thames, to the industrial estate and technology park where Leon Brecht worked.

Paradigm Synthetics was a two-storey building within one of the smaller industrial parks; a strange location for a man who claimed to be the Swiss architect of AI technology. Apparently, Declan had expected something along the lines of *Apple*, or even *OpenAI;* exciting chrome and glass buildings with futuristic technology inside. As it was, the building was quite pedestrian, basically a panelled white frontage with long open-planned offices within.

Downstairs was what looked to be a warehouse space with various items and pallets of technology there. It also seemed to be, as Declan recalled, very similar to what the Batcave looked like in the Christopher Nolan *Batman* movies – neon lights and low ceilings, brutalist pillars holding up the floor above.

Walking up the steps, led by the young male assistant who had come to meet them at the car park, a pair of black-framed glasses making him look like a hipster that hadn't got the memo about beards, Declan found themselves entering into a run-of-the-mill open plan office with a utilitarian grey theme running throughout. There was a burgundy sofa to sit on while they waited, and clear-walled offices and board-rooms ran along the left-hand side, while on the other side of the building there were at least three side-by-side desk units, face-to-face with another row, three rows long – which Declan estimated gave about eighteen to twenty people working here at any one time.

At this point there were only three or four workers there, though.

Finally, at the end was another glass office. This was where Declan and Monroe, after a twenty-minute wait, were eventually led.

Leon Brecht was a man in his late fifties or early sixties. Declan wasn't sure; he had that timeless expression that could vary decades. His hair was brown, but almost seemed bottled rather than natural. He was lean and tanned, and his cheekbones were so sharp you could cut paper with them. His eyes were piercing blue, and he wore jogging bottoms and a fleece zip-lined jersey. Declan couldn't help but notice as he sat down that the glasses Brecht wore didn't seem to be prescription, even though they were clear-lensed, with the slightest hint of orange or even yellow to them.

On Brecht's wrist was an Apple watch, but on the other side seemed to be a separate watch, although Declan wasn't sure if he was reading that correctly – *why would someone need the time so badly?*

Brecht walked back to his desk, a very basic, grey,

wooden, standing desk, sitting down behind it on what looked to be an ergonomic, black carbon chair, and gave Monroe and Declan a smile.

'Detective Chief Inspector, Detective Superintendent,' he said, nodding to each in turn. Declan was impressed; they hadn't given their names at the door, but it was almost as if they'd been expected. 'Sorry for the delay.'

'You know us?'

'As soon as you arrived, our cameras picked up your faces, and our AI ran a facial recognition,' Brecht smiled. 'Don't worry, we weren't intruding on your personal space or your privacy laws. We were purely taking from paparazzi shots from the various cases you've solved over the years. It came up who you were, and I guessed that you'd be arriving anyway.'

His voice had a slight Swiss lilt to it, but there was a twang, almost as if, although being Swiss, Leon had spent time in America.

'Impressive stuff,' Monroe muttered, although his expression didn't show one of surprise and excitement. 'You got any other tricks you can show us?'

'What tricks would you like?'

'Maybe telling us who killed Stephen Kline? That'd be a good one.'

'I could give you a list,' Brecht replied. 'It's quite a long one, unfortunately.'

'You don't seem surprised or saddened by the murder,' Declan remarked.

In response, Brecht simply shrugged, reaching over to the side of his monitor, taking a sip from a water bottle. Declan wasn't sure, but he was convinced that the water bottle lid glowed blue for a moment.

Brecht, noticing Declan's attention diverted to the bottle, held it up.

'It uses UV light to filter antioxidants from the water, which, to be honest, is alkaline heavy anyway, and specially blended.'

'You blend water?'

'It's getting as popular as blending coffees now. The right water can change your mood, change your settings, alter your entire day. Why drink fluorine-infested tap water when you can have the champagne of life?'

Monroe knotted his eyebrows together as he considered this.

'So, you have this water blended and made especially for you?'

'Yes.'

'But you still purify it.'

'You can never be too pure, Mister Monroe.'

Sunlight slanted through the floor-to-ceiling window behind him, casting a long shadow across the polished concrete floor. The office, like the reception area, was minimalist, clean lines and muted greys, with a single strikingly modern sculpture occupying one corner. Against one wall was a dizzying array of graphs, charts and scrolling data on a wall of screens; the overall effect was like stepping onto the bridge of a futuristic spacecraft that was still under construction; sleek tech on one side, and concrete brutalism the other.

Brecht waved them towards a selection of strange-shaped chairs by the wall, a glass partition beside it revealing a state-of-the-art laboratory. Through the windows, Declan could see technicians, all wearing the same, black-framed glasses, moving amongst gleaming equipment, which looked more suited to a sci-fi film than a modern lab. He couldn't quite pinpoint it, but Declan felt he'd been here before, and it was only as he sat down on the sofa that he realised the aesthetic was very much the offices of the movie *Men in Black.*

'Quite the set-up you have here,' he said.

The chairs were ergonomic and they surrounded a low table. As they sat, the table's surface came to life, displaying a holographic representation of human DNA slowly rotating around it.

Declan glanced at Monroe to see that the older Scot was genuinely impressed by this, leaning forward and glancing down through the glass top.

'Mirrors and projectors on a glass screen,' he muttered. 'This isn't as *Star Trek* as I thought it might be.'

Brecht shrugged.

'It's a trinket to impress investors,' he said. 'Unfortunately, it's pressure-set so that any time someone sits down on the chair you're in, a real-time visualisation of my own genetic structure appears.'

He nodded towards the laboratory.

'We're constantly monitoring for the slightest changes that might indicate cellular ageing or regeneration, you see.'

Declan nodded, even though he only understood about half of that.

'What do your monitors say?' he said, gesturing at the screens.

If Brecht was annoyed that Declan had bored of the hologram already, he didn't show it, as he mimicked Declan, showing the screens against the wall.

'They analyse and monitor health data from hundreds of volunteers, including myself and other anti-agers,' Brecht raised his wrist, tapping on his Apple Watch. As he did so, a complex graph appeared on a nearby screen. 'This for instance shows the correlation between sleep patterns and cellular regeneration rates.'

Monroe, always a sci-fi fan, leant forward, intrigued.

'Fascinating,' he said, before looking back at Brecht. 'The other watch you wear?'

'A complicated heart rate fitness tracker, nothing more,' Brecht shrugged. 'I like to make sure I have redundancies.'

He shifted in his chair as he looked at the two detectives.

'I'm sorry to ask this, but can I see your phones?' he asked. 'We have a lot of proprietary hardware and software here, and I need to ensure you're not recording.'

'We take notes in our pads,' Declan started, but Brecht shook his head.

'I'm sorry, but I cannot answer any questions until I am sure you're not recording.'

'We can drag you down the station and interview you there,' Monroe grumbled, tiring of this game. 'We'll definitely be recording you there.'

'Of course, and I'm happy to go there and be recorded, with my solicitor beside me,' Brecht smiled. 'But here, in my office, and alone, I need to be sure I'm not being recorded, officially or candidly, in case I give away some NDA controlled secrets.'

He shrugged.

'All I need is to see the voice recording app is off. That's it.'

Sighing, Declan and Monroe pulled out their phones, showed Leon Brecht they weren't recording, and then placed them onto the table, as if daring him to argue the case now.

Instead, Brecht smiled widely, motioning for the detectives to begin, now comfortable with the situation.

'So, Mister Brecht, please, can you tell me about your

involvement in the Rejuvenation Royal Tournament?' Declan asked.

'The Rejuvenation Royal Tournament is more than just a contest, no matter what people say,' Brecht began carefully, and Declan wasn't sure, but he felt that Brecht had paused, choosing his words carefully. Of course, with English being his second language, he could have just been making sure he didn't say the wrong thing. 'It's not the only reason for doing such a thing.'

'Oh, I don't know, laddie,' Monroe smiled. 'Two million dollars is quite a good reason.'

'Two million dollars is nothing,' Brecht shook his head.

'Ah, so you mean the American finals, the extra, what is it, five or ten million that you get if you get through to the very end?'

'Again, it's what you call "beer money",' Brecht said, shrugging as he relaxed back into the chair. 'It is true many people want the fame and glory of becoming number one, but then in two years – it's a biannual contest – there will be *another* number one and two years after that, another. The tournament will continue no matter what. It's been going for almost eight years already. Every time, the money goes up. The contestants build in numbers, as more people learn about it, and the challenges become greater. But it's not life-changing.'

'I don't know, two million would be pretty life-changing to me,' Monroe mumbled. 'Ten million more so.'

'True, for a normal person living the life of a sedentary worker, going to the gym once, maybe twice a week, maybe a park run on Saturdays, it would be.'

Declan, who did like to run in his spare time, noticed that

Monroe kept very quiet about his singular lack of exercise regimen as Brecht continued.

'Someone like you might spend money on multivitamins, possibly some face creams and anti-ageing eye creams that you buy in Boots or Tesco, Sainsbury's, Amazon ... you might spend a couple of hundred, maybe a thousand in a year, and people would look at you and go, "A thousand pounds spent on tablets? You're a fool. Just buy a multivitamin, get some sun." But this is the normal person. It is the same as a child playing with a toy sword, while next to him a coliseum of gladiators fight.'

'You liken yourself to gladiators?' Declan smiled. 'We've had our own run-in with those recently.'

'Oh, I don't mean that we *are* gladiators, although some people in the tournament might suggest they are,' Brecht gave a weak, cold smile. 'What I mean is the training that people would take to become gladiators in the arena is the kind of training that many of the people in a tournament would do.'

He pointed back at the hologram.

'As I said, I monitor my DNA constantly. It is very important to me that I win, or at least get into the top five, globally. Not just for the money, you have to understand.'

At this, he waved around the office, the glass walls into the strange laboratory next door.

'This all costs more than two million a year.'

'What exactly is this, then?' Declan frowned.

'My brand,' Brecht smiled. 'I'm using AI and machine learning to optimise health outcomes and, well, potentially reverse biological ageing. My approach, unlike the others, involves constant data collection and analysis, all so superpowered AI algorithms can make informed decisions about diet, exercise and supplementation. Everything I do is decided by data.'

Declan frowned.

'Okay, I get having AI telling you what to do can help, but why is that more important than winning millions in a tournament?'

'Because winning the tournament is one tournament and one prize,' Brecht replied. 'Imagine what would happen if I could bottle my training? Turn it into an elixir that anyone could have. Macrobiotic dense food, drinks, smoothies, olive oil; it'd make money, but all of that is commonplace. But now, imagine AI-based proprietary software to keep you on track, a personal trainer in your pocket that reacts to real time, taking all the latest research, the second it's released, using it to make you better, catching every moment of your health data from your smartring, smartwatch, bracelet, whatever, sending it to your augmented reality smart glasses ... the branding is there. We even have our own marketing team.'

He tapped on his watch, and a screen on the wall lit up with a single word.

EXIST

'It's not really a marketing slogan, is it?' Monroe said. 'It's more of a word.'

'It's a mission statement,' Brecht replied. 'Exist. Forever.'

'You should change the font, it's a little harsh,' Monroe, still not warming to Brecht, continued. 'Maybe Papyrus, or Comic Sans.'

Declan ignored his boss, continuing to write notes down.

'And how did you know Stephen Kline?'

At this, Brecht's expression didn't change. Declan had

expected maybe some sadness to appear, but like when he was first asked, there was nothing. His expression was completely neutral.

'Stephen and I were competitors, but we also had a professional relationship,' he explained. 'He was interested in integrating some of my AI-driven health monitoring systems into his cryotherapy spa.'

He glanced at his smartwatch before looking back at the detectives.

'We met years before, before the RRT was even created, but reconnected a couple of years back. We had several meetings about potential collaborations; in fact our last meeting was just three days before the London Summit.'

'But not after?' Monroe asked.

'No, he pulled away from everyone then,' Brecht gave a dark smile. 'It was quite the event, so I heard.'

'Heard? I was told you spoke there?'

'I did, but I didn't network afterwards,' Brecht shrugged. 'That involves interacting with people, and I'm not a fan of that.'

'Okay then, so this meeting before the event, can you tell us about that?'

'Certainly,' Brecht said. 'It was a great meeting. It was here in this office; Stephen was excited about the potential of combining his cryotherapy techniques with my data analysis. He believed it could give him an edge in the tournament. Even gave me a tour of them.'

Brecht stood, walking over to a corner of the office where, on a side table, was a small bonsai tree. As he continued, he started trimming a leaf from the bonsai.

'Like this tree, detectives, our work in longevity requires

constant, careful pruning. Stephen understood that. He was a worthy competitor.'

'Yet, we've been told he wasn't in the competition.' Declan looked up at the comment.

'No,' Brecht replied, his face now showing the first signs of emotion. 'That's not exactly correct. He was on the lists, but not publicly. He wanted to make a splash, only appear when he became top three, most likely later this year. The finish line is New Year's Eve, after all, still a couple of months left to get some solid press. However, he stepped down at the Health Summit, a couple of days after our meeting.'

'Do you know why?'

Brecht shook his head.

'As I said, I left the moment my panel was over. The people who organise it are philistines and don't understand AI. They think I'm cheating, although in the game of staying alive, how the hell can you cheat? It's a binary decision. You either live or you die. The longer you live is still a one, even if the zero is death.'

Declan noted this down as Monroe leant forward.

'Mister Brecht, where were you last night, around eight or nine pm, the time of Mister Kline's death?'

'Last night?' Brecht turned back to face them. 'I was here working late. The building security logs can confirm that, and I'd be happy to provide you with my biometric data from that night as well.'

Suddenly, an alert started ringing from one of the screens. Brecht quickly moved to check it, walking over and examining the data that was scrolling down it.

'Excuse me just a moment,' he said, tapping a few commands on his watch. 'It's an anomaly in one of my data streams. Nothing to worry about. We're still learning.'

He walked back to his ergonomic chair, sitting down with a smile.

'Now, where were we?'

'You get that a lot?' Declan looked at the screens, which following the outburst, seemed to have relaxed.

'You can't make an omelette without initiating a controlled shell fragmentation process,' Brecht smiled. 'New technology always has glitches, and I've initiated a few controlled fragmentations recently.'

Declan noted this down, especially the over-the-top quote, but Monroe took this as an opportunity to change direction.

'What are your thoughts on the other competitors?' he asked. 'Eli Green, for instance? We understand there was a confrontation between Stephen and Eli at the Summit?'

'As I said,' Brecht shrugged. 'I wasn't networking at the Summit and I feel it would be unfair of me to comment on such a thing. Biohackers are such bitchy little queens at the best of times. They love data, but they love to hear about other people *failing* in their data more. Eli's approach is ...'

He trailed off as he considered this.

'*Traditional*. Effective, perhaps, but lacking in innovation. Now, Aria Milton, her work is intriguing. Have you uncovered any details about *her* experimental treatments?'

'We're not at liberty to discuss other aspects of the investigation, Mister Brecht,' Monroe said coldly.

'Of course, I understand. I merely ask out of scientific curiosity.'

Declan looked around the office one last time. It sounded like Brecht had an alibi, and was hoping to gain some information of his own here, but for the moment, there wasn't much more they could gather.

'What are your views on the competitive nature of the tournament?' he asked. 'It does seem to be a little dog-eat-dog, if you know what I mean.'

Brecht leant forward now, his eyes bright at the question.

'Competition drives innovation, Detective Chief Inspector. The tournament pushes us to the limits of what's possible in longevity research. It's not just about winning—'

He waved around the office.

'—It's about advancing human potential.'

As he finished, he straightened, and Declan realised that as far as Brecht was concerned, the interview was now over.

'I hope I've been helpful,' Brecht continued. 'Please don't hesitate to contact me if you need anything further.'

As they rose to leave the office, picking up their phones and placing them away, Declan paused.

'There's a strange smell,' he said, frowning. 'It's been here since we arrived, and I can't quite place it.'

'Ah,' Brecht smiled. 'That's a mixture of my herbal essences and ozone.'

'Ozone?'

'Of course. I have an advanced air filtration system. The perfectly regulated temperature of the office filters through with this scent to relax me during the day.'

Brecht continued walking them towards the glass door to his office. On the other side of it, Declan could see the same assistant who had brought them into the office now walking back over to them, holding what looked to be a nutrient shake.

'Let me guess,' he said. 'The ingredients are measured with scientific precision?'

Brecht smiled as he took it from the assistant, waving for him to lead them to the exit.

'Of course,' he said as he passed a business card across. 'I can see that of the two of you, *you* are the one who is more likely to go down this path. And if you ever do, give me a call, Mister Walsh.'

'No longer "Detective Chief Inspector"?' Declan smiled.

'That's for this terrible murder enquiry,' Brecht shrugged. 'If you're a potential client ...'

He let it trail off and walked back into his office.

Their farewell now given, Declan and Monroe followed the assistant as he led them out; Declan noted at one point he tapped at the side stem of his glasses. *Perhaps these were all smart-engineered too?*

Declan stared at the card in his hand.

'Thinking of using them, laddie?' Monroe asked, but Declan simply slid it into his pocket.

'I'll stick with multi-vitamins for the moment,' he smiled as they walked to the car. 'I just hope Anjli's doing better than we are.'

6

MEDICAL LABS

As Anjli and Warren entered the Canary Wharf building where Aria Milton was situated, she looked up at the frontage; the building looked like every other finance and legal building surrounding them, but the sign above the reception read:

Luxor Aesthetics – where science meets serenity.

'Luxor, that's the Egyptian temple, right?' Anjli muttered, half to herself. Warren, however, said nothing as she stared around. It was like a modernist's dream, a sweeping structure of glass and sustainable bamboo. In the reception area were images and paintings; large frescoes of manicured gardens filled with medicinal herbs and flowers, a small, serene lake – or, rather a pond – to the side, its surface broken by the occasional leap of a fish.

It seemed as out of place as you could possibly get for Canary Wharf.

Walking up to the reception, Anjli showed her warrant card.

'Detective Superintendent Warren and Detective Inspector Kapoor to see Aria Milton,' she said. 'She's expecting us.'

'Yes,' the receptionist rose, passing Anjli and Warren each a wooden card. Anjli frowned as she stared at it.

'It's our visitor's pass,' the receptionist explained. 'They're made out of sustainable bamboo wood. The RFID chip's inside, like a normal card would be, but we don't have plastics.'

'How forward-thinking of you,' Anjli replied as the receptionist, nodding to her assistant to hold the fort, continued away from the desk and towards the stairway at the back.

The offices were high in the building, and the elevator they got into took them to the fourteenth floor before Anjli and Warren were led through corridors lined with soothing abstract art and living walls of lush greenery. The air as they walked was infused with a subtle, almost invigorating scent. Anjli assumed it was some kind of blend of essential oils designed to enhance calmness.

The receptionist, seeing Anjli's sniff of the air, gave a smile.

'It's a proprietary blend of essential oils designed to enhance cognitive function and promote cellular health,' she said. 'Aria's own recipe.'

Anjli gave a smile and a nod; it felt a little like she'd understood about half of what the woman had said. The receptionist paused and tapped on a door – which looked like it had been made of pine-stained mahogany – before she opened it and invited the two detectives in.

Aria Milton rose from a plush ergonomic chair, moving with the fluid grace of a yoga master. She looked to be in her early forties, but Anjli knew from Billy's files she was a good fifteen years older than this, and there was an agelessness about her that made it difficult to pinpoint her exact number. Her skin had a radiant glow, although Anjli wasn't sure if this was fake tan or half a dozen other skincare routines, and her eyes sparkled with an intensity as she walked across to shake their hands. She was dressed in flowing, pastel-coloured leisure wear, which seemed slightly odd for the woman. Anjli assumed it was probably some kind of advanced fabric that adjusted to her body temperature – but it was probably just comfortable to wear.

Milton extended her hand, her voice melodious in the office, as she nodded a *thank you* to the receptionist, who disappeared, shutting the door behind her.

'Detectives, welcome to Luxor Aesthetics,' she said. 'I hope you don't mind meeting here, I'm in the middle of a rather intensive treatment cycle.'

She shook hands with them both, and as she did so, Anjli noticed a very faint tremor in Milton's fingers, quickly masked as she gestured for them to sit.

They sank into chairs that seemed to mould to their bodies, with a glass coffee table between them promoting a decorative arrangement of rare, likely health-promoting flowers, judging from the aesthetics of the office. On one wall, a large aquarium housed exotic fish, their scales shimmering as they swam lazily through crystal-clear water. On the other was a wall of shelving, with a variety of self-help books, awards and ornaments.

A staff member entered silently as they sat, bringing a tray of what looked to be health smoothies. The drinks were a kaleidoscope of colours: deep purples, vivid greens and sunny yellows, each garnished with a flower.

'Would you care for a rejuvenation blend?' Milton said as the tray was placed in front of them. 'It's packed with antioxidants and my latest nano-nutrient formula.'

Anjli smiled as she picked one up, sniffing it.

'It smells like Nicky Simpson's drinks,' she said in passing.

'I know who Nicky Simpson is,' Milton's face darkened. 'He says he's a health guru, but we all know he's a gangster. It doesn't surprise me you'd know him, what with you being police.'

Anjli gave a smile. Aria Milton hadn't been wrong. Although Nicky Simpson was a YouTube "health guru" with his own spas and gyms, he'd also been part of a crime family that ran South London for generations.

'Anyway, I can guarantee you,' Milton replied almost smarmily, 'regardless of whatever snake oil he's fed you, you've never received one like this.'

She waved at the flower.

'For a start, the flowers here are edible, created specifically to provide nutrients for you. Please, try one.'

Warren picked up one of the drinks and sipped at it curiously, while Anjli gave a smile. With talk of edible flowers, Aria Milton was sounding more and more like a health-guru Willy Wonka by the second.

'Miss Milton, we're here to ask you about your involvement in the Rejuvenation Royal Tournament,' she said. 'As well as speak to you about the death of Stephen Kline, to see if you can give any additional information on the victim, and your relationship.'

'Of course,' Milton replied, taking a sip of her own smoothie. 'I'm an open book, detectives. The tournament is the perfect platform to showcase the efficiency of my treatments.'

'And your relationship with Stephen Kline?' Warren asked.

There was the slightest of flickers of emotion that crossed Milton's face at the name, but she quickly masked it.

'Stephen was a visionary, a competitor, yes, but he was also a colleague. His death is a tremendous loss to our field.'

'When did you last see him?' Anjli asked.

Milton considered this and looked into the distance as if trying to recall.

'It was a checkpoint meeting here about a week ago. We had a heated discussion about the ethics of certain experimental procedures.'

'So, you didn't see him last night when you had a cryotherapy session?' Anjli asked. 'We ask because we have you on CCTV leaving. You were the last client of the night.'

'No, of course, I was at Ionosphere. I have no reasons to hide that,' Milton said quickly. 'It's just you asked when I last saw Stephen, and I didn't see him yesterday. It was his assistant Alexis who provided the service.'

'Provided the service?' Warren frowned.

'Oh, you know, laid out the clothing and then when I got into the chamber she timed me, let me out, measured my temperature going in and coming out.'

'What was your temperature?' Anjli asked out of idle curiosity rather than any other reason.

'Thirty-one, maybe just under thirty-two degrees when I went in, and about fourteen when I came out. A nice drop. I didn't have the fan on, so it could have been a bit lower, but it was what I needed.'

Anjli nodded, writing this down in her notebook. She'd

have to confirm later on with the assistant whether Milton was telling the truth or not.

'You said you had a heated discussion,' she said. 'Could you elaborate?'

Milton placed her half-drunk smoothie down, sighing.

'Stephen believed I was pushing boundaries too far. He threatened to expose some of my more avant-garde research, but he was just concerned, nothing more—'

Suddenly, she broke into a coughing fit. She quickly composed herself, waving back a concerned movement from Anjli.

'The smoothie went down the wrong way,' she said, forcing a smile. 'It's because I was talking while drinking. Now, where were we?'

'Miss Milton, we have you leaving Mister Kline's cryotherapy centre shortly before he died,' Anjli read from her notes. 'Can you give us more information on where you were last night after you left?'

'Absolutely, I was here in my private lab. I'm running a critical phase of an experiment. My staff can corroborate this.'

'A list of names and numbers would be good.'

'Of course.'

'What time did you leave?'

Aria considered the question, tapping at her lip as she did so.

'You know, it was probably about five,' she admitted. 'I almost stayed over, crashed on the sofa there, but my back wouldn't have thanked me.'

'You often work long nights?'

'Oh yes,' Aria nodded. 'Sometimes you have to. I'd guess you have a cot or a camp bed somewhere in your offices for when you pull an all-nighter.'

Anjli smiled.

'We might have one or two,' she replied, and Aria Milton looked around as she did so.

'I think anyone who works hard needs one,' she said, leaning back into the seat. 'Eli, for example? He has his pod.'

'Pod?'

Aria laughed now, as if this was some kind of known joke.

'In his office he has a side room that's basically a den,' she said. 'Bed, big screen TV, fridge and kettle, everything you'd need for an all nighter. But he also believes in naps, probably because he used to practice polyphasic sleep, specifically the Uberman sleep schedule.'

'Is this different to normal sleep?' Warren frowned. 'Like in a bed or something?'

'In a way, yes,' Aria replied. 'This schedule involves taking multiple twenty-minute naps spread throughout the day, usually around six naps in total, resulting in about two hours of total sleep.'

'I need eight or I'm a monster,' Warren shook her head. 'Two hours would kill me.'

'It's a little more complicated than that,' Aria smiled. 'People often try it to increase productivity, as polyphasic sleep schedules aim to maximise waking hours, by focusing on short naps that quickly drop into REM sleep – the most restorative phase.'

'So, what, he gets twenty-two hour days? I can see why that'd be good on a deadline.'

'It's also used by those with demanding or irregular schedules, like shift workers or sailors,' Aria replied. 'However, while it can work in the short term, it's generally not recommended for long-term health, as it disrupts natural circadian rhythms and can lead to sleep deprivation—'

'So, while you're trying to lower your age for a competition, I'm guessing this isn't a good thing to do.'

'I wouldn't know, as I've never tried it,' Aria shrugged. 'Although I will say there's a definite corroboration between Eli trying this, and his number rising to the point he's currently at in the top twenty.'

She sighed.

'Anyway, he built this little sleep pod to use while practising polyphasic sleep in the office, and now it's turned into a hidey hole where he can keep away from the world. Like the novel *Rogue Male*.'

'And your thoughts on the other competitors? Leon Brecht, for instance?' Warren asked, moving away from the current subject, probably because she didn't want to start some kind of book club conversation.

Milton's expression hardened slightly at the name.

'He's brilliant, but cold. All data, no intuition. Eli's more my speed. Innovative, willing to take risks.'

She pulled out a handkerchief, dabbing at her top lip, which was starting to sweat.

Anjli leant closer.

'Miss Milton, forgive me for being blunt,' she said, 'but you seem ... unwell.'

'I assure you, detective, I'm in peak condition,' Milton replied, tensing visibly. 'My treatments are ...'

She was cut off this time again by another coughing fit, more severe. When she gathered her breath, she looked back at Anjli.

'Miss Milton, is there something you're not telling us?' Anjli asked, softer this time, more concerned.

There was a long, quiet moment in the office and eventually Aria Milton deflated slowly.

'What I'm about to tell you must remain confidential,' she said softly, almost as if making sure that nobody outside the office could hear. 'Not to be written in notes or used publicly. Can you give me your word?'

Anjli glanced at Warren and placed her hand on Milton's wrist in an empathic manner.

'I can give you my word that if it isn't relevant to the case it won't be used, and only my team will be told,' she said. 'If that's good enough.'

Milton considered this and then sighed.

'I'm afraid I'm dying,' she said. 'It's a rare, aggressive form of Amyotrophic Lateral Sclerosis, or ALS. You know it?'

Anjli wasn't sure, and seemed to remember some kind of ice in a bucket challenge a few years ago in relation to this, but shook her head rather than bluffing the woman in front of her.

'It's a neurological disease, also known as Lou Gehrig's disease, where the nerve cells that control voluntary muscles start to die off. In the UK, we call it Motor Neurone Disease, but ALS has become more common recently. It begins with little things – like a tremor in my hand or a cough I can't quite shake,' Milton explained. 'But as it progresses, it'll eventually affect everything; my ability to walk, talk, even breathe. The type I have is particularly aggressive, meaning it's moving faster than usual. Most people with ALS have a few years; the one I have stays dormant but visible for years, and then when it kicks off, it gives you *months*. I've known about it for a while, and there's no usual treatment to stop it, just ways to manage the symptoms as they come. The treatments, the tournament, they're my last hope.'

Anjli stared in shock at the woman in front of her.

'How long do you have?'

'Oh, I don't know. Doctors told me I had six months, but that was two years ago. I've managed a bloody good job of keeping the Devil from my door, so far. But, it could happen at any moment. One day I could be fine ... the next day, pop. All I can do is find ways to keep it at bay, which I've been doing at my own expense.'

'Did Stephen Kline know this?' Warren asked.

'He knew about my condition. He was sympathetic, even offered to collaborate on a treatment. But I would never ...'

She paused.

'I'm not a murderer, detective. I'm a scientist racing against time.'

As she said this, she touched a barely visible patch on her arm. Anjli assumed, with this new information, that she was possibly administering some kind of micro-dose of medication through it.

'Is there anything we can do to help?' Anjli asked.

'Just find whoever did this,' Milton replied sadly, as she rose, mimicking the two detectives as they did the same. 'He didn't deserve what happened here.'

'Can you think of anybody else who might have wanted him dead?' Anjli asked as they all stood in the office, the meeting almost over.

Milton nodded.

'Eli Green, as much as I like him, he'd had issues with Stephen recently. Mira, as well, should be spoken to. She wasn't exactly happy.'

'About what?'

'About her DNA,' Milton smiled. 'I'm afraid it's not my place to say anything, but you really should have a look into it.'

'Were you there when the fight happened at the Summit?'

'There was a confrontation,' Milton nodded. 'There were a lot of secret conversations going on at this year's Summit. When you hit this amount of money, this many intelligent people, and this much opportunity ... it's simply another one of those kinds of things.'

She sighed.

'People go to the Summit to learn things, sit in the audience, gain information from the experts,' she said. 'But, these people, they're not the important ones. The important ones are the attendees who pay for the sessions and *don't* go into the auditorium, preferring to have hushed conversations in the bar while the talks go on. And, although I'm technically one of those, as I can't really learn from the talks anymore, I'm too old now for games.'

'You don't look it,' Warren smiled.

'Oh, I don't mean in looks,' Milton smiled back in response. 'I mean in my soul. Fighting an enemy that wants to kill you every single day takes it out of you, you know. All of this, these machines, these recipes, everything ... it was created to save my life. I would hate to think that something I did caused the death of someone else. However, if I can answer any questions, please let me know.'

At this, the meeting was obviously over, and Anjli and Warren nodded, shaking Aria Milton's hand one more time, Anjli noticing again the tremble in the hand, understanding now with hindsight what it truly meant.

AS THEY TRAVELLED DOWN THE ELEVATOR, ALONE, WARREN looked at Anjli.

'Do you think she did it?'

'No.' Anjli shook her head. 'I think Stephen Kline was possibly one of the few people who was keeping her alive. You don't kill someone like that unless you have a reason.'

She looked around as the elevator opened and they walked out into the opulent reception area.

'I do think, however, that we need to have another chat with the assistant, Alexis,' she said icily. 'I think there's more here than we're seeing.'

7

FIRST MOVEMENTS

'I CAN TELL YOU THAT ALEXIS KOVALENKO DIDN'T GO HOME last night,' Billy said. 'That is, if she did, it wasn't by a usual route.'

'How do you mean?'

Billy sat at his bank of monitors, pointing at his screens. On it was a list of numbers and spreadsheets.

'These are Alexis Kovalenko's Oyster card details,' he said. 'Every transaction she makes. When she's catching a train or underground, DLR, you name it, if an Oyster card is used, it gets clicked on. The money is taken off the card, and she updates it every month.'

He tapped on his keyboard, and more screens started to appear.

'You can see here, that when she wasn't at University, twice a day she would travel from Cutty Sark station in Greenwich to Canary Wharf using the Docklands Light Railway. I'm guessing this is her going to work in the mornings and coming home in the evenings, as she lives near the Waitrose on Jubilee Place.'

'That's money,' Anjli said, looking at the map. 'Lots of expensive apartments there. I remember seeing a few when we were solving the Rupert Wilson case, a couple of years back. So, she used the Oyster every day?'

'Well, there *are* a few gaps that don't match up with the books.'

'The books?' Warren frowned.

'Oh sorry,' Billy said, pointing at a second monitor bank. 'This is the signing in and out book for Ionosphere. There are four members of staff: Stephen Kline, Alexis Kovalenko, and then two other assistants, Laura Miller and Derwin Mak. All four of them cover the shifts, eight in the morning until eight at night, Monday to Sunday, although Sunday is only till six. Going through the rotas I get a pretty good idea of what days Alexis is in, as they match her University timetable, and they match quite consistently to the Oyster card.'

He shrugged as he split his attention from screen to detectives.

'Granted, every now and then there isn't a link, and the chances are she might have forgotten the card and tapped on the reader with her contactless card or used a smartwatch. The problem with that is we'd have to ask for her credit records – and we don't have enough right now to ask for that.'

Anjli nodded.

'This is the problem when you don't live in a draconian dictatorship,' she said. 'Maybe she walked home? Canary Wharf to Greenwich isn't that hard. Perhaps she went to Millwall and took the pedestrian tunnel? Maybe she was going somewhere else?'

'Maybe, all I have are the facts, and they say she didn't use the card last night, and she didn't use it this morning when she arrived to open up,' Billy leant back. 'Whether this means that she stayed somewhere else, or she walked doesn't matter, as it actually means that we don't have any confirmed travel for her, which puts her back on the suspect list, even though she claims she went home before this all happened.'

He smiled.

'That said, I am checking all the CCTV footage at local DLR and tube stations, to make absolutely sure. Also, I might be playing in some "grey" areas to see if I can track the route her phone took.'

Anjli nodded.

'Well, if you find anything, find a way to make it more legitimate,' she suggested. 'Also, we should have another chat with her. Any news on Eli Green?'

'Yes, according to the flight plans, Elias Green landed in Heathrow at lunchtime. He had an Addison Lee car booked from the airport which would have taken him to his Hampstead home at around two,' Billy said, looking at his watch; it was almost five in the afternoon now. 'By now, he's probably there, chilling out. Or whatever biohackers do when they do it, probably having exercise and shining the sun on his bum or something.'

'Shining the sun on his bum?'

Billy reddened.

'Something about the perineum being an energy spot?' he muttered sheepishly. 'Bullman mentioned it.'

'You should stop listening to Bullman,' Anjli replied. 'Or I'll tell Sam on you.'

Billy forced a smile.

'I'm just trying to be on top of things. No, that's not what I meant, that's bad phrasing ...'

Anjli chuckled as Billy kept digging.

'Anyway, he's not answering his phone, so he might be

taking a nap, or hiding from any business calls while he beats the jet lag, so we've scheduled a meeting with him tomorrow through his office PA.'

Monroe, hearing Billy talking, now emerged out of his office to see what was happening. His face soured as he saw Warren.

'So you're still with us then, lassie?' he asked, half-mockingly.

Anjli looked at Warren.

'You should have a word,' she said.

'Now's not the time,' Warren muttered, barely imperceptible, as she looked back at Monroe. 'And you're still sober, that's a good start.'

If the comment had surprised Monroe, he made a good job of hiding it.

'What do you have?'

'I've got some information on Milton, possibly something on the assistant. Nothing yet from Doctor Marcos.'

'Aye, that's coming in a minute,' Monroe said. 'De'Geer's bringing it up as Doctor Marcos wanted to have a look at the machinery.'

He started back towards the briefing room.

'Come on, Walsh,' he shouted. 'We're going to have a wee chat.'

Declan emerged out of his own office.

'You know, this whole rejuvenation thing is fascinating,' he said. 'There's tons of YouTube sites that talk about it. I hadn't even heard of half of this before.'

'Oh God,' Anjli muttered to herself. 'Are we going to have *another* thing you're getting into? Are we going to have you waking up at five in the morning and sun worshipping and all that?'

'It might mean I'll stay young and healthy for longer.' Declan gave a smile to Anjli. 'Wouldn't you want that?'

'Hell no,' Anjli grinned. 'I want you dying quickly of a heart attack so I can gain the house.'

'And thus Lady Macbeth was born,' Monroe said sadly. 'Come on, everybody, let's go see where we stand right now.'

MONROE STOOD AT THE HEAD OF THE BRIEFING ROOM IN FRONT of the plasma screen, his eyes scanning the faces of his team. It was late in the afternoon now, almost early evening. Declan and Anjli were sitting in their usual seats to his left, Billy at his usual spot by the laptop, with, annoyingly, Warren sitting to his right. Doctor Marcos had yet to arrive, but at the back sat Sergeant De'Geer and PC Cooper.

The briefing room was quiet as they waited for him to begin.

'Right then,' he said, his Scottish brogue thick with fatigue from the day. 'Let's see what we've got so far. Laddie, you start.'

Declan, who the 'laddie' had been aimed at, nodded.

'Leon Brecht?'

'Aye, let's bring the others up to speed.'

Declan turned to speak to the room.

'As we know from Billy's earlier breakdown, Leon Brecht's the AI guy, and he's got an alibi for the night of the murder. He was working late at his lab, we have a couple of witness statements claiming he was definitely there, and security logs apparently back him up.'

'Apparently?' Billy leant forward, raising an eyebrow as he looked up from his laptop.

'We'll need to verify it,' Declan nodded. 'And, by that I mean *you'll* need to verify it, but he seemed …'

He paused, trying to find the right word.

Monroe stepped in.

'He seemed detached from the whole thing, like Kline's death was just another data point in his grand experiment.'

'He said he knew there had been issues with the others, but he wasn't part of it as he didn't talk to people,' Declan continued. 'I got the impression he barely spoke to them at the best of times. Although, I've since found on a YouTube page that he worked with David Lester back in the day when AI was an emerging novelty, so I'll check into that.'

Declan leant back into his chair as Monroe shook his head.

'He was a cold fish, and that's for sure. Definitely something more going on there, and I think we need to look into him. Anjli, you went to see Selene Carter and Aria Milton with our guest. What did you get?'

Declan saw Warren flinch at the term "guest" but kept quiet as Anjli pulled out her notebook.

'Selene wanted us gone the moment we arrived, claimed we were spooking the teenage girls she was teaching,' she explained. 'Said she knew Kline through David Lester, who was helping her with her Olympics achievements eight years back.'

'David Lester again, aye? That man's popular.'

'Yes, Guv. She showed us she was at some event in Piccadilly last night until ten, and then …'

'Pretty much told us to piss off,' Warren continued.

'Okay, we'll stick a pin in that for a moment. And Milton?'

'Aria Milton's story is complicated,' Anjli continued

reading from the notes. 'She claimed she was at her lab during the time of death, and her staff can corroborate.'

'Don't we have her on Ionosphere's CCTV leaving?' Monroe asked.

'We do, but apparently Stephen Kline wasn't there at the time, or if he was, maybe he was in his office and didn't want to speak to her. Either way, this was before he would have died.'

Anjli looked over to Warren, as if hoping she would continue. Taking the hint, Warren did.

'Alexis, the assistant at Ionosphere, apparently looked after Aria Milton, and they both left shortly after the end of the session,' she explained. 'Alexis is being scheduled to come in tomorrow, so we'll find out more about what happened there, but after seven-thirty in the evening, Stephen Kline was on his own. Aria was seen to leave on the CCTV, and so was Alexis about five minutes later ... but there's more.'

She paused, weighing her words carefully, before looking across at Anjli.

'I think this should be mentioned.'

'What should be mentioned?' Declan frowned.

At this, Anjli nodded to Warren, looking back at Monroe.

'We promised this wouldn't go past the team in this room, so please don't make a liar out of me.'

'Of course,' Monroe was confused now. 'Go on.'

'She's dying, Guv,' Anjli explained. 'ALS. She says the tournament's her last chance of finding a cure.'

A heavy silence fell over the room. Monroe, however, broke it with a grunt.

'Motive enough to kill, some might say.'

'I don't think so,' Anjli shook her head. 'If anything, it looked like Kline was helping her. She seemed genuinely upset by his death, and the impression we both got was that with Kline now gone, the chances she had of staving off ALS until she could find a cure, or until technology caught up, were now massively reduced.'

'Okay then,' Monroe nodded. 'What about the assistant Alexis? Should we be waiting until tomorrow? Apparently wee Billy here was saying her story doesn't add up, that she lied about going home.'

'We don't know if she lied yet,' Billy shook his head. 'She could have walked – it's an easy walk to do – but it does raise questions. Why, on these particular sessions, didn't she use her card, or, if she did, why didn't it register?'

At this point, the door opened and Doctor Marcos walked in, pausing Billy as he trailed off.

'What did I miss?' she asked.

'You haven't missed much,' Monroe said. 'I'm hoping—'

'Good, then you'll want to hear this,' Doctor Marcos interrupted without preamble. 'The cryotherapy chamber was tampered with.'

All eyes turned to her as she took her seat.

'The safety protocols were disabled,' she continued. 'Normally, the chamber would shut off after a set time if the session wasn't physically ended. Someone deliberately overrode that feature.'

She looked over at Billy.

'Also, there was a timer, so that at night the cryotherapy chambers would be brought up to the minimum temperature they could safely be kept at, without breaking anything in the machinery. It was a cost-saving energy bills decision, but it would have brought them up to a manageable level until an hour before opening, when they lowered back down in temperature. Stephen Kline could still have passed away from exposure and hypothermia; we're not talking room temperature here, but he would have had a better chance of surviving, especially wearing clothing.'

'The cryotherapy chamber had been left on all night and was deliberately set that way?' Monroe's eyes narrowed. 'So, we're definitely looking at murder, not accidental suicide.'

'Possibly,' Doctor Marcos replied. 'Again, if Stephen Kline *wanted* to kill himself, he could have overridden this to make sure it worked. People do talk about dying in snowy landscapes being peaceful; extreme hypothermic levels may bring out symptoms that make death akin to merciful sleep, even if that's not the case. Maybe that's what he wanted. But if it wasn't, and it was murder, then whoever did it knew exactly what they were doing. This wasn't some kind of amateur job.'

Billy cleared his throat.

'There's something else, Guv,' he said, diverting everyone's attention back to him. 'You asked me to look into the Summit, the one everyone's been mentioning? Turns out it was quite the event.'

'Go on, lad.'

'Well, it seems Kline made a big announcement there,' Billy tapped on the screen and pulled up a blog post from a Substack page. 'Apparently, he said he was dropping out of the tournament. Caused quite a stir, apparently, because half the people there didn't even know he was *in* the tournament. A lot of people were pissed off that he'd been doing it secretly, and that others had known but kept it quiet.'

'That fits with what Leon Brecht said,' Monroe nodded. 'He gave the impression Kline was on the lists, but not publicly – and wanted to make a splash when he became top three.'

'Was there any reason given for why he dropped out?' Declan asked.

Billy nodded, returning his attention to the screen.

'That's where it gets interesting,' he said. 'I found some communications on a biohacking Discord server forum, talking about an argument someone saw while there between Kline and the tournament organiser, tech billionaire Rupert Cray. They were arguing about Mira Nakahura, the investment banker.'

'What about her?'

'Well, according to the message, and remember this is third person and possibly an unreliable narrator, Kline was concerned about her DNA,' Billy replied. 'I don't know why, but there was anger. He felt he should have been informed about her DNA results. Even though he's nothing to do with the contest—'

'He *was* a sponsor, and he worked with them,' Declan reminded Billy, but Billy, in response, shook his head as he continued.

'True, but he was also a contestant, so they would have had to have kept it from him,' he explained. 'All I can tell is that it was something to do with DNA testing. The tournament involves extensive genetic testing, and I'm assuming that if he'd stayed in, something must have been about to come out.'

'So, Kline drops out to protect something about Mira?' Warren asked, shaking her head. 'Why kill him over that?'

'I think we need to find out what it was about Mira that made him drop out,' Anjli suggested. 'There could be a motive there, especially as she was using his cryochamber for the last eighteen months. Aria Milton also suggested we speak to her about her DNA... also, if other people were angry or resentful at him showing up ...'

'Maybe Rupert Cray, for example,' Declan added. 'If there is a scandal here, it could torpedo the whole tournament.'

Monroe drummed his fingers on the table as he considered this.

'Aye, laddie,' he said. 'We need to know what this scandal is though, before we can work out how big it was. Declan, you and Detective Superintendent Warren go speak to Eli Green tomorrow. He'll have had a good night's sleep by then, and I want to know more about this falling out with Kline. Anjli, dig deeper into Alexis Kovalenko's background. There's something not right there. We've got her coming in tomorrow as well, so let's leave no stone unturned there. Billy, I want everything you can find on Mira Nakahura and this Rupert Cray character. And somebody get me more information on this bloody tournament. I want to know every rule, every loophole, every potential angle for foul play.'

He stood, signalling the end of the briefing, having been leaning against the table for most of it.

'Remember, we're not just dealing with a murder,' he said. 'We're dealing with what looks to be a whole world of people trying to cheat death itself. And now we've got family secrets in the mix. Be careful out there.'

8

WORK DINNER

EVEN THOUGH MONROE HAD SAID TO CARRY ON TO THE following day, as it was already moving into the early part of the evening, the team didn't stop investigating at that point – it wasn't in their nature. And so it was almost another three hours until Anjli knocked on Declan's office door.

'How long have you been there?' Declan looked up, rubbing at his eyes.

'About a minute,' she replied. 'I wasn't going to interrupt, but you looked so tired. I thought you could do with a break.'

Declan nodded, rising.

'Yeah,' he sighed as he looked down at his laptop. 'It's not just the case. I'm still trying to sort out this whole Schnitter's will situation.'

'I thought it was done? MI5 opened up and said they were involved.'

'Still got to sell the house, and all the other bits and pieces,' Declan shrugged. 'I can't magically pass the will off to other people. We still have to deal with it all until it's done ...'

He trailed off, and Anjli understood. Karl Schnitter,

before he died, had left Declan everything in his will. It had been done to make Declan look complicit, but luckily for him, others had taken the blame instead.

He walked over to the window, staring out into the Inns of Court outside.

'I can understand why Monroe wants to get out of the office all the time,' he said. 'Back when I was out there in the bullpen, I used to get annoyed that he'd keep coming out, following us on excursions, when he should've been sitting in here doing his job.'

'Let me guess, now you're in here doing the same work, you'd rather not be doing it?' Anjli asked.

Declan grinned.

'You see, this is why we work so well together,' he replied. 'You understand me.'

'I think it's more of a case of watching you and realising this is definitely the road less travelled for me,' Anjli leant against the doorframe. 'I think I'm happy being a Detective Inspector. I think DCI might make me want to strangle people.'

'Well, if it did, we'd come and arrest you,' Declan shrugged. 'So, I was thinking maybe getting some takeout when we get back? I've got to speak to Jess later on tonight—'

'Actually, I had another option for you,' Anjli replied. 'We've been invited out for dinner.'

She laughed at Declan's stricken face.

'Don't worry, it's not an important one. It's the pub across the road. Sam's popped by, and it's an opportunity to drag Billy away from his laptop.'

Declan nodded, turning away from the window, leaning against the windowsill. Sam Mansfield was a reformed forger – well, at least Declan *hoped* he was reformed – who had helped them on a couple of occasions. In the process, he'd met and seemingly fallen for Billy, who had done the same. Recently, however, Billy hadn't been seeing that much of Sam, and Declan had wondered whether the relationship was falling apart.

'Let me guess – pub dinner, nice and relaxed; we're there as what, chaperones, judges, marriage counsellors?'

'Possibly all of the above,' Anjli replied, walking over.

Declan frowned, looking past her, out of the window that looked into the office.

'Where's everyone gone?'

'Home. Everyone's left apart from us.'

'It was packed a minute ago,' Declan frowned again.

'It was packed an hour ago,' Anjli replied. 'You've been deep in whatever you're doing. It's just gone half-past eight; as I said, I almost didn't want to interrupt you.'

She patted her stomach.

'I'm bloody hungry though, and if you're not coming, then I'm going on my own.'

DECLAN AND ANJLI WALKED IN THROUGH THE MAIN ENTRANCE of *The Old Bank of England*, seeing Sam and Billy at the side, sitting at a high table, with two seats spare on the opposite side. Over the years, and positioned on the other side of Fleet Street from the entrance to Temple Inn and the Last Chance Saloon, the busy pub had become one of the favourite locations for the team when any of them were working late in the office. An imposing Grade II-listed building, the pub was once the Law Courts branch of the Bank of England from 1888 to

1975, but after falling into disrepair, it was restored by Fuller's brewery two decades later in neoclassical style, complete with marble, specially commissioned murals, chandeliers and sculptured high ceilings. Now a McMullen's brewery, the pub was homely and welcoming; exactly what was needed, from the looks of the conversation Sam and Billy were having.

Sam was, as ever, dressed casually; jeans, T-shirt and a leather bomber jacket, while Billy was, as ever, in a bespoke three-piece suit.

The two couldn't have looked any more from different worlds if they'd tried.

They were deep in conversation, but as Sam saw Declan and Anjli arrive, he gave them a small wave.

'We haven't ordered yet,' Billy said as they sat down facing him. 'I was going to go up to the bar now.'

'I'll come with you,' Declan replied, looking at Anjli. 'Usual?'

'You know me so well.'

Declan walked up to the bar with Billy, but from the moment they started across the pub, he could sense something was off. Billy looked nervous, slightly over-energetic, as if trying hard to make things look like nothing bad was going on. Eventually, Declan held him by the arm before they were served, and turned to face him.

'What's going on that's got you in such a tizzy?' Declan asked.

Billy went to reply and then stopped himself, frowning.

'You know, I never thought you'd be someone to use the term "tizzy",' he replied.

Declan glared at him, and Billy wilted under the gaze.

'It's Sam,' Billy said. 'I really like him, and he really likes me, and we've spent a lot of time together, and things are moving forward.'

'That's what's supposed to happen with relationships,' Declan said.

'I know,' Billy nodded. 'But it's not even been a year since Andrade.'

At the name, Declan suddenly understood exactly what was going on in Billy's mind. Andrade Estrada had been a Colombian diplomat Billy had fallen for, connected to one of their earlier cases. When Johnny Lucas had been accused of murder – while under the belief he was his brother Jackie – Andrade had been sent by his superiors to pass along information on Jackie Lucas dying in a Colombian prison years earlier; a trip made in person, as the Colombian Embassy hoped word would get to Prime Minister Charles Baker – through Declan – that they'd helped, and he'd look favourably on them.

As it was, Billy and Andrade had gotten together and fallen for each other to where, when Andrade was being transferred from the embassy, Billy had considered dropping out of the force and going with him. But Andrade had turned out to be less than honest; involved with the Los Lideres Cartel, and lying to Billy throughout their relationship. Billy had been forced to arrest him, and Andrade had gone into witness protection. He had even offered Billy a chance to join him, changing their names forever, but Billy, feeling betrayed, had said no.

Declan understood why this could alter a man's impression of love.

'You can't compare everybody to your ex,' Declan said. 'That's like me comparing Anjli to Liz or to Kendis—'

'Or to Tessa Martinez.'

'I never went out with Tessa Martinez,' Declan cuffed Billy on the back of the head, knowing this was Billy's way of trying to change the subject away from his own issues.

'I get what you're saying,' Billy said as he looked back at the table. 'But ...'

'But Sam's good for you. He makes you live a little, rather than sitting in your space cockpit in the office.'

'Is that what you call it?' Billy laughed.

'You're surrounded by monitors in what seems to be a flight chair,' Declan said. 'You even have a joystick that can attach to the arm. What would you call it?'

'A gaming chair,' Billy replied as they moved up to the bar. 'Where I sometimes play space pilot games. So, sure, space cockpit works.'

They gave their food and drink orders, Declan opting for a Guinness even though he was originally going to have nothing more than water. Billy had already turned back, staring over at Sam.

'What if he hurts me like Andrade did?' Billy said.

'Then you move on,' Declan replied. 'You find someone else. There's plenty out there. You're still quite young. I mean, Christ, I found Anjli in my forties.'

Billy shuddered. 'I don't want to wait that long, Guv.'

'Could be worse,' Declan laughed. 'Monroe waited until—'

'Oh, I *really* don't want to wait *that* long,' Billy laughed. 'I just worry that Sam ...'

'You're worried he'll hurt you, that he'll go back to his old ways, that something else will happen ...' Declan nodded. 'I get that. I worry Anjli will find someone else, or that she'll be transferred, or get an opportunity far away for a better career. And if she does, she does. You have to decide what you want to do. Are you going to go for quality or quantity?'

Billy nodded, grabbing the drinks.

'Shall we?' he asked, and Declan knew the conversation was over. Sighing, he allowed Billy to lead him back to the high table, where they found Anjli and Sam deep in conversation.

'Something I should be worried about?' Declan smiled as he sat down.

'Sam's given me his interpretation of the case,' Anjli replied.

'I didn't think we were supposed to talk about the case,' Billy said, looking embarrassed.

'How much did you tell him?' Declan looked over at Sam, who shook his head.

'Billy didn't say anything,' he replied stonily.

'It doesn't matter,' Declan replied. 'I trust you. So does Anjli. How much did Billy tell you?'

Sam looked briefly at Billy, who shrugged, and then smiled back at Declan.

'Pretty much everything,' he said. 'Mainly about this contest and anti-ageing and all that sort of stuff.'

'Do you have any thoughts on it?' Declan asked.

At this, Anjli nodded.

'Actually, he's got a good take,' she said. 'Coming at it from a forger's point of view.'

'I'd like to say more as a scholar of human behaviour,' Sam leant back in his chair. 'Forger sounds so ... last year.'

Declan took a sip of his pint, before continuing.

'Go on then. Tell me what it sounds like to you,' he said. 'Using whatever Billy's told you and whatever Anjli has now added while we were getting drinks.'

Sam considered, took a sip of his own drink, a whisky with ice, and placed his elbows on the high table, leaning forward.

'If you ask me, there's something off about the whole situation,' he said. 'Everyone in this tournament seems to be selling a story about how they've turned back the clock with their own drinks, or their own equipment, or their own AI. But there's nothing concrete to back it up.'

Anjli nodded in agreement as Sam continued.

'It sounds like it's all smoke and mirrors, but you'll probably find that you won't be able to put your finger on what's real, and what's just a really good PR campaign.'

'He's got a point,' Billy said. 'We know Aria Milton is creating her own technology to try and keep herself alive. We know Leon Brecht is trying to prove that AI isn't the monster people say it is. I'll guarantee you when we speak to Eli Green, he'll have something to do with the items he had in Ionosphere that he removed. And then, of course, there's Stephen Kline himself and his anti-ageing benefits of cryotherapy.'

Sam, leaning back on his chair, casually swirled the ice in his glass before speaking again.

'You know,' he began, his tone conversational but edged with what felt like a knowing smirk, 'when you're in my line of work—'

'Forgery,' Anjli offered.

Sam ignored her.

'When you're in my line of work, creating a believable story is half the battle. It's not just about forging a signature or faking a document. It's about crafting something that people want to believe.'

'How do you mean?' At this, Billy shot Sam a curious look.

Sam glanced around the table before continuing.

'OK then, take the contestants in this tournament. Each one of them seems to have built a narrative around their success – a miracle diet, a cutting-edge treatment, whatever it is. But the thing about a good forgery, or in this case a good lie, is that it has to fit the person it's attached to. It has to make sense, even if it's not true.'

'You're saying some of these people could be faking it, but doing it so well we wouldn't notice?' Declan asked, taking another sip from his drink.

'Exactly,' Sam replied. 'The best lies are the ones that are just close enough to the truth. And if someone's trying to pass off some treatment as their own success, they'd make sure everything about them – their behaviour, their look, even how they talk – fits that story.'

He paused, considering what he was saying, his mouth twitching to the side as he thought about it.

'But if you look closely, you might notice small inconsistencies, little details that don't quite match up – like how they avoid certain topics, or how their habits don't line up with the lifestyle they're selling. These sorts of things are what give you life or death in the world of forgery or cons.'

'This "crafting something that people want to believe",' Billy said now, 'you wouldn't be talking from personal experience, would you?'

Sam glanced at Billy with a smile, but then softened his expression as he saw Billy's concerned look.

'Oh hun,' he said, patting Billy on the cheek. 'I might've done it in my business life, but I've never done it to you.'

'This thing about habits not lining up with the lifestyle they're selling,' Anjli raised an eyebrow, and changing the subject back to the case. 'This could be someone who claims they're on an extreme calorie-restricted diet but seems a bit too comfortable ordering a full plate at dinner, right?'

'Exactly,' Sam confirmed, returning his attention to Anjli now. 'Or someone who's supposedly into all-natural remedies but has more than a passing interest in the latest synthetic treatments.'

'Which would fit a couple of the people on our list,' Declan said.

Sam took a measured sip of his drink before responding.

'If it were forgeries or con artists – my world – you could use this inconsistency to your advantage,' he explained. 'Find the cracks in their story, start pulling at the threads. If their whole narrative is a well-crafted forgery, eventually it'll unravel.'

'Therefore, we look for the details that don't add up – the little things that betray the bigger lies.'

'Exactly. The truth will be hidden in those small inconsistencies. And remember, everyone's trying to sell you a story here. Our job is to figure out which ones are real and which ones are just a clever forgery.'

He considered this.

'How many of them work together?'

'How do you mean?' Declan frowned. 'They're all rivals.'

'Yeah, but they're all in the contest together,' Sam said. 'Sure, they want to beat the others, but they could form alliances, work together. There's no winner until the American leg in Vegas, right? Who's gaining from someone else's help?'

'Well, I would have said Kline,' Anjli replied. 'But he hasn't exactly gained much here.'

Sam shook his head, as if disbelieving Anjli.

'I'll bet you a tenner right now that at least half of them are working together,' he said. 'I know I would have. You know, in my old life. Which I no longer miss in any way.'

There was a moment of silence before Anjli raised her glass to Sam.

'You know what? You might have missed your calling. You've got a knack for this detective stuff.'

Sam chuckled, leaning back in his chair.

'I think I'll leave the badges and paperwork to you lot,' he said. 'I'm just here for the free food.'

As Sam finished, the server turned up with their meals, with Anjli realising she needed to pick up some condiments from the side counter. Declan went with her, feeling a hankering for some mustard on his food, even though the pie he'd ordered was already quite spicy.

As he reached the side counter where the condiments lay, Anjli looked at Declan as he raised an eyebrow.

'"You've got a knack for this detective stuff",' he laughed. 'You are aware eighty percent of what Sam said we've done ourselves?'

'I know,' Anjli nodded. 'But I think Billy needed a moment to realise Sam's more than just a forger.'

'He spoke to me when we went to the bar,' Declan said. 'He's worried about having another "Andrade" situation.'

'Which is why we need to make sure Sam stays as close to the police as possible,' Anjli grinned. 'That way, it won't happen again.'

She patted Declan on the arm.

'Anyway, my fearsome Detective Chief Inspector, I'm sure you can tell me exactly how we can get things working on this case, with no forger to help.'

'Sure,' Declan picked up some mustard. 'But can I eat first?'

9

OVERHEATING

THE LONDON LONGEVITY COLLECTIVE, OR "LLC" AS IT WAS known on social media, was a loosely grouped collective of biohackers and wannabe anti-ageing specialists that met weekly on a Thursday night in London, downstairs in a private bar called *Walkers of Whitehall*, a pub that was found down a side road opposite the Trafalgar Theatre, and mere minutes from the Houses of Parliament and the buildings of Whitehall.

David Lester had found the place when booking a Christmas party a year and a half earlier and had been repeatedly booking it, secretly covering the cost out of his own pocket, even though, as far as everybody else was concerned, he was just an attending biohacker. The collective was primarily filled with young people, and this made David feel young as well. He was in his late forties, and although he liked to tell people that *other* people said he "looked in his thirties", he was more than a little aware, and a little annoyed, that he actually looked in his *slightly younger* forties.

He was tanned with long brown hair pulled back into a

ponytail, a muscular physique, and orange-lensed glasses that he wore to keep the blue light from his eyes. That was the official statement, of course. The real reason he wore them was because he thought it made him look cool and futuristic. Also, one of his eyes was slightly differently pigmented to the other, and by wearing the shaded glasses, it blended the blue one and the grey one together.

Apparently it was something David Bowie had, but David Bowie also had crooked teeth for most of his life; it didn't mean that David Lester wanted to be the same.

The collective had now been running for almost eight months; David had started it as a way of gaining information on the latest trends in the biohacking community. He employed a solid team of people who gave him information on what he should be doing on a daily basis, but they were quite steady and standardised in their practices. He needed people who wanted to push the envelope, who were curious; people who would ingest things that nobody else would take.

Also, there was a slight element of Messiah complex, if he was being brutally honest. He liked the fact that the people at the collective looked up to him. They knew of him. They wanted to know *more.*

Especially some of the younger, prettier ones.

David had spent his life on the West Coast of America, in San Francisco and then Cupertino, where he'd made his money young, as a Silicon Valley entrepreneur. He had bought and sold companies, usually at a significant profit. And because of this, he was able to sponsor his hobbies. One of them was anti-ageing and longevity, but he had other, less public hobbies; ones that had eventually had him disbarred from the competition in San Francisco and forced to move to London, if he wanted to carry on building his brand.

As far as people were concerned, David Lester was the perfect Christian father. But beneath the sheets, he was a little more Sodom and Gomorrah than Joseph and Mary.

Shame. Mary was probably a hottie.

As he looked around the collective, there were two or three women he'd already *plucked*, so to speak, all of which were grateful for the information he'd given them ... and the experience.

Some people would have called it a cult.

David Lester called it a *weekday*.

The event was finishing up; they'd been talking about breath-work with some Indian guru who he didn't have a clue about. He wasn't a fan of the new-age bullcrap that people wanted to talk about, but it brought people in, and that's what he wanted. The more people who came in, the more people who would buy his books, who would follow his talks, who would download his apps.

Who'd build his *brand*.

He wasn't a billionaire because of his altruistic nature, after all.

The event was ending now; couples were hooking up, friends and colleagues were walking out together. The solo biohackers, having learned what they needed to, were also moving on to their next location, wherever it was. There was a man in his forties, toned and wearing a fleece jumper with a zip-lined front, standing to the side, talking to a group of younger women. Although there was nothing particularly wrong with it, Lester found himself filled with a pang of jealousy. *He* was the one who ran these events. *He* was the one who was supposed to have the pretty girls talking to him. The women seemed enraptured by every word the stranger said. Irritated by this, Lester eventually stood up, walked over, and tapped the man on the shoulder.

'Hi,' he said. 'I'm David. I don't think we've met.'

At the introduction, the stranger straightened and extended his hand. 'David Lester? I'm a big fan of yours! I've followed you on the leaderboards and everything.'

'Oh, are you a player in the tournament?' Lester asked, slightly surprised.

'Oh God, no,' the man laughed. 'I'm not at your level! The name's Joseph Lawrence.'

There was something familiar about the name, but it didn't kick in right away.

'Is this your first time here?'

'I've been to a couple of your events, stood at the back, but yeah, I decided to come along tonight.'

'Well, you've definitely made some friends,' Lester smiled, trying to hide his annoyance.

'Joseph was telling us about the body,' one girl, whom Lester vaguely recalled was called Francesca said, her eyes wide with curiosity, as if listening to some deep, dark secret.

'The body?' Lester wasn't sure where this conversation was going.

'He found Stephen Kline,' the second girl added, matter-of-factly.

'You found Stephen's body ...' Lester echoed, his tone now flat, emotionless.

Joseph, in a state of awkwardness, nodded, not realising he was stepping into a minefield.

'This morning, at Ionosphere,' he explained. 'I booked an early session. I was the first in.'

'He was explaining about what he saw,' Francesca gushed with gossipy excitement.

'Well ... it was more explaining that I'd had a doughnut,' Joseph said, his expression one of someone now trying to dig himself out of a hole he realised he'd been jumping into.

'A doughnut?'

'Yeah, I had a doughnut last night. Now I'm regretting it,' Joseph admitted, the last two words sounding as if he was regretting *talking* about it more than eating it.

'Awesome,' Lester said. 'Can I have a quick word with you?'

Taking Joseph to the side, Lester placed a reassuring arm around his shoulder as he led him away from the others.

'I don't know you, and I'm sure you're a nice man and everything, but I run this event, and I want to keep it quite relaxed.'

'No, I totally get that,' Joseph nodded enthusiastically.

'Yeah, I don't think you do,' Lester replied. 'You see, Stephen Kline was a friend of mine.'

'He was a friend of mine as well,' Joseph agreed. 'Well, more of a client, really, but you know, I spoke to him lots.'

'With the best will in the world, Joseph,' Lester started, his tone forced to be balanced, 'you working with Stephen Kline doesn't give you the right to turn up to places and start telling people all about *what he looked like when he died.* I was a *close* friend of Stephen's. And I don't appreciate people turning up to my events, telling people about dead bodies. More importantly, other people who come to these events, who, if they hear somebody bad-mouthing Kline—'

'No, I'm not in any way ...'

'You're talking about his dead body and how you found it,' Lester shut him off quickly. 'I know how he died; I've been told. He died in a horrid, terrible way. Frozen to death, the last hours spent hammering on the door, trying to escape, before he succumbed to the cold.'

Lester leant closer now.

'You look like you're somebody who's into the scene,' he whispered. 'Let me make it very simple for you. If I hear you talking about Stephen Kline's death to anybody who isn't a police officer, I will make sure that you are banned from every single anti-ageing establishment in London, of which there are quite a few. And of which all owe me favours. Do I make myself clear?'

Joseph Lawrence nodded, and Lester patted him on the shoulder.

'You have a good night,' he said, walking over to his seat once more.

Joseph, realising he'd made a massive error in judgement, grabbed his jacket and walked out, deciding, rather prudently, not to talk about this to any others. However, as the collective started to leave, there was one biohacker who was arriving.

One David Lester was surprised to see.

'What are you doing here?' he asked with a dry smile as Mira Nakahura walked into the bar, down from the steps that led to the main kitchen area. 'This is for biohackers, people who want to push the boundaries. This isn't for nepo babies and wannabes.'

Mira said nothing as she moved past a couple of jealous women, annoyed that their lord and saviour was talking to some stranger off the street. She walked up to Lester, now sitting on the end of the leather booth seat, leant over and rammed the forearm of her right arm into his throat, pushing his head against the wall.

'Did you do it?' she hissed. 'Did you kill him, you *utter wanker?*'

Two of the young men who had been at the biohacking event saw this and started forward, but Lester waved them off.

'Of course not,' he gasped.

Mira, now releasing her hold, straightened, giving him space.

'I might not have liked Kline, but I wouldn't have killed him,' he shuddered as he continued. 'Terrible way to go as well.'

If Mira was considering this, she wasn't making it public. Lester stood up, facing her, eye to eye.

'I didn't kill him, even though I wanted to,' he said. 'If anything, he would have tried to kill me, yeah? After everything that happened at the Summit, especially what he found out.'

Mira looked away, as if embarrassed or ashamed of what Lester was talking about, before she gathered her composure and looked back.

'Private talk, now.'

'There's a room we can use,' Lester said, nodding to the barman. He'd been allowed to use it a couple of times in the past. The barman thought it was because David Lester was talking about million-dollar proprietary apps, or cutting edge biohacking technology, but in essence, it was mainly because he needed a quick place he could go visit with one of his young female conquests.

It wasn't that large, but when a woman was kneeling down in front of you, there wasn't much space needed.

Some of the biohackers were curious about what was

happening as they saw him moving to the door, and he waved a hand.

'Guys,' he said, loud enough for all to hear, 'I'd like you to meet Mira Nakahura, currently number five on the Rejuvenation Royale Tournament leaderboard.'

This caused a definite rumble of interest. Anyone who was *that* high on the RRT list was almost royalty in the London biohacking scene. Even the jealous women were suddenly gushing about her, and suddenly the people who were suspicious of her, wondering who she was, were now crowding to speak to her.

'In a minute, please,' she said. 'I'll talk to you in a minute, but first Mister Lester and I need to have words.'

The pair of them left the disappointed crowd, walking past the entrance to the bar area and heading into the back room, to the side.

Lester opened the door, indicating for Mira to enter, following her inside.

Once the door was shut, she turned to face him.

'You're serious,' she said. 'It wasn't you?'

'No,' he said.

'Do you know who it was?'

'It could have been Selene, she's a cold bitch. Leon's a robot and doesn't understand how emotions work. It could have been Eli, although he was back from Taiwan today, so pretty much impossible ...' Lester smiled. 'Maybe it was you. It's not as if you don't have a reason.'

Mira stared at David Lester for a long, cold moment, and then, without warning, she lunged forward, slamming him against the wall, her mouth pressing hard against his.

As they tumbled to the side, falling onto a large box of crisps, they were already tugging at each other's clothing, with a familiarity that showed this wasn't the first time that this had happened.

'Are you going to ram your forearm against my throat again?' Lester asked, as they broke for air.

'If you want,' Mira said as she moved down his body.

'Mmm,' Lester replied. 'That could be just what the doctor ordered.'

IT WAS GONE TEN THAT NIGHT WHEN THE SMOOTH PURR OF THE metallic-purple Porsche Cayenne came to a stop outside Eli Green's house in Hampstead.

The engine cut off, and Selene Carter stepped out. The chill evening air brushed her skin as she glanced up at the imposing house; the SUV's sleek dark frame blended into the misty street, but its luxury was unmistakable. It was a car that symbolised power, success, and control – three things Selene Carter wasn't really feeling at this moment.

She had an athletic lean frame, the result of years as a former Olympian triathlete. Her blonde hair, usually neat, was slightly tousled, dark shadows under her green eyes hinted at sleepless nights, and her jaw was tight with tension, the stress of Kline's death, or something equally large, clearly weighing on her.

In front of her, Eli's house loomed, all glass and sharp lines, standing in stark contrast to the older homes that lined the rest of the street. Hampstead had always had an air of old wealth, but Eli's modern build screamed *new money*, with its rooftop patio and a subtle glow from the windows, where the blue light dampeners would have turned on by now.

The neighbours had been unhappy when he started

building this monstrosity; they would've been even unhappier if they had known what he'd done in the basement, effectively building his own home cinema underneath their own homes without their knowledge. The building was a bold statement, a *screw you* to the locality, and Selene Carter hated it. She'd been here before, several times in fact, but tonight the house felt different – something felt off.

She slammed the car door harder than she intended, her irritation and anxiety bubbling over, and paused for a moment in the quiet street, as if expecting someone to come to a window and shout at her to keep the noise down. Stephen Kline's death earlier that day had shaken her, but this – Eli's silence, the unanswered calls – this was pushing her to a breaking point.

She needed answers, and she needed them now.

She stormed through the gate and up to the door, her breath quickening.

'Eli!' she shouted, banging her fist against the solid wood. There was no sound from within. Her heartbeat drummed in her ears as she rang the doorbell several times; it was a video doorbell, the kind that allowed you to be seen through the camera lens on a mobile device, and she leant into the camera, staring directly into it.

'Eli, you son of a bitch, open up! I need to talk to you.'

Again, there was no answer.

Stepping back from the door, she glanced up at the upstairs windows where a faint light flickered.

He had to be there.

She started ringing the doorbell and hammering the door again, harder this time.

'Come on!'

After a few more seconds, the door finally creaked open.

A housekeeper, or maybe an assistant – a middle-aged woman with a short brown perm – peered out, looking uncertain. Selene had met her before, but had never bothered to learn her name or her role here. Probably a mistake, right now.

'Can I help you?' the woman asked, frowning as she stared at the bedraggled woman in front of her. 'Ms Carter?'

'I need Eli,' Selene cut her off before she could ask any questions. 'Where is he?'

'Mister Green cannot be disturbed,' the housekeeper began as Selene brushed past her into the hallway. 'He only just got back from his trip this afternoon.'

But Selene was already moving, walking through the hallway. The quiet, pristine space felt unnervingly empty. Eli's house had always been like this though; too clean, too perfect. It felt more like a showroom than a home, the kind of place designed to make everything look beautiful, while hiding too many things behind the plaster.

'Is he in the main room?'

'No.'

'His bedroom? Study?'

'I don't believe so.'

He might not be in the main rooms or even his bedroom, but Selene had a good idea where he'd be. When Eli was flying multiple time zones and trying to kill his jet lag, he would always retreat to his rooftop patio when he didn't want to be disturbed. It was one of the reasons he'd designed the building this way.

Selene started taking the stairs two at a time, her nerves tingling with every step. Kline's death had been brutal, but Eli's silence, his absence, felt wrong. Regardless of whether he'd flown back today or not, he would've come back in business class at least – first class, most likely. He'd have had Wi-Fi.

He could've sent messages.

She could be wrong – she often was – but tension was coiling tighter in her chest as she reached the rooftop door.

'Has he spoken to anyone today?'

'His son came by, but that was to drop a book off, before leaving,' the housekeeper replied. 'He's spoken to me by text.'

The lights on the patio glowed softly, heat already radiating through the cool air as she entered it. Eli had created this patio as his personal wellness retreat; there was a Zen garden, trellises partially blocking the view of neighbouring buildings, laced with Christmas tree fairy lights, all a warm white, glowing in the night, but also creating a sense of peace and tranquillity. To the side was a small wooden sauna, with a plunge pool built into the decking next to it, the source of both warmth and light.

'How long's he been in here?' Selene shouted back to the housekeeper, her voice strained with impatience.

The woman hesitated, standing just inside the door as if afraid to come any further.

'He went in this afternoon. He should've been done ages ago.'

Selene's gaze darted to the sauna, the soft glow of the lights casting long shadows across the deck. Her heart pounded harder in her chest as she stepped towards it. There was no reason to be this nervous, of course; she knew Eli. He was probably lounging inside, enjoying the heat after his long flight, probably alternating with the bloody plunge pool for shits and giggles. And yet, something about this entire situation felt wrong, like there was a thread of tension strung too tightly, ready to snap.

'Well, someone's in here,' Selene muttered under her breath as she reached for the handle of the sauna door. 'Eli?' she called softly, almost afraid of what she might find.

No answer.

Her fingers gripped the warm handle, and with a sharp intake of breath, she pulled the door open.

Steam billowed out of the sauna, but it didn't take her long to see that there was a body inside. Eli Green slumped against the side of the sauna in nothing more than a pair of swim shorts, unmoving; the remains of a smoothie spilt over the floor, the cup still in his hand.

For a second, everything seemed to stop. Then the cold realisation hit.

He was dead, just like Kline was.

Two deaths, and this time she wasn't just suspicious that something was wrong. Now she was terrified.

'We need to call the police,' the housekeeper said, stepping back from the sauna as she stared in horror through the door. But before she could move, Selene spun, grabbing her by the arm.

'Not yet,' she said. 'Take me to his study. *Now.*'

10

UNRELIABLE NARRATIONS

When the call came through, Monroe was the one who took it.

It was late in the evening, gone eleven; Declan and Anjli had already returned to Hurley, and the other members of the Last Chance Saloon would have been wrapped up in their beds, ready for another day.

Monroe, however, had been out with a friend while Rosanna Marcos worked on the case over at the Lambeth pathology offices. However, he'd realised on the way home, thanks to a timely reminder on his phone, that he'd left his laptop in his office. Therefore, when the call came through, he was actually in his office, beside his desk.

That wasn't the first conversation he had on arriving though; strangely enough, that was from Detective Superintendent Warren, sitting in the bullpen, working at a desk.

'What the bloody hell are you doing here, lassie?' Monroe frowned, looking around. 'You *are* aware you don't work here, right?'

'While we're working on the case, I do,' Warren replied,

straightening. She was obviously as surprised to see Monroe as he was. 'I'd managed to gather some information from my team back at Canary Wharf, and I was just running through it.'

'You know, we have a lad for that,' Monroe smiled. 'He's superb. He could be the best in the world.'

'I don't care,' Warren snapped back. 'I'd like to find out myself.'

'Ah, you always did,' Monroe grumpily turned to walk back to his office.

'Did you forget something?' Warren called out after him. 'A bottle, perhaps?'

Monroe let the insult slide, hearing the phone go in the main office and ignoring it as he gathered his laptop, placing it in his messenger bag. He was, however, conscious of a low-spoken surprised voice and, as he turned, he saw Warren putting down the phone and looking up at him.

'Eli Green,' she said.

'Aye, what about him?' Monroe replied, walking out of his office and facing her across the bullpen. 'Let me guess, he's confessed to everything?'

'Not quite. He's dead,' Warren was already gathering her jacket. 'Found in his Hampstead house, on the roof.'

'On the roof?' Monroe frowned. 'Was he going to jump?'

'No, he has some kind of patio up there, and they found him in the sauna.'

'Aye, of course, he'd have a sauna on his roof,' Monroe replied, shaking his head. 'Wait, are you telling me he was found broiled?'

'I don't know what you'd call it, broiled, cooked, whatever, but yes,' Warren replied. 'I'm happy to head over if you want to finish and call it a day.'

Monroe considered this for about a second before shaking his head.

'No, I'll come with you,' he said. 'We'll go in my car.'

'Are you sure?' Warren replied. 'If you recall the last time we were on a case together ...'

'The last time we went on a case together, it was a different world,' Monroe replied. 'Give us the details, you can brief me on what they said while we're driving there.'

THE TRIP FROM TEMPLE INN UP TO HAMPSTEAD WAS QUITE busy for this time of night. Pubs were emptying, and the late-night traffic had built up. But the journey gave both Warren and Monroe a chance to break the ice. Although in Warren's case, it seemed like she wanted to break it with a very large hatchet, and preferably in the middle of Monroe's face.

'Your team seems good,' she said. 'I'm impressed with DI Kapoor.'

'Aye, she's a keeper,' Monroe nodded. 'They wanted to kick her out of the force, but I fought to keep her in the team.'

'Why would they want to remove her from the force?'

'She was caught beating the shite out of a domestic abuser.'

'I like her even more,' Warren grinned. She sat back in the passenger seat, considering her next words.

'You seem happier here,' she said, 'you know, than you were in Newbury.'

'Newbury was a tough time,' Monroe replied.

'You're telling me,' Warren breathed. It was supposed to have been under her breath, but it ended up coming out, and Monroe glanced at her, his eyes narrowing.

'If I recall, lassie, *you* were the absolute nightmare, not me.'

Warren looked back at him.

'Oh, aye,' she said, mocking his tone. 'And how would that be?'

'Well, if I recall correctly. I came in to help out with your team, and you were the most miserable bitch I'd ever met,' Monroe snapped. 'You looked like you were constantly chewing a mouthful of thistles. Every time I wanted to get something done, you'd argue with me, and you'd question what I was doing. You were constantly watching me. I get it if you wanted to learn from me, lassie, but it looked like you were trying to work out how to get me fired.'

'And this is why you think I don't like you?' Warren asked, her voice now cold. 'You think I don't like you because you, what, came in and took my job?'

'Well, I'm guessing you're annoyed I came in and took Pearson's role, when you felt that you could have done it quite perfectly yourself,' Monroe shrugged. 'So, aye, I do think that. But you have to remember, lassie, you'd only just become Detective Sergeant. He was a DCI. There was no way you—'

'I didn't want to head the department,' Warren snapped now, her voice rising in the car, making Monroe jump in surprise. 'I just wanted somebody running it who wasn't *pissed* all the time.'

There was a long, uncomfortable moment of silence in the car. Warren released a pent-up breath, shaking her head.

'That's not how I meant it,' she said. 'I wanted to talk about it, but not ...'

'No, that's exactly how you meant it,' Monroe said, turning to face her briefly as he paused at a roundabout. 'And you're right to be like that. I had my demons back then, I was crawling into a bottle more times than crawling out. I thought I was functioning, but it took a few people down the line to point out that I was just using it as a crutch.'

He turned back to the road.

'Maybe I could have been better.'

'There's no *could* about it,' Warren argued, not allowing him to concede the point. 'You *should* have been better. You were a legend. You coming in from London, you'd been involved in some of the biggest stings in the East End. And there you turn up, this washed-up drunk, who just keeps going on about the glory days. You were supposed to teach me, make me a better detective.'

She looked back out of the window now, angry.

'I look at Declan Walsh, and I see what I should have been,' she said.

'Declan was his own man before he came to me,' Monroe replied, looking back at her. 'And aye, maybe I did drop the ball. But blame is a two-sided street, Lenette.'

'So I'm supposed to have been the one to say "excuse me, Guv, but you seem a little too bollocksed to run this case right now. How about I do it for you?"' Warren chuckled. 'Don't make me laugh. You gave no shit about me at all. You were just concerned about yourself. All you wanted to do was get back to London, get away from this provincial shithole that you'd been dumped in because you were an embarrassment. What was it at the time? Possible corruption? Working for Johnny Lucas?'

'I never worked for Johnny Lucas,' Monroe growled.

'Yeah, okay, that's what I heard afterwards,' Warren replied. 'You see, I kept close ties on you. I wanted to see whether you would actually drink yourself into an early grave. But no, every time you screwed up, they'd do the same thing.'

'Which was?'

'They gave you a promotion.'

'I screwed up more times than you understand,' Monroe shook his head. 'But don't for one second think that you got the shitty end of the stick.'

'Oh yeah?' Warren shifted in her seat now to turn to face Monroe. 'Do you remember Savernake Forest, where you turned up with Walsh, knowing it would kick a fight off, and then as you're having a go, you're sending in Rosanna Marcos behind me, dressed like one of my crew? I almost got fired for that. Christ knows why they didn't.'

'Would you like to know why they didn't?' Monroe asked calmly.

'What, you know?' Warren frowned.

'Aye, I know why they didn't fire you.' Monroe gave a small smile now. 'It's because I asked them nicely. Actually, if I'm being honest, I put the fear of God into them. You see, you make a joke about how I had high-level friends that kept me alive and stopped me getting fired; I used those same friends with you. You allowing Doctor Marcos into that crime scene got you into trouble, but it also helped us solve a crime that eventually led to a Cabinet Minister and a member of a very specific Westminster Star Chamber keeping his freedom. Your boss back then ... who was it now? Detective Superintendent Chatham?'

'Peter Chatham, yes.'

'Well, Peter Chatham got a phone call in the middle of the night, telling him that if you hadn't assisted us, we wouldn't have been able to fix this, and the person who called him was so high up the chain there was no way he could avoid it. Before he could even have the conversation, the phone call had been made, thanking him for allowing us to use you, and how you'd been such a help in our case.'

They'd reached Hampstead, and Monroe pulled the car to the side, turning off the engine as he looked back to face her.

'You see, Lennie,' he started, 'you're so busy blaming others for what they haven't done, you're not noticing the fact that they're actually doing what they can for you. Now I am sorry that I was a horrid and terrible drunk when I worked with you, but that's the past. I've come to terms with what I was back then, and how close I was to finding myself ...'

'Fired?' Lenny suggested.

'No. Dead in a ditch,' Monroe finished. 'This wasn't going to end with me losing my job. This was going to end with me losing my life. And the reason I didn't die was because I had friends who looked out for me. Who kept me going. Who cleaned up my screw-ups.'

He gave out a pent-up sigh, years in the making.

'How about we bury that hatchet, aye? Preferably not in my head. And move on, like professionals.'

'I've held on to this anger for years,' Warren also sighed. 'It's kept me warm at night, and you're asking for me to just toss it away?'

'Aye,' Monroe held a hand out to shake. 'How about it?'

Warren stared at the hand, looked up at Monroe, and her face twisted into one of anger.

'Screw you, old man,' she hissed as she left the car.

Monroe retracted his hand, chuckling to himself.

'Well, that went better than I expected,' he said out loud, before joining her.

MONROE HADN'T EXPECTED TO SEE ANY FAMILIAR FACES WHEN he had arrived at the Hampstead house. For a start, it was the middle of the night, and he was only there by pure chance. So, it wasn't surprising when the officer controlling the scene was a face he didn't recognise.

'Sergeant Ashad, sir,' the man replied as Monroe showed him his warrant card. 'Your doctor is checking the body right now.'

'Do we have a time of events?'

Ashad pulled out his notebook, flicking through it.

'Selene Carter arrived around ten-forty pm,' he read. 'She was quite insistent to speak to Mister Green. The housekeeper, a Marjorie Halliwell, claimed she wouldn't take no for an answer; it was almost as if she felt that something was wrong. They hurried up onto the roof, where they found Mister Green in the sauna.'

'Dead, I'm guessing,' Monroe replied. 'It would be a completely different conversation, wouldn't it, if he was still alive. Do we know how long he'd been dead for?'

'Your doctor's checking now, I believe ...'

Ashad swallowed.

'You look like you want to say something,' Monroe noticed the pause.

'It's just ...' Ashad frowned, looking around, as if concerned he was being overheard. 'The housekeeper said that Selene Carter had turned up on the doorstep, ringing the doorbell and banging on the door, demanding to see Eli Green.'

'OK,' Monroe replied. 'What's triggering your concern here?'

'There's no doorbell footage,' Ashad replied, nodding at

the front door. 'It's a video doorbell. You can be seen by the house owner, and it turns on by ringing the bell.'

'No motion detection?'

'Apparently they have cats in the area that kept triggering it, so they turned it off,' Ashad shrugged. 'We asked to see the footage, and when the housekeeper opened up the app to show any movement or ringing doorbells, there's nothing.'

'Maybe she didn't ring the doorbell, maybe she just banged on the door?' Warren suggested.

'Absolutely, ma'am. It just felt strange that the housekeeper said that it happened.'

'Okay,' Monroe pulled out his phone. 'Luckily for you, I've got a lad who can check into this. Anything else?'

'Not really,' Ashad replied. 'It just felt a little strange.'

Monroe nodded, already texting a message to Billy. They had worked on a similar doorbell in the "Posies Killer" case only a couple of weeks earlier. Billy had managed to gain good knowledge then on how to find deleted video footage.

Walking up the steps, they paused as Doctor Marcos met them halfway.

'I thought you'd be with the body,' Monroe replied.

'It's about to be taken to the morgue,' Doctor Marcos shook her head. 'There's nothing here.'

'How do you mean?' It was Warren who asked.

Doctor Marcos stared back up the stairs as if using x-ray vision to look back to where the sauna was.

'From all intents and purposes, it looks like Green came back from Thailand, did some exercise, which a lot of people do to try to stave off jet lag, and then used his plunge pool and sauna. Both were on. The plunge pool had been dropped down to three degrees, which is about right for somebody wanting to do a session, and the sauna, well, it's a sauna. They're hot.'

'But ...' Monroe asked, knowing there was always a but.

'But if I was looking at it as somebody off the street, I might think that he was jet-lagged and tired, the sauna was warm, he fell asleep,' Doctor Marcos shook her head. 'You know, the kind of sleep where no one ever wakes up.'

'You said if you were someone off the street,' Monroe raised an eyebrow. 'What would you say if you weren't?'

'I'd say there's something dodgy as hell here,' Doctor Marcos shook her head. 'No one falls asleep and dies in a sauna unless they're drunk. This is unnatural.'

'Like Stephen Kline?' Warren asked.

'Possibly,' Doctor Marcos nodded. 'The difference here, though, is that Eli Green could have left the sauna whenever he wanted. The door wasn't locked. If anything, it was almost open. The clock on the sauna had even turned off, lowering the temperature.'

'So, how did he die?' Monroe asked.

'That's a question for the Met pathologist,' Doctor Marcos replied. 'Who I will be going to speak to right now. He had a smoothie in his hand he'd dropped to the floor. This wasn't a slow doze, this was out like a light, instantaneously.'

She glanced back at Monroe.

'You're going to have to make your own dinner, darling. Mummy's going to be home late.'

Monroe grimaced at the term and noted that Warren stifled a snigger.

'Anything else?'

Doctor Marcos shook her head.

'Not yet. We know that the driver brought him back here from the airport, arriving somewhere around half-past two.

That's an eight-hour window in which he could have been in the sauna. I'll know better how long he was in there once I've seen the DNA cells. They'll alter, you see, with the heat.'

'Will you have a briefing for tomorrow?'

'Do I get to sleep?'

'That's your call,' Monroe asked. 'I'm more than happy if you want to bring somebody else in. De'Geer, I'm sure, would happily drive in right now.'

'De'Geer's gone home, and he should sleep,' Doctor Marcos was adamant. 'I've got this. It'll only take a couple of hours. I'll go back to the unit and crash out on one of the cots. I'll get more sleep than if I was at home with you, anyway.'

Monroe reddened, looking back at Warren.

'She means I snore.'

'Believe me, Alex, I wasn't considering anything else,' Warren replied. 'The thought of you in any way … like that … would put me off romance for the rest of my life.'

'Don't knock it till you've tried it,' Doctor Marcos grinned. 'Either way, the body's on its way to the morgue, so I'll get on it immediately. I'll let the forensics keep checking around.'

She stopped.

'Have you spoken to the witness yet?'

'The housekeeper?'

'No, Carter,' Doctor Marcos looked around, possibly looking for the woman she spoke about. 'She was leaving as I arrived. She'd given a statement and was being taken away by a friend of hers.'

'And?'

'And it felt a little "crocodile tears" if you ask me,' Doctor Marcos replied, 'I can't explain why, but for somebody who turned up banging on the door and screaming for help, it just seems a little odd that nothing else happened.'

'I'll look into it.'

'Good,' Doctor Marcos patted Monroe on the arm. 'Have a look around, speak to a few other people, but I'm done here. I'll speak to you later.'

Doctor Marcos left Monroe and Warren together, standing in the upstairs hallway.

'Do you want to go look at the sauna?' Monroe asked.

'Well, I'm already here, it'd be rude not to,' Warren replied, but then stopped. 'I'm sorry for what I said in the car, yeah? When I said screw you. It's just ...'

Monroe shook his head.

'No need to apologise at all, lassie,' he said. 'I get it. Some people just don't gel. And I'd rather you were honest, rather than give me the "crocodile tears" Rosanna just mentioned.'

'Thank you,' Warren gave a brief smile. 'Oh, and for the record ... *not* keen on being called lassie either.'

'Aye, I thought as much,' Monroe grinned. 'Let's go have a look around, Detective Superintendent.'

11

BACKUP FILES

DECLAN WAS ANNOYED THAT HE HADN'T BEEN INFORMED OF THE second murder when it happened, but he understood why Monroe had gone on his own, rather than getting Declan to come all the way back from Hurley, shortly before midnight. However, he'd have preferred a heads-up on the case, especially as he walked in to find a sleeping Doctor Marcos in a cot in the day room. She'd explained everything groggily while Declan made her coffee, then he'd wandered back to his office, already planning out the day ahead.

Originally, it was going to be a day for interviews, but considering the fact that his first meeting was supposed to be with Eli Green, who was now dead ... that seemed a bit of a moot point, now.

As it was, Billy had some information for him.

'I think I've found something,' he said, scrolling through lines of data on his computer.

'When you say you think you've found something, usually it means you've solved the case for us,' Declan smiled. 'So, I'm hoping that's the situation this time.'

'No, but I've found some abnormalities,' Billy replied, tapping the screen. 'I think I've worked out what the problem was at the Summit.'

'Go on,' Declan waved a hand, sipping his coffee with the other.

Billy tapped on the screen.

'All the candidates have to give their DNA to be checked by independent researchers,' he explained. 'The moment Stephen Kline was murdered, we contacted Rupert Cray, explaining the situation, and all the DNA of the London candidates was sent to us.'

'And of course, that's probably against half a dozen EU rules,' Declan muttered.

'It's a private competition, and they sign away the rights when they apply,' Billy shrugged.

'Okay then, so what do you have?'

'Well, the first thing that's noticeable is that Stephen Kline's DNA isn't there,' Billy said, 'which makes sense if he officially wasn't a contestant.'

'But he was looking to join in,' Declan pointed out.

'Yes and no. He was looking to come in late to the event. The impression was that he'd only do it once he knew he could hit the top three, but then he chose at the Summit to step down – or, rather not actually officially enter in the first place,' Billy replied. 'Which means his DNA wouldn't be on record.'

He turned around to face Declan.

'However, since he was the victim, we have his DNA on record, anyway.'

'Okay,' Declan leant against the desk behind him as he waited for Billy to continue.

'And going through it, I've realised that his DNA is incredibly close to another contestant. So close, in fact, that they are definitely related.'

'Are you saying that Stephen Kline had a brother or sister in the competition?'

'No,' Billy replied, turning back and opening a browser window. On it was a picture of Mira Nakahura. 'I'm saying he had a *daughter*.'

Declan leant closer, staring at the image.

'Do you think she knew?'

'I think she might have found out during the conference,' Billy shrugged. 'It would explain why there was an argument.'

'She'd been using his cryotherapy centre for the last eighteen months,' Declan frowned as he stared at the screen. 'She had to know.'

'Possibly,' Billy leant back. 'But until we speak to her, we won't know.'

'I was going to speak to Mister Green today, but maybe I'll have a chat with Mira Nakahura instead,' Declan looked over to Anjli, sitting at her desk. 'Fancy a trip to speak to ... well, apparently Stephen Kline's daughter?'

Anjli frowned and then shrugged.

'Sure,' she said. 'It's not crazier than half the other things we've had to do over the years.'

'That's not the only thing I wanted to talk about,' Billy said. 'So, last night, Eli Green died in his sauna.'

'We know,' Declan said. 'Monroe kept it from us, so that we couldn't go and have fun with him on some patio roof.'

'True,' Billy replied, 'but he sent me a message close to midnight, telling me to find a way of checking deleted video files.'

Declan looked at Anjli as if she would magically understand what Billy was talking about.

'Let's pretend for one minute that neither of us were here when that happened, yeah? We've only just arrived in the office and started our first coffee of the day,' he said.

'Basically, Selene Carter had arrived and started hammering on the door, demanding to speak to Eli Green,' Billy explained. 'But one of the coppers, a Sergeant Ashad, pointed out that the housekeeper, during her statement, had said that Selene Carter had been ringing the doorbell *and* banging on the door.'

'Two separate things,' Anjli said, now rising from her desk. 'Let me guess, it was a video doorbell.'

'Yes,' Billy said, turning his attention to her. 'The problem is that when they checked the video doorbell footage, there was no sign of any doorbell being rung, which means either Selene Carter didn't ring the doorbell ...'

'Or someone deleted the footage.' Declan nodded. 'So, how do we get the footage?'

'Backup server,' Billy grinned. 'You see, Ring doorbells, Nest doorbells, and all the other doorbells, if there's some kind of Wi-Fi collapse, or your phone gets broken, they save the data on the cloud. And if you accidentally delete something, they hold it for a few days to make sure you *meant* to delete it.'

'And if someone deleted it at the source, they might not have known to delete it everywhere?'

'I was able to hack into Eli Green's system—' Billy paused, frowning, '—is it technically hacking if you've got the details because he's dead, and his phone's in your boss's hand? Either way, I could check, and up in the cloud, there *was* video footage of Selene Carter banging on the door and ringing the front doorbell. Now, there's every chance this was just a technical issue, and it disappeared by accident ...'

'Go on, you've obviously got something else you want to say,' Declan looked across at Anjli. 'He's got that look. The bloody annoying one.'

'You're right,' Anjli peered closer at Billy. 'It is bloody annoying.'

'They called the police at twenty to eleven,' Billy continued, ignoring the jibes. 'They said that Selene Carter had come in, argued, demanded to see Eli, stormed upstairs, and found his body. This matches the banging on the door seen in the video.'

'So, what's the problem?' Declan and Anjli asked together.

'The problem,' Billy replied, 'is that they called the police at ten-forty at night, but the video footage is time stamped, and shows her arriving over fifteen minutes earlier.'

He gave it a moment for Declan and Anjli to understand what he was saying.

'There's no way Selene Carter took over fifteen minutes to find the body, if she was in that much of a hurry,' Declan said. 'So, what were they doing in the time between discovering the body and phoning the police?'

'That's a question I think we'd need to ask Ms Carter,' Anjli said, her eyes narrowing.

Declan was about to continue to reply to this, but movement out of the corner of his eye distracted him, and he turned to the main doors to see Bullman walking through. He must have had an expression that was readable though, because the moment she saw him, her eyes narrowed and she paused in the doorway.

'What?' she asked. 'Do I have lipstick on my teeth?'

Declan glanced back at the others. It was known that Bullman had a history with Kline. It had also been told to him yesterday by Bullman herself that she'd had a more romantic history.

'Ma'am, I have to ask you a question,' he said. 'It's not something I really want to ask.'

'Go on.' Bullman carried on into the office, walking over to Declan and Anjli.

'Did you know that Stephen Kline had a ... daughter?'

Bullman shook her head.

'He never had a daughter,' she replied, and then paused, frowning. 'Well, at least he told me he never had a daughter. He didn't have kids, full stop. He was so concerned about it that fifteen years ago he had the snip.'

Declan nodded at this, more in an automatic fashion than in agreement.

'That's as may be, ma'am, but it seems that might have been a little bit too late,' he said.

Billy looked up from the computers now, realising that neither of the other two people in the room were going to tell Bullman what needed to be said.

'I've got the DNA, ma'am,' he said. 'Stephen Kline has a very strong DNA connection to Mira Nakahura, the kind you would have if you were father and daughter.'

'I see.' Bullman's face was impassive as she took in the information. 'Does she know? Does he ... *did* he know?'

'We're not sure,' Declan replied. 'Billy's only just gained the information.'

'Right. Well, we need to get her in then, don't we?' Bullman replied, walking over towards Monroe's office. 'Is he in yet?'

'No ma'am, he worked late in Hampstead.'

'Excellent. I'll be using his office today then,' Bullman looked back to Declan, and he could tell she was trying to be light-hearted, giving a throwaway comment, but it came away cold and harsh. 'You two can bunk up for the day in yours.'

'I think I might be spending a lot of my time in interview rooms and in meetings,' Declan replied candidly. He was about to continue, but PC Cooper appeared at the doorway, motioning for Declan's attention.

'What is it?' he asked.

'We have Alexis Kovalenko downstairs,' she said. 'We'd arranged for her to come in today to answer some questions. It seems like she's turned up fresh and early.'

Declan glanced at Bullman.

'We should wait for Warren to turn up,' he said. 'She was the last person to interview her at the scene. If there's any discrepancy, she'd pick it up.'

Bullman nodded at this.

'She should be arriving soon,' she replied. 'I spoke to her last night after the, well, sauna event. She said she'd be in early.'

Checking his watch, Declan looked back at Cooper.

'Could you put her in one of the interview rooms?' he asked. 'Provide her with whatever she wants. Make her aware that she's not a suspect. We just need to corroborate some information.'

'Is that true?' Anjli asked as PC Cooper left. 'That she isn't a suspect?'

'At the moment, everybody's one,' Declan replied. 'We just need to work out what the hell we're doing.'

There was new movement at the door, and Cooper brought Alexis into the office, walking past the desks as she walked towards the stairs at the back of the room. The usual way to do this was to go up from the car park, avoiding the front entrance and the march through the main office, but

Cooper simply shrugged as the others in the room looked at her.

'She asked to go this way,' she said. 'And there's problems with the rear staircase. We've got some pipes issues.'

'We only just got the bloody place renovated,' Bullman moaned.

'Obviously some corners were cut,' Declan suggested.

Alexis seemed calmer than she had been when last they met, but she also looked nervous, slightly hyper.

'Hi,' she said, nodding to everyone. And, as Bullman rose from the chair she'd been sitting on, Alexis made a beeline for her before Cooper could stop her.

'Sophie – I mean Miss Bullman – I mean Detective Chief Superintendent Bullman, I wanted to apologise,' she said in hushed, almost reverent tones. 'I shouldn't have hugged you. You're a client, not a friend. And you're like the woman running the case and all that. It's weighed on my mind for a while.'

'It's fine,' Bullman replied. 'You were in shock. Happens to the best of us. Are you okay?'

'Not really,' Alexis admitted. 'I'm a little hopped up on caffeine right now. I have lessons later today and work that needs to go in.'

She showed her messenger bag.

'I brought my laptop, so if you need me to go sit somewhere quiet, I can – oh, shit.'

The last part was aimed at her bag, sliding off her shoulder as she moved nervously around, and falling onto the floor, spilling everything out onto the carpet. As she fell to her knees, picking up the discarded items, she bumped into Anjli's leg as a pen rolled under her table.

'Sorry, sorry, sorry ...' she muttered, eventually getting

back to her feet and ensuring the bag was closed. 'If I missed anything, just let me know. Shit, I'm so clumsy. Shit, I shouldn't have sworn—'

'It's fine,' Bullman's face was still smiling, but Declan could see it was forced. 'PC Cooper, can you take Miss Kovalenko to an interview room? Allow her to take her bag in too, she can do some homework while she waits.'

Alexis went to hug, but then thought better of it and gave Bullman a nod, before following Cooper up the stairs.

As she left, Billy let out a pent-up breath.

'And I thought I was clumsy and nervous around the boss!' he exclaimed.

At this, everyone looked at him.

'Yeah, I know,' he said. 'Move along, nothing to see here.'

IT WAS ANOTHER TWENTY MINUTES BEFORE WARREN ARRIVED; and from her expression, and the bags under her eyes, she had obviously not slept the night before. Interestingly, she arrived almost at the same time that Mira Nakahura did, with De'Geer, having gone out to collect her.

'Miss Nakahura,' Declan said as they both entered the main office. 'Thank you for coming in. We have some questions.'

'I'm sure you do,' Mira replied. 'The question I'm going to ask though is, are we doing them here or are you going to stick me in an interrogation room?'

'We call them interview rooms, and we do them there because they're able to be recorded,' Bullman said, now standing at the door to Monroe's office. 'And yes, you will be having your conversation in one of them.'

'Am I a suspect?'

'Actually, yes,' Declan replied honestly. 'And we'd very much like to know what happened at the Summit two months ago.'

Mira nodded, as if expecting this.

'I can tell you that right now,' she replied.

'We'd rather have it on record.'

Mira pulled out a phone and turned on her recording app.

'I'm happy to do it here.'

Declan, again, shook his head.

'I'm sorry, Miss Nakahura, but I'm afraid we must insist.'

Mira seemed to deflate at this, as if all the bluster and bravado she'd shown was gone. Saying nothing, she gave a curt nod and allowed De'Geer to lead her upstairs to where the interview rooms were.

'Interview room two,' Bullman shouted out after her. The last thing they wanted was for her to walk into the same room as Alexis Kovalenko, although Declan wasn't sure if it would have affected anything, anyway.

He turned back to Warren, making herself comfortable at a desk.

'Are you okay if I take command for a moment?' he asked.

Warren shrugged, rubbing at her eyes.

'Walsh, I am just about awake,' she said. 'You can control me any way you want to.'

'Right, then,' Declan cocked his head, hoping that wasn't some kind of flirtation; although from Warren's expression it really didn't seem like it, as he turned his attention back to Bullman now. 'Also Guv, if you're okay with this, I would suggest that Detective Superintendent Warren and I speak to

Alexis, and Detective Inspector Kapoor and yourself speak to Mira.'

Bullman nodded curtly, and Declan wondered if she was still trying to take in the fact that Mira seemed to be Stephen Kline's secret daughter.

'Billy, keep doing what you do,' Declan smiled. 'There's something else we're not noticing, I'm sure of it.'

'And when the Guv comes in?'

'Tell him he can have my office for the day,' Declan grinned. 'He'll be over the moon.'

12

INTERVIEW ROOMS

MIRA NAKAHURA LEANT BACK ON THE CHAIR, HER ARMS FOLDED in front of her. She was wearing a tweed jacket over what looked to be a loose-fitting t-shirt, a pair of jeans, and a pair of Chelsea boots.

'I came in to answer questions,' she muttered, 'not to be treated like a suspect.'

'And yet here we are.' Bullman gave a tight, humourless smile as she sat down, turning on the recorder.

'The time is nine-fifteen am,' she said into it. 'Mira Nakahura in conversation with Detective Inspector Kapoor and Detective Chief Superintendent Bullman.'

At the name, Mira straightened.

'Are you *Sophie* Bullman?' she asked.

'You've heard of her?' Anjli was the one who replied, realising that there could be some kind of conflict here.

Mira nodded.

'You knew Stephen up in Manchester, didn't you?' she asked. 'Before he moved down?'

'I did,' Bullman replied.

'He was a friend of yours?'

'He was,' Bullman again replied, before placing her elbows on the table as she moved closer. 'But I'm not the one answering questions today, Miss Nakahura. You are.'

'Okay, sure, go ahead.'

'How long have you known Stephen Kline?'

'Just under two years,' Mira replied. 'It was the last Rejuvenation Royale Tournament. They do them every two years, you see. Several of the UK's contestants had used cryotherapy in their regimens. I was curious, I thought I'd look into it. Started going there as it was convenient for me, as I work in the Wharf.'

'Okay,' Bullman nodded, 'and that was the only reason you sought out Stephen Kline and Ionosphere?'

'What other reason would there be?'

Bullman clicked her tongue against the top of her mouth as she watched Mira for a long, uncomfortable moment.

'I'd like to ask you about the Energy Optimisation Summit,' she said. 'I understand there was an argument, and that you were involved in it.'

'I wasn't involved as such,' Mira replied calmly. 'There was a load of us in that, well, more of a kick off than anything else.'

'A load of us?'

'Most of the UK contestants. We were annoyed.'

'About?'

'Stephen wasn't a contestant in this year's competition,' Mira continued. 'That is, he hadn't entered. You can enter as a contestant any point up to the thirty-first of December this year. As long as the data's in the system by the cutoff, you're good to go.'

She shook her head at this. This was obviously something that had annoyed her in the past.

'You know, it takes the piss though,' she continued, conversationally. 'I mean, there we are, putting our data out for months on end, and if someone could just turn up on Christmas Day, decide, “hey, I'm gonna do this” with their shiny new Christmas present data capture kit, whack it into Cray's system—'

'Rupert Cray?'

'Yeah, the guy who created the event, and *wham bam boom,* suddenly they're third place, and whoever was behind them is now out of the contest.'

'I thought it was the top ten numbers, not just first, second, third?' Anjli asked.

'I was being rhetorical,' Mira corrected herself quickly. 'But if someone comes in and takes a position above you, that pushes you one down. If you were nineteenth globally, then now you're twentieth. What happens if someone else turns up the day after, pushing you out of the finals?'

She shook her head.

'There should be a cut-off point,' she said. 'Like, you know, at the start of the year. That way we all know what's going on. It's a level playing field.'

'Is it a level playing field, though?' Bullman asked. 'The impression we get is you all have your own secret recipes to help you.'

Mira smiled at that.

'You do what you can. The whole point of this is to show what works and what doesn't. And that's what we do. If I'm doing some regimen that gives me a 0.63, while, I don't know, Leon Brecht's AI is giving him a 0.67, then realistically, although we're doing well and we're going to live longer than most other people, I'm still doing better than him. My *regimen* is doing better than his.'

'And what is your regimen?' Anjli asked.

'Proprietary,' Mira replied coldly, looking back at her. 'If you want to know, you'd better get a court order.'

'I thought everything was open.'

'Our rankings are open,' Mira replied. 'That's the only thing you can talk about openly in the competition. You might be using illegal drugs, or technologies, non-FDA approved items. You might even have a fatal disease that's slowly eating away at your body. No one would know in the local rounds.'

Anjli sat up at that.

Mira Nakahura was subtly mentioning Aria Milton's disease.

'You haven't yet said why people were angry at Stephen Kline.'

'Because he said he was joining the competition. Gave his data in, wanted to see it all.' Mira muttered, shifting on the seat. 'Look, the leaderboard gives you the score, yeah? The zero-point-whatever. It doesn't give you all the markers though, all the individual epigenetic changes, metabolic efficiency, cognitive health, stuff like that. That's kept secret. But Stephen wanted to see it all. He wanted to see the markers.'

'Why?' Anjli frowned. 'What advantage would he get from that?'

'Most of us, we're checking our data monthly,' Mira explained. 'That way you can track what goes up, what goes down. This shows us what we need to do to go higher up the board. We don't get to see what the next person's doing, regimen wise, and we don't get to see whether they've gone up or gone down in their individual areas; the only way we know is when we see that final, composite number. If you've gone from 0.64 to 0.66, you know something's changed. It could be you had fast food for a couple of days, or maybe you've been travelling internationally, and you've got a bit of jet lag. It doesn't matter. We don't see that. Only Rupert Cray and his team do.'

'But Stephen Kline wanted it?' Anjli asked.

'Yes. And from what we could work out, Rupert Cray gave it to him.'

'Why would he do that?'

Mira chuckled.

'You tell me,' she said. 'Knowing Stephen, it was probably some kind of con artist scam.'

'You thought Stephen was a con artist?'

'He was definitely more "carny folk" than most people realised,' Mira replied coldly. 'But anyway, it didn't matter because after we started complaining, and after he got a look at our data, he decided he wasn't going to enter after all – probably realised we were all way above him. It turned into a storm in a teacup. I think we all felt betrayed.'

'And why would you feel betrayed?'

'Because he'd helped us all. We'd all used Ionosphere at some point. Christ, people like Eli had once been in business with him. Aria Milton had some of her products there as well. He was supposed to be our friend, our ally. And instead, all he did was take us for a ride.'

'And you don't think there was any other reason Stephen Kline might have not wanted to be in the competition?'

Mira didn't answer. And from her expression, Anjli knew that she'd *just realised* what the next question was going to be.

'How long have you known that Stephen Kline was your father?' Bullman asked.

There was no denial. Mira leant back and sighed.

'All my life,' she replied. 'And if your next question is, how long did Stephen Kline know he was my dad? I can answer that as well. Day two of the Summit, when he saw my DNA after Rupert Cray gave it to him ... and he realised the truth.'

ALEXIS KOVALENKO SAT NERVOUSLY AT THE TABLE, HER FOOT tapping rhythmically, her hands clenched together and forced into her lap as if to stop herself shaking. Declan and Warren came into the interview room, sitting down opposite her, Warren giving a small smile.

'Don't worry,' she murmured, 'we're just following up. I'm going to record it because my friend here is getting on a bit and has a worm eating his brain. It's a lot easier to have these things recorded so he doesn't confuse himself.'

Declan made a face at this but kept it humorous, knowing that the plan was to keep Alexis relaxed. With Warren done, he leant forward, turned on the recorder.

'Interview starts at nine twenty-five. Detective Superintendent Warren, Detective Chief Inspector Walsh, and Alexis Kovalenko in the room.'

He leant back, straightening as he stared at the woman in front of him.

'What do you study at Greenwich?' he asked.

If Alexis had expected that as the first question, she made a damn good impression of being surprised.

'My what?'

'What do you study at Greenwich? You're there doing a university degree, right?'

'Yes.' Alexis nodded. 'It's a Batchelor of Science, with honours, in Genomic Medicine and Artificial Intelligence.

Basically, we're exploring the role of genetics and epigenetics in ageing, while mastering AI technologies that analyse complex genetic data, optimise health protocols, and predict biological outcomes.'

'I see,' Declan nodded. 'Thank you. And why didn't you catch the underground or DLR when you finished your session the day before yesterday?'

Even though it'd been positioned to throw her off balance again, as he spoke it Declan felt this was more a question she was expecting, and her expression didn't change as she shrugged.

'I wanted to get my steps in,' she explained.

'Your steps?'

Alexis nodded calmly, settling back into her chair, and Declan felt it was almost as if she was comfortable in the conversation. The question about the university had thrown her; that wasn't something that she'd been waiting for, but this seemed to be one that she'd prepared for.

'I spend a lot of time at Ionosphere behind a counter,' she explained. 'My only walking is really when I take a customer to the cryotherapy chamber, or come and let them out. My step count is low. At the moment I'm supposed to be getting about ten to fifteen thousand steps. Currently, I'm not really hitting them.'

She relaxed her arms now, running a hand through her hair as she continued.

'If you walk a mile, it's about two thousand steps. So, realistically, if I'm walking seven miles a day, I'm doing the amount I needed. Walking down to Deptford from Canary Wharf is two and a half miles. That's another five thousand steps.'

'And you did the same yesterday morning as well, I guess?'

Alexis nodded.

'For the record, Miss Kovalenko has just nodded,' Declan noted.

'Sorry,' Alexis replied. 'Yes. I did that yesterday morning.'

'Thank you. Is this a common thing or a recent change?'

'It's more of a recent thing,' Alexis admitted. 'Only been doing it a few days now.'

'Convenient,' Declan remarked.

'We'd like to ask you about your last client,' Warren now added. 'It was Aria Milton, I believe.'

'Yes,' Alexis nodded. 'She was the last person, maybe seven-thirty appointment, I think.'

'And after that, you were closing up?'

'No.' Alexis shook her head at this. 'I mean, yes and no.'

'Could you elaborate?'

'I mean, yes, I was finishing up for the day, but Stephen had said there was one more booking, one that hadn't gone through the computer system, so I didn't know who it was.'

'Do you get these a lot?' Declan asked. 'Off the system bookings?'

'No, not really,' Alexis shook her head. 'To be honest, I assumed he was just trying to butter up a financier. We get a few of them turning up. You know, it's Canary Wharf. If you're not working in finance, you're working in law.'

Declan knew little about Canary Wharf, so simply nodded.

'Okay,' he said. 'And why would Stephen be looking to "butter up" financiers?'

At this, Alexis chuckled.

'Because he's always desperate for money,' she replied. 'The guy's broke, has been ever since I started work there.'

She leant forward.

'Can I be candid?'

'Sure,' Declan waved. 'Go wild.'

'Stephen was a nice guy, but he was lousy with money,' Alexis explained. 'He was constantly getting new investors into his company, getting them to give him seed money which he would then use to pay off the *old* investors, who by then were demanding where *their* money was. He was constantly robbing Peter to pay Paul.'

'If he was such a lousy entrepreneur, why did you work for him?'

At this, Alexis looked at him as if he was mad.

'Okay, sure, I was working for, you know, basic wage,' she said. 'But he never screwed up my wages. And besides, where else would I be able to get the amount of treatments that Ionosphere offered for free? It was one of the perks of the job. I could have as many cryotherapy sessions or hyperbaric chamber sessions, even red light therapy sessions, as I wanted. Hundreds of pounds of treatments a week, all given to me as part of the deal.'

Declan wrote this down. It indeed sounded like a perk, especially for somebody who was involved in the industry, so to speak.

'Do you know if Stephen met with this unknown person?'

Alexis shook her head.

'I left shortly after Aria Milton went,' she explained. 'There was a booking for first thing in the morning, which I should have been there for, but I was told by Stephen not to bother. Eli Green had the first session of the day, but he'd already dropped Stephen an email saying that he was in

Thailand, landing the following afternoon and wouldn't be there till later. I think they had moved his appointment to mid-afternoon.'

'I thought Eli and Stephen weren't talking?'

'They weren't, but he still used the chamber. The email had been sent to the main "info" email. Stephen had been the one who picked it up, nothing more.'

'What about Joseph Lawrence?' Declan asked. 'How did he find himself there?'

'He ate a doughnut,' Alexis chuckled. 'Decided he'd had too much sugar or carbs or something like that. He was a wannabe; not one of the RRT experts, just somebody who really wanted to push his longevity. He would use all the anti-ageing equipment next door in the gym, and when they couldn't help him, he'd come to us and use whatever we could do here. Apparently, he'd woken up feeling bad and decided he wanted a last-minute cryo session. When somebody cancels, the app shows it. So, when Eli Green had his appointment moved, Joseph Lawrence could book it.'

Declan nodded.

'Does this happen much?'

'Oh God, no,' Alexis shook her head. 'This was a unicorn, you know? Nine times out of ten, it takes a good couple of hours for the system to update. You'd have to be looking at like six in the morning to see the booking come up. I guess that's what Joseph was doing; I didn't know until I arrived and found him standing there.'

Declan nodded at this.

'You're telling me that when you arrived, you weren't expecting to find Joseph Lawrence there or Stephen Kline still in the office?'

Alexis shook her head.

'No,' she replied. 'But I wasn't surprised that he was working late.'

'Because of the financiers?'

'Because he was always working late,' Alexis smiled. 'If it wasn't financiers, it was the contestants.'

'You mean the services he was offering them?' Declan asked. 'I know Aria Milton and Eli Green utilised his services, as did Mira Nakahura, but are you saying the others did as well?'

'Oh, everybody did,' Alexis smiled now, warming to the task of whistleblowing. 'It was the only way they could have their meetings.'

'Their meetings?'

'Sure,' Alexis smiled, settling down in her chair. 'The ones where they worked out how to take everything from Rupert Cray.'

13

TEAM UPS

ALEXIS MUST HAVE KNOWN THAT THIS WAS A BOMBSHELL statement because, as she spoke, her eyes glittered with malice and glee as she leant forward, as if about to "spill the tea", as the cool kids liked to say, about her employer – or rather *ex*-employer.

'You see, the problem with those anti-ageing pricks,' she muttered, all pretence at concern now gone, 'is they don't look at the *menials*, they don't consider that we might know what's going on, or have a clue what's happening. But I saw everything. Stephen paid me my money and allowed me to have my playtime in the toy boxes. But whenever they turned up to chat, I wasn't supposed to see them.'

'So, how *did* you see them?'

'I'm not an idiot,' Alexis replied. 'I saw the security footage. I had it connected to my phone in case I was in the toilet when somebody came in through the main door. Sometimes you have to answer the call of nature, and if you're alone on the shift, you have to find ways of still being able to see what's going on, yeah? There were several times when the footage would disappear the following morning, so I started noting down when they were having them, and started watching live.'

She grinned.

'There's a Starbucks in one of the malls. I'd go sit in there and watch it on my phone. I couldn't hear what was going on, as there's no audio, but I'd see who turned up. And I worked out what was happening, from chatting to Eli and to Aria when she came for her sessions. They thought *I* was part of it as well, by the simple fact that I worked there.'

'Okay, you're going to need to explain to us what "it" is,' Declan said, 'because currently all you're saying is they had a secret talk and you knew something about it.'

Alexis's smile dropped as she was chastened, and she nodded.

'Of course, sorry,' she said, the excitement of giving gossip now suddenly removed by the harsh reality of what she was about to say. 'You understand how the tournament works, right?'

'Yeah. Some mental billionaire wants to give money to people who can live forever,' Warren replied irritably.

'Yes, but there's more to it,' Alexis explained. 'You see, there's a global competition that happens around the world. There are group stages in Europe, one in London, America which includes New York, Chicago, Austin and the west coast Silicon Valley area, there are also ones in Asia, India, Africa ... you name a continent, there's a global group stage, if not two in the area.'

'We know the basics,' Declan said, mainly to speed things along. 'We know, for example, that of these global areas, they all link to a group leaderboard.'

'Yes, exactly,' Alexis nodded with an expression of relief,

probably that she didn't have to explain everything in great detail. 'So everything's based on one score. Your percentage. Are you ageing at 0.6 or at 0.7? The ones who have a lower number do better.'

Declan nodded; Billy had explained this the previous day.

'And the top twenty overall go through,' he said. 'From all the tournaments.'

Alexis pointed a "finger gun" at Declan like a Las Vegas singer.

'Exactly. From everywhere. And, the finalists get to fight it out in Las Vegas, where at that point things become more exposed.'

'How so?'

'For the first round, the group stages? All you have to do is prove that you have a slower age rate. Once you get to Vegas, you get to really push what you use. If you're buying your way in, using other people's technology and skills, then *those* people will benefit from this, because it shows that they know how to make you live longer. If you're a tech industrialist, and you're using your own software, *you* become the brand.'

Declan nodded. It was very similar to what Leon Brecht and Aria Milton had both said in their interviews the previous day.

'But how does this all come into secret meetings? Surely they don't want to be helping each other, they actively want to be above each other on the leaderboard.'

'The enemy of my enemy is my ally,' Alexis shrugged. 'It was David Lester who started it. Have you spoken to him yet?'

'He's on the list,' Declan replied. 'Did you know why he worked with Stephen?'

'Because he wanted his help,' Alexis grinned widely again, back to giving the gossip that she so desperately obviously wanted to give. 'You see, Lester, he was kicked out of the West Coast group. I don't know why but it pissed him off, almost had him booted out of the whole competition. But he convinced the bigwigs who run the thing that he should be able to enter the London tournament. He had an office here or something, I don't know the full story. But the people who had kicked him out weren't just the people who ran the West Coast competition, it was the competitors themselves. He wasn't liked.'

'Okay,' Declan said, allowing Alexis to continue. 'He's hated. So what?'

'So, David watched the UK leaderboard,' Alexis said. 'Start of this year, maybe a bit later, the top five was pretty much settled. David was in it, as was Milton, Brecht, a couple of others who dropped out since. But in the top ten, you could see that people were varying.'

'Varying?' Warren noted.

'Wildly varying numbers,' Alexis clarified. 'Someone was on 0.67, someone was on 0.79. There was quite a wide scope in the top ten. And Lester didn't want that.'

'Why would Lester care?' Warren asked.

But Declan was starting to understand.

'David Lester wanted London, *all* of London, to get into the top twenty, didn't he?' he asked. 'It wasn't about him getting into the finals. It was about removing his old competitors, the ones that tried to remove him, *from* them.'

Alexis nodded.

'After I worked out what was going on, I looked into the figures,' she explained. 'You can check up all the tournaments, see who's winning in each zone. The highest ranking person on the West Coast grouping was 0.71. Lower than usual. There was one that was on 0.68, but they dropped down to 0.73 in the last month. When the London contestants started having their meetings, two were under that. Currently, at least five, maybe six of the London candidates are under that.'

'Do you know what they said during these meetings?' Declan asked.

Alexis shook her head.

'You'd have to ask one of them,' she explained. 'All I know is that David Lester started having these meetings, and suddenly all of them started doing better.'

'They pooled their information,' Warren muttered. 'Surely that's cheating.'

'How can you cheat when there are no rules?'

'Any of the people who were in these meetings would have known what was going on, yes?'

Alexis nodded.

'Good,' Declan said, typing on his phone. 'Hold on a moment.'

ANJLI WAS ABOUT TO ASK ANOTHER QUESTION TO MIRA, WHEN her phone beeped; pulling it out, she read the message from Declan.

'For the record, DI Kapoor has received a text message,' Bullman said as Anjli stared down at the screen, nodded to herself and then passed the phone across to Bullman, who also read the message, before pursing her lips and staring coldly at Mira Nakahura.

'Right,' she said. 'We've already had to get one secret out of you, that Stephen Kline was your father. How about you explain to us about your secret meetings with your other contestants in order to remove the West Coast candidates from the top twenty?'

Mira's mouth opened and shut twice in quick succession, almost as if her brain was commanding her to *say something,* but her mouth simply couldn't work out what to continue with.

'I don't ... don't—'

Anjli slammed her hand down on the table, the sharp retort making Mira jerk back, her eyes wide.

'Two men are dead in as many days. One of them was your father. So how about we cut the shit and you tell us what's going on?'

Calming, Mira let her head loll back, looking up at the ceiling for a long minute.

'For the record, Miss Nakahura is refusing to answer the question,' Anjli said.

'No, no, I'm not,' Mira retorted, shaking her head. 'It's just ... I'm not sure how to explain it.'

'How about you just tell us?' Bullman replied.

Mira nodded.

'It was David Lester's plan,' she explained. 'He was pissed off, butt hurt over the Americans telling him to piss off, yeah? And there was a couple of people on the list over there that had done really well in the previous tournament, made it all the way to Vegas, but David had come third in Vegas two years ago and they were annoyed at him, saw him as a threat. So, they started making up stories, saying how he was a groper, a creep, you know, hashtag-MeToo, all that stuff.'

'And is he?' Bullman asked coldly.

'No, he's misunderstood,' Mira replied a little too quickly, flushing as she spoke. 'He's a good man. They hated him.

They decided to destroy his reputation. He had to leave, come to London to carry on.'

'Okay, let me get this right,' Anjli checked the text message one more time. 'He decided that all the London people should get together and stick it to his old competitors.'

'Well, when you make it sound like that, it doesn't sound good, but it was good competition,' Mira said. 'The needs of the many outweigh the needs of the one and all of that. He thought that if we could all pool our resources, we could find the ultimate anti-ageing premise. We could get ourselves down underneath the Americans, underneath the Indians, underneath even the Japanese. And trust me, *those* guys were really going for it. It wasn't just that the winner of the London group would win two million dollars. The top twenty *global* all win two million dollars. We could all win here. So he started having meetings.'

'At Ionosphere?'

Mira nodded.

'First off, it was at Eli's insistence we had them at Ionosphere. Eli was working with Stephen and they'd just dissolved their partnership; it was a year back, at the time they were still amicable. Stephen was fine with it, and allowed us to use one of the hyperbaric rooms. There was enough space for us to sit around and talk, and if anybody asked, well, we were having treatments, or Aria was selling us one, as she made them. We would pull resources, we'd explain what we found worked and what didn't, what supplements seemed to be doing good ... sure, for the first couple of months we varied all over the place. At one point I was second in the list, then I was down to eight. But we stabilised. And for the last couple of months, we've been, if you don't mind me saying it, kicking the arses of the Americans.'

'So, this is all revenge,' Bullman said.

'For David, maybe, but for us it was a chance to get in there. You've got to realise it's not just about the money.'

'Oh, we're aware of that,' Anjli said. 'We know that just getting to Vegas helps you build your brand. What I can't work out is what do you get out of this?'

'How do you mean?'

'You're an investment banker, Miss Nakahura. You don't have any company that makes money from people's wellness. If anything, you winning only makes you the money that you make from the winnings, nothing more.'

Mira gave a smile, but it was a bitter, harsh one.

'I was there to prove to my father that I could do it,' she said. 'That was it. I'd heard rumours he was thinking about doing it this year, so I decided to enter. I'd been following him for years, and I thought I could get into it, make a name. At the start, I was getting nowhere. But then David kind of took me under his wing, helped me out.'

She smiled at that point, and the harshness of the previous expression was replaced by warmth ... or maybe hope.

Oh my God, Anjli thought to herself, recognising the look, and leant forward.

'How long have you been sleeping with David Lester?'

'It's not like that,' Mira instantly argued, and in doing so gave away that it was very *much* like that.

'What would you call it, then?'

'Professional admiration,' Mira suggested. 'He saw in me somebody who could build his dream into reality. And yeah, working together, what do you expect? There was a chemistry, which turned into a sexual relationship.'

'We looked into David Lester when we first checked the

list,' Bullman said. 'Do you know why America wanted him out of their league?'

'Yeah, they didn't want him to win,' Mira replied. 'He was giving away secrets to people who weren't part of their elite cadre.'

'No,' Bullman replied. 'It's because he kept sleeping with teenage girls.'

'No ...'

'Still, it's good that he's found someone to settle down with,' Anjli was surprised at Bullman's tone but then remembered that Stephen had been a close friend. 'So why the fight? Two months ago?'

'I've already said,' Mira explained. 'He found out that I was his daughter and he was annoyed that I hadn't told him. The others had kind of adopted me at that point and ...'

She trailed off, as if realising the lie was no longer working.

'He was a friend of Rupert Cray,' she admitted, her voice quieter now. 'There was talk he might have been telling him what we were doing, and why we were doing it. He claimed he was on our side, and was allowing us to use his location, but you know ... smoke without fire ...'

She looked aside and Anjli couldn't work out whether she was actively saddened by what she was thinking about, or if she was trying to work out the best way to speak about this without looking bad.

'Look,' she eventually continued, 'my deadbeat father, as much as he was, had a fling with my mother twenty-five years ago. I don't think he even knew that she was pregnant. By the time she found out, he was off on his travels, hunting blue zones or something along those lines. By the time he returned to the UK, settling in Manchester, I was eleven, maybe twelve. I didn't know who he was. My mother had never explained it to me. And then he was on some TV show. One of those kind of, you know, "the future of technology" shows on BBC One.'

Her expression soured as she remembered the moment, reliving it in the interview room.

'And my mum sat up straight and started swearing at the screen. I didn't know why. She just pointed at him and said, "that's your father". From that point on, I was obsessed. When he found out that I was his daughter at the Summit, it was almost as if he felt betrayed that I hadn't sided with him earlier, when at the same time, I still felt that he had betrayed me.'

'But if he didn't know that you existed, how could he have betrayed you?'

'I didn't say it was a rational belief,' Mira snapped back. 'But while looking into him I learned about his debts. I learned how he'd almost gone bankrupt several times. How he'd screwed over various partners. There's a guy out there he owes two million to, who he just basically ran from. He's got creditors as long as my arm. I know he'd gone to David and asked for some money. A kind of "all friends together" loan if he was going to be helping David defeat the Americans. David felt it was more of a blackmail request and told him to go fu— well, you know, to get lost.'

She shrugged.

'Rupert Cray was at the Summit two months ago and he was seen talking to Stephen more than once. Quite friendly, close even. Now, sure, Ionosphere was a sponsor of the London stage of the competition, and maybe there was an element of innocence here but as I said a minute ago, no smoke without fire.'

Anjli nodded.

'When it all kicked off about you, I'm guessing it got a bit chaotic.'

'Yeah,' Mira nodded. 'He banned me from the cryotherapy centre until I pointed out that he couldn't legally do that. After that, he made sure that whenever I turned up he wasn't there. He didn't want to know me.'

'Who else knew about this?'

'About him being my father? Everybody who's part of the group.'

'And that would be ...' Bullman insisted.

'Selene, she thought it was hilarious, Eli, he was more angry than anything else, David of course. Leon wasn't that fussed, but he's a sodding robot and would have known ...'

Mira trailed off.

'That was about it, I think. Maybe Rupert,' she shook her head. 'But none of those would have ended this with his death. And none of those would have ended with Eli's death either.'

'How did you know that Eli was dead?' Bullman asked. 'We haven't said anything.'

'You didn't need to,' Mira replied. 'It's all over our WhatsApp. Selene told everybody last night.'

There was a moment of silence, as Anjli and Bullman glanced at each other.

'One more thing,' Bullman asked. 'Did Stephen know you were sleeping with David Lester?'

Mira nodded.

'He learnt when the fight kicked off,' she explained. 'Couldn't understand why David was leaping to my aid. When he found out – when they all found out – it went badly. Kept saying David was old enough to be my dad, while

I was saying when we were all in our hundreds it wouldn't matter.'

'If you manage to live that long, as currently your average is dropping daily. Interview paused, nine-thirty-seven am,' Bullman said, checking her watch and turning the recorder off. 'You're going to have to stay here a little while, if that's okay. We need to confirm a couple of things. Do you have an alibi for last night?'

'Yes, I do,' Mira smiled, relief crossing her face. 'I was at a biohacker meetup. So was David Lester. I'd gone to speak to him. It was at Walkers of Whitehall. It's a pub.'

'I know the pub,' Anjli nodded. 'You won't mind if we speak to them to confirm this?'

'Of course.'

Anjli looked at Bullman and, as if by unspoken agreement, the two of them walked to the door.

Mira just stared off at the wall, lost in thought.

As they walked outside the interview room, Anjli turned to Bullman.

'Okay,' she said. 'Let's talk hypotheticals here. Stephen Kline was about to out the group as working together to remove the American contingent. Maybe that was enough to have them take him out.'

She frowned.

'Although technically, I'd consider that with this whole "there are no rules until there are rules" point, they could have said there was nothing to say *against* teaming up.'

Bullman was staring off down the corridor as she listened.

'If they killed Stephen because he was telling on them, then they're all to blame, no matter who did it,' she muttered. 'But it does give us a solid motive. Somebody winning two million dollars is one thing. Three or four, even five people, each losing out on two million? That's a completely different story.'

'Also, of course, if Stephen finds out that he has a daughter, and David Lester's screwing her ... that could cause a fight or two.'

'Or, someone else is using that,' Bullman's eyes narrowed into slits as she considered this. 'But then the question becomes, why kill Eli Green? From the sounds of things, he was one of the people who suggested having the meeting there. He wasn't talking to Rupert Cray, from what we know. If anything, we know he'd had an argument with Kline months ago and withdrew his support. So, if this is anger at Kline tattling on them causing his death, then Green's death makes little sense.'

She stopped in the corridor, Anjli almost bumping into her with the suddenness of the pause.

'The only thing we know so far,' she said, 'is that if you want to live forever, you need to be very happy to kill everybody else. Let's see if Doctor Marcos has learned anything. Maybe that'll explain to us what's been going on.'

14

AUTOPSY FINDINGS

Monroe wasn't filled with his usual Scottish swagger and attitude as he stood at the front of the briefing room, staring at his unit.

It was late morning; Mira Nakahura had been allowed to leave because of lack of evidence, while Alexis Kovalenko had agreed to hang around, now working on her laptop in the canteen area while the unit worked out how much of a suspect she truly was. For the last hour, the detectives and officers of the Last Chance Saloon had been working through the statements, to see if there was anything that could be used.

'First off, I'd like to thank you all for your sterling achievements,' Monroe muttered, 'leaping headfirst into these interviews before I could attend.'

Declan gave a small smile at this. Monroe had turned up twenty minutes into the interviews, and had been rather annoyed that he wasn't able to join in. However, it had been pointed out to him he'd got to go to a murder scene without anybody else, and so they were still equal in the grand scheme of things.

The room was filled for the late morning. Doctor Marcos, De'Geer, and Cooper sat at the back. Warren sat in her now seemingly regular spot beside Billy, who was working on his laptop as ever, streaming the images across to the plasma screen behind Monroe. Bullman stood in the doorway to the side of Anjli, who was beside Declan.

On the screen was a picture of Stephen Kline, taken from the Ionosphere website.

'We've got a lot to go through. And possibly a short time to do it in,' Monroe said. 'First off, Doctor Marcos, I'm guessing you've got some new data on the bodies for us?'

Doctor Marcos nodded, rising and walking to the front of the briefing room. The last time Declan had seen her, she'd been downing copious amounts of coffee, trying to wake up. She'd then spent the next hour and a half going over the data of both murders once more, hunkered down in her office on the ground floor.

'I've got information on both Stephen Kline and Eli Green,' she started, checking her notes on the iPad in her hand. 'We've examined both bodies. Last night, well, earlier this morning, I went back and examined Stephen Kline's body again, going over the location once more.'

She looked over at Warren.

'I'd like to thank the Detective Superintendent for answering some questions as well,' she said. 'Her unit being the first on scene meant they were able to get some crime shots I hadn't seen beforehand.'

She turned to Billy and nodded. Billy pressed the button on his laptop, and the screen behind Monroe and Doctor

Marcos turned into a crime scene photo of the frozen Stephen Kline in the cryochamber.

Declan couldn't help it; his eyes flickered over to Bullman, but her expression was stony and cold, holding her emotions in while she watched.

'Yesterday we weren't sure whether Kline had somehow committed some weird kind of suicide or had been locked into the cryochamber without his consent,' Doctor Marcos started. 'His death was consistent with extreme hypothermia. We've already gone through that, and I'm not going to do it again.'

She also looked over at Bullman as she spoke, and Declan knew she was doing this to help out her friend.

'However, we've now been looking at the chamber itself.'

She nodded to Billy, and the image changed to showing a close-up of one of the two slatted locks that had been placed on the glass.

'We believed these locks had been secretly placed on the door, so that when Stephen Kline went into the cryochamber, it would lock behind him,' Doctor Marcos explained. 'We've now had a chance to properly look at them, and I can tell you that's not the case. These screw in to lock on the outside, so they had to have been placed on the door *after* Kline had entered, and he would have to have stood there and watched it happen.'

'Or he was unconscious,' Declan suggested.

'There were no drugs in his system, and there were no signs of bruising,' Doctor Marcos shook her head. 'If anything, it made us wonder whether the suicide option was true because, for all intents and purposes, it looks like Stephen Kline willingly walked into the cryotherapy chamber and stood there as they locked the door.'

There was a moment of silence in the room as everyone took in what Doctor Marcos had just explained. The thought of standing in minus ninety-two degrees, watching your killer lock you in ...

Declan shook his head.

'What about the cutoff switch?' he asked, looking around the room. 'Okay, the killer turns up, forces Stephen Kline in, locks the door as he enters... either way, I thought there was some kind of cutoff switch for the cryotherapy. It would turn off at night to save energy or something.'

'You're correct,' Doctor Marcos nodded. 'However, it looks like it was overridden remotely two nights ago.'

'Convenient,' Monroe nodded. 'Okay, we now know that the killer had to have been there with Kline. It couldn't have been set up in such a way that they could do it remotely – apart from changing the temperature settings, that is. Alexis Kovalenko and Aria Milton were both there at the end. We need to have a chat with them again.'

'Alexis Kovalenko is still upstairs, sir,' Declan said. 'We could have a chat.'

'Do so,' Monroe nodded. 'Although she's been quite open with everything that's going on, I'm not sure she's not playing us. What about Eli Green?'

'We've now had the autopsy into Eli Green,' Doctor Marcos replied, swiping the screen of her iPad, nodding to Billy. She was preparing for a lecture, and behind her, the image changed to the body of Eli Green, in his shorts, lying on the bench in his sauna.

'We know he was found in the sauna, but this wasn't simply a case of heatstroke – there's much more going on here,' she explained. 'First off, after running a couple of toxicology tests, we found Green was drugged with midazolam, a powerful sedative. It's commonly used in medical settings to induce deep sedation or even anaesthesia, especially before surgeries or invasive procedures.'

A nod, and now the chemical compound diagram of midazolam appeared on the screen.

'It's a benzodiazepine that acts on the central nervous system by enhancing the effect of GABA, a neurotransmitter that inhibits brain activity,' Doctor Marcos continued. 'In high doses, it essentially shuts down parts of the brain responsible for awareness, muscle control, and respiratory function. Mister Green wouldn't have been able to fight back, let alone realise he was in danger. His muscles would have relaxed, his breathing slowed, and within minutes, he'd have been completely unaware of his surroundings.'

'Where do you get midazolam? Anjli asked.

'Midazolam's classified as a Schedule-three controlled drug under the *Misuse of Drugs Regulations 2001,* meaning it's closely monitored,' De'Geer spoke from the back now, checking his own notes, likely gained from his own data – working with Doctor Marcos seemed to rub off on people. 'It's commonly used in hospitals for sedation before surgeries, or for patients in intensive care units. It's also used in palliative care for its sedative properties.'

'You'd typically find it in injectable form, and it's stored under strict controls in hospitals and care facilities,' Doctor Marcos took over again. 'For someone to get their hands on it outside of a clinical setting, they'd likely need access to healthcare resources – perhaps through a hospital, pharmacy, or someone in the medical field.'

'Looks like we need someone who knows a doctor,' Monroe muttered. 'Which is likely bloody all of them, considering the crap they dump down their throats.'

'But that's not all,' Doctor Marcos looked over at him. 'We also found traces of riluzole in his system. This works by inhibiting the release of glutamate, and in smaller doses, it helps reduce nerve overactivity. However, in Eli Green's case, combined with the midazolam, the riluzole would have further dampened his neuromuscular functions, compounding the effect of the sedative. This cocktail of drugs rendered him completely immobile and unable to react to external stimuli.'

'The stimuli being the sauna?' Declan asked.

Doctor Marcos nodded, her face tight.

'Normally, when someone enters a sauna, the body responds to the rising temperature by initiating thermoregulation; primarily sweating, increased heart rate, and faster breathing, to dissipate heat. But, in Mister Green's case, midazolam suppressed his body's natural ability to regulate heat. His respiration was slowed, and his nervous system was effectively offline. The riluzole would have further reduced his muscle control, including the muscles involved in breathing, making it impossible for him to hyperventilate or increase his oxygen intake. In effect, his body couldn't adapt to the rising heat.'

Another nod, and Billy showed a crudely designed image, likely drawn by Doctor Marcos on her iPad, of a body overheating. Declan wasn't sure, but it was almost as if this had been primed because Doctor Marcos knew he'd be asking the question.

'When the body is unable to cool itself, core temperature rises dangerously,' Doctor Marcos walked over to the plasma screen now, pointing at the figure shown. 'In Mister Green's case, trapped in a hot sauna, his external body temperature likely spiked past forty degrees centigrade, or a hundred and four Fahrenheit – the point at which cellular damage occurs. His cells would have started to break down because of hyperthermia, and his organs, particularly the brain and heart, would have failed. His heart would have been under immense strain, unable to compensate for the rising body temperature, ultimately leading to cardiac arrest.'

She grimaced.

'Essentially, his body "boiled" from the inside out,' she added, allowing that thought to be taken in by the team.

'One important thing Doctor Marcos noticed during the autopsy, is that Eli Green wasn't sweating when he died,' De'Geer continued on Doctor Marcos's behalf. 'Even in extreme heat, a conscious person would have shown signs of hyperhidrosis, which is profuse sweating as the body attempts to cool itself down. The absence of sweat indicates that the drugs had fully incapacitated him before the heat had a chance to trigger those normal physiological responses. He didn't even feel the heat coming on; his system was too sedated to react.'

'Therefore, what we're looking at is a carefully orchestrated death,' Doctor Marcos continued. 'Someone knew exactly how these drugs would interact with his body and the environment. The midazolam and riluzole created the perfect storm, and his body was effectively paralysed while the heat took its toll. Left in that sauna, it was only a matter of time before his organs gave out.'

'Do we know how the toxins entered the body?'

'The smoothie he was drinking had traces,' De'Geer spoke up again. 'We believe he drank it as some kind of anti-jetlag cleanser, and was finishing it when he went into the sauna. However, he lost consciousness, and the cup spilt the remnants to the floor.'

Declan frowned at this.

'Surely, though, the sauna would have had some kind of failsafe?' he asked. 'To stop it staying on for so long?'

'They do,' De'Geer replied. 'And this one should have too, as apparently it was set for a thirty-minute session.'

'But it continued on past that?' Monroe furrowed his brow at this. 'So, a cutoff switch has yet again been removed. That seems mighty suspicious.'

There was a moment of quiet in the briefing room, and Monroe took the moment to look at Anjli.

'Okay then, moving on. Who could have done this?'

'Well, straight away I can tell you that Mira Nakahura, David Lester, and Alexis Kovalenko all have alibis for yesterday afternoon and last night,' Anjli replied, looking up from her notebook. 'Alexis was at University, and then at a birthday party for a fellow student. We've already spoken to the person who was running it, and they've confirmed that Alexis was there. We even have video and photos of when a birthday cake was brought out on social media; Alexis is seen in the background, and even has a slice of the same cake in her laptop bag, probably for later.'

'What flavour?' Billy asked, instantly regretting it. 'Sorry, carry on.'

'As for Mira Nakahura and David Lester, there was a biohacking meet-up last night in London, in Whitehall,' Anjli gave Billy a glare before continuing. 'We've already spoken to a couple of people who went, and the pub itself. All of them have confirmed that David Lester was there all night and that at one point of the evening, Mira Nakahura was definitely there.'

'One point of the evening?' Warren asked, looking across.

'Yes, Guv,' Anjli replied. 'It seems she did turn up, but it was late as the event was ending. There's a chance she could have somehow got from Hampstead to Whitehall at that time of night, but even by courier or cycle ...'

'It's unlikely,' Declan nodded.

'One other thing, it looks like Joseph Lawrence, the man who found Stephen Kline was there, but we think it's coincidence,' Anjli continued. 'London biohackers at a meeting isn't that surprising. He didn't speak to Mira, and the only time he spoke to Lester was, well, a telling off.'

'Telling off?'

'Apparently, David Lester didn't take kindly to Joseph Lawrence talking about finding Kline's body,' Anjli replied. 'Took him aside and had a chat. No idea what he said, but Lawrence grabbed his jacket and ran.'

'I'm starting to like this guy,' Declan nodded. 'What about the afternoon?'

'We have Mira confirmed to be on a Microsoft Teams meeting,' Billy read from a document. 'This went from mid to late afternoon.'

There was another pause, and Declan held a hand up.

'Oh for God's sake—' Monroe started, and Declan gave a sheepish grin as he stood, turning back to Doctor Marcos.

'Sorry,' he asked. 'You mentioned what midazolam is used for, but we skipped past riluzole?'

'Oh, yes, that's the super-fun part,' Doctor Marcos replied, looking across the room at him. 'It's a more specialised drug, prescribed primarily to patients with amyotrophic lateral sclerosis.'

'Wait, ALS?' Anjli sat up. 'As in what Aria Milton has?'

'As in its not something you'd find in a general pharmacy,' Doctor Marcos nodded. 'In the UK, it's usually dispensed through neurology clinics or specialist pharmacies that deal with rare and chronic conditions. Given how specific its use is, someone with access to ALS treatment programs or neurology wards might have obtained it.'

'I think we need to chat with Miss Milton again,' Monroe growled. 'Especially with her love for smoothies.'

'Or someone's using this to aim us at her,' Doctor Marcos added. 'They would have known we'd find it. Unlike midazolam, it's not a controlled drug, but it's still only available on prescription, and wouldn't be something people were likely to come across, unless they were directly involved in treating ALS patients. It's quite a specific clue.'

'Did he have any other visitors apart from Selene Carter?' Warren asked. 'Someone who could have done this?'

De'Geer now held a hand up.

'Laddie, you don't have to put your hand up every time you have an answer,' Monroe laughed. 'I've only just weaned that out of wee Billy, here. And if you're trying to follow in Walsh's footprints as an excellent role model, you're shite out of luck there.'

'We spoke to the housekeeper,' De'Geer said, ignoring the jibe and nodding to Cooper, who now joined him, standing up and reading from her notes.

'Marjorie Halliwell,' she read. 'She'd worked for Eli Green since he arrived in London about four years earlier, lives in the house on the ground floor. She's staying with her sister at the moment for obvious reasons. She said his son came by to drop a book off after his dad arrived back from Thailand, but left just before she went out to get some supplies at about two o'clock. She was out for about ninety minutes, returned at three-thirty. Eli Green already left a message by then basically saying, "Do not disturb me, I'm in the sauna." She'd called up at dinnertime, but again, when she texted him, he texted back, saying he'd be down later.'

'Why couldn't she just go and knock on his door?' Declan asked. 'If they're living in the same house—'

'It's a large house,' Monroe interjected. 'And when we looked at it, it seemed a bit "upstairs-downstairs." You know, "neither the two shall meet" and all that.'

He sighed.

'She probably only contacted him through WhatsApp or text. But that means anybody could have replied in his absence.'

'True, sir,' Cooper replied. 'But they would have had to have had access to his phone. And from what we can work out, his phone was in his study the entire time.'

'Okay, check into that,' Monroe said. 'So, there's a period of time when Marjorie wasn't in the house when he could have met with somebody.'

'But again, the ring doorbell only shows one person turning up,' Billy now replied. 'A cycle courier. They drop something off and then leave.'

'Can we see what that was?'

'It was a package, about A4 sized, quite thin. The video footage didn't show much else. The courier had a logo on his vest, so we've called them, hopefully they can give us a better idea of what it is.'

'Hopefully it's not just a bloody Amazon parcel,' Monroe muttered.

'She did mention one other thing,' De'Geer took over now. 'She said that when Selene Carter turned up and they found the body, she wanted to tell the police immediately, but Carter forced her not to, told her to hold off until she could grab something from the study.'

'Oh aye?' Monroe asked.

'She didn't see what it was. Selene was in the study for ten minutes, then came out making the call.'

'So, Selene Carter had something in the office she wanted to remove, before the police turned up,' Monroe nodded. 'That is what I call suspicious activity.'

He drummed his fingers on the table for a long moment.

'Okay,' he said. 'We know the group were looking to rig the tournament, but we need to see why Eli Green would have been killed if that was the reason for Kline's death. Also, we need—'

'Actually Guv, I have something on that, too,' Billy said, tapping on his keyboard, and a leaderboard appeared on the plasma screen. 'The US figures updated this week, and you can see here that at least five of the West Coast tournament have lower percentages than the London people.'

'Which means for all their secret teaming up, they're not succeeding in their plans,' Monroe nodded. 'Good pick up. Okay. We need to go back to the canteen and speak to Alexis again about the night Kline died, speak to Selene Carter about whatever she took from the study, and have a chat with Aria Milton over whether she's missing any drugs recently. Anjli, have a chat with David Lester, if you can find him. Anything else?'

'Actually, yes,' Bullman spoke from the door now. 'So, as you all know, I knew Stephen when he was in Manchester. And everything said so far is true, he was a chancer who was always hunting the next big payout. But I spoke to a couple of friends on the Manchester beat who were around when he was, and they reminded me of something. It might be relevant, it might not be, but six years ago, when he was still up there, he borrowed a lot of money from a gangster named

Connor O'Rourke. Apparently, he never paid it back, always covering the interest, but never the full amount.'

'Which was?' Declan asked, already knowing the answer.

'One and a half million,' Bullman replied.

'Which, with exchange rates, is almost the same as the first round winner's pouch,' Declan whistled as he leant his head back. 'Okay, so do they know anyone up there we can speak to about this?'

'Actually we have a source way closer than Manchester,' Bullman gave an evil smile now. 'A Manchester DI who worked on the O'Rourkes all the time Kline was there, who knows exactly what happened.'

Declan groaned the moment he heard the words "Manchester DI". There was only one person he knew who fitted that, who'd been a Manchester detective since 2011, leaving the force two years earlier ...

'Bloody hell,' he muttered. 'I'm going to have to chat with Tessa Martinez again, aren't I?'

15

OLD FLAMES

When Declan had last seen Tessa Martinez, she hadn't been happy to be there at the time; a tell-all book about him was about to be released, a ploy by a disgraced government official to try to force the Prime Minister's hand, using Declan as a bargaining chip. Luckily, Declan had managed to head this off at the pass, but it still left an unpleasant taste in his mouth that the last time he saw Tessa, she had acted so standoffish with him.

She worked for Sean Ashby, the editor of *The Individual* newspaper as a private investigator, a job that had been offered to Declan when he thought he was losing his police position. Tessa herself had lost her own police position a couple of years earlier when, because of PTSD and pain medication, she'd found herself played by one of her childhood friends, and the truth about her position in a group of teenage sleuths called *The Magpies* was released.

She'd been involved, through this connection, in a variety of severe crimes, and had spent eighteen months in prison before being released due to mitigating circumstances, a knee injury taken in an explosion years earlier, that left her constantly in a fugue state and addicted to pain medication. There was more to the release of course, primarily the fact that *The Magpies* had been connected to a government scheme that still had people in high places who didn't want the whole story mentioned.

But, once out, and cleaned up, she'd needed a new purpose.

Declan hadn't realised, however, that the purpose seemed to be at odds with helping him.

There was also, of course, that Declan had feelings for Tessa. She had been a teenage crush, a poster on his wall from when she was in *The Magpies*. He'd even joined the force, in a roundabout way, because of his teenage love for the books. And when they'd worked together, there was definitely chemistry, both professionally and physically.

However, in the time that Tessa had been in prison, Declan had started his relationship with Anjli, something he wouldn't have changed for anything. But there was still a thought in the back of his mind, that *what-if* feeling. If Tessa Martinez *hadn't* been arrested, if she hadn't been guilty, what would have been the road travelled there? Would she have stayed a police officer up in Manchester? Would he have moved to her, or would she have moved to him?

Or would nothing have happened and he would have ended up with Anjli anyway – destiny and all that claptrap ...?

As it was, Tessa Martinez had been quite happy to meet him for an early lunch.

They had met at a *Pret A Manger* near Cannon Street station. It was close to both of them, with *The Individual's* offices being in the city. Declan was jumpy, slightly nervous even, as he waited for her to arrive, sipping at a sparkling water bottle and picking at the croissant he'd picked up. Eventually she did arrive, and Declan took a breath as he saw her.

She was beautiful, but then she always had been. It was a different beauty to Anjli, who was equally as stunning, And although he wasn't there to consider Tessa as an option romantically, his breath still caught in his throat.

She was slim and toned, Mediterranean in looks with curly black hair over brown eyes, a charcoal suit and a pastel pink shirt underneath it. She wore glasses – *this was new* – and she smiled as she approached, sitting down next to him.

'Before we start, I need to apologise,' she murmured.

'No apology needed,' Declan replied, knowing where she was going with this. 'I was in a bad spot, and a ton of shit was about to rain down on me. Understandably, you couldn't be seen in public with me.'

He smiled.

'As it is, you provided me with that book in advance. And that saved my career, so I can't really complain.'

This brought a smile to Tessa's lips. And again, Declan felt his heartbeat race a little faster.

'So, what can I do for you?' she asked, leaning back in the chair.

'No small talk?' Declan raised an eyebrow.

'Sure, okay. You still with Anjli?'

'I'm still with Anjli.'

'Then I'm done with the small talk,' Tessa gave a little smile as she winked at him.

Declan placed his hands on the table, deciding it was best if he went fully professional at this point.

'I need to speak to you about Manchester,' he said. 'Connor O'Rourke.'

At the name, Declan saw a visible transformation in Tessa's posture and attitude.

'O'Rourke,' she muttered. 'I haven't heard that name for a while.'

'When was the last time you heard it?'

'Four years ago, I think,' Tessa replied. 'He took his business out of Manchester, decided he'd rather live in Spain.'

'Really?'

Tessa smiled.

'He was finding it a little too argumentative there.'

'Rival gangs?'

'More like hassle from the police on a regular basis,' Tessa smiled. 'I'd made it my job to take him down.'

She looked around the sandwich and coffee shop, likely considering her next words carefully, considering the topic of conversation.

'What do you need from me?' she asked. 'I mean your boss's boss was at Manchester too. I didn't deal with Bullman, didn't really know of her at the time, but she would've had her own run-ins, and therefore information on O'Rourke.'

'She said you were a better choice to speak to,' Declan muttered. 'Also, it's connected to somebody she knew.'

At this, Tessa leant closer, her interest piqued.

'Really? Someone I might know?'

'Did you ever meet a man named Stephen Kline?' Declan asked.

Tessa considered this.

'Yeah, I met Kline,' she said. 'Several times, in fact. I'm guessing you knew that?'

The comment seemed strange, and Declan frowned. As he did so, Tessa's eyes widened.

'Oh God,' she exclaimed, 'you *didn't* know. What is this, a test?'

'No,' Declan replied. 'Two nights ago, Stephen Kline was murdered. It's part of a case, and we've already had two bodies, so we're checking every avenue right now.'

'Who's the second body?'

'A man named Eli Green.'

'Oh,' Tessa said simply. 'No wonder you're here, then. Yes, I spoke to Stephen Kline a few times. I kinda had to.'

'Oh? Why?'

'Well ... you see, ten years ago, he was one of our confidential informants,' Tessa smiled.

There was a long moment of silence as Declan stared across the table at Tessa.

'I'll be honest, I didn't expect that one coming,' he eventually muttered.

Tessa, however, simply shrugged.

'He owed O'Rourke money,' she explained. 'Large amounts. I think he thought that if he could get him put away, he wouldn't have to pay him.'

'That's a little naïve,' Declan replied.

Tessa gave a *what-can-I-do* kind of shrug.

'Are you buying me lunch or what?' she asked.

'Pick what you want. It's on me.'

'Wow, last of the big spenders.' Tessa rose from the chair and walked across, picking up a sandwich and a bottle of still water, paying for it at the counter. Sitting back down, she crossed her arms while waiting for Declan to continue the conversation.

'Did O'Rourke know he was informing?'

'Not that I know of,' Tessa shook her head. 'I think it's one reason why Stephen moved down to London. O'Rourke was wondering who was grassing on him. Too many things he'd been involved in were falling apart. No one's that unlucky. By that point, however, I wasn't paying as much attention as I should've.'

Declan knew what she meant. Near the end of her tenure, she'd been more addicted to pain pills than anything else, keeping them in an Altoids box, pretending that they were breath mints. He pursed his lips together, considering what she'd told him.

'Do you think O'Rourke could have killed him?'

'I wouldn't have,' Tessa smiled. 'Until you mentioned the second body.'

'Eli Green? What about him?'

'He was part of the crowd in Manchester too,' Tessa explained. 'He was in with Kline, a major investor in his "dream". Maybe a million and a half, two million tops. A smidge more than O'Rourke was in with. But the thing with Eli was, that he was getting profits from the business. He was a partner rather than a financier. He also had his own line of equipment rented in there and God knows what else that he was working on.'

'Was he making money from that?'

'Renting out the pieces and taking the money as effectively side-hustle money? He was probably making more money than Kline was,' Tessa shrugged, starting on the sandwich. 'But if O'Rourke is behind this, he would have known that Green and Kline were thick as thieves.'

'Not at the end they weren't,' Declan added.

Tessa paused mid-chew.

'What do you mean?' she asked through a half-full mouth. 'The two of them were inseparable.'

'Something happened,' Declan replied. 'A year ago, right after they arrived in London, Green pulled his funding, sold his shares ... then only a couple of months back, he took his items from the spa.'

'Well, well, well,' Tessa said, wiping at her mouth with a napkin. 'For Eli Green to walk away from money ... there's something definitely going wrong there.'

She shook her head.

'I only met Green once, maybe twice total. Obviously, Kline wasn't happy for people to know he was talking to us. When I did, it was at an event, a party. I had to go to see Kline to grab some information from him, and Green was there.'

She thought back to the day, staring off, her eyes unfocused.

'There was another guy there. Yank, stupid ponytail, that's all I remember. Couldn't tell you what he was talking about, but the three of them seemed deep in conversation. Then, a couple of months later, bang, woosh, Kline's off to London. Suddenly been given money, suddenly got an opportunity to hit the big time.'

She picked up the sandwich, about to continue.

'Or, he realised he had to get out of town before he was murdered, brutally, by a gangster he owed money to.'

'Do you know if O'Rourke had connections in London?'

At the question, Tessa laughed.

'O'Rourke worked in London tons,' she said. 'He had friends. You might know them.'

'Let me guess. Jackie and Johnny Lucas,' Declan sighed.

'Ah, you spoiled the punchline.' Tessa opened the still water, holding it up in a mock toast. 'Cheers.'

Declan joined in the toast, grimacing slightly as he considered the upcoming conversations. At least he could aim someone else at Johnny Lucas. Perhaps Monroe or even Anjli could have a chat with him; they both had better histories with him.

Tessa, watching him, frowned.

'You've got that look,' she muttered. 'Are you okay?'

Declan sighed, shrugging, giving the same *what-can-I-do* kind of expression that Tessa had given earlier with his hands.

'I thought we'd get at least a week off between cases,' he explained with a shrug. 'But no sooner are we finishing the posies case than we're immediately moving on to this. I could do with a break.'

At that, Tessa started laughing.

'You think *you* could go on holiday?' She shook her head. 'Declan Walsh, you are copper through and through.'

'I wouldn't be too sure,' Declan replied, almost argumentatively. 'When I quit the force, before I went and took the case up in the Peak District, I was hunting the apparent death of Francine Pearce. I was in St David's in Wales. Spent a couple of weeks there, and I learned how to surf.'

'You learned how to surf?' Tessa shook her head. 'The things I missed while in prison ...'

'Well, if you do the crime, you do the time,' Declan laughed. 'I was getting quite good as well. I only smashed my face three out of five times.'

'How did you smash your face?' Tessa leant forward. 'Surely water isn't that hard.'

'The water might not be hard, but the surfboard bouncing on it is,' Declan shrugged. 'Let's just say it was an acquired skill.'

'Did you enjoy it? Or were you just trying to fit in with the locals?' Tessa gave a wolfish grin. 'Do you have any photos? You know, of you in your wetsuit? Was it super tight? Did it show your muscles?'

'Yeah, we're stopping this conversation now,' Declan replied.

'Ah, shame,' Tessa grinned. But then the smile faded. 'I'm guessing it was after this that you got together with Anjli.'

Declan nodded.

'Someone tried to kill her,' he said. 'Someone tried to kill me as well, but between the two of these, we kind of, well ... you know.'

'Yeah,' Tessa nodded. 'I know, I was in prison. There was nothing I could do.'

'So ... since you got out, have you gone out with anybody?' Declan asked, mainly trying to change the subject, but realising as he spoke that it sounded like he was now prying. 'I mean, just curious – just because you had a bad issue with your previous partners doesn't necessarily mean you—'

'Should live the life of a hermit?' Tessa finished for him. 'No, I've been on a couple of dates. Sean set me up with a friend of his, although that was one of the worst things I ever did. I'm even with an app that tries to use AI to match me to my perfect companion.'

'Oh yes,' Declan grinned. 'And who does it say that is?'

However, instead of answering, a change came over Tessa and she rose from the chair, turning to leave. Declan was quite surprised because up to that point, he thought he was having quite a pleasant conversation.

'It shows me a picture of *you*,' she replied, and she walked off.

Declan should have commented that wasn't a funny joke

or made light of it, but instead he just stared, surprised at the statement, as Tessa Martinez left the *Pret-a-Manger*.

He sighed, leaning his head back. Two years ago, he would have killed for the opportunity to be with her. She was, after all, his childhood crush, and she was everything he'd ever thought he wanted.

But she wasn't Anjli.

Strangely, Declan almost felt guilty because Tessa had flirted with him, even though it wasn't technically his fault and he definitely felt he hadn't encouraged it. But there was something Tessa had said about AI, that had triggered a memory.

Leaning back in his chair, he pulled out his phone and dialled a number.

'Billy,' he said when it was answered. 'Do we have a time of death for Eli Green?'

He could hear Billy typing.

'Doctor Marcos is still confirming that,' Billy's voice came down the phone. 'Apparently the sauna has made it more difficult to set the time exactly, but she thinks it was around three in the afternoon, which would match the time of someone turning up, providing him with whatever it was, and him then going to sleep.'

'Thanks.' Declan put the phone down on the table, the call disconnected, and stared at it. *What was it he wasn't getting?*

At the table beside him, there was a young couple talking, and one of them suddenly had an alarm go off on their phone. She turned it to face her, tapped it, spoke to their friend, gave him a kiss on the cheek, and then left. Obviously, the alarm had told her it was time to leave, but with that one singular motion, Declan remembered what it was.

Leon Brecht's watch, and the alarms that had happened on the screens when they went to see him the previous day.

Rummaging in his pockets, Declan looked for the visitor's pass that had been given to him by the receptionist; the one that had taken him up the stairs when they'd visited Brecht in *Paradigm Synthetics*, in Kingston-Upon-Thames.

It was a printout. But there, on the paper, was the time it was printed.

14:40

Declan leant back. They had spent some time waiting, before they'd been led to Brecht's office, which would have made it after three. There was every opportunity that somewhere between three and three thirty, Leon Brecht's system had alerted him – while they were in the room.

Was the alert telling him that Eli Green was in the sauna? Had he found a way to use his technology to remotely turn off the sauna's kill switch? And if so, was this something that could have happened the previous day, remotely disconnecting the cryotherapy channel?

Kline had been talking to him about the cryotherapy, and had even let Brecht have a look around. It didn't matter if Leon Brecht had an alibi. If he was in his laboratory and could have done it by remote control, he could have been anywhere and still been the killer.

Declan rose up, but as he did so, his phone suddenly rang. He had certain ringtones: *Dixon of Dock Green*, if Monroe called; *Charlie's Angels* theme, if Anjli dialled. Most of the time he had the phone on silent, so he just had the vibration. But this was the stock phone call, with no caller ID.

He answered the call.

'Detective Chief Inspector Walsh.'

There was a pause. And then a voice, computerised, spoke down the phone.

'If you want to know who killed Stephen Kline,' it said, 'you should look in Eli Green's safe.'

With that, the call ended. Declan stared at the phone, annoyed at a lack of a number he could work from here.

But now, Declan had to put aside his thoughts on Leon Brecht. He'd come back to them later on.

First, he had to check a victim's house.

16

VISIBILITY

Ever since he had joined the Last Chance Saloon, Billy Fitzwarren had regularly faced death while out in the field. Whether it be from his own side, armed SCO-19 officers charging at him thinking he was one of the enemy, corrupt gangland cartels, or even serial-killer daughters with an axe to grind, Billy had found it was far safer to stay in the office behind his desk. Even then, he'd still been hurt. Friends and colleagues had been killed as messages over the years, the most recent being Rufus Harrington, a man he had vaguely known at school, who over the last couple of years had become more of a friend ... who'd then been killed as a message by a serial killer.

Therefore, it was quite a surprise for Sergeant De'Geer to have Billy knock on his door, downstairs in the forensics department where De'Geer now worked, asking him to go with Billy out to Canary Wharf.

They had driven in Billy's car, a Mini Cooper which, although perfect for Billy, was a little cramped for the seven-foot-tall Viking sergeant, who had spent most of the journey shifting and muttering that a squad car would have been far easier.

If Billy was listening, he wasn't paying attention.

Eventually, they arrived at Ionosphere. The building was still closed, police tape still around the frontage, but De'Geer had a set of keys provided to Doctor Marcos by the forensics team once they'd closed up shop; likely the keys Stephen Kline had used, now just spare.

Entering Ionosphere, De'Geer turned off the security system. Turning back to Billy, who was already searching around the room, he asked, 'Can I ask what you're looking for?'

'It was something said by Alexis Kovalenko,' Billy explained, tapping the plaster of the walls, 'when she talked about the others all turning up and having meetings here.'

De'Geer nodded, following Billy through the rooms.

'It clashed with something else that I'd been told,' Billy continued, entering the room where the hyperbaric chamber rested to one side, a red light therapy station to the back. He looked around, examining the walls. 'When we first arrived, we were told there was no CCTV in here because customers would be getting changed. Likewise to cryotherapy chambers.'

De'Geer pursed his lips, understanding now.

'The question you're wondering is how Alexis was able to see this without an official camera?'

Billy was already turning in a circle, his phone up in the air as if trying to find some kind of signal.

'If, hypothetically, someone had placed a wireless camera up here, there's every chance it would be on its own network. You know, so when you turn on your Bluetooth, it would appear.'

'So, you're just searching for Wi-Fi devices in the room?' De'Geer grinned. 'I thought we'd done that.'

'You would have,' Billy replied. 'But at the time, you wouldn't have been looking for CCTV devices. You would have seen various names come up and just assumed it was the tech in the room. There was no context.'

He tapped at his screen.

'The red light therapy session works with an app. You can see here that it's looking for a connection. The hyperbaric chamber also works via Bluetooth, so that too has its own personal signal. But this ...' he tapped at a selection of words and letters, '... this isn't the Wi-Fi, it's neither of the devices in here, the Cryo chambers are turned off, and if I'm right, this is unknown.'

He glanced around, looking up into the corners.

'Which means somebody's put something in here ... there.'

He reached up into the corner but couldn't quite make it. Sheepishly, he turned back to De'Geer.

'If you could—'

'For a start, let's do this properly,' De'Geer muttered irritably, putting on a pair of blue latex gloves and reaching up with ease, casually pulling at a piece of plastic in the corner. After a few wiggles, it came free, and De'Geer brought it down. It was a 3D printed piece of plastic, in the same colour as the brown cladding of the corner moulding to hide it. Behind the print was a tiny wireless CCTV camera, a second wire embedded in the plastic beside it.

De'Geer checked it over before presenting it to Billy to look at, his eyes narrowing warningly as Billy went to touch it. Billy, nodding in acceptance, pulled out his own pair of latex gloves and examined the small camera, pulling it from the 3D casing.

'That's weird,' he frowned, shaking his head.

'What is?' De'Geer took a baggie out of his vest pocket and placed the new piece of evidence into it.

'This is a security camera that was placed here purely to spy on someone,' Billy looked around the room. 'Surely you'd pay a little bit more and grab one that has a microphone.'

De'Geer was already examining the plastic casing, and he grinned.

'You're right,' he said. 'There's a separate microphone, but the casing's been made to hold them both together. Here.' He pulled out the second wire, and revealed what looked to be some kind of a Bluetooth piece from the side, connected by a USB-C connection.

'I'll need to examine these,' Billy added, as De'Geer replaced the items into the baggie. 'But you might want to check them for fingerprints first. We might be lucky.'

De'Geer had already moved over to the corner, examining the wall.

'There's less reason for people to be up here, so the fingerprints won't be just anybody's,' he replied, as he had already started examining.

Billy, meanwhile, had left the room, walking back into the foyer area where the reception was. There was still something not quite right and he couldn't work out what it was; the glass-fronted entrance was closed, nobody walking past at this time of day, especially with the police tape around, and he found himself exiting Ionosphere, standing outside the glass doors as he looked around.

There was a CCTV camera behind the reception, aimed at the door. Alexis had basically said as much, and there was every chance that this camera could have been placed in by Stephen Kline himself, and connected to the network. Alexis could have been innocent, not understanding about it, logging on by accident when she made sure she could check the front door when having a sneaky wee.

But why would the camera be placed in the office?

Perhaps Stephen wanted information? Blackmail perhaps? But then if he was wiping footage, that didn't gel. Something was still niggling, something about cameras. That the security footage had been doctored, with parts deleted, infuriated him.

But, as he looked around, he realised what had been niggling at him, and started walking over to the storefront next to Ionosphere; situated between the cryotherapy spa and an upscale gym, he noticed it was some kind of nail bar. Billy liked a manicure as much as the next person, but he didn't frequent nail bars that much. It was open, and Billy entered, nodding to the receptionist as she stared at him, probably surprised to see such a dapper-looking gentleman walking into the room currently filled with middle-aged women.

'Do you have an appointment?'

'No,' Billy said, reaching into his jacket pocket and pulling out his warrant card. 'I'm here in connection with next door. I was hoping I could speak to the manager?'

'She's busy over there at the moment,' the receptionist replied, nodding to a woman at the far end, painting nails. 'I can call her if it's really important, but if it's something that I can do ...'

'No, that's fine,' Billy nodded. 'Do you have security cameras here?'

'Do you mean CCTV? Sure,' the receptionist nodded at

the corner behind her, where a small black camera in a glass dome could be seen. 'It's nothing major. It's just, you know, in case somebody tries to smash a window or something stupid like that. It doesn't aim next door, though, if that's what you're looking for.'

Billy smiled.

'It's kind of like that, but not quite,' he said, noting the receptionist's confused expression at the comment. 'Basically, I was hoping to see your security footage for two nights ago, or at least get a copy of it.'

'I think that can be arranged,' the receptionist said, 'but I don't know what we can give you. We offered when the police first came by, but once they started checking it and realised it didn't cover next door, they stopped being bothered.'

Billy looked back at the door.

'Anybody who leaves Ionosphere has to walk past your shop,' he said. 'I'm hoping we might see something.'

'That's not exactly true,' the receptionist said, nodding over to the left, out of the front entrance. 'There's a set of stairs that go up to the street. People could go up there.'

'Well, let's hope they didn't,' Billy passed a business card across with his email address on it. 'If you could get something sent over there, it'd be greatly appreciated.'

The receptionist examined the card as if looking for a forged banknote and placed it on the counter.

'We keep everything for a week on the server in the back room,' she explained, 'but it's also uploaded to the cloud. I can send you a login link if that's good?'

'Perfect,' Billy tried to give a reassuring smile, but realised it came across more as a leer. 'I'll be going now.'

As he exited the nail bar, Billy saw De'Geer hurry out of Ionosphere, noting that Billy had disappeared.

'If you're looking for CCTV, we've already looked there,' he muttered. 'Checked the footage the same day. Unfortunately, you couldn't see anything; nobody walked past at that time of the evening, bar a couple of late night workers.'

'Because of the stairs over there that people leave by,' Billy nodded. 'The receptionist just mentioned that.'

At this confirmation, De'Geer pointed over at the offending staircase.

'You can't see the stairs, they're too far to the side,' he explained. 'It's a low range of view. In fact, that dentist opposite? That's literally as far as you can see. So anybody coming into Ionosphere from that way ...'

He shrugged.

Billy looked over at the dentist window display, primarily showing large images of cheerful people with perfectly straight, white teeth, and, pursing his lips, returned his attention to De'Geer.

'Do me a favour,' he requested. 'Stand back at the entrance to Ionosphere for a couple of seconds, will you?'

'Sure,' De'Geer replied, confused as to what the plan was here.

Billy wandered back into the nail bar, giving another smile to the receptionist, who was surprised to see him again. Then, pulling his phone out, he aimed out of the shop window and took a photo. This done, he thanked the receptionist and left once more.

Walking over to De'Geer, he showed the photo he'd just taken.

'See?' he pointed at the dentist.

De'Geer nodded. It was just visible, but he could see the

reflection of his fluorescent police vest in the window opposite.

Billy placed the phone back in his pocket.

'We might not be able to see anybody coming in or out of the store,' he noted, 'but we might get a reflection.'

He rubbed at his chin as he looked back at the nail bar.

'Or not, of course.'

17

BOXING STING

Monroe had offered to speak to Johnny Lucas, following Declan's text from his lunch meeting, but it was Anjli who took the trip, explaining that she was going to be heading into the City to speak to David Lester, so she might as well have a slight diversion.

Johnny Lucas ran a boxing club in Globe Town, in East London; for a while, it had been his in name only, while he was attempting to save the nation as the latest MP for Bethnal Green and Bow, a position he was able to win in an almost landslide victory, after clearing his name of all previous crimes.

Well, Anjli smiled to herself as she looked up at the building, *by throwing them all on his imaginary half-brother, who turned out to be real after all.*

She entered the boxing club and took a deep breath. It used to smell of leather and sweat, an old-school boxing ring in the middle with heavy weights around it, but in recent years, Johnny had moved with the times and now there were cardio machines, electronic testing areas, and even a plunge pool – or ice bath, as they called it here – at the back wall, as this was less a newfangled science, and more the traditional way for boxers to recuperate.

Even the EastEnders are moving in with the anti-agers, Anjli considered to herself, and she nodded to one of the trainers.

'Leroy, is he around?'

Leroy nodded, pressing a button on the wall.

'Not shouting out?' Anjli laughed.

'The boss prefers a more subtle approach to being called,' Leroy smiled. 'Shouting out his name is so old school, while this is a new world.'

He nodded at the doorbell he had pressed, and the small Wi-Fi webcam drilled into the wood above it.

'Chimes in his office, lets him know there's somebody to see him. It also turns on the monitor next to him, and that camera there shows who it is.'

There was movement from the back offices and Johnny Lucas walked out, all smiles and with his hands outstretched, possibly for a hug, which was incredibly unlike the man.

Anjli almost did a double take; usually, Johnny Lucas would be wearing a black suit with a blue shirt, his almost white hair quiffed back in a stylised cut. But this man was completely different. For a start, he was wearing jogging bottoms and a sweater, a pair of expensive-looking white trainers on his feet. His hair, usually bouffant and blow-dried back, was cut in a trendy style. If anything, he looked a good five or ten years younger.

He smiled as he saw Anjli's expression.

'Go on, get your mid-life crisis jokes out of the way,' he said. 'And come give me a hug.'

Anjli shook her head.

'Johnny, to have a mid-life crisis you must be in the middle of your life,' she said, 'and we both know you're way down that line. Also, since when do you bloody hug?'

Johnny Lucas clutched at his heart in mock horror.

'Et tu, Brute?' he muttered, before shrugging it off and wandering over to the water dispenser at the side, pouring himself a glass. 'I warmed up in Westminster, shall we say. Happier to let people closer these days.'

'Westminster made you soft,' Anjli replied.

'So, is this Anjli or DI Kapoor I speak to here?' Johnny smiled. 'Are you here for a spar, maybe a gym session ... or am I once more the go-to guy for gangster shit that you guys need to know?'

'You know me too well,' Anjli shrugged. 'It's official, I'm afraid.'

'Am I in trouble?'

'Should you be?'

Johnny gave a smile as he shrugged. Anjli decided to leave it at that.

'Go on then, if it's not me, it's something else you need,' he glanced across at Leroy. 'It's always bloody something. They should pay me a consultancy rate.'

'Connor O'Rourke.'

'Christ,' Johnny almost spat the water out, as he turned his attention back to Anjli now. 'When you come up with names you really go deep into the past, don't you? What about him? What's he done now?'

'Possibly nothing,' Anjli replied. 'But we think he might have killed a confidential informant from Manchester, a man named Stephen Kline.'

'Heard the name,' Johnny shook his head. 'Don't know him. And as for O'Rourke, I've not seen him for a good three, four years now. His son does a lot more of the business these days.'

He gave a small, almost wistful smile.

'The sons are taking over from a lot of people.'

Anjli nodded slowly, but her expression was that of someone unsure of what was going on here. Johnny Lucas, a man who seemed at peace with everything? It felt wrong, somehow.

'Right,' she replied. 'Well, unless you've got any secret sons I need to know about, I'm not gonna worry too much about that here, right?'

At the line about secret sons, however, Johnny gave a small smile.

'Spoke to Ellie Reckless recently?'

'Our paths barely cross,' Anjli said. 'Why?'

'Just curious.'

Anjli made a mental note to call the woman when she got back to the office. There was something going on here that she didn't know about and it annoyed her. But, in the meantime, it sounded like O'Rourke wasn't the suspect here.

Johnny, meanwhile, was refilling the small water cup.

'Go on then, let's see if I can help you,' he said as he turned back to face her.

'Connor O'Rourke was apparently owed money by Kline,' she said. 'Back in Manchester, a few years back. It's looking like Kline ran on the debt. We're still waiting to find out all the information, but ...'

She trailed off.

'You're wondering whether the son, Mickey, would have

come on strong?' Johnny asked. 'Deciding to get any money he's owed to his father?'

He looked away, pondering the statement.

'He is a bit forceful, I'll give him that. He could have done it. But murder? Nah, that's not his type. He might be the muscle in the next generation of O'Rourkes, but he's not stupid like his dad was.'

'Connor wasn't that bright?'

'He loaned money to Stephen Kline and allowed him to run on him, if what you're saying's true,' Johnny laughed. 'That don't sound that bright to me.'

'You don't think he'd ...'

'Kill someone? Nah, Mickey's all about computers, like your lad Billy,' Johnny replied. 'He'll destroy you online, rather than kill you. Wipe out your credit rating. Use deep-fake and AI to show you doing terrible things to children. Funny enough, it's a bigger threat these days than "I'm going to break your legs if you don't give me what I need".'

'Or dump you in an ice bath,' Anjli said, glancing across at the bath to the side.

'You should try it,' Johnny Lucas said. 'It's amazing. Absolutely focuses you better than anything else.'

'You use it?'

'Hell no!' Johnny laughed. 'I ain't stupid. My trainers tell me. I live vicariously through them.'

His smile dropped, and suddenly, once more Anjli stared at the more familiar cold, hard face of Johnny Lucas.

In the past, she would have said this was the moment when *Jackie* appeared, the second personality inside him. But for a while now, Johnny and Jackie Lucas hadn't been sharing a mind.

Now, she wondered whether that was in *name* only.

'Though I have been told, however, an ice bath is a superb way to make someone speak,' he said, his voice now emotionless, almost robotic as he considered the option. 'Being held under water, it freezes your brain. People will do anything rather than go in it.'

'I'll keep that in mind,' Anjli said, deciding not to make any more jokes while he was in this state. 'If you hear anything about Connor O'Rourke, please let me know.'

Johnny Lucas paused as he was returning to his office, turning back to her.

'Is that you saying, "if I hear anything, let you know?" Or is it you saying, "please go ask your various criminal friends and see if there's something I can find out?"'

Anjli shrugged.

'Whichever sounds easier.'

Johnny considered this, nodded and then walked off into the back offices.

'Don't be a stranger,' his voice echoed out in the corridor before he was gone.

Anjli looked back at Leroy who had been watching the conversation with interest.

'How often is he doing that?' she asked.

'Doing what?'

'The personality shift.'

Leroy shrugged.

'He's always done it, ever since I've known him.'

'Yeah, but back then, he was two personalities,' Anjli replied. 'Is this why he left Parliament? There was a chance he was going a little more "Jackie", than the Right Honourable Member?'

Leroy said nothing, looking back at the door.

'He's fine,' he replied. 'He's with friends. And sometimes you need to be a bit cold and callous in this business.'

'The boxing business?' Anjli offered, knowing what Leroy truly meant.

'Sure, that's what I meant,' Leroy said, his expression unreadable.

Anjli shook her head, looking back at the offices.

'That was more than that,' she said. 'And you bloody well know it. Do me a favour, yeah? Let me know if he starts getting worse.'

Leroy nodded and turned away, back to work as Anjli left the boxing club. Once outside, she pulled out her phone, dialling a number she'd barely ever called.

'Reckless,' the voice of Ellie Reckless spoke down the line. 'How can I help, DI Kapoor?'

Anjli glanced back at the club.

'I've just been to see Johnny Lucas,' she said carefully, in case he could hear her somehow. 'You seen him recently?'

'Here and there. What's the problem?'

'Have you noticed his attitude change, mid conversation?' Anjli asked. 'You know, like it used to do when Jackie was turning up?'

'You think Johnny and Jackie Lucas are becoming a thing again?' Ellie sounded concerned. 'I hadn't noticed, but I can keep an eye on it. He's been falling into his old ways since quitting Parliament. I was hoping his split personality *wasn't* one of those ways.'

'I'd appreciate you keeping me in the loop,' Anjli said as she walked over to her car. 'More if he becomes a threat to anyone.'

She stopped.

'Oh, something else,' she added. 'I made a joke about

secret sons, and he asked if I'd spoken to you. Is there something I don't know?'

There was a long pause down the line.

'Yeah,' Ellie eventually replied. 'You heard of Arun Nadal?'

'In passing,' Anjli nodded, even though Ellie couldn't see it down the phone line. 'Small-time gangster. Seems to have funding though. We think it's Seven Sisters related. Why?'

'He's Johnny Lucas's great-nephew,' Ellie replied. 'Anita Lucas's grandson, from a relationship she had with the Turk, who ran Soho thirty years back.'

'Jesus,' Anjli whispered. She knew all about Anita; she'd tried to take over the Lucas empire – it was what Johnny used to clear his own name, throwing the crimes "Jackie" did onto her, and his actual, long-dead brother. 'Let me guess, he's being funded by Johnny?'

'Maybe,' Ellie replied. 'And the fact he learned he has a gangster family member was another reason he quit parliament.'

Anjli thanked Ellie for her time and disconnected the call before climbing into her car, taking one last look at the boxing club. If Johnny was turning back into the "Twins", this was bad for the area. And if he had a young, upcoming, hungry gangster under his thumb, then that was a recipe for something big and bad happening in London very soon.

She'd discuss this with Monroe later, though; first she needed to solve this case. The thought was halted, however, as her phone beeped; a message from Declan.

> Bringing Selene Carter in, and heading to speak to David Lester. Will send details on why she's coming in, can you run the interview? X

She frowned, re-reading it. She knew Declan had met with Tessa Martinez, but the "x" at the end was a little over the top.

Still, if he was going to see Lester, there was no need for her to see him as well. Sighing, she started the car, and headed back to Temple Inn.

18

SECRET AND SAFE

By the time Declan reached Hampstead, Eli Green's house was back to normal. The crime scene tape had been taken down, probably as soon as the police had disappeared, knowing the neighbourhood; after all, nothing screamed "lowering house prices" like police tape hanging around.

When he knocked on the door, there was a clattering of locks before it opened slightly to reveal a scared-looking woman. Declan hadn't been sure who would be there, if he was being honest; he'd only realised the house could be empty and impossible to get into as he pulled up. He knew there'd be a key somewhere, he just didn't expect the housekeeper to be back at work so quickly.

'Are you Marjorie Halliwell?' Declan asked, showing his warrant card as the scared-looking woman nodded. 'I'm Detective Chief Inspector Walsh.'

The now-confirmed-to-be-Marjorie nodded, opening the door wider.

'Please, come in,' she said, as Declan entered, closing the door behind him.

'Are you sure you should be back here?' he asked, with more than a hint of concern visible in his voice. 'I mean, it's not exactly the best of places to be when somebody's …'

Marjorie, however, had already started walking off.

'My boss is dead,' she said matter-of-factly. 'As much as I don't want that to be the case, I kind of have to accept it. As soon as things get settled, the house will be sold. His estate and his son will start sniffing around, and they won't want to keep me employed. I might as well get everything sorted, shipshape, pack my bags, and leave.'

Declan paused in the doorway. He hadn't considered how much Eli Green's death would affect the housekeeper in more ways than just emotionally.

'I'm sorry,' he said. 'Do you have a place you can go?'

'Oh, absolutely,' Marjorie smiled, but it felt forced. 'I own a cottage in Tunbridge Wells. One thing about working for Eli for the last couple of years is he's always been good to me, money wise, ever since he arrived in London.'

She wiped a tear.

'I will miss him.'

Declan didn't know what to say to that, so he gave a nod and a slight shrug.

'Look, I'm really sorry to pressure you,' he said, 'but I'd like to look in his study, where Selene Carter went.'

At the request, Marjorie nodded.

'Of course,' she said. 'I'll take you straight there.'

However, instead of going upwards, she walked towards a door underneath the stairs.

'I thought we were going to the study?' Declan asked.

'We are,' Marjorie gave a small knowing smile, as if she was giving a secret that nobody else knew about, as she opened the door. 'This is where Selene Carter went.'

The door itself led to a set of stairs that went downwards. At Declan's expression, Marjorie smiled.

'Mister Green had a specially created basement when he tore down and rebuilt the house,' she explained. 'He has a ten-seater private cinema, as well as several of his louder inventions. The basement is soundproof, which meant the neighbours wouldn't have to suffer listening to the machinery.'

'What kind of things did he have here?'

'Mister Green was always looking at new ways to create anti-ageing equipment,' Marjorie shrugged. 'I never bothered asking him what he did. But he would often work on them. It was almost like his ...'

She paused and stared off as if searching for an answer.

'Have you seen *Iron Man?*'

'The movie? Sure. Robert Downey Jr.'

'So, in the film, he has a basement where he builds his armour, but it's also where he builds all his high-tech equipment and energy sources, all that kind of thing,' Marjorie explained. Declan was quite surprised that a woman who looked like Marjorie would know so much about this. 'Well, this was Mister Green's manufacturing room.'

'I would have thought he would have had some kind of off-site office to do all that,' Declan said.

'Oh, he does.' Marjorie was opening the door at the bottom of the stairs now, ushering Declan through. 'However, there are things he's working on ... and there are, well, things he's *working* on.'

The second line was said with such mystery that Declan couldn't help but wonder exactly what was being worked on in this subterranean basement of a workshop.

Entering a corridor, he stopped beside a door marked

CINEMA. He couldn't help himself; opening the door, he peeked in, whistling as he looked.

'It's impressive,' he said. 'It looks like the smallest screen in a multiplex.'

'He was very proud of it,' Marjorie said. 'Of course, I think he only ever used it twice in all the time he was here.'

'That's a shame,' Declan said, emerging back out into the corridor, noting that Marjorie was now unlocking another door. 'The study?'

'Yes.' Marjorie opened it and allowed Declan to enter.

The study was exactly as Declan had seen before, so many times. A desk. A bookcase. A couple of side cabinets. A filing cabinet.

To the side, a potted plant kept the room looking relaxed and cosy, and the chair was ergonomic, which was expected for someone like Eli Green.

He hadn't walked around to it yet, but Declan pretty much guessed that when he saw the front side of the desk, he'd see it was a sit-stand desk or something equally as healthy. Maybe even with some kind of walking-pad treadmill to place underneath it.

What he didn't see, however, was a safe visible anywhere in the basement office.

'I need to know where the safe is,' he asked. 'We have reason to believe there's something in there, or something now missing from there, rather, following Selene's visit.'

Marjorie baulked at the question.

'Oh no, sir,' she said, 'I wouldn't know what was in such a—'

'I didn't ask you if you'd been to the safe,' Declan interrupted. 'I asked where the safe would be.'

He looked at the walls. There weren't many spaces where

a safe could be hidden. If Eli Green had the house built specifically for him, he would have been involved from the very beginning, during the architect planning stages. He could have placed the bloody thing anywhere.

In fact, as he looked around, there was something that felt *familiar*.

Walking back out of the room, he looked down the corridor.

'Is there anything else down here?' he asked.

'The room on the right is the manufacturing room, and the room down the very end on the left is the toilet,' Marjorie said. 'He has a small guest bathroom there in case he gets sweaty.'

Declan nodded. *His workshop's in the basement, his sauna's on the roof, and in between was nothing more than a posh, expensive-looking house he barely spends time in.*

Declan couldn't help himself; he walked down to the end and opened the door, looking into the room. It comprised a shower, toilet, sink, and a changing area.

Declan measured it by eye, and then paced back to the study's door, entering it, now pacing again to the back of the study, and the bookcase behind the desk.

'It's roughly thirty paces,' he said to Marjorie, 'from one end of the corridor to the other. If I take away the paces I've just made in this room and in the bathroom, I'm short twelve, maybe thirteen paces. That's about three metres.'

Marjorie looked confused at this statement.

'There's a room missing,' Declan explained.

'How would you know such a thing?' Marjorie asked, her face whitening.

'My father once made a secret room in his house,' Declan

shrugged. 'Long story really, but it gave me a knowledge of how these things work.'

He started examining the bookcase.

'I'm guessing as you've been his housekeeper all these years, you know if there's a secret place here.'

'... yes.'

'It would save a lot of hassle if you just told me how to open it.'

Looking over at the housekeeper, Declan could see Marjorie chewing at her lip, torn as to what to do.

'Or I could bring you into the station as an accessory,' he said, knowing it was harsh to speak of such things to a woman who had lost her livelihood. 'Refusing to aid an officer in the pursuit of ... well, whatever.'

Eventually, Marjorie nodded, walked over to an ornament at the side of one shelf, and pulled at it. It was connected into the shelf itself, and there was a click, as the middle of the bookcase opened.

Declan smiled. This was way more high-tech than his father's one had been. But then that had just been created to look like a room filled with junk.

Entering the room behind the bookcase, the motion-detected light turning on as he did so, he saw it was a small three-metre square room, and designed like a survivalist would create a bunker.

A bed was to the side, a TV in front. There was a fridge, a microwave, a hot plate and a blender, likely for smoothies, an ottoman, likely filled with clothing, and a traditional-looking safe against the wall. The safe itself was chest height, and about two feet wide by three feet deep, with a number lock on the front.

It looked like sometimes Eli couldn't be bothered to walk back to his bedroom. Anjli had mentioned that when talking to Aria Milton, she'd said he had a "sleep pod" in his office for when he tried some newfangled way of sleeping, and Declan wondered whether this was the same.

If you're spending ten minutes walking to your room and back for your twenty minutes' sleep, this was a better choice.

Declan turned back to Marjorie.

'What's the code?' he asked.

Marjorie shook her head.

'He never gave it to me,' she said. 'He never let me in here. I didn't even know this existed until ...'

She stopped herself. But Declan knew the rest of the statement.

Until Selene Carter had come in there the previous night.

'You were with her, weren't you?' Declan said. 'In your statement, you said that you stood outside when she went into the study, but you were here. You saw how she got in.'

'My statement—'

'Is under review,' Declan said, pausing whatever excuse she was about to give. 'We're concerned there are irregularities. So, anything you do here to help me ...'

Marjorie nodded, sighing, but didn't move to help in any way. Declan walked over to her, staring down at her. There was a good foot in height between them, and he used this to his advantage.

'I'm going to ask one more time,' he said. 'We can do this here, or in an interview room.'

'One-seven-five-six-five,' Marjorie eventually said. 'I don't know what it means, if it's a date or anything, but ...'

Nodding a *thank you*, Declan walked back to the safe and tapped the code into it. There was a lock button, and as he finished the numbers, he pressed it, hearing the whirr and click as the door opened.

Pulling the door aside, he stared into the safe.

There were three shelves. One shelf, the middle one, had a black box resting within. Pulling it out and opening it up, he found it had stacks of gold coins in little plastic cases. He'd seen these before; Gold Britannias, exempt from capital gains tax and a way for a lot of rich people to save their money. There were twenty, maybe twenty-five coins inside the box; he didn't know what the current price of gold was, but he guessed there was probably something along the lines of forty or fifty grand's worth of gold there. Beside it were wads of fifty-pound notes, in sets of thousands. Pulling on his blue latex gloves before touching anything else, Declan counted out the piles. Again, another twenty thousand pounds was here.

There were some contracts on the base shelf, as well as a couple of expensive-looking watches, and Declan spent a couple of minutes flicking through before placing them back as they didn't seem relevant, but the top shelf was strangely empty. What was interesting, however, is that there was a shape; the dust over many years had obviously settled, and there was a clear mark that something had been removed.

Declan now understood why Marjorie Halliwell was back in the house so soon after the murder. The chances were she knew that someone would turn up eventually, and once they opened the secret safe they would find at least eighty, maybe ninety grand's worth of assets here, depending on how much the watches were worth. With no way for anyone to know exactly what had been in here, and with no Eli around to explain where it went, it was an excellent severance package for a woman who no longer had a job. All of her comments about being well off with her house in Tunbridge Wells now felt like ashes in his mouth as he turned to face the housekeeper.

'When were you going to take it?' he asked calmly.

'I don't know what you mean.' Marjorie put her hands on her hips, as if to dare him to continue this line of questioning.

Declan stepped away from the safe.

'You didn't know about this safe until last night, right?' he asked. 'But Selene Carter did. She comes in, you find the body, and then she demands you let her down here, into the study. You say the police need to be contacted. Yet she convinces you that you should keep quiet until she's done. You, who have worked for Mister Green for so many years.'

He glanced back at the contents of the safe.

'That is a pretty good reason to keep quiet,' he continued. 'But, you couldn't take it when the police turned up, could you? You had to keep quiet. That's why you said you didn't come in with her. You could still claim plausible deniability to what happened in here. You "didn't see a secret door get opened". You "didn't see her go through the safe". And then, when the dust had settled and before the lawyers came in to work out what to do, here you are, less than twenty-four hours after he's died, back in the house, doing your job.'

He shook his head.

'I'll ask one more time; when would you have taken the contents of the safe?'

Marjorie's eyes filled with tears, possibly at the embarrassment of being found out, or maybe even from the anger of knowing that she no longer had this windfall she had expected.

'I would have taken it today,' she eventually said. 'He owed me my last month's money. This would have paid the debt.'

'Eighty thousand's worth?'

Marjorie said nothing for a long, hard moment.

'Are you going to arrest me?' she eventually whispered.

Declan shook his head.

'To be honest, I don't know. Maybe. I'll have to mention, of course, that there were coins and money in here, but I haven't audited it. Only his son would know what was in the safe, and that was only if he'd ever looked. I'm sure if anything small disappeared, no one would care. All I want to know is *what did Selene Carter take*?'

Marjorie, who had seemed to brighten up a little the moment she realised she might get something out of this, straightened.

'There was a photo,' she said, 'in a frame. I only glimpsed it. It looked old.'

'Okay,' Declan asked. 'What was in the picture?'

'It was the Olympics. Not the last one, but the one before,' Marjorie continued. 'It was Eli. And Mister Kline. He was there. There was another man. I didn't recognise him. And there was Selene. It was a celebration because she was wearing her Team GB tracksuit and had her silver medal, which she'd won that year.'

Declan frowned at the description. *Why would somebody break in here to take that photo?*

'Did you get a good look at the person in the photo you didn't recognise?' he asked, already flicking through the images on his phone.

'Yes,' Marjorie replied. 'He was young, maybe forties. He had a ponytail.'

At that, Declan paused, remembering a line Tessa had said only hours earlier.

'There was another guy there. Yank, stupid ponytail, that's all I remember.'

Flicking through the contestants on the rejuvenation tournament page, he stopped at David Lester. In the picture, David was wearing a fleece jacket over a t-shirt, orange-tinted glasses, and his hair was slicked back, pulled into a ponytail.

'Was it this man?' he asked.

Marjorie, seeing the photo, nodded.

'I think so,' she said. 'I mean, he was younger, but yes.'

'And was there anything else?'

'No. Although Selene, in the photo, was hugging the man you just showed me. They looked close. I think that's why she wanted it.'

'What makes you say that?' Declan put the phone away as he asked. As a response, Marjorie pointed at the desk in the other room.

'She took the picture out of the frame there,' she said. 'Left the frame on the desk as she left.'

Declan closed the safe now, walking back into the study. On the desk, to the side, was the empty frame. Picking it up, he opened the back, staring at the space where the picture would have been. They'd had a case a while back where something had been hidden in the back of a photo frame, and here, on the cardboard backing, Declan could see an indentation.

Something had been placed behind the photo, the backing then forced back on.

Something that had been removed by Selene Carter.

Was the photo even important, here?

Pulling out a clear baggie and placing the photo frame into it, Declan took a last look around the study. Someone had gone to a lot of effort here to send him to this location, and he wondered why ... and who.

'Did you mean it?' Marjorie asked, confusing him as he looked back to her with a frown. 'That I could take some stuff?'

'I never said you could take anything,' Declan said. 'I just said I hadn't counted it.'

He pursed his lips as he contemplated the next line.

'Of course, someone else might know exactly how much was in there. Elias Green junior, for example. And if there's something missing, well ...'

This stated, Declan decided it was time to leave, and left the study. He didn't know what Marjorie would do. He didn't care, to be honest. Eli Green had a secret basement safe that held money, contracts that didn't seem relevant on first perusal, and a photo with something hidden in the back, something so important that Selene Carter had removed it before calling the police.

Which, of course, raised other questions.

For a start, how did Selene Carter know that there *was* a secret safe, if Green's own housekeeper didn't?

One thing was for sure ... David Lester was becoming more interesting by the second.

Quickly, he dialled Anjli's phone.

'It's me,' he said when she answered, a habit as she would have seen his name. 'I'm leaving the Hampstead house now, and I'll be heading to David Lester. I know you're going there after speaking to Johnny Lucas, so instead, can you get back to Temple Inn and interview Selene Carter when she gets in? I'm about to text Cooper, and tell her to go pick her up.'

There was a pause, a long, surprisingly quiet moment

from Anjli on the phone, and for a moment Declan worried she was angry with him for his meeting with Tessa, a jealousy he hadn't expected.

'Anjli?'

'Yeah, sorry,' she replied down the line. 'I just don't understand why you've called. I'm already at Temple Inn, and Cooper's already out to pick Carter up.'

There was a moment's hesitation, before Anjli finished.

'As per your text.'

'What text?' Declan felt as if he was in the wrong conversation here. 'I haven't sent one.'

'Half an hour back, you sent me a text as I left Johnny's boxing club,' Anjli's voice was concerned now. 'Are you sure you're okay?'

Declan scrolled into his texts, to see if he was going mad, and his eyes widened as he saw his conversation thread with Anjli. At the end was a message, sent almost half an hour earlier.

> Bringing Selene Carter in, and heading to speak to David Lester. Will send details on why she's coming in, can you run the interview? X

'Anjli, I didn't send this,' he said slowly. 'And I only just got out of the Hampstead house.'

'What do you mean you didn't send it?' Anjli's tone was irritated. 'Maybe you should come back and I'll go to Lester's. Maybe your "lunch" has got you all flustered.'

'Anjli, I'm serious,' Declan shook his head. 'Get De'Geer to pick up Lester, and make sure Billy's at his desk. I'm coming back in, and I want him to go over this with a fine toothcomb.'

Disconnecting the call, he stared at the phone message before looking back at the house. He hadn't even arrived there when the text was sent.

It had to be remotely, but how, and *from whom?*

19

HACKED

'I SWEAR TO GOD, I DIDN'T SEND THIS TEXT,' DECLAN SAID AS he stood over Billy, who was currently checking through Declan's mobile phone. 'Also, the times don't match up. I was telling Anjli here to call in Selene Carter before I even knew *why* I'd be pulling her in.'

Billy nodded. He'd plugged Declan's phone through its USB-C port into a device connected to his computer system, and lines of code were scrolling down his vertical screen as he periodically checked it.

'There's every chance something could have come onto your system,' he said. 'But the thought of somebody remote controlling your phone is a little concerning.'

'Aye,' Monroe said, walking out of his office – well, rather, the office he was now using instead of Declan's, with Bullman having taken over his once more. 'First you start having texts from yourself sending to people, the next thing you know you're giving away your secret passwords to Indian call centres.'

The joke was made in jest, but Billy took it seriously.

'They're getting better,' he said, looking back at Monroe. 'I had a call yesterday from Greater Manchester Police.'

'You did?' Monroe raised an eyebrow. 'Have you been a naughty boy, Billy?'

'It wasn't really the police,' Billy said, 'but it was bloody close. A "PC Lewis Hardon" called, said a laptop had been found during an arrest, with some compromising data.'

'Compromising in what way?' Declan smiled. 'Have you been taking photos again?'

Billy reddened and glowered at Declan.

'I don't mean *that* kind of compromising,' he muttered. 'I mean they said they'd found passwords for things like my emails and stuff. They were concerned that this arrest they'd made, and the laptop they'd found, had hundreds of details on it, from hundreds of innocent victims, and I was one of them. And then they started talking about my cold wallet.'

'That's crypto, right?' Declan frowned at this.

'Well done,' Billy almost clapped but probably realised it would be a bit too patronising at this moment in time. 'I have a cold wallet that doesn't connect to the internet, where all my crypto funds are. If I lose my password, I have to use a selection of seed phrases. When they phoned, they told me that this laptop they'd discovered from the arrest had a text file under my name holding twenty-four phrases, and they needed to confirm with me whether I had such a wallet, and if these could have been connected. There was no way they could have known this.'

He leant back in his chair.

'The number matched Manchester Police. They even asked me to check the main website to confirm that the number was correct while giving me a crime number.'

'And at no point did a PC named "Hard-On" warn you

that this could have been some kind of scam?' Anjli waggled her eyebrows suggestively.

'It was an embarrassing surname, probably used to stop someone asking,' Billy shrugged. 'Anyway, they started saying that I needed to go to my local police station to discuss it. And that's when the alarm bells started to ring. I mean, I was suspicious to start with, and I wouldn't have given my details, but I said Temple Inn was the closest, and just carried on as if nothing was going on. And at no point did they click that I was actually a serving officer—'

'Which they would have if they were really from Manchester Police and had your details in front of them,' Declan finished. 'Of course. So, what happened then?'

'Nothing,' Billy said. 'They said to have a chat with Temple Inn the following day at ten o'clock. I left it at that. By that point, I'd guessed it was a scam. Then half an hour later, "customer support" from my cold wallet's company contacted me to let me know that Manchester Police had called them, and they were now checking into it.'

He grinned.

'The problem was they forgot to change their spoof number, the one I saw on the phone. There was no reason why the American call centre for my cold wallet would have called me from Manchester Police Station,' he shook his head. 'I looked into it. There's a lot of people on social media who'd been caught by this. God knows how many people had given away their seed phrases. Hundreds of thousands in crypto coins have probably been removed in that process.'

'And this is related to us how?'

'What we put on social media, on the internet, it can be scraped,' Billy said. 'I'd obviously mentioned crypto somewhere, at some point, and this scraped up, passing it to the scammers. Your AI guy that you went to see yesterday, Brecht? He said they'd worked out who you were from the moment you arrived, purely by checking your face and letting the AI do its thing, scraping news articles and photos. The chances are, at some point, your phone has been placed somewhere, where a small app was able to be stuck onto it. Maybe a piece of coded malware that connects to something off-site.'

He looked back to his monitors, tapping at the left-hand screen, where a picture of Eli Green, taken from his website, was visible.

'The housekeeper said that Eli had been sending her texts when he was already dead. The chances are it was using something similar to what you've got here. Either somebody was replying to her, or it was an incredibly intelligent AI chatbot, responding with answers that the algorithm assumed it actually would need.'

'I have a chatbot on my phone?' Declan asked, half mockingly. 'Can it solve the case for me?'

'The chances are yes,' Billy gave a shrug, 'because it's probably one reason why the case is happening. You want to see something horrific?'

Of course everyone did. Billy grinned, opening up a video. On it, Monroe faced the screen, the background of the office as it was now.

'Billy, I just wanted to say, laddie, that you're a credit to the force,' Monroe said on the video. 'You're like the son I never had. I want to adopt you. The entire team would collapse without you.'

He paused it, looking back at Monroe, who stared at the screen in horror.

'What the shite?' was all the Scot could say.

'It's the latest thing in AI,' Billy replied. 'You put in photos and it can create fake "you" videos. It's being used for company training videos, stuff like that. You add the voice, and that can be generated by a few minutes of real-target audio, and suddenly you can have Taylor Swift endorsing a candidate in an election, or—'

'Or the Guv saying how you're the little gay son he always wanted,' Anjli laughed. 'Projecting much?'

'That was a script, sure,' Billy looked around. 'But tech these days? I could have the AI "be" the Guv. You give it enough data and he could answer questions, chat in real time. There's talk of doing this with historical characters in museums.'

There was a moment of pause before everyone asked Billy if this was the only video he'd made. Billy, reddening, opened up another. It was De'Geer, in full Viking gear, on a mountain.

'Odin!' he shouted before Billy turned it off.

'It was a birthday gift for Cooper,' he muttered sheepishly.

'In fairness, I can see him doing that for real,' Declan said.

'Guv, can I ask a question?' Trying to change the subject now, Billy looked over at Monroe.

'It's never stopped you in the past,' Monroe replied. 'Or, perhaps you ask your wee mini-me it?'

'When Eli Green was found,' Billy started, ignoring the jibe, 'you'd already gone home.'

'Aye.'

'But you came back because you'd left something in the office.'

'Yes, my laptop,' Monroe replied, and then frowned. 'I'd had a reminder on my phone that I had figures that needed to be checked over before midnight. I'd forgotten to do it during the day.'

He sighed.

'In fact, I hadn't even realised I had it on my list, but when I checked my to-do list, it was there, and, well, I was driving past the office, anyway.'

His eyes narrowed as he stared at Billy.

'Are you telling me that my phone's been hacked as well?'

Billy didn't reply, simply holding out a hand, expecting Monroe to pass his phone over, which, surprisingly, Monroe did, without any qualms. Billy attached it via another cable into another port on his computer.

'Two phones helps me a lot more,' he said. 'If you've both got the same coding somewhere, I'll know that you've both been hacked. Where were you last night?'

'Visiting an old friend,' Monroe replied. 'A desk sergeant I used to work with when I was in Mile End. He's retiring. There was a bit of a gathering.'

'Was it in your calendar?'

Monroe considered this and then nodded.

'Are you saying to me that whatever this is saw I was at a pub event, knew that I'd be driving home past the offices, and sent me a reminder to pop in and check my laptop – all so I could be in the offices at the same time that a message comes through that Eli Green was dead?'

Billy shrugged.

'Stranger things have happened,' he replied. 'I mean, in previous years, we've had the DCI there possessed by a spectral hand.'

'That was amateur hypnotism, and we debunked that,' Declan replied quickly. As he looked over at Monroe, he added, 'Leon Brecht. We were both there. We know he uses

AI. We both placed our phones down on that weird table of his that showed his DNA, after he was very insistent we showed we weren't recording him. Maybe there was a way he could hack into our systems through their Wi-Fi?'

'Look into it,' Monroe said, glancing back at Billy. 'Good work. Carry on. I'm not overjoyed that we're being suggested to do things, even if it seems to help us with the case.'

He looked back at the screen.

'Somebody is buggering around with us. They wanted us to be ready for Eli Green's death, and also bring in Selene Carter for something we didn't even know at that point. We're being led by the nose, and I don't bloody well like it.'

'Speaking of Selene Carter,' Billy said, looking up as his screen flashed a message, 'Cooper's just brought her in.'

'Good,' Monroe smiled. 'I'll have a chat with her. Declan can go speak to Leon Brecht, as the AI seems to want him to speak to Lester instead, and I'll be damned if I'm letting it control the case. And Anjli, we still need to have a chat with Aria Milton about the ALS medication.'

'Warren's doing that,' Anjli replied. 'She was feeling a little left out, so I suggested it. She was with me when we first spoke.'

She sighed, cricking her neck as she did so.

'Any news from the courier at Eli Green's house?'

'Actually, yes,' Billy pulled up an email. 'Apparently it was powdered supplements; there was a note on the box saying this. No information on where it came from, though, as the sender's details were corrupted on the server.'

'Convenient,' Declan replied. 'Also, since when does someone say "powdered supplements" on a package?'

'Probably so security don't think it's drugs or something if it goes through a scanner,' Billy looked back at him. 'I use texturing powder in my hair, and if I fly with it, I put it in a little labelled tub so people don't think I'm smuggling cocaine.'

Declan sighed, looking back at Monroe.

'He gets very excitable,' he said.

'Right then,' Monroe looked over at Bullman, who had now exited his office and was leaning against the door, watching them. 'Before Billy here digs himself into any more holes, would you like to go speak to an Olympic silver medallist?'

'Go team,' Bullman said, but her expression and her tone gave the impression that "team" was the last thing on her mind.

Declan actually felt sorry for Selene Carter.

20

SILVER MEDALLISTS

Selene Carter looked nervous and tired, which, considering that less than twenty-four hours earlier she had found a body in a sauna, was understandable. She looked up from the interview desk as Monroe and Bullman entered the room.

'Good morning, Miss Carter,' Monroe said, as he sat down. 'I'm a big fan.'

With no other preamble, he leant across and turned on the recording device.

'Interview at five thirty-two pm. Selene Carter, Detective Superintendent Alex Monroe, Detective Chief Superintendent Sophie Bullman in attendance.'

'Should I have my solicitor here?' Selene asked.

Monroe leant back in his chair, scrutinising her.

'Would you *like* your solicitor present?' he asked.

'I don't know if I need him or not,' Selene replied. 'This feels a little bit more official than I was led to expect. I thought I was coming in to confirm my statement from last night.'

'Oh aye, you are confirming your statement,' Monroe nodded, 'but we also have a few other questions.'

'Like what?'

'Like why you didn't tell us you'd gone into Eli Green's safe in his underground office before you called the police,' Bullman said, her tone sharp.

'I think I need to speak to my solicitor,' Selene said, more adamantly this time, looking from Monroe to Bullman.

'Aye,' Monroe said. 'You probably should do that. We're happy to wait as well. Or ... you could just answer a couple of quick questions for us while we're killing time.'

'What sort of questions?' Selene's eyes narrowed suspiciously.

'Well, we were confused about last night,' Monroe continued. 'You see, I attended the murder scene and saw the body, and it was a very busy house at the time. Lots of forensics already wandering around and scuffing up the carpets. But even I, even with a conversation with a divisional surgeon added into that, managed to get up to the rooftop patio in under four minutes.'

'So?'

'Well, my question is, if you were so concerned about speaking to Mister Green once in the house, you wouldn't have spent as much time as I did standing around,' Monroe explained. 'You would have run to the roof where you knew he would be. And once there, you would have found the body in a matter of a minute or two. Yet you took fifteen minutes before you phoned the police.'

Selene shook her head vigorously.

'No, that can't be right,' she said. 'There was no way it was that long. I don't know, maybe we were confused. I mean, there was a lot of standing around and staring.'

'Was there now?' Monroe asked. 'Because the impression we got from the housekeeper, Mrs Halliwell, is that you demanded she *didn't* call the police, and immediately went down to his underground study.'

Selene Carter shook her head again, but this time her expression was one of calm, almost as if she had expected this question to turn up at some point and had already prepared her answer.

'Mrs Halliwell was hysterical,' she said, 'running around all over the place. She ran down to the study, trying to find his phone. It wasn't by the sauna, and she was convinced the phone would explain everything. He had texted her, you see, and she couldn't understand how that would have happened.'

'And you went down as a shoulder to cry on?' Monroe asked.

'That must be where the extra time turned up,' Selene nodded.

'Aye ... so, it wasn't you entering the study, opening the secret door that led to the safe room, and removing items from it ...'

It wasn't a question. It was stated coldly.

Selene Carter said nothing, simply staring at the two detectives.

'I don't know what you mean,' she eventually blurted out.

'I can see that this has been a testing time for you,' Bullman spoke now. 'So, let me give you a little more context here. You see, we have *also* been in that safe room.'

She placed her elbows on the table, leaning closer as she continued, her voice lowering.

'We found that nothing seems to have been removed apart from a photo frame. A photo frame that was left broken open on Eli Green's desk next door, the photo within removed, as well as the item that had been packed in behind it.'

'I really don't understand why you're telling me this,' Selene spoke, but her voice was rising, more desperate.

'Oh, that's easy,' Bullman smiled. 'You see, we have the photo frame, the safe, the keypad that was used to open it. Even the ornament that opened the secret door. I'm guessing you were flustered; you hadn't expected Eli Green to be dead when you arrived. You thought perhaps he was the one that had killed Stephen Kline. But when you found he was dead as well, you realised there was a moment of opportunity for you. Maybe Eli was holding something on you, something you could now get rid of.'

She looked at Monroe before returning her attention to the onetime Olympian.

'The problem you have, Miss Carter, is when you have a moment of opportunity, you don't often consider the preparations you need to do,' she explained. 'You're not a career criminal, after all. And that means that you didn't think of putting on gloves when you grabbed these items, when you opened doors, when you typed in codes ... which means you left not only your DNA but also your fingerprints.'

'Now, we don't have your fingerprints yet,' Monroe added. 'We don't have proof that your DNA is there. But we have one of the best forensics departments in the world examining it right now. How long do you think it will be before we find you were the one who removed the photo frame from the safe, and then opened it on the desk?'

'I get that this is probably nothing connected to the murders,' Bullman's voice softened now as she continued. 'But you have to understand that *if* you found something that

Eli Green had over you, this is a motive for you murdering him.'

'I was at a school, teaching inner-city students how to run track when he died,' Selene said. 'I was nowhere near him.'

'Then you'll be fine,' Monroe replied. 'But, in the meantime, you can still explain to us what you took. I understand it was a photo taken at the Olympics, where you won your silver medal? A photo that included Eli Green, Stephen Kline and, we believe, David Lester?'

'You're all friends, right?' Bullman interjected. 'All part of the same tournament, so why would you be so concerned about a photo? Although we do wonder what had been folded up and placed behind it? Something that was important enough to stick in a safe for, well, pardon the pun, safekeeping?'

Selene said nothing, her eyes widening. Most likely, she realised the noose was around her neck and had already been tightened, and that Monroe and Bullman were just waiting for the nod to pull the lever that opened the trapdoor beneath her.

'We can wait for your solicitor,' Monroe said. 'If you feel we should.'

Selene sighed and shook her head with resignation.

'I cheated,' she said. 'The Olympics. I was micro-dosing.'

'Go on.'

'I'd trained my whole life for that Olympic medal, and I was so close, but I wasn't fast enough. Not by myself, anyway,' Selene explained. 'That's when I ... I did something I'm not proud of. I used a micro-dosing regimen of EPO – a hormone that boosts red blood cell production. More oxygen, more endurance, better performance.'

She shifted uncomfortably on her chair.

'It was something I shouldn't have touched, but I didn't see another way to stay competitive. Most athletes who get caught using EPO get busted because their levels spike during a drug test, but I had a way around that.'

'Let me guess, one of the others in the photo?'

'David Lester was part of a team that had been helping me,' Selene explained. 'I'd met him at some event years ago. He was working with another company at the time – one he's long since sold on – but he'd showed me some rudimentary AI; we're talking early days stuff. It was a way to get around the sanctions and the rulings. He's obsessed with optimisation, with pushing the limits, and he had this system. It was ... advanced.'

'Advanced enough to beat the drug testing?'

Selene nodded.

'We're talking micro-dosing and AI-monitored blood work, things that could slip right under the radar. Small, carefully timed doses of EPO that would peak when I needed them, but drop back down to safe, legal levels by the time any tests were done.'

As if realising she wasn't explaining herself properly, she straightened in the chair.

'It wasn't just the drugs, it was the technology that made it possible,' she added. 'And then there were blood transfusions. My own blood, pre-stored and reinfused before the race. Again, small enough to give me that edge but not enough to set off any alarms.'

'How did that work?'

'We had clean blood bags, which meant I could transfuse myself with my own blood, previously extracted and stored under controlled conditions,' Selene explained. 'This allowed me to increase my red blood cell count without leaving traces of synthetic EPO. Lester had this AI that tracked everything – my heart rate, oxygen levels, blood viscosity. It was like having a coach inside my body, making adjustments on the fly, telling me exactly how much I could push before the system would notice.'

'So you knew you were cheating,' Monroe said quietly.

'I'm a British triathlete,' Selene snapped. 'My funding was next to nothing under the National Lottery. I was having to take out loans. I was being sponsored by people like *Sports Direct*, for Christ's sake. People in America were being given millions to train, with state-of-the-art VO2 max buildings to work in. I had a lido in Kent.'

She shook her head.

'I convinced myself this was a way of levelling the scales.'

She stopped herself, shaking her head.

'No,' she corrected. 'I was cheating from the very first moment. I didn't expect to win; I thought I'd get a good score, but I didn't expect to be on the podium. When I did, I realised the world was going to be paying a lot more attention to me. And then, when another competitor was removed for doing similar, I realised—'

'You'd broken the law.'

'I was under the assumption it was okay, I swear,' Selene insisted. 'But by then, it was too late. And when I won the silver, my career took off. Suddenly, I could become the brand I'd always wanted to be. My endorsements rose. But there was a secret that was hanging over my head. And there in the audience, when I gained it all, were the people who had helped. Kline, Green, Brecht and Lester.'

'Brecht?' Monroe asked. 'He wasn't in the photo, from what we heard.'

'He doesn't "do" photos,' Selene nodded. 'He was the one

who had brought the AI to the table. David understood it, but he wasn't a slant in the field like Brecht was. This is all my fault, really.'

'What is?'

Selene waved around, and Monroe felt she wasn't meaning the room they were in.

'Because of me and my problems, David Lester reached out to Brecht, brought him on board. Without me, we'd likely never know the guy.'

'You're not a fan?'

Selene said nothing, but after a moment she continued, ignoring the question.

'Anyway, back when it all happened, I made sure that there were no photos of me with any of them. I couldn't have anybody start looking, yeah? Armchair detectives checking the internet and realising there was a story here. I mean, you saw what happened to Lance Armstrong when he played with EPOs and bloodwork.'

She sighed.

'But there was a photo. Taken while I was still on a post-podium high. Brecht took it on his camera.'

'And then what,' Monroe asked. 'You started training for the next Olympics? Commonwealth Games?'

'No, I then said I couldn't do this again, and retired while I was "on top", as they say.'

'So, hold on,' Bullman held a hand up to pause Selene now. 'I see what *you* got here; a medal and endorsements. But what did David Lester get for helping you?'

'David? He gained a real-world trial of his micro-dosing techniques, which he could later market as a high-performance, legal biohacking solution, mainly for those looking to enhance their endurance, without breaking the rules,' Selene shook her head. 'Of course, it was all breaking the rules, in a way. Still, it was the start of his biohacking journey.'

'If you were team "David", why the blackmail photo?'

'It was the Rejuvenation Royale Tournament,' Selene continued. 'When David decided he wanted to go up against America.'

She paused, the weight of her confession settling in.

'I had considered joining, and hearing this, Eli had pushed for me to get involved. I was a name, someone who could help Rupert Cray on the socials, you know? But the first year I came in high, like 0.80 high. I was so far away from the leaderboard it was painful.'

She smiled, and Monroe wondered if it was a memory crossing her mind.

'Anyway, Eli came to see me. He'd helped here and there when I was ... working ... with David—'

'Cheating,' Bullman offered.

'When we worked together,' Selene ignored the comment, 'I didn't think he knew the full extent of the grey areas I was playing in then, believing it was above board—'

'And why would he think that?'

'Because I told him, and I was incredibly persuasive,' Selene snapped irritably. 'But over the years since, he'd collaborated with David on a biohacking supplement for the tournament. He was never going to get *his* age down enough, but he saw a winner in David. Anyway, a couple of years back, he sold his shares with Ionosphere after there was some kind of falling out with Stephen, and he used the money to lean more into this. David was an open book.'

She grimaced, looking up at the ceiling in anger.

'And of course, Eli loved reading books,' she muttered. 'He found my old case studies in David's archives, digging into my past health records and training data, which had been quietly collected by David's monitoring systems. He stumbled across the EPO irregularities, pieced together the truth about my doping.'

'He realised you hadn't achieved your Olympic success naturally?'

Selene nodded, and for a moment she continued to stare upwards before turning her attention back to the two detectives.

'David wasn't the one blackmailing me, Eli was,' she said. 'He realised he had me. While he had the photo and the data, he could make me do what he wanted. Which, weirdly, was to be part of his little cabal.'

'Let me guess, the data he found was printed out and placed in the photo frame?'

'Not that basic,' Selene shook her head. 'An old school SD card wrapped in paper. On it was a folder containing everything he'd leeched off the server.'

'Where is it now?'

'It no longer exists.' Selene's eyes narrowed, and Monroe decided better than continuing along that path.

'When did you find out about this?'

'Oh, he told me he had it at the start of the year,' Selene muttered. 'Needed me to be a "team player" and help herd the others into the meetings at Ionosphere. There we'd take these supplements, work out what worked best on each of us, and see what worked for all.'

'And Kline was there?'

'Oh hell, no,' Selene shook her head. 'Eli and Stephen hated each other by this point, but nobody knew why. Stephen allowed the room to be used, but would leave, staying in reception while we talked about the important stuff. Eli had demanded from the start he wasn't involved. Something to do with Stephen double-crossing him in a deal, probably something to do with when he sold his shares, although I never worked out what it was.'

Monroe leant back on the chair.

'You're aware that all this gives you motive to kill Eli Green?' he asked.

'I didn't want him dead,' Selene countered. 'I just wanted him to give me back my secrets.'

She paused as realisation set in.

'But yeah, I can see how that would look.'

'Interview ends at five forty-six,' Monroe sighed as he rose from the chair, leaning across and turning off the recorder. 'I think we need a wee break here.'

He paused as he looked at the confused expressions.

'A wee as in small break, not as in...'

'We'll come back to you,' Bullman said to Selene as she rose to join Monroe. 'We need to confirm a couple of things, but if you can think of anything else we need to know, solicitor by your side or not ... I suggest you tell us sooner, rather than later.'

21

THE BENDS

AS THE SQUAD CAR REACHED THE INDUSTRIAL ESTATE IN Kingston-upon-Thames, De'Geer – currently driving – turned to face Cooper.

'Be wary of this guy,' he muttered. 'If what the Guvs say is true, then he's going to be able to out-think us before we even turn up.'

'Well, I don't know about me, but no one's really worried that much about out-thinking you, Morten,' Cooper smiled, climbing out of the car and walking towards the main entrance.

De'Geer grinned at this. For everything he did in forensics, he was still jokingly classed as the Big Dumb Viking by Cooper, which he totally understood. She had mentioned in the past that the moment she realised she'd fallen for him, was when he charged off a boat wielding a boat hook like an axe. It was hard to push the scientific side of your personality when all Cooper could see was *Valhalla*.

That said, from what he'd heard about AI videos, Cooper *liked* that side of him. For her quiet, *special* times.

'I'm serious,' he said as they walked towards the doors, shaking away that thought. 'Don't give your phone to anybody.'

'I know how AI works, Morten,' Cooper replied. 'And I would just like to say right now that I'm a fan of AI. I think AI is great and wonderful, and I look forward to the day when our AI overlords take over the planet.'

'What the hell are you going on about?' De'Geer frowned at the comment.

Cooper tapped the side of her nose.

'They're listening,' she said conspiratorially. 'If they can out-think Walsh and Monroe, they can definitely out-think us. And I, for one, want to be treated as well as the useful "good" meat suits when they take over the planet.'

De'Geer punched her lightly on the arm, and the two of them, laughing, walked into reception.

The receptionist was already waiting for them. As they entered, she placed on thick, black-rimmed glasses, and repositioned an iPad in her hand. DCI Walsh had mentioned the glasses, that the company seemed to want their staff to cosplay as Buddy Holly, but De'Geer immediately realised there was something more here.

'PC Esme Cooper, Sergeant Morton De'Geer,' she announced. 'I'm guessing you want to speak to Mister Brecht?'

De'Geer glanced at Cooper, and already gathered from her expression that she hadn't called ahead either.

'Let me guess,' he said. 'AI?'

'More human observation,' the receptionist continued to smile. 'When your colleagues turned up yesterday, the system told us everything we needed to know about your unit. Seeing a seven-foot-tall blond, bearded officer arrive meant it wasn't that difficult to work out who you were. And there aren't that many female police officers in your unit, especially ones you date.'

If it was meant as a show-off comment, it didn't come off as much.

'Great,' Cooper shrugged. 'You know all about us. So how about you answer a question instead?'

'Of course.'

'What did you do to our bosses' phones when they arrived?'

'I don't understand.'

'There's malware on our bosses' phones,' De'Geer continued. 'The only time it could have happened was when they were here.'

'Do you have proof of this?'

'Do we *need* proof?' De'Geer asked, a little *too* pleasantly. 'We can happily get proof. It won't take long to get a warrant to search everything here. And trust me, we have people who can forensically search through computers, no matter how advanced you think they are.'

The receptionist shook her head at this.

'I think it might have been a misunderstanding,' she replied. 'They would have joined the Wi-Fi system when they were sitting and waiting for the meeting. There might have been a small package that was downloaded at the time; you know, in the same way that when you go to a coffee shop and you turn on the Wi-Fi, you have to go through a particular signup page.'

'Are you telling me that our bosses deliberately downloaded malware that could affect their phone?'

'Oh no, not at all,' the receptionist replied quickly. 'I

personally don't think they did at all. But you seem quite insistent and I wanted to see if I could help you.'

The way she spoke was so emotionless, De'Geer was wondering whether she was a robot as well.

'Anyway, we'd like to see your boss,' he said. 'We've been asked to bring him in for questioning.'

'Bring him in?' The receptionist paused at this. 'You came to us last time, we didn't have to ...'

De'Geer held a hand up to stop her. He didn't know if it was the way she spoke, the familial way she dealt with them, or the fact she kept saying 'we' when in fact it should have been 'he', but he'd just about had enough of talking to the underlings.

'Leon Brecht, now,' he snarled.

'Of course.' The receptionist tapped the side stem of her glasses. 'Location request. Leon Brecht.'

She paused and then nodded.

'He's downstairs in the main warehouse.'

'I'm sorry, how did you know that?' Cooper asked.

The receptionist pointed at the glasses.

'AI in the frames,' she said. 'It's connected to our server. It's the same style as what you get if you were to buy a pair of Meta Ray-Bans, although we're not allowed to listen to music through them. It means that whatever we're doing, if a message comes through we get it instantaneously. If meetings are changed, we get given the revised schedules. And with the tap of a button, we can ask where somebody is, and get an answer.'

She smiled, and it was the beatific smile of a zealot.

'We all wear them, this is the future,' she said. 'Now, let me take you to Mister Brecht.'

As they walked down into the ground floor warehouse area, De'Geer could see why DCI Walsh had claimed it was a "Nolan Batcave". However, he felt it was more like *Unbox Therapy's* YouTube channel, where a man would open up packages in a similar-looking room. It was filled with various devices and machines, though – and, for a second, De'Geer wondered if this was Leon Brecht's version of Eli Green's "Iron Man" cave they'd found in his basement.

'What's he doing down here?' Cooper asked, checking her watch. 'Surely at the end of the day he wouldn't be moving things around or ...'

'Oh no, he doesn't come down here to work.' The receptionist pointed at the far corner. 'He comes here to rest. We have a hyperbaric chamber down at the end.'

'Like the one that Ionosphere have?' De'Geer asked. He'd seen it while they were examining the spa after Kline's murder, and it had interested him to the point he'd started checking into it.

'Well, I mean, it's the same by description,' the receptionist said, and De'Geer could tell that from her tone she was a bit unimpressed with the statement. 'In the same way that you can look at a McLaren and a Fiat five hundred, and call them both "cars".'

De'Geer gave a small, humourless grin.

'Of course,' he said. 'Mister Brecht is obviously way more advanced?'

'AI technology infused with a blended oxygen mixture,' the receptionist started her spiel now. 'The pressure can therefore go to a higher level while still feeling lower. We also have a rotating set of LED lights that goes through a visual entrainment mask.'

'I'm sorry, a what?'

'Visual entrainment masks are devices with pulsing lights you wear over your eyes, while keeping them closed,' the receptionist's tone had changed; it felt like she was talking to a five-year-old now. 'The lights flash in patterns to influence your brainwaves, kind of like how certain music can pump you up, or calm you down. These masks help you relax, focus, or meditate by syncing your brain to different frequencies, like sleep or alertness. Simple as that – lights flash, brain responds, you feel different.'

De'Geer was starting to *not* understand the words she spoke, but he understood the basic gist. Leon Brecht had created his own high-pressure sleep pod, something that would help him when he needed a nap.

'And how long has he been down here?'

'Oh, no more than an hour,' the receptionist said. 'He only does this for ninety minutes. More than that could, well ...'

'Fry his brain?' Cooper offered, and De'Geer was sure he heard the faint tone of optimism in it.

'No, but if he was to go higher in the hyperbaric pressure, it might not help,' the receptionist replied, picking up on the tone as well. 'If we haven't heard from him by then, we'd come down and check on him, but usually his system automatically restarts himself.'

That she was using terms like "automatically restarts" and "systems" for a human being hadn't been missed by De'Geer.

The thought of Leon Brecht being more than man was definitely a branding here.

'Yeah, all right,' he said, deciding to bring the *TED Talk* to a close. 'Shall we wake him up then?'

As they walked over to the hyperbaric chamber, however, the receptionist started to hurry in front.

'That's not right,' she said, nodding to a table beside the chamber, where his phone, his smartwatch and his wallet had been left. 'He rarely takes them in with him, but *that's* new.'

The new item she was referring to was a small plastic bottle with what looked to be some kind of green liquid inside. De'Geer frowned at this; it reminded him of the kind of nutrient smoothies you could find in health stores like Holland & Barrett. It also had a surprisingly familiar texture and look to the spilt smoothie that had been left beside the body of Eli Green.

'Where did he get that?' he asked.

'No idea.' The receptionist walked over and was about to dip her finger into the smoothie, perhaps to taste it, but De'Geer was able to grab her before she did.

'I wouldn't,' he warned. 'If it's what I think it is, you won't have a good day. We need to open this now.'

'We can't,' the receptionist muttered, her eyes widening in horror. 'He's pressurised. If you were to immediately open it—'

'Then how do I open this door?' De'Geer interrupted.

'You have to do the close down sequence and allow it to naturally move,' the receptionist's eyes were wide, like saucers now as she read the display. 'Oh God. It's at 2.5 ATA now.'

'What's that mean?' Cooper walked to the chamber door and looked to be about to start yanking at the handle.

'Usually you go in around 1.3 ATAs, or atmospheres,' the

receptionist typed hurriedly. 'The pressure inside is double that.'

'Is that a problem?'

With trembling hands, the receptionist turned off the chamber.

'Of course it bloody is!' she snapped, all attempts at being "emotionless" now gone. 'At that pressure, oxygen toxicity kicks in fast. We're talking seizures, pulmonary toxicity, lung damage – he could collapse at any moment! And if he tries to come out too quickly, he'll get the bends. He needs to stay calm or this'll kill him.'

De'Geer noticed that although inside the chamber there were purple neon lights lighting up Leon Brecht, he wasn't moving. There was spittle at the side of his lips, the same colour as the smoothie, possibly from maybe throwing some up while unconscious.

But he didn't seem to be breathing.

'Can you go faster?'

'And risk barotrauma and pneumothorax if he doesn't equalise properly? I don't think so.'

Eventually, the reading reached "1", there was a beep, and the hyperbaric chamber turned green, the lights inside giving it the all clear to be opened. De'Geer immediately yanked it open, possibly harder than he should have, hearing a crack as something probably broke inside. He didn't really care though at that point, pulling out the unconscious Brecht, checking his pulse, and then bringing him to a sitting position beside the chamber.

'Ambulance, now,' he instructed Cooper, who was already dialling for one.

The receptionist, ashen-faced, knelt down, staring at her boss.

'We've got to pump his stomach or something, right?' she glanced around frantically. 'We don't have the equipment for that – nothing that's safe—'

'If we try to make him throw up, he could choke,' De'Geer shook his head. 'What about charcoal? It's in some first aid kits, might slow down the absorption.'

'We don't have a first aid kit down here,' the receptionist tapped her glasses frame. 'First aid kit to the warehouse, now.'

'To be honest, it'd only be worthwhile if he's conscious enough to swallow,' Cooper, now finished with the call said as she leant in and checked his pulse. 'He's barely responsive – we can't risk it.'

She shifted Leon onto his side, careful to keep his airway clear.

'At least this way he won't choke if he vomits,' she said.

'Okay,' the receptionist said, trying to steady her voice as she looked from De'Geer to Cooper, her panic barely contained. 'We just need to keep him stable until the ambulance arrives?'

'Check his breathing,' De'Geer ordered. 'If he stops, we're doing rescue breaths, got it?'

Cooper nodded, focusing on the shallow rise and fall of Leon's chest.

'He's probably okay now,' she said. 'If it's what Green had, it was a sedative more than a poison. They wanted him to sleep out the end, as the pressure rose.'

'Who's "they"?' The receptionist stared around the room, as if expecting someone to appear, twirling a moustache and going "mu ha ha".

'Actually, I was kind of hoping you could tell us,' De'Geer

forced a tight smile. 'First, by finding out how that bloody smoothie got here.'

The receptionist walked off, spoke into her glasses, and then returned.

'It was a delivery,' she said. 'Not the smoothie; we have our own. But apparently Mister Brecht received a powdered supplement. Luxor Aesthetics sent it.'

'Did they now?' De'Geer looked over at Cooper. 'I'll stay here and check the scene. You go with Brecht.'

He glanced back at the chamber.

'Let me guess,' he said. 'It can be connected from anywhere, and AI controls it?'

The receptionist dumbly nodded.

'Do you know who did this?' she whispered.

'Well, if it was anyone else, I think my superiors would probably have fingered your boss for it,' De'Geer shrugged. 'But I think that's a little unlikely now.'

22

A TURN FOR THE WORSE

IT WAS LATE IN THE AFTERNOON AT LUXOR AESTHETICS WHEN Warren arrived. She'd borrowed one of the pool cars for the journey; even though she'd had a car when in Newbury, Canary Wharf didn't really require having one usually, or she'd gain a lift from one of the squad cars. The joys of living in Central London, it seemed, was that there was always a bus or a train within a few steps.

Of course, it didn't exactly help when you needed to go to see a suspect.

Anjli Kapoor had originally been planned to go to speak to Milton, but Warren had been at a loose end – and, as she'd been there the first time as well, she'd offered to go in instead.

Warren also got the impression that although the team seemed happy enough to have her there, she was still very much a third wheel on a bicycle.

She'd gritted her teeth a little at that. She'd *always* been the third wheel when it came to these sorts of things. Still, at least there'd been some movement with Monroe. She still thought he was an arrogant, drunken prick, But at least *one* of those three things seemed to be a lot less these days.

Arriving at the building at Canary Wharf, she'd been surprised to find that the doors were closed. After repeated banging for about three minutes, a young woman, most likely the receptionist, came running over, looking frantic. She was waving her hand and shaking her head as if trying to say that *no thank you, we're busy*, but Warren pulled out her warrant card, and slammed it against the glass, her expression one of somebody who was not giving any shits about people being busy right now.

The receptionist had paled, opened the door, and allowed her in.

'I'm sorry,' she mumbled. 'It's just we've got a bit of a problem.'

'Unless it's Aria Milton dying, this is not a problem that I care about,' Warren replied and then paused as she saw the stricken expression on the receptionist's face. 'Christ, I'm sorry, *is* Aria Milton dying?'

The receptionist was already hurrying back towards the elevators, and Warren followed.

'Seriously, is she okay? Should we be calling an ambulance?'

'No ambulance,' the receptionist shook her head. 'Anything a hospital would do is nowhere near as advanced as we have here. It's best if we stay.'

'Is it the ALS?'

The receptionist paused, almost as if she were surprised that Warren knew about this.

'Miss Milton told us when we were last here,' Warren explained.

'She'd been coughing and had tremors for a while,' the

receptionist nodded. 'Last night it got worse. Stress isn't great for people with ALS; she'd been coughing over the day, and had some tremors, but then late in the evening she'd had a fit and felt really rough. Then this morning, she had difficulty swallowing, and her temperature was dangerously high. We've been trying to think of anything we could possibly add into her supplements to try to force it back.'

There were tears brimming in her eyes now.

'I don't think we've got anything else.'

Warren understood. Milton had said when they first met, that the form of ALS that she had was so aggressive that once it started it'd hit hard and fast, and wasn't going to stop anytime soon.

'Did she have anything?' she asked. 'Yesterday evening? Any drinks, smoothies?'

'Only what she usually would have.'

'Did she send any out?'

As Warren asked this question, the doors of the elevator opened and they hurried in. The receptionist slammed the button for the fourteenth floor.

'We don't deliver,' she said. 'Our blended mixes are too specific, and temperature-cooled. It's not like we can sell them at *Holland & Barrett* or something.'

'You're saying you didn't send smoothies to Eli Green?'

At this, the receptionist frowned.

'No,' she replied. 'Also, there's no point. Eli Green has his own supply.'

'He does?'

'Oh, yes.' The doors now opened and she almost ran out onto the fourteenth floor. 'Aria designed it with both Eli Green and also Leon Brecht. The nutrient macro process was created by Mister Brecht's AI, and also through Mister

Green's machines. There'd be no point her sending him product when he can make whatever he needs.'

Warren wanted more than anything to pull out her notepad and start writing this down, but she knew that this wasn't the time to be seen as asking questions connected to the crime; temperatures were too high right now and the data could get skewed. As they hurried through into Aria Milton's office, there, laid out on the couch like an ageing movie star on a chaise longue, was Aria Milton.

It had been twenty-four hours since Warren had seen her last, but the change was dramatic. She was twitching uncontrollably as if she had the onset of Parkinson's. Her hands were gripped as if clenched tight, and she had a sickly pallor to her skin.

'Miss Warren,' she said with a faint smile, 'I'm afraid I'm not really up to seeing guests today.'

Warren didn't argue. Instead, she came and sat beside her, grabbing her hand.

'I'm sorry to see you like this,' she said genuinely. 'I'd come to speak to you about something else, but it can wait.'

Milton shook her head.

'No, please. It would be a diversion from what I'm having to do at the moment.'

She indicated what looked to be a saline drip coming out of her other arm.

'I'm being pumped with every single vitamin and anti-inflammatory cocktail that you can possibly think of,' she said. 'I won't have to eat for a week after this, my nutrient levels will be so sated.'

She coughed, a racking fit that flushed her face, giving it the first colour it had seen in a while.

The receptionist, who by now Warren had realised was

more than just that, who had seemingly been working as a personal nurse for the last few hours, started fiddling with the bags on the stand, and Milton irritably waved her away.

'If they're not working already, they're not going to work if you squeeze them some more,' she muttered. 'Just leave them. Let me be for a moment.'

She looked back at Warren.

'What is it you wanted to ask?' she inquired. 'I'd suggest you ask it here. I'm not really in a state to travel at the moment, and by the time I am, it might be too late.'

Warren went to reply but paused as her phone buzzed with a message. Apologising, she pulled it out to check.

It was from Temple Inn.

> Leon Brecht found unconscious in a hyperbaric chamber, same cocktail in body that Eli Green had. If you see Milton, ask her about this too. Email coming with more.

Her email app pinged with more information, and she quickly checked through it. The information was light, basic even, but from what she could see it'd only happened within the last hour or so.

Regaining her composure, she looked up at Aria Milton.

'I wanted to ask about Eli Green ... and Leon Brecht,' Warren started. 'You know that Eli Green was killed?'

'I'd heard he died,' Aria nodded. 'Selena was telling everybody on the WhatsApp. No offence, detective, but I kind of felt that she was gloating a little.'

'Well, she can gloat in a cell,' Warren muttered to herself, not realising it had come out loud. 'I'd actually come to ask about Green's death, but I've just had a text that says Leon Brecht has also succumbed to one of your smoothies.'

'My smoothie?' Milton frowned. 'I don't understand.'

'Apparently, and I'm not a hundred percent sure on the former as it's just happened, but both Leon Brecht and Eli Green were found with one of your Luxor Aesthetic smoothies in their hands,' Warren explained, checking through her notes to make sure she had the right information. 'Inside both was a homemade concoction of midazolam and riluzole, the latter of which I believe you're quite familiar with.'

Milton started coughing, nodding as she did so.

'You can check my medical records,' she said. 'Every item of medicine I've been given I can account for.'

'Which raises the question of who gave them to you,' Warren asked, finally pulling out her pen, ready to write in her notebook. 'You see, I'm guessing that with your ALS being secret, you're not gaining your supplies over the counter at the chemist.'

'No,' Milton sighed. 'Eli was providing me with the riluzole, through some clinic in Switzerland, and actually, he was helping me with midazolam as well. I used it as a muscle relaxant when taking my more taxing treatments. It would sooth my muscles, make it easier to sit.'

She shook her head as Warren's statement now caught up with her slightly drug-fuzzied brain.

'Are you telling me Leon's dead as well?'

'No,' Warren replied. 'From what I can tell, we got to him in time. But someone was trying to remove him from the looks of things. Or he'd done it to himself. The thing that both situations had, though, was that your drink was with them, laced with this sedative cocktail, delivered in a powdered supplement form and stirred in by the unknowing victim.'

Aria Milton gave a weak nod.

'Leon Brecht and Eli Green wouldn't take it from me,' she replied. 'They'd use their own supplies if they were taking it.'

'Yes, your receptionist mentioned that—'

'My receptionist,' Aria Milton chuckled. 'She's my niece. She's been beside me ever since we started.'

Warren looked over at the receptionist/niece.

'Sorry,' she said. 'It was just because you were downstairs.'

'I'm fine with it,' the niece replied. 'My name's Carole, with an E. I can show you the manifest for all of our drinks if you want. If somebody gave doctored versions, it certainly wasn't from Luxor.'

'And supplement powders?'

'We do make those, but they're bulk produced and hard to alter from the outside,' Aria admitted. 'If someone's added medications, they're bespoke, and not made here.'

Warren nodded. *This was not the time to be asking questions about motivations and such.*

'I asked Carole before we arrived here, but I thought I'd ask again,' she said. 'Did you take anything different, or out of the ordinary last night?'

'Just my medicines,' Aria replied. 'And these have been provided to me specifically by Eli and Leon. I've been taking them for months, all designed from Leon's AI algorithms. I can't see him giving me a bad batch, if that's what you're about to ask.'

'We would like a listing of your current medicine intake, with samples—'

'With respect, Detective Superintendent, I'm not going to do that,' Aria Milton sat up with great effort to face the woman sitting next to her. 'I'm sure your forensics people are incredibly good but, my forensics people are *geniuses*. I'll have them look at it and whatever they find I'll let you know, because believe me, if I find that somebody's trying to kill me by hastening my crippling and chronic illness, I'll want them brought to justice even if it happens after my death.'

After this statement, Aria leant back and shut her eyes.

'Listen, before I go,' Warren said, straightening up, 'if there's anything, any statements you can give in relation to this – and what happened with Stephen Kline – now would be the perfect time to do it.'

'What, some kind of last confession?' Aria laughed, though the sound lacked humour. 'I've taken a turn for the worse, Detective Superintendent Warren. I'm not dead yet. I don't *intend* to be dead yet. This is a blip. I'll fight it. I'll work out what's happening and I'll beat it, like I have the last couple of years.'

She frowned as a thought surfaced.

'I will say something, though. It might not be relevant. I didn't really see Stephen that evening. He'd been distant for a few weeks. I don't know if it was still fallout from the Summit or if other things had happened, but ...'

She shrugged.

'Alexis looked after me, as I said when I spoke to you before. She's an intelligent kid, but a little too caught up in Leon's AI messiah nonsense. She's not the clumsy, innocent person you think she is, though. I've watched her. She plays the mousy assistant, but that woman's a stone-cold killer.'

'You think?' Warren's expression darkened.

'She wanted to know all about Mira after it came out that she was Stephen's daughter. I didn't know how she'd found out. I assumed Stephen had mentioned it, but later, I found out he hadn't said a word to anyone—'

Another racking cough cut Aria Milton off, and Carole

with an E stepped closer, her eyes warning Warren off from continuing. Warren, realised this was probably not the time to pursue the line of questioning, gave her apologies to Carol with an E, and with a final hand squeeze to Aria, partly for support, but also because she didn't really know what else to do, she turned to leave the office – however, Aria Milton reached out and grabbed her by the arm.

'You're not part of them, are you?' she asked.

'How do you mean?'

'The police investigating the case. They're City police. But you're not, are you?'

Warren's face set, as she now stared coldly at Milton.

'Are you saying I'm not a copper?'

'No, of course not. But you were there first, weren't you? Because your area covers Canary Wharf. You're Met police.'

'What about it?'

'Did you know that Stephen Kline was an informant for the police?'

Warren nodded as she crouched back down beside Aria.

'It's one reason he left Manchester,' she explained. 'One of the officers I'm working with dealt with him when he was up there.'

'I don't mean in Manchester, I mean in London,' Aria shook her head weakly. 'He said it once, in passing. He mentioned that in his old life, which I'm guessing was Manchester, he informed on the father, while in London, he informed on the son. They would meet in his office. And somebody in your unit, I think someone of your level, even, would take information from him. I assumed it was you ... you know, with you being from the area.'

Warren shook her head.

'It's not me,' she replied, 'but I can look into it. Thank you.'

This promised, Warren gave Aria Milton another nod, and then made her own way out of the building.

WALKING OUTSIDE INTO THE EVENING AIR OF CANARY WHARF, Warren glanced back at the building, hearing the door lock behind her. The building was dead to the world once more, and Warren doubted anyone else would be entering that night, unless they were a genius level medical professional.

She pulled out her phone, sending a message to her own team, rather than Temple Inn. If Kline was informing to someone there, she was pretty annoyed that nobody had considered mentioning this to her. The message sent, demanding answers, she turned to head towards the car park, but then stopped abruptly; across the road, a man, his jacket hood up, glanced furtively in her direction before quickly looking away and walking off in the opposite direction. It could have been nothing, but something about him niggled at her instincts.

Without thinking, Warren started walking towards him.

'Hey!' she shouted. 'Stop right there!'

The man quickened his pace, and Warren, muttering under her breath, broke into a run.

'I said stop!'

The man glanced over his shoulder, and for a moment, it looked as if he was about to bolt. Warren knew if he started sprinting, she wouldn't stand a chance of catching him – she wasn't exactly known for her track and field abilities. But just as she braced herself for a chase, it was as if he decided it wasn't worth the hassle.

He stopped, hesitated, then slowly pulled down his hood,

revealing the face of David Lester behind his orange-tinted glasses.

'I was coming to see Aria,' he said, his voice steady, though his eyes darted around nervously. 'I was worried she was ill.'

'She is,' Warren replied, glancing back at the building. 'And I'm pretty sure you're already aware how ill.'

'Do you work at Luxor?' Lester asked, and Warren almost smiled; he'd never met her before, and had assumed, as she'd left the building, she was an employee.

'No,' she replied, reaching into her jacket. 'I was just visiting. Funny enough, I was going to visit you, too.'

'Oh?' Lester frowned at the statement, and Warren straightened.

'You're a hard man to find, Mister Lester,' she smiled once more as she pulled out her warrant card, showing it to him. 'And we'd like to have a chat with you.'

Lester looked as if he was going to run again, and Warren prepared to grab at his arm, but instead he seemed to come to an internal decision.

'I'll come with you on one condition,' he said.

'And what's that?'

Lester looked around the clearing, taking a deep breath, and letting it out slowly.

'Keep me alive,' he stated.

23

EVENING VISITORS

Right then, I know it's late in the day, but things are a little all over the place,' Monroe said, leaning against a desk in the main office. 'And I really can't be bothered to go into the briefing room right now. Give me updates.'

'Selene Carter has been released,' Cooper said from the side of the office where she leant against the glass wall, notepad in her hand. 'She had alibis for both murders.'

'What about the CCTV?' Anjli asked. 'The nail bar?'

'Just come in,' Billy replied as he looked back from his monitors. 'There's a figure by the door, but you can't make him out.'

'Him?'

'He's balding, you can see the scalp,' Billy showed an image; it was blurred, distorted by the glass, but visible. 'He comes in at eight, and leaves about nine thirty. In a hurry, too. Waiting for enhancements to give me more on his face, but rendering it is taking time.'

'Could be Eli Green, but he's in Thailand. Brecht, perhaps? He's thinning on top,' Declan suggested.

'Well, I would have said it was Brecht, but now he's in hospital,' Billy said, looking over at Cooper. 'Do we have an update?'

'He's fine,' Cooper replied. 'I mean, he wouldn't have been if he'd stayed in there longer. Bad things would happen the more the pressure went up. Apparently, things can happen slowly at normal pressure, but when you double or even triple the pressure, they get real crappy, real quick.'

'Do we know who sent the supplements?' Monroe asked, looking over at Anjli sitting at her desk. 'I'm guessing Aria Milton's the obvious choice.'

'She *is* the obvious choice,' Anjli replied, leaning back on her chair, 'which is why I don't think it was her.'

She looked around at the room.

'Think about it. An obvious Luxor Aesthetics smoothie is filled with drugs, including ALS medicine, specifically aiming us at Aria Milton,' she shook her head. 'Considering the fact that both Eli Green and Stephen Kline were actively trying to keep her alive, I can't see her being a murderer. Also, Warren's spoken to her, and she reckons she can provide receipts for every scrap of medicine she's been given. Which means that if someone's using riluzole, it's not from Aria Milton's supply.'

'Do we know who *was* supplying her?' Declan asked. 'I mean, if she's keeping it quiet from everybody, this has to be something that's being done under the table, right?'

'It was,' Anjli nodded. 'According to Warren's quick call on the way back here, she was gaining it from Eli Green.'

There was a moment of pause before Declan started to bitterly laugh.

'We're going around in circles,' he said. 'Eli Green's killed by the same medication that he's providing Aria Milton.'

'But where's *he* getting it from?' Anjli asked. As she spoke, however, the doors opened to the office, and Warren walked in. The man standing with her was a familiar figure, wearing his hair down for a change, not keeping the ponytail he was more known for, his orange-tinted glasses hiding his eyes.

'Meet Mister David Lester,' Warren said, waving a hand vaguely in his direction. 'It seemed he wanted to go into hiding.'

'And you found him? Good work,' Monroe nodded at Warren before turning his attention to Lester. 'You're a hard man to find.'

'Do you blame me?' Lester snapped back angrily. 'Stephen and Eli dead, Leon near as dammit, Aria suddenly having symptoms hit her that she hasn't seen for years? Who's next?'

'We were hoping you could tell us that,' Declan said, looking over at Cooper. 'Could you put Mister Lester in interview room one, please?'

'I'm not a suspect,' Lester replied, glaring across the room. 'I'm a victim.'

'Aye,' Monroe said. 'You're very much a victim. And if you keep staying out there in public, you're going to become a victim *way* quicker.'

David Lester grumbled to himself as Cooper motioned for him to follow her – although he didn't argue the case, probably because he knew that staying in a police unit was the safest place he could possibly be right now.

Warren walked over to the desk that she'd claimed when arriving and sat down, staring around at everybody.

'What have I missed?' she asked.

Monroe went to answer her ... and then paused.

'How did you find him?' he asked.

'What do you mean?' Warren frowned. 'You're saying I can't do police work?'

'No, not at all,' Monroe sighed, deciding not to argue the point. 'It's just, I'm curious whether you found him on your own steam, or whether somebody helped.'

'Ah,' Declan nodded from the side, looking back at the confused face of Warren. 'You weren't here earlier on, so you won't know. AI seems to be running our case for us.'

'Okay, what?'

'Both the Guv and my phones were hacked, giving text message orders from me to bring in suspects before we even knew they were suspects. Last night, when you and the Guv went to see the Hampstead house, it was this AI hack that made sure he returned to the office to be here when the call came through.'

He leaned back, looking around the room.

'Leon Brecht's AI knew exactly who we were. It knew everything about us. It was able to work out what we were going to do, what we thought, even, based on the public reporting of our previous cases.'

He turned his attention back to Warren now.

'Therefore, as you can appreciate,' he continued, 'if you found yourself with a sudden clue leading you in a particular direction, it could mean that they've got you as well.'

'Or have they?' Billy asked, half-rising out of his seat before Warren could reply. 'No, seriously, think about it. Sure, they've got us. They found press on us and the algorithms have deep-dived, and the AI knows exactly what we're doing before we do, but Detective Superintendent Warren isn't part of our team. She's only here because she gained a job at Canary Wharf.'

'Thanks for making it sound so small,' Warren said, but she wasn't angry; it was almost said in jest.

Billy reddened.

'I mean, Guv, there's every chance that whoever's doing this hasn't entered you into their system yet,' he said. 'Every contestant is in there. All their thoughts, their regimens, everything is in this, whatever this is.'

He looked up towards the door that led to the stairs, where moments earlier Cooper and David Lester had walked.

'David Lester worked with AI,' he said. 'Maybe he *is* doing this—'

'Or maybe it's Brecht,' a new voice spoke as Doctor Marcos entered the office. 'Don't you find it convenient that *just* as we were about to look into him as a suspect, and bring him in for questioning, he's suddenly attacked?'

'You think he faked his near-death experience?'

'Have you ever read an Agatha Christie novel?' Doctor Marcos smiled as she walked over to one of the empty desks, wiping the surface clean as she continued. 'How many times have the bad guys shot themselves in the arms, so people think they've been attacked by the killer? This could be the same sort of thing. Think about it. Here you are, about to be taken in. You gulp down some smoothie, knowing all it's going to do is give you a nice sleep. Stick yourself in a hyperbaric chamber. Crank it up and have a lay back down.'

'What if nobody entered?' Anjli argued. 'What if De'Geer and Cooper had been kept back from seeing him?'

'But they weren't, were they?' Doctor Marcos smiled. 'I think even though Brecht is a candidate for victimhood here, maybe he's not, if you know what I mean.'

Declan went to reply, but stopped himself.

It made sense.

'Anyway,' Doctor Marcos held up her iPad. 'I've got news.'

'Go on,' Monroe offered, pinching at the bridge of his nose, probably trying to stave off a headache.

'So, I've been examining the DNA markers,' Doctor Marcos sat on the desk, reading from the iPad as she continued. 'I was curious whether anything else had happened at that Summit, and I found a very interesting thing. Everybody who worked with David Lester at taking down the Yanks – so, we're talking Mira, Eli, Selene, Aria – all of them have the same genetic abnormality.'

'That doesn't sound good,' Monroe said.

'It isn't,' Doctor Marcos replied. 'To explain why, I have to explain about something called Gen-Clear. It's a novel, experimental therapy, patented by Eli Green, created by one of his pop-up laboratories a couple of years back, that falls under what we would classify as senolytics. Essentially, these are compounds designed to eliminate senescent cells – cells that have stopped dividing but refuse to die, contributing to inflammation and accelerating the ageing process. In theory, by clearing out these cells, you can improve overall cell function and potentially slow down or even reverse certain aspects of ageing.'

'That's why Bullman does cryo therapy,' Declan said. 'She told me in the car.'

'Sure, there are a lot of ways to improve cell function, but what makes Gen-Clear unique – and banned in a dozen countries, hence why he probably hasn't done much with it – is its modified telomerase activator, which doesn't just clear out senescent cells but also tries to repair telomere length,' Doctor Marcos continued, reading her notes as she spoke. 'Telomeres are the protective caps on your DNA strands that shorten as you age, and shorter telomeres are linked to age-related diseases. The compound they used – and by "they" I mean these bloody idiot biohackers – incorporated a rare peptide chain that could alter how telomerase behaves, potentially allowing cells to regenerate for longer. But it left a distinct marker in the genome, a marker that all the contestants who used this treatment now share.'

'You're saying it's branded them at a genetic level?' Anjli raised an eyebrow. 'Permanently?'

'Well, here's where things get tricky,' Doctor Marcos shrugged as she looked across the office. 'The long-term effects of this are unpredictable. There have been cases of unregulated cell growth, which can lead to benefits like faster muscle regeneration or tissue repair, but it can also cause cells to behave erratically, creating a higher risk for cancerous growths. Whoever created Gen-Clear for Eli – as it's way higher than his medical ability – added this peptide chain to track its distribution, but they may not have fully understood – or disclosed – the risks involved.'

'And how do we know about Gen-Clear?' Monroe frowned now. 'I mean, for us luddites?'

'Eli Green had the notes on his desk,' Doctor Marcos explained. 'I picked them up when we examined the Hampstead house, and I've been deep diving all day. Fascinating, if you really fall down the rabbit hole.'

'But you said Milton had this too,' Anjli was noting this down, frowning as she looked up. 'Surely she was playing with fire, what with her ALS?'

'Maybe, maybe not. ALS – Amyotrophic Lateral Sclerosis – is a disease that degenerates motor neurons, leading to muscle weakness and eventually paralysis. One of the more controversial theories is that stimulating telomerase activity could help with neurodegenerative diseases by promoting cell repair and protecting neurons,' Doctor Marcos was pacing now, the iPad forgotten. 'In Aria Milton's case, the unpredictable cell growth might have actually stabilised her symptoms temporarily, giving her more motor function than she would have otherwise. But the downside is that the same mechanism might cause erratic or uncontrollable cell behaviour elsewhere. Essentially, it's a double-edged sword; it helps her in one way, but it could also put her at extreme risk.'

She let the information sink in.

'What we're dealing with here isn't just a case of off-the-books treatments. It's a ticking time bomb. Everyone who took this experimental treatment has altered their DNA in ways that could help them in the short term, but hurt them in the long run. And the question we need to answer is who knew this, and who was willing to kill to keep it quiet?'

At this, Monroe whistled.

'They've changed their DNA.' He shook his head. 'That's insanity. Why would you do that?'

'It's a common thing in some places,' Doctor Marcos replied. 'In America, you can have the genomes changed in an unborn child, if you really want, while it's still an embryo. You know, clean it out. Make sure it's the perfect baby when it's born. Genetically superior, intellectually acclaimed. And don't even get me started on CRISPR.'

'Isn't CRISPR, like genetics for rich people?' It was almost as if Billy, now sucked in, couldn't help himself. 'And before you all play the obvious response, I mean richer than me people. *Way* richer than me people.'

'CRISPR's a tool that lets scientists cut and edit DNA, like a high-tech pair of scissors,' the venom in Doctor Marcos's voice was audible as she replied; not at Billy for asking, but at the fact this actually existed. 'It helps them target specific genes, remove or fix them, and it's being used to potentially treat genetic diseases and improve crops. The technology's adapted from bacteria, which use it to protect themselves from viruses.'

'You sound like you're not a fan,' Declan said carefully.'

'While it has incredible potential, there's still concerns about its safety and ethical implications, especially when it comes to human gene editing,' Doctor Marcos replied. 'And that's where it can become questionable. At what point does ethnic cleansing start being used, things like that.'

'That's how the eugenics wars started in *Star Trek*,' Monroe muttered to himself. 'We're not supposed to be living in a world that sounds like the bad things in *Star Trek*.'

'Well, that's not the only thing,' Doctor Marcos replied. 'We know that at the Summit, Stephen Kline had a stand-off fight, right? We know Eli Green was so angry that he stopped providing his items to be sold in Ionosphere. And we know that Stephen Kline stepped back from even attempting to enter the competition.'

'Because Mira was his daughter,' Declan said.

'I'm not sure if that's the whole story,' Doctor Marcos replied. 'You see, Stephen Kline had the same Gen-Clear abnormality as well.'

'How?' Declan frowned at this. 'He said he wasn't part of the meetings. He wouldn't have known what they were doing ... unless, of course he was listening through that secretly hidden CCTV that Alexis Kovalenko told us about.'

'He could leave them to their meeting, go to another room and just listen to them,' Billy suggested. 'Whatever they were doing, whatever tests worked, he would go off and do it himself, nice and quiet, like.'

Anjli shook her head.

'So, what? He realised that he had the same abnormality, and that if he joined the tournament publicly, he'd be found out?'

'I'd guess,' Declan replied, considering it. 'I mean, if it was an obviously "secret group" thing, and he rocks up with the same DNA abnormalities, they'd know immediately that he was doing that. That he was spying on them. Could be enough to kill him—'

He paused, looking back at Doctor Marcos.

'There's one name you didn't mention, when you said who had this. Leon Brecht.'

'Yeah, that was deliberate,' Doctor Marcos replied. 'You see, Leon Brecht doesn't have the Gen-Clear abnormality. Whatever they did that gave them it, he never took that treatment. I would guess it was probably because he's so convinced his AI will win, anything that wasn't suggested by the AI just isn't being looked at by him.'

'Or, he knew better not to,' Warren suggested.

The team considered this as the phone in Declan's office, currently commandeered by Monroe, started to ring. With nobody in there to answer, after a couple of rings it stopped, and the phone on Anjli's desk copied it.

Answering it, Anjli listened, thanked the person on the other end, and looked back to Declan.

'That was Sergeant Mastakin on the front desk,' she said. 'He called to tell you your girlfriend is here.'

She smiled as she glanced at a confused Monroe.

'I added that last part. I meant Tessa Martinez is downstairs, says it's important.'

Declan rose from his chair, internally wincing that Anjli took the call.

'It could be connected to the case,' he said. 'I'll go check.'

'Aye, you do that,' Monroe wasn't really paying attention. 'We need to work out what we're missing here. I feel we've finished the jigsaw, but the pieces aren't in the right places.'

EMERGING INTO THE RECEPTION AREA, DECLAN GLANCED across to the desk sergeant, who nodded out of the main doors.

'Seemed stressed,' he said. 'Said she needs some air.'

Following Mastakin's nod, Declan walked out of the crime unit, into the cool evening air of King's Bench Walk. Ahead of him was a small car parking area, and beside what looked to be some kind of Mercedes SUV, Tessa stood waiting.

'I'm sorry, Declan,' she said as he approached, and this almost paused him mid-stride, but as he walked closer, the doors opened and two large, vicious-looking men emerged from the driver and passenger-side doors.

Declan stopped now, cocking his head.

'You're outside a police station. You sure you want to do this?' he looked back to Tessa. 'What the hell?'

'I didn't have a choice,' Tessa was already backing off, heading towards the entrance to the Inns of Court. 'He wanted a chat, nothing more.'

As this was said, the door to the side of the SUV opened, and a man, sitting on the back seat leant over. He was young, maybe in his late twenties or thirties, built like a wrestler and wearing what looked to be a bespoke suit and tie. His head was almost shaved, the cut leaving nothing but stubble, and at some point he'd had a nasty injury to his nose, which was flattened slightly to the right.

'I'm Michael O'Rourke,' he said. 'I understand you've been looking into my father?'

Declan took a moment to adjust, then walked to the car.

'There are easier ways to do this,' he snapped. 'Rather than using my friends as bait.'

Michael considered this, nodding, and then looked back at Declan, his eyes now in the evening light a steel grey.

'Has the AI started out-thinking you yet?' he asked, simply. 'Have you realised you need to act out of character to force it to reset yet?'

He indicated the two men, who'd not moved since exiting the vehicle.

'Well, this is me acting out of character,' he said with a shrug. 'So how about you get in, we'll go for a little drive, and I'll tell you why Stephen Kline was murdered.'

24

DRIVE TIME

DECLAN SHIFTED IN THE BACK SEAT OF THE SUV, PULLING ON THE seatbelt as Michael, or rather Mickey O'Rourke, son of Connor O'Rourke stared out of the window at the Thames. They'd turned southwards after leaving Temple Inn; Declan had the impression they were on a particular route, but he wasn't sure.

He was also a little concerned that he didn't have his phone with him; Billy had still been checking it over, and when Declan had gone downstairs, he'd not expected to be going on a trip.

'Who's your main suspect?' Michael asked, suddenly breaking the silence. 'I mean, it's obviously not Green, as he's dead too.'

'You seem to know a lot,' Declan kept his voice level, relaxed. 'How about you explain why you're kidnapping me?'

'It's less a kidnapping, more a "time-out" in a way,' Michael shrugged. He turned back to the window, his face conflicted, as if he wanted to say something but didn't know how to. Eventually, he looked back at Declan.

'You know he was a scumbag, right?'

Declan raised an eyebrow.

'You're going to have to give me more than that,' he said.

'Stephen Kline. He was an utter scumbag. Cheating bastard. Con artist of the highest order,' Michael O'Rourke spat the words. 'He took my dad for a ride, and when Dad asked for his money back, he ran.'

He settled back into the seat now.

'Cheating, grassing wanker.'

As much as Declan was impressed by the various expletives used, he felt there was more here than just a rant. So, he paused from replying, allowing Michael to continue.

'My dad met him when he was in Manchester,' Michael continued. 'My granddad, yeah? He had Alzheimer's. Took him away from us years before he died. Poor bugger didn't even know who we were at the end. I don't think he even knew who *he* was. Terrible illness. They say it's genetic, that families can have it come down the line.'

He turned to face Declan.

'My dad saw it happen to his dad, and he was terrified it was going to happen to him,' he explained. 'So he looked for ways to stop it happening. Miracle cures that could save his dad and then, when that failed, make sure that he'd never have that problem. He'd always said he'd rather die in a drive-by than lose his brain piece by piece.'

Declan was getting an idea of where this was going.

'Let me guess,' he said. 'Stephen Kline offered him a way out.'

'Kline reckoned he had the way to keep cognitive function going,' Michael nodded. 'Said he had data to back it up. He'd been working with American tech magnates and Swiss AI experts. Said he knew exactly what to do to make sure that my dad would never have to worry about it.'

He wound the window down, leant outside and spat.

'It was all snake oil though,' he said. 'Utter bullshit by a con artist who just wanted money. His company was collapsing, and he needed to keep getting investors in. Took my dad for one point five million in the end. Claimed that this was a small price to pay for immortality.'

He wound the window back up, returning his attention to Declan. His eyes flashed angrily.

'I'm glad he's dead, but I didn't do it,' he said. 'I'm stating that right now. I wish I'd never met the guy.'

Declan guessed that this was something important to Michael. After all, kidnapping a police officer wasn't exactly something you'd do if you weren't that bothered.

'I understand he was paying the debt's interest, but nothing else,' he said.

Michael nodded.

'Not only was he arguing about paying the debt piece by piece,' he said, 'he'd also decided he didn't want to pay the bloody thing in full. He'd begun informing for the police. I think he hoped that if he could get my dad put away, he wouldn't have to pay the debt. Bloody naïve, if you ask me.'

His eyes narrowed.

'You always pay the debts you owe.'

Declan really didn't want to owe Michael O'Rourke a debt. He was like Jackie Lucas on steroids. It made him wonder exactly what debt Tessa had owed, and whether it stemmed from Manchester.

'What happened next?'

'Bugger tried to get my dad arrested, and when that failed, he ran away to London,' Michael sighed. 'My dad? Well, someone like him relies on his reputation, you know. You piss off the O'Rourkes, you get hurt, you screw with us, you disappear.'

He smiled for the first time.

'Hypothetically, of course, Detective Chief Inspector.'

'Of course,' Declan replied, still unsure what was going on here. By now they were moving eastwards towards Tower Bridge, turning left – north, heading to Shoreditch. It felt like they were looping, but Declan couldn't be one hundred percent sure of this.

'People heard that my dad had been played.' Michael shook his head in anger. 'All those gangsters, all those rival gangs ... and it was a sodding biohacker, a second-rate scumbag that managed to make my dad doubt himself. After a while, it got to where unless Kline paid the debt, Dad was a laughing stock. In the end, Manchester became somebody else's playground. Didn't help that the police were still trying to arrest him while this was going on. My dad had done nothing.'

Declan kept quiet. Tessa Martinez had been the one who was trying to bring Michael O'Rourke's father down. He hoped she wasn't in the crosshairs of whatever this was.

'I understand you're the next generation of O'Rourke,' he said, 'in more than just a name.'

'Let me guess, Martinez told you that?' Michael replied, now taking an interest in what Declan was saying, shifting around to face him. 'Did she say what I do?'

'She said you're more computer-based,' Declan replied. 'That it's easier for you to destroy somebody online than it is to break their legs.'

He let the moment draw before carrying on.

'We have someone like that too. He's very good at what he does as well.'

It wasn't a threat; just a reminder that if Michael tried anything, Temple Inn would be there waiting. But instead of arguing this, Michael O'Rourke just laughed, bitterly.

'I thought I was shit hot at it,' he replied. 'Dad gave me the best education, sent me to university ... I was going to become the next UK-based tech millionaire, get away from the business, you know? And then I realised that with all my knowledge and everything I had, I was still non-league compared to the Premier League hackers out there.'

He leant forward, tapping the driver.

'Three random turns,' he said. 'Just in case.'

'You've kidnapped me,' Declan said, raising an eyebrow. 'Which, although I don't really know you, does seem to feel a little out of character. And now you're getting your driver to take random roads. How long have you been scared of AI watching you?'

Michael shrugged, using the opportunity to stick his head out of the window and look around once more. Declan realised this wasn't a contemplative look – it was concern.

He believed he was being watched.

'AI like patterns,' Michael said. 'You change the pattern, you confuse the AI, if only for a second.'

He turned and smiled.

'Has it told you what to do yet?'

'You mean AI?' Declan asked, intrigued.

'*It*,' Michael corrected, not bothering to hide his disdain. 'We started finding messages we hadn't sent, things that had hacked into our system. I'm not exactly a Fortune 500 company or anything, but when you realise some of your men are being told to do things you didn't ask them to, you figure out quickly you're being set up for a fall.'

'Leon Brecht,' Declan nodded.

'Yeah, he's a candidate,' Michael replied. 'Him and that Yank with the ponytail.'

'But, why are you so scared?'

At the question, Michael gave a short laugh.

'My dad was owed money by Stephen Kline, and I had a go at him – publicly. Then you've got Eli Green, who, when my dad was conned by that scumbag, was Kline's partner. Another man who could've been taken out by me for revenge. And now I've got an AI out there trying to convince people I'm the murderer. Once it's decided on the best course, it'll keep convincing you until it works. Algorithms upon algorithms bouncing around. Why do you think I'm worried?'

'Do you know who killed Stephen Kline?'

'I've got my suspicions,' Michael replied cagily. 'To be honest, I thought it was Eli himself – until he died.'

'Eli couldn't have done it,' Declan replied. 'He was in Thailand.'

'No, he wasn't,' Michael shook his head slightly, a knowing look crossing his face. 'He never went to Thailand in the first place. It was all a con.'

'We've got data that shows he flew out.'

'But, as I've been saying, data can be altered. Sure, Elias Green bought a ticket. Sure, the system says Elias Green flew. But which one? Show me CCTV footage of him going through customs. Show me footage of him in Thailand. Whatever he was doing, *he* wasn't there. But if you tell people you're going there on the social media sites, and then you send your namesake son so the name matches? Well, then the AI doesn't realise yet. It's not up to that level. The narrative isn't changed.'

Declan chewed at his lip.

'Are you saying Eli Green could've killed Kline?'

'Yeah, although I don't think he would've though,' Michael replied. 'He was trying to get my money back, but needed Kline alive for it.'

He laughed, but it was a bitter, mirthless one.

'This bloody tournament thing Kline was involved in – he was convinced it was going to make millions.'

'Tournament?' Declan asked, narrowing his eyes. 'You mean the Royal Rejuvenation one?'

'Two million dollars given when he got through to Vegas, ten million when he won,' Michael explained. 'He told me, the last time we spoke, that I'd have the money by the end of the year, guaranteed. Then two months ago, Kline rings me, saying he's dropped out of the tournament and can't deliver. But, don't worry, he's got a new plan. He's going to inform on someone again, but this time, it's to a yank organiser for a carload of money. Next thing I hear, Eli Green's telling me he has another plan to get Kline to sell his shares over, so I have a hundred percent. I ask why the hell I want his bloody spa, but Eli says it's not just the spa, it's the data. Starts talking about genomes and access to immortality. But it was just a hard sell for a shit franchise.'

Declan paused, thinking through what he'd just heard.

'Wait,' he said, his voice sharp. 'Eli Green sold you his Ionosphere shares a year back?'

Michael leaned forward, grinning.

'Didn't you know? Kline and Eli were thick as thieves. They both took out the loan. Sure, Green made a big show of selling his shares and walking away, but he was priming me for whatever was going on, selling me a million quid's worth of assets for a pound. Clearing his debt with paper, rather than money. Promised me Kline would follow suit, but that ... well, it was taking time, especially as they had a massive row a couple of months back.'

'You know what the row was about?'

'Of course. Kline didn't want to give me his spa,' Michael shrugged. 'Reckoned he could find the money another way; another of his bullshit "get rich quick" schemes. But Eli had sold his half, made a massive loss, and still found himself tied to Kline while he wouldn't play ball. It's why Eli didn't go to Thailand. He was giving himself an alibi.'

'For the murder?'

'Christ, no!' Michael laughed now, the first genuine humour Declan had seen from the man. 'For his torturing of Kline! Forcing him to sell to me rather than some yank billionaire who'd pay him enough to run away again!'

Declan was understanding now.

'But I'm guessing it didn't happen, because Kline died,' he said. 'Who gets the company now?'

'Whoever Kline left his shares to when he died,' Michael replied, his tone returning to one bordering on anger. 'And now I find myself with shares I can't sell, and a debt I still can't get.'

He chuckled.

'So I guess I'm as bad as my dad, after all. We're here.'

Declan looked up and saw they were at the Fleet Street entrance to Temple Inn, having driven in a randomised circle. The SUV pulled over, to the annoyance of the cars behind, and Declan climbed out.

'One last thing,' he asked, looking back at Michael. 'You said you had your suspicions on who killed Stephen Kline?'

'Yeah, because Eli called me yesterday afternoon,' Michael replied. 'He was furious about Stephen being dead, convinced someone screwed with the cryotherapy chamber. Kept saying it had to be him.'

'Him?'

'Brecht,' Michael continued. 'Said the only one who could have hacked the system was Brecht. Said he'd even had a row with him that morning, saying he knew, and he was going to make sure *everyone* knew.'

'Well that sounds like a reason to kill Eli Green if ever I heard one,' Declan replied as he stepped away from the car. 'Problem is, Brecht wasn't there at the time, as he was with us, and now he's in hospital as someone tried to do the same to him.'

'Whatever, DCI. Solve the case, so I can sell my shares,' Michael shouted out. 'And don't trust anything Brecht says or does. That man's so advanced, he can land a doughnut on your table one day so you find a body on the next.'

Before Declan could mention that Brecht was in hospital, the car had driven off, and Declan was alone on the street.

Well, that was interesting.

He looked up, following the SUV as it drove off, Michael O'Rourke's last line in his thoughts.

'Don't trust anything Brecht says or does. That man's so advanced, he can land a doughnut on your table one day so you find a body on the next.'

There was something about it, something familiar. He narrowed his eyes, trying to recall ... and then the conversation with Alexis Kovalenko came to mind.

'But, what about Joseph Lawrence? How did he find himself there?'

'He ate a doughnut. Decided he'd had too much sugar or carbs or something like that.'

'Apparently, he'd woken up feeling bad and decided he wanted a last-minute cryo session.'

Was Michael O'Rourke saying that Leon Brecht's AI was so advanced, it could create a witness from a tasty sweet the night before?

As Declan hurried back to the offices, he had a rather concerning feeling that it was.

And the thought terrified him.

25

PONYTAIL

David Lester looked haunted as he stared up from the interview table at Bullman and Warren. Monroe had wanted to go in, but Billy's suggestion of Warren being a wild card weighed heavily on his mind, and he was happy for anything that helped at this stage – so Lenette Warren now sat to Bullman's side.

'It all started after I was kicked out of the West Coast group,' he began, his voice trembling. 'They accused me of inappropriate behaviour with younger women. It was all lies, but it didn't matter. I was out, and I was angry.'

Warren leant forward.

'So, you came to London?'

'I had offices here. It was enough to qualify for the UK tournament,' Lester nodded. 'But I wanted revenge. That's when I met Brecht again.'

'You knew Brecht already, right?' Bullman asked. 'Worked with him?'

Lester shook his head, and was about to reply when Bullman raised a hand to pause him.

'For the record, you didn't work with Leon Brecht when you helped Selene Carter cheat her way to a silver medal?'

Lester really hadn't been expecting that as a question. His mouth opened and shut as his brain caught up.

'No, I mean I think he was involved, but I never worked with him, on a personal level,' he explained, with the blurted tone of a man improvising a new line of narrative. 'I'd met him a few years back, sure, and we were part of the same scene and all that, but he was Europe-heavy, while I was still in the States. I only helped Selene because she reached out to me.'

'You help people who reach out?' Warren gave the impression of a woman who did *not* believe that. 'Out of the goodness of your own heart?'

Lester gave a sheepish, almost embarrassed smile, a slight shrug of his shoulders as he replied.

'One of her competitors was Gail McLean,' he mumbled. 'I don't know if you remember or if you paid attention at all ... she was the American prospect for the gold medal in the triathlon – and she was my ex.'

'Are you telling me you joined with Selene Carter, turning against your own national team because you were *pissed off with your ex-girlfriend*?'

'Well, when you say it like that, you make it sound so petty,' Lester muttered, with a laissez-faire attitude that quickly faded. 'But she was my wife, if only for a year. And then she left me for her coach. It felt bigger at the time.'

Warren looked at Bullman, and saw that she too had realised that this was likely some kind of mask.

'It seems to be a common thing with you, doesn't it?' Bullman now spoke, leaning back in her chair as she faced the American. 'You're pissed at your ex-wife, so you team up with a rival, purely to what, beat her? And then years later, you're pissed off at your own country's biohackers and you team up with a whole load of others to do the same.'

'It wasn't just about the emotional side,' Lester argued, straightening as he spoke. 'There were financial reasons as well. I knew that if we could get this working, find a way of getting the micro-doses correct, there was a chance ... well, there was a lot of money being made in the sporting community.'

'You were illegally micro-dosing augmented blood, something that was prohibited.'

'It was a grey area,' Lester replied, although his expression seemed one of someone who didn't really believe what he was saying. 'Anyway, she didn't win, Gail still got gold, and I tired of the project.'

'You mean you didn't get your revenge, and you decided not to play anymore? Take your toys and leave?' Bullman shook her head.

'Go on then, explain to us what happened next,' Warren said, and her tone showed that she definitely wasn't a fan of David Lester.

'I bought and sold some more companies,' Lester replied with a hint of arrogance, almost as if he was arguing with the woman in front of him, proving a point as he did so. 'I started taking part in the RRT when it started, but when I was in the finals, in Vegas two years ago, there were some problems.'

'I understand you wanted to sleep with teenagers or something,' Bullman offered.

'It wasn't like that at all,' Lester retorted. 'Sure, I've an interest in younger women. That's the point of the anti-ageing community, to make ageism a thing of the past! I know people in their eighties who are making friends with people in their fifties, because when you're in your eighties and in *this* community, you've got the brain and body of someone in their sixties, and your eighty-year-old friends are dead, so you start hanging out with people younger.'

'I think there's a difference between fifty-year-old people hanging out with eighty-year-old people, and fifty-year-old people sleeping with teenagers,' Bullman replied.

'Nothing I did was illegal,' Lester snapped back. 'Everybody I had a relationship with was at least twenty-one years old, legally allowed to drink.'

'And that made it all okay.'

David leant back in his chair and, for the first time in that talk, gave a smile.

'Yeah, actually it does,' he said. 'You guys can't talk. Your age of consent's two years younger than ours. So don't start going all "holier than thou" on us. We've got more morals than you have, it seems, when it comes to sex with younger people.'

He shook his head, realising he was diverting from the topic at hand.

'Anyway,' he continued, 'I made the mistake of sleeping with the daughter of one of my rivals. They were pissed. And when I came third, and looked like I was becoming a rising star – which is a stupid thing to say when you're someone of my age, as by now most people are retiring and thinking of their next career – they started bad-mouthing me, smearing my name.'

He sighed.

'There was a chance my previous indiscretions could have come back out, and by that I don't mean women.'

'You mean the micro-dosing in the Olympics,' Warren finished for him.

'In a roundabout way, yes,' Lester replied. 'Anyway, Rupert Cray was pissed about it.'

'Why did Rupert Cray care?'

'I might have slept with his daughter as well.'

At the revelation, Bullman raised an eyebrow.

'It's starting to sound less that you had a thing for younger women, Mister Lester, and more a thing for daughters of people who you classed as rivals.'

'As long as they're of age, it doesn't really matter, does it?' Lester replied, effectively confirming her deduction. 'Anyway, Rupert wanted me out, a lot of the Americans wanted me out, but what could they do? I was number three in the rankings, and I was putting a lot of money into the industry. I'd even sponsored half the events. They needed to keep me in, but out of the way, so I made it easy for them.'

'You moved to London.'

'I was coming over here anyway,' Lester shrugged. 'I'd met Brecht at a bio-hacking event in San Francisco. As I said, I'd barely known him before, but we had a relationship of sorts, and while we were talking, it came up about what had happened after Vegas, and my anger and frustration with the Rejuvenation Council.'

He laughed at this.

'That's what they call themselves, the Rejuvenation Council. Like they're some kind of elite cabal of immortals or something, rather than some fat Americans with money who think they can live forever if they just pump themselves with NAD boosters and suck on some methylene blue.'

He realised he was ranting and paused.

'Anyway, talking to Brecht, I realised he was unhappy with the scene as much as I was.'

'And why would that be?'

'He was an AI guy,' Lester replied. 'If there's one thing that people hate more than, well, people like me, it's AI. But Brecht was still donating, and he'd kept in contact with Kline and with Eli Green. I'd known them during the Olympics agreement, too.'

'Is that what you call it? The "agreement"? How noble a term for such a small venture.'

Lester didn't reply, simply glaring at Warren across the table until Bullman waved for him to continue.

'Both of them have been friends of Rupert for years, and they agreed to talk on my behalf. At this point, Kline was looking for anybody who'd be his friend. He'd managed to piss off most people by that point, was hanging with Manchester gangsters and he owed money to pretty much everybody. I helped him out, sorted out a small angel donation to his company and the next thing I know, they've all gone to speak to Rupert and convinced him that, "hey, let the American play with us for a while, he'll be out of your hair and the chances are he won't even hit the top twenty, yeah?".'

'And that's why you joined the London leaderboard.'

'Don't get me wrong,' Lester said, and by now his fear had eased, the confidence returning as he spoke on things he knew. 'I'd still have to be one of the top twenty biohackers in the world to get through. That's a percentage that is infinitesimally small.'

'You make it sound bigger than it actually was, though, don't you?' Bullman replied. 'I mean, saying that you're the top twenty, it's like when people say they're the fittest man or woman in the world because they won an international CrossFit event, when actually they're only the fittest out of all the CrossFitters who joined in that particular event. You're the fastest marathon runner out of the marathon runners.

You're the youngest person, out of all the other people who are trying to be the youngest person – it's not exactly billions.'

'You don't think that billions are trying to live longer?' Lester asked. 'You don't think billions are trying to add a few years, make themselves look more youthful? The anti-ageing industry is one of the biggest growing industries in the world right now, Detective Chief Superintendent. There are billions upon billions of dollars being made *every day*. Trust me, it's not as niche as you'd like to think it is.'

He drummed his fingers on the table for a moment; the rhythm zoning him out before he continued.

'Anyway, as I said, after I moved to London, Brecht approached me at a biohacking event.'

'In London?'

'No, San Francisco. I was bouncing back and forth at the time,' Lester replied. 'Somehow, he knew everything about my situation. He suggested we could do more than just win the tournament – we could destroy the American competition entirely. Brecht had this AI system. He said it could analyse patterns in human behaviour, predict outcomes, all that shit, yeah? At first, I thought it was just for optimising our anti-ageing treatments. But it was so much more.'

'How so?' Warren pressed.

'We used it to choose our team,' Lester explained. 'And by that, I mean who we thought would be up for joining us, pooling resources, "greater good" and all that. Brecht's AI analysed every promising contestant in the UK tournament, with a predilection to ones who were in London, or connected to us in some way. We felt it'd be easier to gain people if we already knew them. It predicted who would be most likely to collaborate, who had the best chance of lowering their biological age significantly ... that's how we ended up with our group: me, Aria Milton, Selene Carter, Mira Nakahura, Leon Brecht and Eli Green.'

Bullman's eyes narrowed.

'And Stephen Kline?'

Lester shook his head.

'Eli brought us Selene, saying she was a good name to have on the team, and she owed us, so wouldn't be able to turn on us, in case we destroyed her career. And it helped I knew her. Mira had been suggested by Brecht; at the time we didn't know she was Kline's kid. Just that she was fixated on him. More so than his creepy assistant.'

'Alexis?'

'Yeah, she was another one of Brecht's suggestions too,' Lester laughed. 'He had worked with her through some summer internship, part of her college degree. You call it university degree here, right?' Maybe you should be talking to Leon about his predilection for young girls, eh? Either way, she was his eyes and ears at Ionosphere.'

He continued to drum on the desk as he chose his next words.

'Aria Milton, she was the most desperate of us all. ALS is eating away at her nervous system; she told us she had maybe a year left, tops. This tournament wasn't just about glory for her; it was quite literally her last shot at life. She believed that if she could win, she'd have the funds and the platform to push her experimental treatments through FDA approval, and maybe gain something from Leon's AI. She was all in, even before we asked.'

'We understand Eli was blackmailing Selene into doing this.'

'Well she didn't really have a chance to opt out, but she was still in it for her own reasons.'

'And what reasons were they?'

'She was convinced her "natural" methods—' Lester added two finger "quotes" when saying this '—could beat our tech-heavy approaches. I think she saw winning as a way to launch an entire empire of wellness products and services. Didn't stop her using our tech-heavy ideas when her "natural" ideas shit the bed."

Lester's expression softened slightly as he mentioned the next name.

'Mira Nakahura, she's ... complicated. Brilliant investor, always calm and collected on the surface. But underneath, there was this driving need to prove herself. She'd known for years that Stephen Kline was her father, but he had no idea. None of us did, until recently.'

'How did you find out?'

'They had a screaming match at the Summit, and it came out,' Lester shrugged. 'Obviously it wasn't there with accreditations and legal proof and Jerry Springer, but you could see it once you knew it. I think she entered the tournament hoping to impress him, to force him to acknowledge her in some way. When he found out and reacted badly, it crushed her.'

He looked directly at Warren and Bullman now.

'But here's the thing, right? None of us realised at first how Brecht was playing us all. He knew everyone's motivations, their weaknesses. Aria's desperation, Selene's ego, Mira's daddy issues ... he used all of it. And me? I was so blinded by my desire for revenge against the American contestants that I didn't see how deep I was getting.'

Lester's voice dropped to almost a whisper.

'And Eli ... I think he was the first to suspect something wasn't right with Brecht's AI. That's probably why ...'

He trailed off, unable to finish the thought.

'It was just a strategy to win. Nothing illegal about teamwork,' he eventually finished, but his voice lacked conviction, a far cry from his usual self-assured tone.

'Teamwork that led to two deaths?' Bullman's words hung heavy in the room.

Visibly shaken, Lester recoiled.

'No! I never ... that wasn't supposed to happen.'

'Then what was supposed to happen, Mister Lester?'

Lester seemed to struggle to articulate his thoughts, his brow furrowing in frustration.

'We were just ... I thought ... it made sense at the time.'

'What made sense?' Bullman interjected.

David Lester's eyes darted around the room, as if searching for hidden observers. His voice dropped to a near whisper.

'He always knew. It was like he could read our minds.'

'Read your minds how?'

'His AI,' Lester blurted out, the words tumbling from him now. 'It wasn't just for anti-ageing. He said it could optimise decisions.'

'Optimise decisions for the tournament?'

'I guess.' David Lester seemed jumpy now, looking up into the corners. 'Anyway, Kline wasn't supposed to be part of it. He was just providing the meeting space at Ionosphere, through Eli. But then we discovered something that changed everything.'

Warren's phone buzzed; she glanced at it, looking back at Bullman.

'It's my office,' she said, confused. 'I'd asked them to give me some information. I'll be back in a minute.'

'For the recording, Detective Superintendent Warren is

leaving the room,' Bullman continued as Warren, taking the phone and dialling, left the interview room. 'Did you know you screwed with your DNA?'

David Lester's eyes hooded, as if a great weight had suddenly been pressed upon him.

'Yeah, I knew,' he replied. 'When we worked out that we had the same abnormalities, we started looking into it.'

He leant back in the chair, staring up at the ceiling, and Bullman got the feeling there was more here that he hadn't said.

'This abnormality,' she continued, 'it's not as advantageous as people think it is, is it?'

Lester shrugged.

'It's lowered our ageing,' he mumbled. 'Our telomeres are longer. And in ideal situations, it could add years onto our lives.'

The way he said it, it sounded like he didn't believe it. He glanced down at his hands, turning them over as if searching for wrinkles or lines.

'The problem is, it's like we've injected nitro-glycerine into us,' he explained. 'Our DNA has changed and, well, we've played God a little too much, shall we say.'

'So you could die?'

'It's pretty much a fifty-fifty coin toss at the moment,' Lester muttered. 'One minute you could be absolutely fine, and the next, an aneurysm could appear out of nowhere and kill you instantly. Or you'd find yourself with an aggressive form of cancer that, instead of taking years to kill you, would wipe you out in a matter of days, weeks, even. Think of every terrible illness that could end you, ramp it up to ten, and those are the things that could happen to us now that our

DNA has been altered. Sure, in some ways we might be better off than others, but in other ways ...'

He shook his head.

'I spent millions to create DNA that would make us better,' he explained. 'And now all I can do is hope someone can find a way to reverse it, to kill off the thing that's been changing our DNA.'

26

INFORMANT

As Declan returned upstairs to the office, he saw a commotion around Billy's monitor desk, his "space cockpit", so to say.

'What have I missed?' he asked, frowning.

'That depends,' Anjli looked over at him. 'You've been a while. What have *I* missed?'

'A Manchester gangster who needed a chat,' Declan smiled. 'No need to worry. Again though, what's going on?'

'Billy's found something,' Anjli looked back to Billy, still working on the keyboard. 'And before you see it, I don't want you getting too annoyed.'

Declan raised an eyebrow.

'Why would I get annoyed?' he asked.

'Because Alexis Kovalenko used us, laddie,' Monroe smiled, but it wasn't a humorous one. It was more a "I'm sorry that you're going to be annoyed about this" one.

'Can someone please tell me what's going on?' Declan looked around as Billy reached onto his desk and picked up a pen, holding it up to show him.

'This is the pen that Alexis Kovalenko dropped under Anjli's desk.'

'Okay, so why should I be concerned about that?'

'Because it's not a pen,' Billy continued. 'It's a Wi-Fi based live streaming recording device. She's been recording us.'

'Not so much recording, more listening to us live,' Monroe added, and there was more than a hint of anger in his voice. 'When she came in and dropped her items, she deliberately made sure that this pen stayed. She wanted to be able to hear what we were doing at all times.'

'That's not the only thing,' Billy added, reaching over and picking up a tiny-looking camera. 'This was left in the canteen after she was allowed to sit in there, doing her university work. Cooper found it after I raised my suspicions.'

Anjli sighed, leaning back on her chair.

'Can we just stop letting people walk around out here, planting bugging devices wherever they want?'

'It does seem to be something we do well,' Monroe muttered.

Declan considered what he just heard, his eyes narrowing.

'So, basically,' he said, 'Alexis Kovalenko has been able to hear everything we've discussed in this office and in the break room.'

'And there's a chance this microphone could have picked up what was coming through the briefing room as the doors never shut,' Billy added. 'Video upstairs might not have picked it up, but audio can get into another room even through thin walls. Either way, it does make something a little clearer for me.'

He leant back, placing his hands behind his head, interlocking his fingers as he rested against them.

'Ah, crap,' he suddenly said, rising from his chair and running towards the stairs. 'Back in a minute!'

IN THE INTERVIEW ROOM, DAVID LESTER GAVE A VERY LOUD AND almost theatrical sigh, but Bullman didn't think he was being theatrical. It seemed the weight of everything had finally hit him.

'There's no chance of success here in fixing you?' she asked.

Lester shrugged.

'I don't know,' he admitted. 'The one man who had an idea of how to fix this is dead.'

'Eli Green.'

'It's amazing how industrious you get when you realise you're also in the firing line,' Lester nodded. 'Green reckoned he knew a way to do this. Unfortunately, we'll never know if it worked or not.'

'What was the plan?' Bullman asked.

Lester looked up, and for the first time, started to laugh.

'Apparently, intense freezing,' he said. 'Standing in a cryotherapy chamber beyond the point where you're comfortable – you literally freeze it out of you, multiple times. Why else do you think Stephen Kline willingly walked into a cryotherapy chamber?'

Bullman wasn't sharing the humour.

'Therefore, in a way, Brecht was right not to take it,' she said.

'What do you mean, he wasn't taking it?' Lester frowned.

'We've examined the DNA,' Bullman replied. 'Our divisional surgeon looked into it, and Brecht doesn't have the DNA markers.'

Lester sat up straight now, his expression sharpening.

'But he was taking it,' he muttered. 'We did it together.'

He shook his head, confused.

'I don't understand.'

His fingers started drumming on the table, a nervous tic. Bullman tapped the table gently to regain his attention.

'Are you okay?' she asked. 'I mean, apart from the obvious DNA thing.'

Lester stared at her, his expression hollow.

'I'm making decisions I don't remember,' he said. 'It's like I'm being led in directions I wasn't expecting. Last night, I met the guy who saw Stephen Kline's body. Did you know he was Kline's financial advisor? I looked into him. Made me suspicious.'

'Why suspicious?'

'He worked with Mira. And with Eli's son,' Lester said as if it was the most obvious thing in the world. 'All for the same investment bank. I think he got Eli's son the job, too, as he was dealing with the sale.'

'What sale?' Bullman was getting frustrated now.

'They were selling the business,' Lester leant back, scrunching his eyes as he tried to focus. 'O'Rourke and Eli. They were trying to get Kline to sell, but he wanted to literally give the place away to Cray. The man, Joseph Lawrence? He'd found a way to bypass this. All they needed was Kline to sign one document and it was done.'

Lester pulled off his orange-tinted glasses and rubbing his eyes before putting them back on.

'It's a distraction,' he muttered. 'Everything's a distraction.'

'Who do you think killed Eli Green?' Bullman leaned forward, her eyes narrowing.

Lester paused, then sighed deeply.

'Well, that's a good question. It could have been any of us,' he replied. 'Gen-Clear was his idea, after all. We were giving him one last chance to fix things.'

Tears welled up in his eyes, and he wiped at them with his sleeve.

'I don't want to die,' he said, his voice cracking. 'I shouldn't have to. I've got too much to give. There's no reason Leon shouldn't have that DNA problem. He didn't cheat. He showed us the DNA. The DNA showed that he had the same abnormality.'

'Maybe he showed somebody else, and was using their DNA to lie?'

Lester fell silent, his mind racing. Then suddenly, his eyes widened.

'Oh Christ,' he exclaimed. 'I think you're right.'

He leant back in his chair, stunned.

'And I don't think she knows. Or at least, she didn't.'

Bullman didn't need to ask. She already knew who he was talking about.

Alexis Kovalenko also had the DNA markers – she just didn't know it yet.

She was about to continue when Billy slammed the door open, looking around.

'Don't move,' he said. 'Don't say anything.'

He ran over to the desk between them and crouched down, looking underneath, before reaching up and, with a tearing motion pulled off a taped pen from the underside of the desk.

'What's this, some kind of backup pen?' Lester frowned, confused, as Billy examined it.

'Guv, you need to come see this,' he said to Bullman, already leaving the room, heading back to the main office.

Sighing, Bullman leant to the recorder.

'DS William Fitzwarren is having a moment, and has removed some kind of pen from the table,' she said. 'Interview paused.'

Slowly, she rose to follow, looking back at Lester.

'He's always so dramatic,' she muttered. 'Wait there, yeah?'

BILLY RETURNED TO THE OFFICE, SLAMMING THE NEWLY FOUND pen onto the table beside the one left under Anjli's desk.

They were identical.

'So now we know why she was happy to hang out in the interview room,' Declan said. 'Christ, is there anywhere else she could have planted bugs?'

Billy was already examining it.

'I turned the other two off, but this was still going,' he said as Bullman entered the office. 'She was listening to everything in there.'

'Any bombshells we should know about?' Monroe looked quizzically at Bullman, who nodded.

'Leon Brecht wasn't taking the Gen-Clear like the others,' she said. 'But we think Alexis was, unknowingly. And, if she was listening, she's just learned that it's good for extending your age, but it's also a ticking time bomb.'

'Probably not what she wanted to hear,' Anjli whistled. 'I'd like to say I feel bad about that, but she's literally been playing us, so karma's a bitch.'

'At least it explains one thing; this AI that we've been looking at, the one that seemed to be coming up with our ideas before we even came up with them, it's not some amazing super-advanced AI,' Billy, now back at the monitors, stated. 'It's someone listening to everything we say and *then* using AI, extrapolating what the next step is. We talked about bringing in Selene Carter to here. We talked about the case. The AI picked this up, and it's working things out effectively in real time. Without these microphones and without the camera in the canteen, that AI wouldn't have known what was going on.'

'What about the message it sent?' Declan asked.

'Oh, your phone is definitely compromised,' Billy replied. 'It turned on the microphone on both yours and the Guv's phones, once it uploaded onto them. You spoke to Majorie Halliwell, and it heard everything. It sent the message to pull in Selene because ...'

'Because I'd gained enough information for it to want to do that,' Declan shook his head, unsure whether to be impressed or furious at this. 'Are you telling me that Leon Brecht is a con artist?'

'In a way, yes,' Billy nodded. 'But this also means that everything that he's been basing this "amazing" AI on hasn't been connected to the scientific figures that he's been stating. We know they were recording everything in this room, the briefing room, on your phones, and the canteen. And if we go back, we know someone was recording in Ionosphere, as I found the Wi-Fi camera and microphone. Sure, we thought this might be Stephen Kline doing this, but what if—'

'No, it was Stephen.' Warren now entered the office, her face like thunder as she waved her phone like a weapon. 'I've just had a chat with my boss. Stephen Kline was an informant.'

'We know that—' Declan started, but the words died as Warren glared at him.

'Not in Manchester. I mean now, for my predecessor. I didn't know because I'd only just arrived, and they hadn't informed me about all the cases, but apparently for the last year and a half he'd been informing on Michael O'Rourke to the previous Detective Superintendent, who forgot to mention this when they retired. He's been recording the meetings he's had with O'Rourke, and passing these transcripts off to the police.'

She looked back at Declan.

'When you first met me in the Ionosphere office,' she said, 'apparently, in the top corner there's another recording device he'd placed up there. Whenever he had his meetings with O'Rourke, he'd record his sessions. But it also meant that he recorded everything in his office. Probably at some point he decided to add a second one in the hyperbaric chamber room, to learn what was going on with the rejuvenation team.'

She looked over at Billy now.

'He'd given my predecessor the code to watch whenever they wanted. However, nobody told me until just now, and unless somebody's turned it off, it's still recording. They're finding and sending the details now.

'Everything that's happened in that office has been recorded. Stephen Kline knew, but nobody else did,' Billy stared at the screen, thinking about this. We took the camera when we left the office, but we never had the feed. When it arrives, we'll see who met with him, at least.'

'It's Eli Green,' Bullman said now. 'David Lester just told

us he was hunting for a way to fix the DNA issue. Apparently, it's a little more dangerous than we thought.'

Monroe leaned back in his chair, rubbing his temples.

'Okay, so let's get this straight,' he said. 'This isn't about money, this isn't about AI. This is about people who made a mistake and are now trying to fix it?'

'No,' Bullman replied. 'This is a story about revenge and how stupid people can be when they try to get it.'

'Go on.'

'We all know there's this group of biohackers who worked together to break into the Rejuvenation Royale Tournament,' she began. 'David Lester wanted to piss off his previous competitors, so he used AI based on Leon Brecht's data and built a team of people he thought could beat the Americans at their own game.'

'And that's how we get our merry band of idiots,' Monroe interjected. 'They would meet regularly, at Eli Green's insistence, at Ionosphere. They discussed the latest ideas, figuring out what worked and what didn't. They took whatever worked without caring about the risks. The only one who didn't fully dive in was Leon Brecht – he had faith in his AI.'

'Of course, that turned out to be smoke and mirrors,' Billy muttered under his breath.

'We'll get to that,' Monroe said. 'Tell me more about the DNA.'

'Eli Green created Gen-Clear, but as it was banned in several countries, Eli shelved it, probably until David Lester and Leon Brecht decided it could enhance their DNA,' Bullman continued. 'They took the data, ran it through their systems, and started working on themselves.'

'The Gen-Clear started working,' Anjli now mused. 'They

kept taking it, and while they gained an edge over the Americans, it wasn't enough.'

'Enough for what?' Declan asked. 'It seems like the real issue is that they weren't expecting the public to find out about their DNA modifications.'

Bullman stepped forward, arms crossed.

'According to David Lester, the DNA changes did help them with their telomeres, but it also turned them into ticking time bombs. At any moment, an aneurysm could appear, or cancer could grow in a matter of days. They had no idea what they were dealing with. They were so far down the rabbit hole they couldn't stop digging.'

Monroe rubbed his chin, deep in thought.

'That's a reason to kill Eli Green. But Stephen Kline? Why kill him? He had the same DNA problem.'

'He did,' Declan said. 'But that was because he was copying what they were doing. At some point, he must have realised he had the same modifications and that if he admitted it, they'd know he was spying on them. He might have pretended to drop out for his daughter's sake, but maybe he didn't want to get caught.'

'It could've been both,' Anjli suggested.

'And don't forget,' Billy chimed in, looking up from his laptop, 'if the DNA changes didn't kill them, they could live a long time. Well over a hundred years, possibly more, with the gene therapy. They were augmenting themselves beyond standard biohacking.'

'But they needed to fix it,' Declan said. 'And that's what Eli and Stephen were working on.'

Monroe nodded again, more certain now.

'So, Eli and Stephen were still thick as thieves, even if they weren't on the best terms. Eli would've wanted to fix this, and Stephen would've volunteered to be the guinea pig. He had nothing to lose. If he died during the procedure, his daughter wouldn't have to try it. If it worked, he could redeem himself.'

'But it wasn't as simple as taking a pill,' Declan added. 'He had to stand in the cryotherapy chamber.'

'Here's where I'm confused,' Warren said, glaring at Monroe as if daring him to make a joke. 'Stephen Kline was left to die. But the DNA showed he still had the modifications. If the therapy worked, why did he have to die?'

She'd timed the question perfectly, as at that moment, Doctor Marcos walked into the main office, holding a stack of papers, hearing Warren's comment.

'He did have to stand in the cryotherapy chamber,' she said. 'I found some of his bloodwork from a week before the accident. Comparing that to the DNA we found after his death, the Gen-Clear aberration had significantly reduced. Whatever they did, it was working.'

'Then why leave him to die?' Monroe asked, puzzled.

'Well, I might have an answer for that,' Declan said. 'Michael O'Rourke.'

'What about him?' Monroe asked.

'Michael O'Rourke was owed money by both Stephen Kline and Eli Green,' Declan explained. 'He told me earlier that he'd bought Eli's shares in Ionosphere, shares Eli had promised would make him rich once he sold them, but this was based on Kline selling too, paying off the debt. However, he didn't. He was looking to sell Ionosphere to Rupert Cray.'

Monroe looked sceptical.

'You're telling me he tanked the deal because he didn't want O'Rourke to get paid?'

'Maybe, but one thing we do know is that something happened that made Eli leave Stephen in that chamber.'

'What if this was a negotiation?' Anjli asked now.

'Hell of a negotiation technique,' Billy replied. 'Stand in the cold until you say yes.'

'Actually, Anjli's right,' Declan interjected. 'O'Rourke mentioned Eli needed Stephen to sign a document to pass his shares across. He believed Eli got Kline into the freezer, probably under the pretext of fixing the DNA, and then locked him in, saying if he didn't sign the shares over, he'd die.'

'But why the secrecy around the flight to Thailand?' Anjli asked, frowning.

'Simple,' Declan said. 'Eli didn't want anyone knowing what he was doing to Stephen. If it went wrong, he had plausible deniability. We thought Eli Green was the one who flew to Thailand. Turns out it was his son, Elias Junior. Billy, send the Addison Lee driver the photo of the two together, see which one he recognises.'

'Okay then, so, hypothetically,' Anjli said, 'Eli goes to ground. He stays hidden, letting his son leave, taking everyone's attention, while he waits it out in the basement. When his son returns, Eli would reappear, clean as a whistle, ready to start again.'

Monroe frowned.

'Then, how was he killed so quickly after that?'

'Because someone was unhappy with him,' Declan replied. 'Someone else knew Eli was to blame.'

'It could have been more than that,' Doctor Marcos swapped her iPad. 'I have the DNA results on Aria Milton, too.'

Warren frowned at this.

'I thought she wasn't sending them?' she asked. 'That she had better people doing it and all that?'

'She does,' Doctor Marcos smiled. 'It's just I know two of them, and they owed me favours. I had an email from them an hour back; they found abnormalities, but they don't have an investigator's mind, you know? They just lumped it all into "hey there's a bad DNA thing so all DNA things are linked.'

'But they're not?'

'Yes and no,' Doctor Marcos smiled. 'You see, as Detective Superintendent Warren saw, Aria Milton's ALS symptoms have returned with a vengeance. But I say the symptoms, not the ALS itself.'

'How can that be?' Anjli asked, and then narrowed her eyes. 'Oh, you're kidding me ... are you saying that Eli Green, while providing Aria with medication to help her, was actually playing her?'

Doctor Marcos nodded. But before she could elaborate, there was a buzz; Declan glanced over at his phone which was vibrating on Billy's desk, and frowned.

'Should I answer that?' he asked Billy. 'Is my phone clean now?'

Billy shrugged, not wanting to confirm an answer, and Declan answered, turning it onto a speakerphone.

'DCI Walsh.'

'Is it true?' The voice of Alexis Kovalenko spoke through the phone. 'What I heard?'

'Well, that depends—'

'I know you found the pen,' Alexis snapped. 'I was listening. I heard.'

Declan didn't need to know what it was Alexis had heard; he waited a moment before replying.

'Yes, it's true,' he said. 'The question is, what do you want to do about it?'

'Kill Leon,' Alexis growled.

'Probably not the best of ideas,' Monroe muttered. 'But, if you want to help us, you could tell us who killed Eli Green, and then we could tell you how the aberration can be safely removed.'

There was a moment's silence before Alexis spoke once more.

'You want me to tell you everything in return for my life?'

'Well, if you put it like that ...' Monroe smiled. 'Yes.'

There was a moment of silence down the line as Alexis Kovalenko considered this.

And then she told them *everything.*

27

WAITING ROOM

MIRA NAKAHURA DIDN'T UNDERSTAND WHY SHE'D BEEN contacted by Alexis, the assistant from Ionosphere, and she definitely didn't understand why she'd been told to go to Leon Brecht's private hospital ward room. However, it'd been insinuated that this was worth her time, and more importantly would explain the Gen-Clear issues, showing how to remove them in time for the end-of-year data upload for the final rankings, while keeping the benefits.

Bloody Leon. Even after almost being killed, he's crunching the numbers.

Mira approached Cromwell Hospital, its glass-fronted entrance blending into the well-kept streets of South Kensington, still expecting something bad to happen. The building itself was modern and understated, giving off a quiet sense of professionalism rather than luxury. There was no need for flashy signs or grand entrances here – this was a place where the rich and discreet came for serious treatment. People like Leon, for example.

As she stepped inside, she saw the reception area was

bright and clean; the marble floors and high ceilings gave it a spacious feel, but there was no unnecessary extravagance. Behind the sleek reception desk, staff greeted her with the kind of polite efficiency that suggested they were used to handling high-profile clients, waving her upstairs when she explained who she was here to see. The whole place had the feel of a well-oiled machine – calm, organised, and focused.

On the third floor, she entered the main waiting area, designed almost exactly like the space on the ground floor, and found herself facing Selene Carter, sitting in a chair to the side, and Aria Milton, in a wheelchair, pushed by a dark-haired woman on the right as she entered.

'Jesus,' she said as she saw Milton. 'Are you okay? Is this the DNA thing ...'

'No,' Aria smiled. 'It's my own DNA thing. I had an ALS flare-up.'

Mira wasn't sure what to say to this, so instead said nothing as she looked around.

'Where's David?' she asked, confused. 'Alexis, the Ionosphere assistant said he'd be here.'

'He will be,' Alexis said, now walking into the waiting room from the other side. 'But he's coming with the police.'

At this statement, the temperature in the room visibly cooled.

'Why are the police coming?' Mira asked, looking nervously around as, through the doors she'd recently just walked through, David Lester entered, three men following him. The first was someone she recognised; Joseph Lawrence, a financial advisor at her company. Beside him was a tough-looking man with a broken nose, and beside them was DCI Walsh.

'Glad you could all come,' he said. 'We're just missing someone.'

There was a moment's pause, and then Mira saw another officer, an Indian woman bring in a rather pissed off Leon Brecht in a wheelchair.

'I heartily object to this,' he muttered as she walked him to the side, placing the brake on his wheelchair to stop it moving.

It was around now that Mira Nakahura realised she was in trouble.

Declan stared coldly at Leon as he whined by the other door.

'You've got a lot of visitors, and they wouldn't all fit in your room,' he explained, as if talking to a child. 'So we'll do this out here. If it helps, imagine you're all sitting in the Ionosphere hyperbaric chamber room, trying to screw the Rejuvenation Royale Tournament out of millions.'

Nothing was said. Everyone glared at him.

'I'm glad you're all here,' Declan said with a smile. 'It would've been so annoying if none of you had turned up.'

'It feels like entrapment, looking at who else is here,' Selene Carter muttered.

'It's not entrapment. It's a story,' Declan said. 'One that I thought I'd tell you. You see, this competition has turned you all into gladiators. It was a term that was said to me by Leon, when we first visited him; gladiators practising for years to become the best of what they could be. But the problem with gladiators was that the sight of blood became, well, nothing to them. They were no longer triggered by death or illness or violence. In the same way that you've had the same happen with you.'

He shook his head.

'You were so desperate to win that money that you would've done anything that David Lester said.'

'David?' Selene spat. 'I wasn't here because of David.'

'No, you were here because of Eli Green,' Declan nodded. 'And that you were being blackmailed. But you all had your reasons.'

He looked at Mira.

'You were looking to get one over on your father. Selene there wanted her freedom back. Aria Milton was looking for opportunities to survive. Leon wanted to prove his AI worked, David Lester wanted revenge.'

He smiled.

'The man to my left? Michael O'Rourke. He just wanted money owed to him. And then we have Eli Green and Stephen Kline; Eli who was so far down the tournament list nobody really cared about him. Eli, who had however been planning things all along. Eli played the long game here and none of you realised.'

Declan walked over and sat down on one of the chairs.

'You see, Stephen Kline always knew Alexis worked for Leon, who was her sponsor at University. He always knew she'd be sending the information back. And he always knew that she would be how Kline would make his money.'

'Bullshit,' Selene muttered. 'He wasn't that clever. I mean, he was a genius, sure, but that involves understanding human psychology, and he hated talking to people. Just like the robot there.'

The line had been aimed at Leon, who simply shrugged in response as Anjli, beside him, continued.

'At the Health Summit thing, you all had a fight,' she explained. 'But it wasn't because Stephen had just learned that he had a daughter. It was because you'd realised he was trying to piggyback into the tournament. However, when he announced he was looking to do this, Eli pointed out that he couldn't, because Stephen had the same DNA abnormality as you.'

'There was no way he could've had the same results from his own research,' Mira muttered. 'He had to have stolen it from us. From Eli.'

'True, as Eli Green created Gen-Clear,' Declan said, 'or at least a lab that he once owned did. But now he needed to cure this abnormality, before it killed you faster than the ALS that's going through Aria Milton's body.'

'Harsh,' Aria said.

Declan turned and gave a smile.

'I'll come to you in a moment,' he replied. 'So there we are, Stephen Kline pissing you all off at the Summit, showing that he's been doing everything that you're doing, whether you wanted him to or not. But of course, at the same time, he finds out that, oh no, Mira Nakahura is his estranged daughter, and someone who for the last eighteen months has been trying to get him to notice her, while she proves in some Don Quixote way that she wants to be better than him. With only one person who she ever confided in about this, Eli Green.'

'There's no way you could know that,' Mira muttered. 'He's dead.'

'Oh, I don't mean Eli senior, I mean his son, Elias Junior, who works as an intern at your firm,' Declan replied, looking at Joseph Lawrence. 'He worked for you, right?'

Silently, and looking like he really didn't want to be here, Joseph Lawrence nodded.

Declan looked over at Alexis now.

'So, the son tells the father, and a secret is shared. But Eli Green senior was playing his own game. You see, people thought that you were working for Leon Brecht. That you were creating the AI through the recordings and through information that you were gathering. But in effect, you were giving it to Eli, as well.'

'Eli was the one who hired me,' Alexis shrugged. 'I mean, Leon is a genius, but at the same time ...'

'So, now you have a dilemma,' Declan turned his attention back to the room. 'You have a rejuvenation tournament that's coming up and your DNA is doing well – but then it stops. The DNA isn't doing as good as it used to and now you're being told that actually you could explode, or get terrible cancer, or half a dozen different things that are not what you signed on for. This is not good. But don't worry. Because Eli Green has a plan. He's going to cure you. You'll all be so grateful to him.'

He shook his head.

'The problem was, from the very beginning, Eli had an idea how to do this if things went wrong, but as it happened, he realised he could now use it to his own advantage.'

'How?' It was Selene who asked.

Declan looked over at O'Rourke now.

'He sold me his shares in Ionosphere,' O'Rourke admitted to the room. 'He'd owed a debt – they both had – to my father for years. He was paying it off. But both of them had to do it, and Kline decided he wanted to sell his shares to some yank prick named Cray.'

'Rupert Cray?' Aria was surprised by this.

'He was working for him,' Alexis admitted. 'Once he knew you were all dosing the new DNA cleanser, he took the details and took it himself. He then sold it to Cray, who took the information and passed it across to the Americans. He understood from Kline that David Lester had deliberately set up a way to remove the West Coast contestants, and he felt turnaround was fair play.'

'I'm pretty sure that if you check the Americans, the ones who have suddenly leapfrogged you back to the top of the charts, you'll see that they too have the same abnormality,' Declan added. 'At some point Eli Green must have realised the only person who would've done this would be Kline, and he also found out around then that Kline was informing to the police on Michael O'Rourke.'

O'Rourke hadn't been told about this, and he looked in surprise at Declan.

'He was? Christ, it really was "like father, like son" for him.'

'You don't seem bothered,' Anjli replied.

'He was a venous, sneaky shite,' O'Rourke muttered. 'I never trusted him, so he had nothing on me. But it does explain why he wouldn't sell me his shares. Probably thought he could run out on the deal a second time. Though Eli promised me he'd fix it.'

'And he believed he could,' Declan nodded. 'You see, Eli believed he knew how to cure himself if things went to shit. It involved going further into cryotherapy than he'd comfortably want to, but it could be done. I'm no scientist, but we know some good forensic ones. And they've told us lots of long words and phrases like "trigger cellular stress responses", "activate heat shock proteins", "initiate cellular repair mechanisms" and various incredibly advanced explanations of how to trigger the body's natural DNA repair mechanisms, while simultaneously slowing down the dangerous acceleration of cellular processes caused by the modification.'

'Basically, "cold good" and "DNA bad",' Anjli added with a smile.

'Anyway, Eli convinced Stephen Kline that there was a way to fix this. Kline, of course, demanded to be the test subject – not out of any kind of selflessness, but because he wanted it fixed, and fast. But this was where Eli played his card.'

'You can't know this,' Leon muttered. 'You weren't there.'

'True,' Declan replied. 'And both men are dead. But his phone was there, Leon. In his pocket, the phone you'd hacked when he was in Paradigm Synthetics at one point, just like you hacked ours.'

He nodded to Alexis.

'She explained to us how you'd had her bug everyone, and how you'd clone a small piece of malware onto the phone of anyone who came close to you. Everyone here probably has it, too. It also turns on the microphones. Alexis showed us how she would listen to the recordings, and it was a simple job for our resident cyber expert to reverse engineer the line – with Miss Kovalenko's help – to find the server you kept them on.'

Leon now spun to stare at Alexis.

'You betrayed me?'

'You broke my DNA you *bastard!*' Alexis shouted back. 'You didn't take the medicine, you knew it'd screw things up, but you let me do it! What was I, your lab rat?'

She rushed at Leon, but Anjli stepped in front.

'Recordings aren't admissible anyway,' Lester said, with more than a little concern in his voice. 'Not unless we agreed in advance.'

'Different if the two men on it are dead,' Declan replied. 'We heard the recording. We heard Kline be given the impression this was the first in several sessions that'd shock his system into fixing things, but Eli had placed locks on the door, ones only he could open. And, as Kline got colder and colder, Eli encouraged, and then demanded him to sign the document Joseph Lawrence had created, that would sell his shares to Michael O'Rourke.'

'I had no idea about this,' O'Rourke shook his head.

'Yeah, you did,' Anjli replied with a shake of the head. 'As we said, we have his calls recorded, remember? That includes the ones Eli had with you.'

'So, he signed over the shares?' Aria asked.

'No,' Declan shook his head. 'Probably "old" Stephen would have, but he couldn't now, could he?'

The last part was aimed at Joseph Lawrence.

'No,' he said. 'Stephen had placed them in a trust for his daughter.'

At this, Mira gasped, and if it was staged, it was incredibly well done.

'He wouldn't change this,' Declan said, and his voice took on a darker tone now. 'He couldn't if he wanted. But Eli didn't believe him, and wouldn't let him out ... until it was too late, and he realised he'd gone too far. At which point, he ran.'

There was a quiet moment of what was likely reflection as the last sentence was stated.

'And that's where Leon, Mira and Selene come in,' Declan replied. 'And the story *really* gets wild.'

28

THE TRUTH

'You have to be joking me,' Leon Brecht now looked around, confused. 'Are you saying that I'm connected to this murder? I'm a victim. Look at me.'

'Yes, look at you,' Declan spoke. ' Incredible how you survived. I'd like to say it was luck, but you don't believe in that, do you?'

He walked closer to Leon now.

'You see, we first thought this might have been Alexis keeping an eye on what was going on, but she was walking home, because *you* told her that thanks to the AI algorithms, she needed to start walking more, gaining more steps. How about walking back to her house in Deptford? That would gain her five thousand steps, but what it would also do was remove any chance she had to prove that she wasn't at Ionosphere. She would walk home, unaware she'd lost her Oyster card alibi while *you* listened in instead.'

'This is crazy talk,' Leon muttered, shaking his head, glancing around the room as if looking for someone to back him up.

'You told us you were in your office that night, and you were,' Declan continued. 'Eli Green ran because of what had happened, but he turned the system off when he realised he'd gone too far, brought it down to manageable settings.'

'As far as he was concerned, the cold chamber would heat up, Stephen would survive, and although he'd have a bad time, he wouldn't be dead,' Anjli added from behind Leon. 'All Eli had to do was stick with his alibi plan. Then, if Kline claimed Eli tried to kill him, he could shrug it off, say it was some kind of vendetta against him from Kline, who had obviously done this to himself, hence the locking of the doors. Maybe even aim police at the O'Rourkes if the whole "being locked in" part was questioned.'

'He also probably hoped Kline would have second thoughts about keeping these shares in his daughter's name, and keep his mouth shut in case he found himself in another such situation,' Declan took the line of questioning back up. 'But he didn't realise, Leon, that *you* were the virus in the system. He turned everything off, but you turned it back on, connecting through the Wi-Fi. And once you did that, you began to play your games.'

He looked around the room at the others.

'I mean, you *are* all aware that, as far as Leon Brecht is concerned, it's not about the ageing. It's about convincing people how to act through AI. There's more money in mind control than there is in biohacking.'

Leon leant back in the wheelchair, clapping his hands slowly.

'You cannot prove any of this,' he said.

'Do you want to talk hypotheticals? Oh, I can talk hypotheticals to you,' Declan said. 'I can say that hypothetically, you would have looked into the system. Possibly checking into Joseph Lawrence, once you heard that he'd been brokering this deal through Eli's phone's microphone. You'd then learn Joseph worked with Mira Nakahura, through his social media scraping, like you did with me. Maybe even see that he was a try-hard biohacker, who worried a bit too much about carb intake.'

Joseph Lawrence straightened as Declan continued, and he couldn't work out if the man was angry he'd been used, or insulted he'd been used so easily.

'Tell me, was it you who arranged that his wife brought a box of doughnuts home, or was that pure luck? Did you nudge her in the right direction, ensure he ate a doughnut which would weigh on his mind the following day? Alexis here mentioned that most people didn't get last-minute bookings when they were first-thing cancellations. Yet Joseph Lawrence had a notification pop up on his phone *telling* him there was a spot available at the exact moment he needed to know, conveniently making sure he was there to see the body.'

'Did you make me part of this?' Joseph stood at the back of the room, staring across at Leon.

'Oh, come on!' Leon shook his head. 'This is bullshit. You cannot prove this.'

'I'm pretty sure that once we look into it, we'll be able to find that you were connected through to the Ionosphere Wi-Fi at a set point in the evening,' Declan replied. 'And sure, we might not prove it conclusively, but I'll guarantee it'll be enough to dig deeper. And we're really good at digging, Mister Brecht. You see, you knew what you were doing when you started Joseph Lawrence on this path. You wanted him to be there, to be told that Eli Green had cancelled his appointment, because you knew that Joseph Lawrence *worked* with Eli Green.'

'That's not possible,' Joseph shook his head, confused. 'Eli Green—'

'Ah, no, sorry,' Declan held a hand up. 'I apologise, I wasn't explaining myself properly. You guys do like absolutes after all. I meant Eli Green *Junior*.'

He realised he'd started pacing and forced himself to stop.

'You see, Eli, or rather Elias Green Junior was an intern at the same company that both Mira and Joseph worked in. In fact, he was an intern for Joseph Lawrence. And when Lawrence was told by Alexis that "Eli Green had phoned in cancelling his session," he was confused, because he knew that Eli Green, *his* Eli Green was in Thailand, and wouldn't have booked a session.'

'No, that's not right,' Selene argued now. 'It was Eli who went to Thailand, not his son. He told us.'

'Of course he told you. He wanted you to believe he'd gone to Thailand so that he could do what he needed to do with an alibi,' Anjli replied. 'Think about it, Eli had told everybody he was going to Thailand, because he originally *was* going to Thailand. He probably booked his tickets, and then when he realised he had an opportunity to sort out Stephen Kline and fix this problem with Michael O'Rourke, he asked his son to go in his place. After all, father and son shared the same name, so "Elias Green" was still travelling. They would have changed the passport number and that would have been it.'

'The day that Elias went to Thailand, Eli went and hid in his basement, which had been set up for when he needed a sleep pod, just like in his office,' Declan continued. 'He had everything he wanted to hide out. And then two nights ago he went to see Stephen Kline, demanded he sign the document, realised things hadn't worked the way he wanted, ran back to his house and waited. Elias Junior, meanwhile, landed back from Thailand the following day, took an Addison Lee cab back to the house, where as far as the housekeeper was concerned, he turned up to drop a book off now his father was magically back. She hadn't even realised he'd left the house.'

'Bloody woman was clueless,' Selene muttered. "I don't know why he kept her on. This is all speculation. Guesswork.'

'True, but the source was someone who knows how these things work,' Declan smiled. 'Someone who suggested a person with AI expertise could look at their rivals, find the cracks in their story, and start pulling at the threads. If their whole narrative is a well-crafted forgery, eventually it'll unravel.'

'How does that affect this?'

'Knowing that could be the case, we looked for the details that didn't add up—the little things that betrayed the bigger lies. The truth is always hidden in those small inconsistencies, even if a story is being sold here. Our job is to figure out which stories are real and which ones are just clever forgeries.'

There was a moment of silence as everyone took this in.

'But here is where Leon's AI really did its job, because Joseph Lawrence mentioned in a meeting to somebody he knew, who used Ionosphere, about what had happened,' Declan looked over at Mira now. 'You.'

'Joseph mentioned it to me, sure,' Mira said. 'He didn't realise I was Stephen's daughter, but he knew I went to Ionosphere. We'd bumped into each other and he'd mentioned the coincidence of names. He hadn't realised that Eli Green was so important, because he wasn't really part of the scene. He was just a wannabe.'

'Thanks,' Joseph muttered.

'But him telling you led you to realise Eli senior was likely the one who had killed your father,' Declan said. 'And so you decided to get your own revenge.'

'I'm afraid this is where you're wrong, Detective Chief Inspector,' Mira smiled now, holding her hands up in a *what-can-you-do* kind of way. 'I was in a meeting that afternoon. I've already told you this.'

'Yes, and we've had a look at it,' Anjli replied. 'You see, the thing about virtual meetings is they're often recorded these days. After we explained the situation, your company sent us the recording, and we saw you spend most of the meeting happily nodding and humming and giving the occasional piece of advice. But our cyber guy, as we keep mentioning, is an expert. Especially on what an AI video looks like when it's placed into a call. The problem we had though, is *you're* not good enough at coding to do that. We think that you would have had help from someone who was an expert in AI, or who at least knew people. Someone like Leon Brecht was an option, but perhaps there was a better one ...'

Anjli looked over at David Lester now.

'You know, like someone you were sleeping with.'

However, the moment she said it, she realised she was wrong – as Lester's face dropped.

'Who did you go to?' he asked. 'Tell me it wasn't him.'

The "him" he indicated was Leon Brecht, who smiled.

'Oh no,' he replied. 'Is there trouble in paradise? Just like I prophesied when you first started sleeping with her. I didn't need AI to know that. I just needed to know how bad you two are at relationships.'

'No,' Mira replied, 'I didn't use Leon. I'm not exactly an idiot, you know. There are apps on the internet that work well with these sorts of things. I just took a five-minute video of myself sitting in front of the camera, put it through the system, and just allowed it to do what it needed to do. I started the call, said I was having internet problems, and it was freezing me out. Said as I could still see and hear, that it was probably better if I just kept quiet for the rest of the meeting. I gave my report, then pretended I had some kind of web link issue, reached across, buggered around with the camera—'

'And then the second video started of you moving back to position,' Anjli continued. 'But this one was now AI-based, while you travelled to Eli Green's house.'

Mira nodded, realising that by now there was no point continuing with the lie.

'Yeah, I went to his house,' she said. 'I didn't go in, though. I sat outside for two hours, trying to build myself up, decide what to do.'

'Why didn't you use David Lester?' Declan asked. 'You know, for the AI?'

'Because I thought he might have been one of the people who killed Stephen,' Mira sighed. 'We'd had a fight a couple of months back at the Summit. Stephen had found out not only that I was his daughter, but I was sleeping with David – and, well, he became a bit fatherly, which was taking the piss, considering he'd avoided me for twenty-five years.'

'I was under the assumption he didn't know about you for twenty-five years,' Declan responded.

Mira shrugged.

'Doesn't matter. Either way, he was an absolute prick about it, started trying to ban me from ever seeing David, and they got violent.'

'By violent, she means there was a minor squabble, a bit of pushing back and forth before people just told them to stop being children,' Selene muttered. 'She's making it sound worse than it actually was.'

'Either way,' Mira replied, 'I didn't trust David anymore. I wasn't sure if he had done it. In fact, when I saw him that night at the biohacking event, I even asked him straight out whether it was him.'

'From what we understand from witnesses, you rammed your forearm against his throat and demanded to know whether he did it. The quote we have was "did you kill him, you utter wanker?"' Anjli grinned. 'I'm actually quite impressed.'

'Well, it doesn't matter,' Mira said irritably. 'I sat outside his house for two hours, realised I wouldn't do anything, and then went home.'

She muttered under her breath, and Declan raised an eyebrow.

'Something you'd like to share with the class?'

Mira looked up and glared at him.

'I can't believe my company gave you the meeting footage,' she said. 'You should have needed a warrant for that.'

'Oh, we would have,' Anjli smiled, 'which is why they didn't give us the footage. We just assumed that if we *told* you we knew, you'd give up and tell us.'

'You *what?*' Mira glanced from Declan to Anjli in horror. 'Are you saying ...'

'Yeah, we bluffed you,' Anjli looked down at Leon. 'Seems like you're not the only one who understands human perception. And we didn't need your fancy AI tools or anything.'

'Did you see anybody go to the house while you sat outside wondering what to do?' Declan asked, returning Mira's attention to the point at hand.

Mira shook her head, but then paused.

'Yes,' she replied. 'I did, actually. Aria Milton.'

Declan looked across at Aria, who shrugged.

'Yes, I went to visit him,' she said. 'It was before I spoke to you, DI Kapoor. Probably while you were talking to Selene.'

'You knew I spoke to Selene Carter?' Anjli paused. 'Of course you do. You all have a bloody WhatsApp group.'

'Anyway, I turned up, knocked on the door.'

'You didn't ring the doorbell?'

'God, no,' Aria replied. 'He has a video doorbell that only records when someone rings the bloody thing. I didn't want people knowing I was there.'

'Any particular reason why?'

'Stephen Kline had just been murdered,' Aria said. 'I didn't want people thinking I was having some kind of secret meeting.'

'But you *were* having a secret meeting.'

'I've already said how my ALS meant I was having to find unconventional ways to find the medication that kept me alive,' Aria explained. 'Eli had it, but I was running low. I turned up, knocked – no answer. I called him, left a voicemail asking if he was there ... I guessed he was asleep.'

'When was this?'

'About half-past two.'

'You didn't send him a package, with a powder supplement to add into his smoothie?' Declan added.

'No.'

'Well, someone did. The courier we saw arrive claimed that's what he delivered an hour earlier,' Declan looked at Leon. 'Something that, when the courier company tried to look into it, corrupted their data. You know, like a virus. I understand you spoke with Eli before he died?'

'And how would you know that?' Leon frowned, and Declan wondered if, for the first time in a while, he'd found something outside of his planned comfort zone.

'Because he *told me,* you robot-thinking wanker!' Michael O'Rourke shouted. 'Said you hacked into the spa and turned the freezers back on when he left! Said he had proof, and he'd told you this. Then later that same day, he's dead – and his sauna, just like the spa, hadn't turned off!'

'Circumstantial,' Leon smiled, now back in control. 'I had no connection to Eli's sauna. I was also in a meeting at the time, at Paradigm Synthetics. With this man.'

He indicated Declan, who nodded.

'True,' he replied. 'But do you remember when you had to step aside during that meeting, when you had an anomaly in one of your data streams?'

'What about it?'

Declan shrugged as he pulled out his phone, tapping a quick message, and sending it.

'Well, it made me wonder whether something was coming through to you, perhaps from the sauna's computer systems,' he suggested. 'But to do that, we'd need to prove it.'

As he said this, Leon's smartwatch started to beep.

'You might like to check that,' Declan smiled. 'You see, while we stand here, one of our team is in Hampstead, directly linking through to the sauna's guts, and sending the same message it did at the time.'

He pointed at the watch.

'Straight to you, it seems,' he continued. 'What was it you said? "You can't make an omelette without initiating a controlled shell fragmentation process"? Well, I think you just fragmented all over the place right now.'

'And don't make out you were attacked as well,' Anjli turned to face the man in the wheelchair. 'We know you did it to yourself. Timed it to look like you'd been taken out, while drinking down the same cocktail you sent Eli Green.'

Declan tapped his temple, a pair of imaginary glasses.

'You see, when you have your staff all wear instantly contactable glasses, it makes it real simple to work out who's where,' he said. 'Your assistant was so scared when she found you, she gave our officers the details, and when we checked through, we found that at the same time our officers arrived at the car park, you had someone locking you in from outside the chamber. Someone who confirmed this when we asked. Amusingly, it was the same guy who brought your shake to you as we left the previous day.'

He cocked his ear.

'You hear that? That's the sound of all the eggs smashing,' he said, as he looked at the others. 'And all of you? You're all complicit in various ways, mainly because he's been manipulating you, a Frankenstein science experiment; whether you're making decisions you didn't mean to, or sending messages you don't recall sending. Or, in Aria's case, having an onset of symptoms that she shouldn't have.'

At this, Aria raised an eyebrow.

'I shouldn't have ALS?'

'Well, unfortunately that part is true, still, but your relapse earlier? Not so much,' Declan replied. 'Your scientists would have found the same, but ...'

'Let me guess, his sodding AI was killing the data,' Aria

glared at Leon, who went to reply, to argue this ... but then simply sighed, leaning back.

Declan, flipping the page in his notebook, read from it.

'According to our divisional surgeon, he replaced your real ALS medication with a mix of drugs that would weaken your body and make it feel like your ALS was progressing. Muscle relaxants, like diazepam and baclofen, which caused your muscles to tire more easily, make it feel as if your condition was deteriorating. In addition, he used beta-blockers like propranolol, which slowed your heart rate, caused fatigue, and made your reflexes sluggish – again, symptoms that could be mistaken for ALS worsening.'

He looked at Leon as he continued.

'He also slipped in sedatives like lorazepam, which would have drained your energy even further, leaving you feeling completely exhausted,' he continued. 'Leon knew you were already emotionally fragile from the discovery of the DNA aberrations, so to amplify that stress, he gave you pseudoephedrine to make your heart race, heighten your anxiety, and leave you constantly on edge. These effects made you feel more stressed, vulnerable, and convinced that your body was failing you.'

He turned his attention back to Aria.

'What you've been experiencing isn't a sudden and violent progression of ALS. It's the result of the drugs Leon gave you, through the unsuspecting Eli, who believed Leon was working for the same cause, combined with the psychological toll of losing your friends. He manipulated both your body and your mind. My guess is he wanted to make you the patsy for all this, and hoped he could stress you out to the point your body gave out before we got to you.'

As Leon rose from the chair, likely to leave, Anjli grabbed his wrist, cuffing it.

'Everyone here has a secret,' she said as she locked Leon's hands behind his back. 'It's not your job to use them. We might not be able to tie you to all the deaths, but we can definitely find enough to dig deeper.'

She looked at the others now.

'Eli Green did find a way to fix the DNA,' she said. 'Kline's DNA had changed. We'll provide you with what we have, so you can work out a way to fix yourselves.'

This said, she walked to the main entrance to the waiting room, where De'Geer and Cooper had appeared, having waited outside.

Declan nodded to himself before following.

'Oh, and I'd hard reset all your tech, and hire someone to check them all for any, well, dodgy looking data packages,' he said. 'Trust me.'

And, with Anjli, De'Geer and Cooper leading Leon Brecht from the room, Declan gave a final, virtual "tip of the hat" to the others, before following.

EPILOGUE

Of course, it wasn't that easy. Leon Brecht hadn't killed Stephen Kline; a rogue AI algorithm had affected the spa's regulatory system – so his solicitors explained – which restarted the systems at the worst possible time, exactly as the unhinged Eli Green attempted to murder Stephen Kline.

Without Green able to speak his side of the situation, it looked as if Leon would get away with it, too – until David Lester, still a minor partner in Brecht's company, allowed the authorities complete access to everything Leon Brecht's AI had gathered from its "scraping" of data, which included the hours of recordings he'd gathered from the hacked phone microphones that Alexis had provided unofficially. Recordings that included, in detail, Eli Green locking Stephen Kline into a cryochamber before demanding he sign his company to Michael O'Rourke, a debate that ended with Kline stubbornly hanging on to his values until he passed out from cold exposure, filled by Green's frantic calls out as he tried to disconnect everything. They also included Green blackmailing Selene Carter to join the group, Kline trying to sell everyone out to Rupert Cray and unfortunately for him, also David Lester's multiple, inopportune relationships with young, innocent, female biohackers.

They also showed that Eli Green had faked his trip, had been sent powdered supplements on the day of his death, a package he believed was from Aria, and that his system, again, had been affected by Leon Brecht's rogue AI algorithm.

The AI killed them. Not Leon.

Unfortunately for Leon, though, what Lester opened up for the police also included his clinical trial notes, where he wrote everything he did, and was *doing*, to the biohackers he now controlled. How he had manipulated them to follow Lester, how he'd built Alexis Kovalenko into the perfect sleeper, intending to bring her in more fully into the next tournament in two years, and how – with at least four of his test subjects in the RRT top twenty – he'd be able to prove he was the king of AI.

That people had died was completely lost on him.

Of course, this wasn't the only fallout. The recordings also proved that the West Coast contestants, given a boost by Rupert Cray, had also performed the illegal Gen-Clear therapy, and the other global groupings kicked off at this, to the point where it went public that Cray had "rigged" the event. As this was announced, the Gen-Clear DNA adaptations were removed, following a regimen of short-burst extreme cryotherapy sessions – both in the UK and in the US. By the end of the month, all contestants had lost any significant gains from this, and by the time four weeks had passed since the arrest of Leon Brecht, the entire tournament had been closed down because of massive negative press.

Selene Carter had her silver medal stripped from her, and was retroactively banned from ever competing professionally again. Mira Nakahura quit her job and took over Ionosphere, claiming she'd work with Michael O'Rourke to make it profitable. This was short-lived, however, as shortly after the recordings were passed across, it was revealed that O'Rourke had also been "scraped", and his phone had given Leon hours of recordings, many of which were involving criminal activities. Before Michael O'Rourke could be arrested though, he ducked out, joining his father in Spain. Which was ironic, really, as there was every chance he could have pushed for a mistrial, claiming these were recordings taken without his consent.

In one of the few positive moments of the culmination of the case, Aria Milton's ALS flare up turned out to be nothing but another experiment for Leon, an attempt to burn her already fragile life out before she could clear her name for the murders he was setting her up for, and once she evened out her medication, she returned to her original levels. However, Declan knew that without Eli and Leon providing her with the medicine, and with David Lester returning to the US to live a "quieter life", there was every chance her supply could be drastically reduced, or cut off permanently.

That said, in a world of millionaires, medicines could always be sourced if the need was great enough. Declan hoped she'd go on for years more.

Also, and this was likely a positive for her rather than for her husband, Melanie Lawrence, wife of Joseph Lawrence, filed for divorce. It looked like his biohacking regimen, as well as his interest in younger women, finally reached breaking point.

Alexis Kovalenko was arrested as an accomplice of Brecht's, but because of her help in bringing him down, she gained leniency. Declan heard she'd also dropped out of her degree – perhaps AI wasn't as cool a subject for her anymore.

And then there was Marjorie Halliwell, who'd been arrested after a suspicious gold merchant found her at his counter trying to sell over forty grand's worth of gold bullion, with no explanation of where she gained them from.

Declan almost applauded her tenacity.

Over a month after the events at Ionosphere, Declan sat at his desk, working through the weekly figures, when he saw movement in the main office through the main windows. Looking up, he saw Detective Superintendent Warren walking in, talking to Anjli as she did so. The two women had built a grudging respect for each other over the weeks, and in a small way, Declan was a little jealous of this. The only people he really spoke to were Monroe and Billy; Henry Farrow no longer took his calls and Alvaro Esposito had in no uncertain terms told Declan to lose his number in recent months.

Anjli stopped at her desk, and Warren continued to the door beside Declan's office; that of Monroe's. She paused, knocked, and entered. Three minutes later she emerged, smiling, then moved to Declan's door, knocking lightly.

'You're smiling,' he said suspiciously. 'You walked into Monroe's office and now you're leaving it smiling. Did you just kill him?'

'You wish,' Warren replied, and there was a lightness in

her voice Declan hadn't heard before. 'I just gave him my news.'

'Which is?'

'I'm leaving Canary Wharf,' Warren shrugged, leaning against the doorway. 'It's been a month and all I've done is break up some small gang fights. I need something more exciting in my life. So, in a month or so, I'm returning to Newbury.'

'I thought the whole point was to get out of Newbury?'

'No, the point was to get my promotion,' Warren replied, the smile dropping slightly as if she expected a fight here. 'Anyway, it's not the same unit, it's about ten minutes down the motorway, but I think I fit the "provincial" stereotype more than "city copper".'

She sniffed, looking around.

'I thought you guys were lucky, but now I see you're just lonely,' she continued. 'You and Monroe are fortunate you found people who love you, because if you didn't, you'd be even more miserable to be around.'

'How did Monroe take your news?' Declan rose now, walking over to her.

'Better than I thought he would,' Warren admitted. 'I was expecting another fight, how he'd be all holier than thou and telling me I was walking out on my team, and all that, but all he did was say I was making the right choice, shook my hand and told me not to be a stranger.'

She winked.

'I think he's drinking again.'

'I'm glad you've sorted out whatever problems you had,' Declan held out his hand and Warren shook it.

'When I first met you, I'd heard about you,' she said. 'The

copper who punched a priest on live TV, who then arrested one of his own. The news followed you around like a cloud. And, as time went on, you added more to it.'

'Yeah, that bloody cloud's massive now,' Declan replied. But, surprisingly, Warren shook her head.

'You've got nothing other than your own insecurities pushing you down,' she said. 'You try to live up to other people's expectations – I get that, your dad was a hard-arse, apparently, and you're trying to be Monroe.'

She leant in.

'Don't,' she whispered. 'Let Monroe be Monroe. He's bloody awful at it, anyway. Be Detective Chief Inspector Declan Walsh, and be damned with everyone else.'

This said, she stared at Declan quietly for a moment and then turned, walking out of the office.

Declan, watching her, looked over at Anjli through the doorway.

'Did you do that?' he asked, but Anjli seemed as surprised as he was, shaking her head.

'I told you she liked you,' she laughed. 'You know, in that "favourite of all the pets" kind of way. Like Bullman does.'

Declan blew her a kiss and walked back into his office, staring around at it. The weeks had been quiet since the Ionosphere case, and he'd spent more time than he wanted in the room.

Grabbing his jacket, he walked back into the bullpen area of the office.

'I'm just going out,' he said. 'Need some air.'

'Need company?' Anjli, concerned, asked.

'If you'd like,' Declan smiled. 'I was going to have a wander around the Inns of Court, see if I can get into trouble.'

'That sounds perfect,' Anjli said as she grabbed her own jacket. 'Where do we start?'

'Everywhere,' Declan laughed as they left the Temple Inn offices together.

Want the next Declan Walsh novel? CLICK HERE, or turn the page...

ACKNOWLEDGEMENTS

When you write a series of books, you find that there are a ton of people out there who help you, sometimes without even realising, and so I wanted to say thanks.

There are people I need to thank, and they know who they are, including my brother Chris Lee, Jacqueline Beard MBE, who has copyedited all my books since the very beginning, and editor Sian Phillips, all of whom have made my books way better than they have every right to be.

Also, I couldn't have done this without my growing army of ARC and beta readers, who not only show me where I falter, but also raise awareness of me in the social media world, ensuring that other people learn of my books.

But mainly, I tip my hat and thank you. *The reader.* Who once took a chance on an unknown author in a pile of Kindle books, and thought you'd give them a go, and who has carried on this far with them, as well as the spin off books I now release.

I write Declan Walsh for you. He (and his team) solves crimes for you. And with luck, he'll keep on solving them for a very long time.

Jack Gatland / Tony Lee,
London, November 2024

ABOUT THE AUTHOR

Jack Gatland is the pen name of *#1 New York Times Bestselling Author* Tony Lee, who has been writing in all media for thirty-five years, including comics, graphic novels, middle grade books, audio drama, TV and film for *DC Comics, Marvel, BBC, ITV, Random House, Penguin USA, Hachette* and a ton of other publishers and broadcasters.

These have included licences such as ***Doctor Who, Spider Man, X-Men, Star Trek, Battlestar Galactica, MacGyver,*** BBC's ***Doctors, Wallace and Gromit*** and ***Shrek***, as well as work created with musicians such as ***Ozzy Osbourne, Joe Satriani, Beartooth, Pantera, Megadeth, Iron Maiden*** and ***Bruce Dickinson.***

As Tony, he's toured the world talking to reluctant readers with his 'Change The Channel' school tours, and lectures on screenwriting, story craft and comic scripting for festivals and conferences such as *Raindance* in London and both *Author Nation* and *20Books* globally.

An introvert West Londoner by heart, he lives with his wife Tracy and dog Fosco, just outside London.

Locations In The Book

The locations and items I use in my books are real, if altered slightly for dramatic intent.

Ionosphere, obviously, doesn't exist. That said, it is based on a Canary Wharf Cryotherapy centre called Le Chalet Cryo, which is a) nothing like the one in the book and b) the place I go weekly, like Bullman does, for a four-minute session. I've been doing this for several years now, and I enjoy it greatly, and I know the nootropic benefits of a session do help me when writing.

On that subject, as it's not an actual location I'll place it here; the Rejuvenation Royale Tournament, or RRT is not a real thing. People do not get paid winnings for staying alive.

It is however loosely based on a real thing - the Rejuvenation Olympics. This is a global initiative founded by entrepreneur Bryan Johnson and Doctor Oliver Zolman, aiming to advance the science of biological aging through competition and collaboration. Participants engage in various lifestyle interventions and anti-aging strategies, with their progress measured using advanced biological age testing methods, such as the DunedinPACE algorithm. The competition ranks individuals based on their pace of aging, fostering a community dedicated to longevity and healthy living.

Famous names (well, famous in the world of anti-aging) in the current leaderboard include Aldo Britschgi, Daniel Lewis, Siim Land, Dave Pascoe, Julie Gibson Clarke, while the most famous currently is "Don't Die" advocate, Olympics founder and Youtube star Bryan Johnson, who at the time of writing is in fifth place.

None of the other locations are based on real places.

The Old Bank of England pub is real, and the description and the history written in the book explain more than I could here, although one thing I don't mention, which was until recently true is that in their 'sun garden' is a double decker bus that you can drink in.

The Boxing Club near Meath Gardens doesn't exist - but the location used is the current **Globe Town Social Club**, within **Green Lens Studios**, a community centre formerly known as Eastbourne House, that I would pass occasionally in my 20s.

If you're interested in seeing what the *real* locations look like, I occasionally post 'behind the scenes' location images on my Instagram feed. This will continue through all the books, after leaving a suitable amount of time to avoid spoilers, and I suggest you follow it.

In fact, feel free to follow me on all my social media by clicking on the links below. Over time these can be places where we can engage, discuss Declan and put the world to rights.

www.jackgatland.com
www.hoodemanmedia.com

Visit Jack's Reader's Group Page
(Mainly for fans to discuss his books):

https://www.facebook.com/groups/jackgatland

Subscribe to Jack's Readers List:
https://bit.ly/jackgatlandVIP

www.facebook.com/jackgatlandbooks
www.twitter.com/jackgatlandbook
ww.instagram.com/jackgatland

Want more books by Jack Gatland? Turn the page...

Printed in Great Britain
by Amazon

57181657R00209